Also by Regina Hart

Fast Break

Smooth Play

"You'd sacrifice your c_____
for your marriage?"

Warrick flicked his fi_____
good husband to Mary firs_____
source of the strain on our marriage."

"But *you're* not causing the strain. The *media* is.
Mary knows that." Jaclyn's reasonable tone reminded
Warrick of his efforts to explain the media madness to
his wife.

"And they'll continue to be a problem as long as I'm
an active player."

"You mean as long as you're a public figure, which
is what they'll consider you for the rest of your life."

"You won't change my mind, Jackie."

Jaclyn wiped her upper lip with her right wrist. "Will
Mary be all right with your giving up your lifelong
dream?"

Warrick recalled an image of Marilyn standing at the
top of their staircase the night she'd told him she hoped
he got the ring this season so he could retire.

Warrick looked at Jaclyn. "It wouldn't be her first
choice. But I don't think a divorce would be, either."

Jaclyn shook her head. "I can't imagine the Monarchs without you. And I can't imagine you retiring
without at least one ring. I really want that title for you.
I'm certain Mary wants that as well. She believes in
you, Rick. And she loves you. She wouldn't want you to
retire with regrets."

The Empire Arena came back into view. Warrick
checked his watch. They were going to complete their
run in less than fifty minutes.

Warrick wiped the sweat from his brow. "Then I've got
one of two choices. I can either retire after this season
without a ring, if it comes to that. Or I could continue my
career until I earn a ring and retire without a wife." He
caught Jaclyn's eyes. "Which would you choose?"

Keeping
SCORE

REGINA HART

Kensington Publishing Corp.

http://www.kensingtonbooks.com

DAFINA BOOKS are published by

Kensington Publishing Corp.
119 West 40th Street
New York, NY 10018

All Kensington Titles, Imprints, and Distributed Lines are available at special quantity discounts for bulk purchases for sales promotions, premiums, fund-raising, and educational or institutional use. Special book excerpts or customized printings can also be created to fit specific needs. For details, write or phone the office of the Kensington special sales manager: Kensington Publishing Corp., 119 West 40th Street, New York, NY 10018, attn: Special Sales Department, Phone: 1-800-221-2647.

Dafina and the Dafina logo Reg. U.S. Pat. & TM Off.

First trade paperback printing: July 2012

ISBN-13: 978-0-7582-5883-0
ISBN-10: 0-7582-5883-6

10 9 8 7 6 5 4 3 2 1

Printed in the United States of America

To my dream team:

- My sister, Bernadette, for giving me the dream
- My husband, Michael, for supporting the dream
- My brother, Richard, for believing in the dream
- My brother, Gideon, for encouraging the dream
- My friend and critique partner, Marcia James, for sharing the dream

And to Mom and Dad always with love

Acknowledgments

Sincere thanks to Stephanie W. Costa, MD, an obstetrician/gynecologist, and C.J. Lyons, MD, a pediatric emergency room doctor and multi-published author, for their help with the hospital information.

1

"Enough's enough, Mary. When are you coming home?" Warrick Evans settled his hips against the kitchen counter. He gripped its smoke and white marble top behind him. It was late Sunday afternoon. From across the room, he pinned his wife of almost two years with a steady stare.

Dr. Marilyn Devry-Evans angled her softly rounded stubborn chin. Her chocolate eyes met his challenge. "I've told you I need time, Rick."

Warrick's palms were sweating. He swallowed the brick of fear in his throat. "It's been a month."

A blush kissed the honey brown skin of her high cheekbones, but her gaze never wavered. "I have a lot to consider. I didn't realize what I was getting into when I married you."

"I told you when we met that I was a basketball player."

Marilyn hugged her arms around her slender torso. "But the Brooklyn Monarchs weren't any good when we met. Now that you're in the play-offs, you're a celebrity."

"I'm still Rick." His grip tightened on the counter until his knuckles hurt.

"You're Rick amplified." Marilyn shook her head. The straight strands of her dark brown ponytail swung around her shoulders. "You're in the newspaper every day. People are gossiping about you, about me, about us. I never planned to live my life in the spotlight."

Knowing she had a point didn't make hearing it any easier. "Neither did I. But that's part of the price I have to pay for a championship ring." The other costs were his swollen knees and the spasms in his back.

"As your wife, the loss of privacy is a price I have to pay, too."

"I know. And I'm sorry. When I fell in love with you, I didn't consider how my career would affect you." Warrick took a breath, then another. "Is the price too high?"

"I don't know." Marilyn's words sliced his heart right down the middle.

What was behind her indecision? Marilyn was an obstetrician/gynecologist. She made sound decisions quickly all the time. Why couldn't she make a decision about their marriage? What—or who—was coming between them? He had his pick of options, starting with her parents.

Warrick rubbed his forehead. His fingers burned as the circulation returned. Terrell and Celeste Devry had warned their daughter against marrying a man who "played games" for a living. Nothing Warrick said or did would change their minds, and he'd done everything short of sending them his college transcripts. Luckily, his in-laws hadn't been able to change Marilyn's mind. Not even their scowls during the ceremony could derail the wedding.

He dropped his hand. Warrick ached as his gaze lifted to Marilyn's profile. Her gleaming mass of dark hair was swept back and restrained at the nape of her neck with her usual clip thing. Warrick wanted to release the device and draw his fingers through her hair. He wanted to pull her into his arms. It had been too long since he'd held her.

He released his grip on the kitchen counter and stepped forward. "I miss you, Mary."

Her wide eyes were filled with sadness and confusion— and it was all so pointless.

"I miss you, too." Her voice was husky.

Relief rushed him, rocking him back on his heels. Warrick closed his eyes briefly. She still cared. He had reason to hope. "Then come home."

Marilyn shook her head, her expression miserable. "It's not that easy, Rick."

He moved closer. Her body's warmth pulled him like a magnet. He wanted to bury his head against her neck and inhale her fragrance—jasmine and talcum. He missed breathing her scent as he fell asleep at night and woke in the morning.

Warrick studied her features one by one—high fore-head, short nose, sharp cheekbones, sexy lips, stubborn chin.

"Do you love me?" His voice was a whisper.

Marilyn dropped her arms. "Of course I do."

His heart healed. "And I love you. It isn't any more complicated than that."

Her rich dark eyes searched his. "But it is. I don't like opening the newspaper or logging on to the Internet and finding stories speculating about our marriage and whether I'm good enough for you. I don't like people attacking you and questioning your character."

"It doesn't matter what other people think. All that matters is what we know, and I know that I need you in my life."

He reached for her, lowering his head until his mouth met hers. Her lips were soft and welcoming beneath his.

It had been more than four weeks—twenty-nine days—since he'd last touched her. Tasted her. He was starved for her loving. Warrick held her tighter against him. He traced the shape of her mouth with his and she opened for him.

Warrick's body relaxed with her acceptance. He slipped his tongue between her lips. His senses were overwhelmed by the sweet, hot taste of her. When she wrapped her arms around his neck and drew him closer, his knees went weak. He traced the curves of her slender shape. The touch stirred the memory of the way her body looked above him. The way she felt beneath him. His blood sang in his veins.

Warrick walked them toward the kitchen table. He loosened his hold on her to pull her soft cream blouse from the waistband of her brown pants. He raised his arms so Marilyn could help him pull his jersey over his head. Her fingers singed a trail across his abdomen as she nudged the material higher. She played with the hair on his torso. Warrick's muscles quivered. His breath quickened at her touch. Could she feel his heart racing? Could she tell how much he needed her?

They shed her blouse and pants with the urgency of their very first time. But it was too fast. He had to slow it down. He wanted Marilyn to remember how good they were together. He needed her to want to come home. Warrick drew in a slow, deep breath. Her scent made him throb with desire. He stepped back, fighting for control. He battled back the desire raging inside him. His body wanted to make this fast and hot. His heart wanted them to last forever.

Marilyn slipped off her black camisole. Warrick's body tightened at the sight of her slender curves in barely there, wine red underwear. Her firm breasts rose above a demi-cup bra. Her slim hips teased him with a strip of matching cloth.

Warrick wanted to stay in these feelings forever. He wanted to charge forward, past the static between them, and save his marriage. He wanted to go back in time and tell the gangly, nerdish adolescent he'd been that one day he'd marry a woman with brains and the body of a goddess.

He closed the distance between them again. Marilyn's chocolate eyes darkened as her gaze moved over his chest, down to the khaki pants riding low on his hips. Warrick reached behind her neck and released the clip binding her hair.

He drew his fingers through the thick, loose mass. It was as soft as a sigh against his skin. Her fragrance wafted up to him. Warrick's muscles tightened. "I love you so much."

"I love you, too." Marilyn balanced her hands on his shoulders. She rose on her toes and touched her lips to his.

Heat shot through him, making him catch his breath. He struggled to find control but need was a fire consuming him from the inside out. Only for this woman. Always for this woman. He clasped Marilyn against him, pressing her breasts to his chest, holding her hips hard to his. Marilyn gasped and Warrick swept his tongue inside her mouth.

Their tongues danced, sliding over and across each other, wrapping around one another in a simulation of the way their bodies would move. Marilyn moaned in her throat. The low, sexy sound made Warrick lightheaded. Her body moved with his, telling him what she wanted, what she needed, what she liked.

On the edge of his consciousness, Warrick felt her fingers at the waistband of his pants, working his belt.

He stepped back and stripped off his khakis and underwear. Marilyn reached out and molded her palms against his pectorals. His heart beat painfully under her hands. She ran her short, neat fingernails down his chest, over his abdomen, and into the hairs at his groin. Warrick's muscles quivered with anticipation.

He pulled her into his arms and held her to him. Her skin was warm and soft. Warrick buried his face in her neck. Marilyn trembled in his arms. His hips rocked her. Warrick hooked a hand behind her knee and drew her thigh high against his side. Marilyn moaned and pressed tighter against him. She covered his chest with nips and kisses, licking his nipples and grazing his pecs. She lifted her head and claimed his lips. Her touch made him feel wanted, cherished. Warrick opened his mouth and let her in. His head spun as she pulled his tongue deep into her mouth. She suckled him, caressed him, stroked him. Each intimate caress stoked his desire.

Her hands moved up his back and Warrick trembled. Her fingertips kneaded his muscles and he sighed. And when her nails scratched his bare skin, he stiffened. Her delicate physician's hands grasped his glutes and worked him against her. Warrick felt her dampen.

He turned with her in his arms, settling her hips on the kitchen table. Warrick reached behind Marilyn and unhooked her bra. He stripped the garment from her and tossed it aside. Warrick dipped his head and kissed Marilyn's nipples, first the left, then the right. He drew her right breast into his mouth. Her taste was full and sweet. He palmed her left breast, its weight familiar in his hand. Her skin was delicate to his touch.

Warrick lifted his head and looked at her. Her hot chocolate gaze scorched him. Her features were tight with a shared hunger.

He kissed her quick and hard. "You are so beautiful."

A slow smile curved her lips. "So are you."

Warrick chuckled and kissed her again. He loved the way she tasted on his mouth, the way she felt in his arms. Marilyn wrapped her legs around his hips and shimmied closer to him. Warrick cupped his hands under her and lifted her from the table. With Marilyn's arms and legs around him, Warrick sank to the floor. Marilyn released him, allowing Warrick to shift back between her long limbs. His gaze touched on her firm breasts and tight waist before returning to her face.

Her eyes glowed with desire. "I need you now."

Warrick reached out and stroked her cheek. "I need you forever."

He closed the distance between them. He kissed her neck, then nibbled his way down her chest to cover her right breast with his mouth.

Heat shot through her breast and settled between her legs. Her head pressed back and her lips parted in a gasp. Warrick's mouth worked her breast. Marilyn ached with desire. She held her breath as his teeth grazed her nipple. His tongue licked and laved it, twirling its tip. His mouth suckled her harder. Her hips pumped against him, matching the rhythm of his mouth.

Warrick released her. Marilyn bit her lower lip, rolling her head back and forth. He'd lit a fire with his mouth that coursed a path between her breasts and her thighs. He paused at her navel, stroking his tongue in and around the dip. He kissed and licked her before moving on to her hips.

His mouth teased and tormented her as it drew closer and closer to her femininity by centimeters before moving away. Again and again she felt his breath nearing her core before Warrick shifted course. He kissed her hip bone. He nipped her thigh. His tongue grazed her belly—but always at a distance.

"Rick, please." Marilyn's fingernails scraped against the smoke and white marble tile flooring.

"What is it, honey?" His breathing stirred between Marilyn's legs.

She gasped. Her heart tried to punch its way free of her chest. "Stop torturing me." Her voice was tight.

Warrick's laughter was low. "All right." He drew her knees up over his shoulders and kissed her deep.

Marilyn screamed her surprise at the intense sensations igniting her body. She arched her back, lifting her hips higher. Wave after wave of pleasure crashed over her, liquefying her bones. Her muscles strained. Her nipples tightened. Blood rushed through her veins. The muscles inside her pulled to the breaking point.

Then Warrick stopped.

Marilyn gasped. Her eyes shot wide. Her muscles shrieked in frustration. Warrick surged over her. He captured her mouth with his own. His hands clasped her hips and he dove into her. Marilyn screamed as pleasure burst inside her. She trembled in Warrick's embrace. His lips gentled on hers until she finally caught her breath.

Warrick's hips moved with hers, longer and deeper. Slower. Harder. He pressed into her. He rocked inside her. Their sweat mingled. Pressure built again. His scent was soap and sandalwood, above her. Warrick released her mouth. His breath came in short, sharp pants like music to her ears. Intense and exciting. She'd missed him. She'd missed this—and so much more.

Tension stretched tight as Warrick continued to move in her. Blood pounded in her ears. Marilyn's muscles strained. Warrick lifted his head and caught her left nipple with his lips. A jolt shot through Marilyn to her deepest muscles and shook again. Warrick's back arched. His hips crushed into hers—hard. He buried his face into her neck. Marilyn wrapped her arms around his shoulders as he shivered above her. She kissed his throat. In this moment, nothing and no one else existed. It was just the two of them. If only they could stay like this always.

Warrick didn't want to move. He didn't think he could. His body was firmly planted to the ground, warm and relaxed. Beside him, Marilyn stirred, pulling a smile from him. "I'm too old for this."

A wicked grin parted her full lips. "Oh, I don't know. I think you're in your prime."

Warrick chuckled, happier than he'd been in weeks. "I mean too old to be making love on the kitchen floor. I need a bed." He rolled to his feet and stood. He stretched his arms above his head. A movement in his peripheral vision drew his attention to the kitchen window. "What the hell?"

Marilyn sprang into a sitting position. "What's wrong?"

Warrick pulled on his pants. "I saw someone at the window."

"What?" Marilyn snatched her blouse and pressed it against her chest. "Someone was watching us?" She leaned over as though trying to make herself smaller while straining her neck forward to see through the window five feet away.

"Stay inside." Warrick circled Marilyn on his way to the back door.

She wiggled around on the floor, trying to put on her clothes and still remain out of sight. "Wait. I'll come with you."

"No, you won't." Warrick pulled open the door and stepped outside, wearing only his hastily zipped khakis.

He crossed the cedar deck in two long strides, then

jumped its four steps and landed lightly on the lush green lawn. He rounded the house toward the left side yard past their vegetable garden. Marilyn had planted lettuce, tomatoes, carrots, green beans, and other vegetables days after they'd moved into the house two years ago. He must have the best diet in the NBA.

The side yard was empty. Warrick glanced at the kitchen window. The blinds were turned up to allow light in while still protecting their privacy. But, if you stepped closer to the window, you could see the kitchen table. A chill rolled down his spine. Warrick continued to the front of the house. The gate was closed and no one was nearby. The movement outside their window must have been his imagination. He was chasing shadows.

Warrick turned back to his yard—and almost walked into Marilyn.

"Did you see anyone?" She leaned to the left, trying to see around him.

Her thick brown hair was tousled. The straight tresses swung around her shoulders with her every move. Her cream blouse hung loose over her baggy brown slacks and revealed much of her cleavage. Her narrow feet were bare. Her neat toenails, polished silver with multicolored sparkles, peeked from beneath the pant legs.

Marilyn's buttoned-up physician's identity had slipped, exposing his wife's sensuality. He wanted her again.

Warrick swallowed to ease his dry throat. "I asked you to wait inside."

Marilyn stilled, frowning into his eyes. "If there was an intruder, I could help you."

She was fit and toned from regular and strenuous workouts. Still the mental image of her confronting an intruder would keep Warrick awake for weeks. "Help me by calling nine-one-one."

With his hands on her shoulders, he turned Marilyn toward the backyard. Warrick wrapped his right hand around her slender waist and escorted her back to the house.

She looked around the side yard, glancing up at the window. "Maybe you were imagining things." She sounded hopeful.

"Maybe." He pulled her closer.

They continued into their home in contemplative silence. The scent of grass and blossoms carried on the late-spring breeze. It felt so good to have her back in his arms after a month without her. *The longest month of my life.* Now they could put the media and public scrutiny of their private lives behind them, and get back to being married. He stepped aside to let Marilyn precede him into their home.

"Rick, I'm going to check into a hotel." Marilyn's words came from behind him as he locked the door. They were like knives slipping into his back.

Warrick forced himself to face her. His voice was tight, controlled. "Why?"

She shrugged as she turned to walk farther into the house. "I can't continue to impose on Em's generosity."

Emma Mane had been Marilyn's best friend since college. She gave man haters everywhere a bad name. What was she telling Marilyn while his wife was deciding whether to stay with him or leave? The possibilities made his blood run cold. Still, the fact Marilyn hadn't asked for a divorce after four weeks with Emma told Warrick their love could survive an apocalypse. Why couldn't Marilyn see that?

Warrick unclenched his jaw. "How much longer are you going to keep us apart, Mary?"

"I don't know."

"You don't know." Warrick dragged a hand over his

scalp. If he hadn't already shaved his head, he'd have ripped his hair out by the roots. Marilyn sounded like a broken record and the lyrics were worse than the bubblegum pop she enjoyed.

He exhaled a soul-deep sigh, trying to lessen the pain that threatened to bring him to his knees. "You don't know how long it will take to decide whether you can live with me. You don't know what to do about us. What do you know?"

"I know this situation would be a lot easier if I weren't still in love with you."

The words weren't enough anymore. "If you love me, come home."

She shook her head, tangling her hair even more. "I don't know if I can live with you *and* the media."

"Then what was this?" He nodded toward the kitchen table and gestured toward the floor. "What were we doing here?"

Color darkened Marilyn's brown cheeks. "I do love you, Rick. But I don't know if love is enough."

Her words were a sucker punch. Warrick struggled to stay upright and breathing. What more did he have to do to prove he was worth loving?

"Not enough for what?" His voice was raspy with fear. Could she hear it?

"I'd never planned to live my life in the spotlight. I don't want strangers judging me, my husband, or our marriage."

"I can't control the media, Mary, no matter how much I want to."

"I understand. That's why I have to decide whether I can live under this constant pressure. What will it do to our marriage? What will it do to us?"

Warrick fisted his hands in the front pockets of his

khakis. Were these Marilyn's words or Emma's influence? "I think our marriage is worth fighting for. Do you?"

She wrapped her hands around her arms. "How do you fight the media? Troy tried and lost his job."

Troy Marshall, the Brooklyn Monarchs' vice president of media and marketing, had had a tough time with the increased press scrutiny as the team had entered the play-offs for the first time in fifteen years.

Warrick closed the gap between him and his wife. "But he kept fighting until he got his job back."

Marilyn waved her arm in an agitated gesture. "Thanks to that newspaper reporter, Andrea Benson."

Troy and Andrea had jumped through a lot of hoops to find their happily-ever-after. In contrast, Warrick and Marilyn's love story had been a slam dunk—until recently. Had their easy courtship made him too confident about their marriage?

Warrick ran his hand over his head again. His fingers shook just a bit. "They make a good team. I think we do, too."

Frustration swept across Marilyn's features. "I don't want to be judged by people, like when the Monarchs Insider wrote that I 'wasn't worthy to be seen on a professional athlete's arm.'"

Warrick's jaw clenched. He'd never get over his anger with the blogger who'd called herself the Monarchs Insider. She'd posted insults about his wife on the Internet, causing them both pain.

"Honey, I'm sorry about that blog, but it was written by a jealous woman with an ax to grind."

Marilyn turned away. Her voice was sad. "And hundreds of readers agreed with her."

"Don't let other people come between us, Mary. What they think or say doesn't matter. All that matters is what *we* think and what *we* feel."

She gave him a cynical smile. "You know you can't fight public opinion, Rick. How long will it be before you start believing what other people write about us? How long will it be before one of those young, scantily clad women who wait beside the tunnel to your locker room catches your attention?"

This wasn't Marilyn talking. Emma's cynicism sounded in those words. "I've been walking past those women since I was in college. You're the one who caught my attention."

She gave him a skeptical look. "Are you telling me you never slept with any of those groupies?"

He crossed his arms over his bare chest. "I'm not going to give you a report of the women I slept with before I met you—"

"Of course not—"

"And I won't ask you to give me one, either. But I do expect you to believe me when I say I haven't slept with anyone else since I first laid eyes on you."

Marilyn's gaze dropped. "I don't want to argue, Rick. I just wanted you to know where I'll be in case you need me."

Warrick took a breath. "I need you now."

She shook her head. "That's not a good idea."

Warrick lowered his arms. "Fine. The team's traveling to Miami Wednesday night."

"I know. Thursday's the first game of your series against the Miami Waves. You e-mailed your schedule to me."

At least she was reading his e-mails even if she didn't always return his calls. "You can move back in while I'm gone. I'm sure Emma wouldn't mind putting you up for another three nights."

Marilyn frowned. "Em's not rushing me to leave—"

"I'm sure she's not."

Marilyn must have heard the sarcasm in his tone. "You've never liked her."

"I'm not her favorite person, either. So will you move back while I'm gone?"

Marilyn hesitated. "You don't mind?"

"Of course not. This is your home."

"Where will you stay?"

Warrick kept his expression neutral. "Don't worry about me. I'll find a place to stay." Their home had a perfectly comfortable guest room.

Marilyn's smile of gratitude was worth the risk he was taking. "Thank you, Rick."

"You can thank me later." Once their marriage was back to normal.

All's fair in love and war. He was in love with Marilyn and would fight anyone and everyone who tried to come between them. His trick to get her back into the house was worth the risk. Hopefully, in the end, she would agree.

2

Warrick jogged across the Monarchs' practice court Monday morning. He and his teammates were running a series of plays, preparing for the Eastern Conference Championship against their rivals, the Miami Waves. He found his position in time to catch the pass from his practice squad teammate, Roger Harris. Roger usually warmed the Monarchs' bench until the second quarter. Why had his head coach, DeMarcus Guinn, assigned Warrick to the team with the bench players for this morning's practice? Shouldn't he be on the squad with the starters? What had he done wrong?

Warrick pressed the doubts to the back of his mind. He dribbled once, then drove hard toward the corner of the court, matching the ball's bounce to his steps.

Jamal Ward cursed as Warrick powered past him. The rookie turned to hustle after Warrick. But, caught off guard, Jamal was too late to defend him. Warrick steadied himself at the corner of the court, leaped, and sent a teardrop shot toward the basket. The ball kissed the backboard before diving through the hoop.

Warrick pivoted to jog back down the court. He caught up with Jamal. "Marlon Burress is going to do the same thing to you that I just did. Didn't you study the Waves' game film?"

"Obviously not; otherwise he would have known that." DeMarcus's voice dripped with disgust. His coal black eyes snapped with impatience. He blew the whistle to stop the practice, then turned to Jamal. "That two-point play should never have happened."

Warrick agreed. The rookie hadn't read the scouting reports and he wasn't giving his full effort during practice. Yet Warrick was in a white jersey with the bench players while Jamal was with the starters wearing black.

Don't let it matter. Just focus on whatever the team needs to get the win.

DeMarcus continued to glower at Jamal. Two years after retiring from the NBA, the rookie head coach's lean, six-foot-seven-inch frame was still in playing shape. "I want you to cover Burress. He can't match your speed. But if you can't anticipate his movements, your speed won't matter."

Jamal, a nineteen-year-old rookie with an attitude, curled his lip. The starting shooting guard's six-foot-four-inch wiry body seemed covered in ink. "Man, that old guy can't get past me."

DeMarcus jerked his head toward Warrick. "Rick is older than Burress, and he's already gotten past you three times this morning."

Warrick searched his coach's expression. Did De-Marcus think he was too old to start? At thirty-four, his age was the reason he had to prove himself with every game, every practice. But DeMarcus, a former NBA three-time Most Valuable Player, had stayed in the league until he was older than Warrick was now.

Jamal cocked a hip. "I'll turn it on for the game."

Snickers and groans echoed around the practice

court. Hadn't Jamal learned anything this season? If the rookie guard didn't change his attitude, it was going to be a long seven-game series.

"Turn it on now." DeMarcus's words were sharp with impatience. "I played with Burress on the Waves for almost ten seasons. He's going to take every advantage you have over him and turn it against you. And he'll take every advantage *he* has over *you* and bury you with it."

Jamal held up his arms. "I got this, Coach."

DeMarcus raised his right hand for the ball.

Serge Gateau, the Monarchs' six-foot-ten starting forward, lobbed it to him. The Frenchman from Lourdes wore his dark blond hair pulled straight back in a shoulder-length ponytail. His lean square features were clean-shaven, his blue eyes sharp.

DeMarcus pressed his clipboard against Jamal's chest. "Take a seat and watch how it's done. I'll guard Rick while he plays Burress."

Jamal took the clipboard. "Why can't I be Burress?"

Vincent Jardine, the team's center, chuckled. "You can't even play Jamal."

Jamal glowered at the other man. "Shut up."

DeMarcus spoke over his shoulder. "Rick does a better Burress than Burress. Sit down."

Warrick watched Jamal trudge off the court. His sneakers squeaked against the gleaming hardwood floor as he crossed the practice facility to stand sulking on the sideline. Would they ever get through to the rookie? Almost a year ago, Jamal had left Michigan State University after his freshman year. One and done. Now, at the age of nineteen, he had a seven-figure contract with the Monarchs. He had the skills, the payday, and the job. When would he get the maturity?

DeMarcus blew his whistle, a wordless command for

the team's full attention. He heaved the ball at Warrick.
"Show me what you've got."

Warrick caught the basketball at chest level. Hadn't
he been doing that all season? What more was his coach
looking for? Warrick dribbled the ball while he considered his next move. He was Marlon Burress playing
against his longtime teammate and fellow future hall-
of-famer. What would Burress do? Warrick got into
character, giving DeMarcus a small, taunting smile. His
coach's eyes widened, then narrowed. Warrick feinted
right, then spun left, switching the ball to his left hand.

DeMarcus moved to Warrick's left. He gestured
toward point guard Darius Williams, a bench player
wearing the starters' black jersey. "Box him in."

Darius crowded Warrick on his right, blocking his
access to the paint. The bench players swarmed the
perimeter in a ring of white jerseys. The starters clad in
black covered them. With Warrick double teamed, one
of the white jerseys was left undefended. Warrick exchanged a look with Roger Harris, his open teammate.
A split second of silent communication.

Get ready.

Warrick heaved the ball into the open lane. Roger
snatched it from the air and slammed it into the basket.
Two points.

Adrenaline rushed through Warrick. He clenched a
fist. From the sideline, Jamal cheered. Warrick turned
to jog back up the court. The sound of DeMarcus's
whistle brought him up short.

DeMarcus stood with his hands on his hips and a reluctant smile easing his expression. "I didn't see that
coming."

Warrick faced his coach. "You thought Burress
would take it in."

DeMarcus chuckled. "He usually does."

Warrick wiped sweat from his brow. "That's why he would've passed."

Jamal ran onto the court and stopped beside De-Marcus. "In your face! In your face!"

DeMarcus gave the younger man a look that humbled him. Jamal joined the other starters.

Oscar Clemente, the Monarchs' first assistant head coach, drew nearer. His intense dark eyes gleamed. "You beat him with your mind."

Warrick nodded. "Burress plays smart as well as hard. If he's up against someone who knows his moves, he'll do something unexpected."

Oscar smoothed back the few gray hairs circling his rounded pink pate. His expression was smug. "You read your opponents the same way Marc does."

That was the second time Oscar had made a comment comparing him to DeMarcus. What was the old guy up to?

DeMarcus took his clipboard from Jamal. "Rick, I'm putting you on Burress. You know his moves and what he's thinking. Jamal, you take Millbank."

Jamal sighed. "Whatever. I just hope we can finish one series without having to go all seven games. I'm tired."

Warrick cleared the sweat from his forehead. "I don't care how many games we have to play as long as we get the ring in the end."

Oscar glanced at DeMarcus. "Spoken like a champion."

DeMarcus jerked his chin toward Warrick. "Rick, get a black jersey. Darius, put on the white one."

Warrick breathed easier. He was still on the starting roster. He hustled to the benches to grab a fresh black jersey. He'd won the fight to save his starting position.

Now if he could win the battle to save his marriage, he'd have everything he'd ever wanted.

Marilyn took a deep breath, squared her shoulders, and exhaled. The meeting room of the Linden Boulevard Women's Health Clinic was scented with peach potpourri. She checked her posture and concentrated on not fidgeting. Her gaze bounced off the Georgia O'Keeffe paintings mounted to the pale peach walls before landing on the two women seated across from her. They looked fresh from the salon. Their tailored power skirt suits dripped with accessories.

She crossed her legs under the round blond wood table. She'd taken an early lunch break this Monday morning to meet with the clinic partners before returning to the hospital. "I'm excited about the prospect of joining your practice."

Janet Crowley gave her a gracious smile. Her cap of glossy black hair framed her thin dark features. "We're excited about our plans for the future of the clinic. Health care lectures, free screenings for women with low income. We're looking for corporate sponsors to partner with us to grow these programs."

Dionne Sproles, the more animated of the two, spread her arms. Her large gray eyes shone with enthusiasm. "Women are the backbone of our families. We're the nurses, chauffeurs, accountants, tutors. We take care of everyone else. Who takes care of us? We do. Well, it's time we got some help and the knowledge to make ourselves better, healthier. The LB Clinic is going to lead the way with that effort."

Marilyn's pulse leaped with excitement. "Those are the kind of programs in which I'd like to get involved.

Women's health care is more than annual checkups. It's prevention and education. I'd like to help you develop those programs and get them started."

She sipped her coffee. The hot, bitter brew made her eyes tear and her tongue itch. Luckily, the clinic had other things than its java to recommend it. Chief among them was the ability to set her own hours and better supervise her patients' care.

Dionne tapped the manila folder beside her coffee mug. "What we've learned about you so far is really impressive. You have a strong résumé and great experience."

Janet leaned back in her seat. "And, of course, your credit report and background are excellent."

Marilyn relaxed by degrees. "I was fortunate to get into Stanford for my undergrad and the University of Pennsylvania Medical School. They're both very strong programs."

The two other women exchanged smiles. Janet lifted her coffee. Her dark brown eyes gleamed over the rim of her mug. "We meant your family. The Devrys of northern California have an impeccable reputation. They're old, established money."

Dionne nodded, her auburn hair waving around her face and shoulders. "Your family is really well respected. They're well regarded for their philanthropy and have a lot of connections all over the country."

Marilyn stiffened. The two partners were tripping over themselves in praise of her lineage. Her fingers tightened around her china coffee cup. "I'm proud of my family's personal and financial contributions to social causes. It's a commitment that's spanned generations and one I'll continue. But I'm not here as my family's representative. I'm representing only myself."

Had she made herself clear? She wouldn't go to her family for financial assistance or business introductions.

If the clinic partners agreed for her to buy into the clinic, they'd get Marilyn Devry-Evans only. She wasn't a package deal.

Janet's smile didn't reach her eyes. "We can't run away from our names, though."

Marilyn returned her cup and saucer to the table. She didn't want to risk breaking them. "No, we can't. But I don't intend to trade on it, either."

Janet tilted her head to the right. Her curtain of ebony hair swung with it. "Do you feel that way with both of your names?"

Marilyn's shoulder muscles tightened. "Yes, I do. My family and my husband have achieved a lot. Now I want to make my own mark as an obstetrician/gynecologist and women's health professional."

The partners exchanged looks again. Janet crossed her legs. "Frankly, Marilyn, as impressed as we are with the Devrys' stature and reputation, we're less impressed with the Evans side of your family."

Marilyn's skin heated. "Have you been checking on my family?"

Janet shook her head. "Only what we've heard in the media."

"And what we've found on the Internet." Dionne smoothed her auburn hair in an odd, over-caffeinated manner.

Marilyn folded her hands on her lap. "Unfortunately, not everything you hear in the media or read on the Internet is true."

Janet checked her manicure. "Your husband makes a living playing a child's game."

Marilyn's face tightened. "My husband is a professional athlete. He works hard and is paid well. But what does that have to do with me?"

Janet swept a hand toward her. "You're his wife.

What he does reflects on you. Frankly, I'm afraid we don't approve of his lifestyle. We don't believe it suits our image."

Marilyn's eyes narrowed. "What is it about his lifestyle that concerns you?"

Dionne shrugged. "We've heard about celebrities' really loose social lives."

Oh, this should be good.

Marilyn's gaze swung between Janet and Dionne. "With how many professional athletes have you socialized?"

Janet smoothed her hair in an almost defensive gesture. "None, but we've heard of the wild parties and loose women."

Marilyn's burst of laughter startled even herself. "My husband's not the stereotypical celebrity. Just like every other demographic in society, some athletes party a lot and some don't. My husband prefers quiet nights at home—with me."

Dionne angled her chin. Her gray eyes were troubled. "It was widely reported that Rick Evans was in a Cleveland bar the night before one of the team's games."

Widely reported? "Actually, it appeared in one online gossip blog and the writer had an ax to grind against the Monarchs." Warrick's words rang nicely—probably because they were true.

Janet waved her hand dismissively. "In any event, we don't want those rumors reflecting badly on our business interests. We don't think you'd want that, either."

No, she didn't. But what were they suggesting? "What would you recommend I do?"

Dionne leaned forward. "Talk with him. Tell him he has to be aware of how his behavior affects your career."

Janet commanded her gaze. "We're looking at two

other candidates. You're well regarded professionally. Our only concern is your husband's reputation."

Marilyn suppressed her irritation. She looked from Janet to Dionne. "I'll speak with him. I'm certain we won't have any cause for concern."

That's because Warrick's reputation was just as impeccable as the clinic's partners', perhaps more.

"We hope so. We'd like you to be part of our team." Janet's expression was more avaricious than welcoming.

"I'd like that, too." Marilyn finished her coffee.

The clinic partnership was another part of her plan to build an identity separate from her larger-than-life parents. But the look in Janet's eyes made her wonder if she could ever put enough distance between herself and her parents.

"The clinic partnership may not work out." Marilyn curled up on the rose-colored love seat in the living room of Emma's condo. Her friend had a penchant for pastels and fluffy furniture.

Emma Mane lowered herself to the matching armchair. Her honey blond hair swept over her left shoulder as she turned toward Marilyn on her right. "What happened? Did they reject your application?"

"No. They said they were impressed with my résumé and my background. They'd checked my credit, which is good. But they seemed more interested in my parents than me."

Marilyn had changed into her baggy red cotton shorts and Warrick's silver Monarchs T-shirt. The comfortable outfit usually helped her relax after a long, stressful day at the hospital. But tonight, she couldn't settle her thoughts.

Emma crossed her legs. Her lemon capris exposed her lower calves and ankles. "Well, your parents are very well known in philanthropic circles. I'm sure your prospective partners have at least considered approaching them for a donation."

Resentment soured Marilyn stomach. "That's an irresponsible reason to invite someone to become a partner of a clinic."

Emma shrugged her thin shoulders beneath her bright white T-shirt. "Maybe. But it's a strategic move that immediately gets them closer to your parents' purse."

Marilyn drummed her fingers against the love seat's padded arm. "I can't guarantee that my parents will invest in the clinic. Besides, they're in northern California. There are plenty of philanthropists in New York."

"But none of them are your parents." Emma sounded drained from her hospital duty hours. As a pediatric doctor, she often treated injuries children should never experience.

Marilyn uncurled her legs from the cushions and folded her arms. "Janet and Dionne are going to take a risk on *me* to get to my *parents*. I don't know who should be more insulted, me or my parents."

She wanted her own practice so she could be her own boss and set her own hours. More importantly, she wanted to go into private practice so she could provide continuity of care to her patients. Marilyn had no interest in mooching off her parents' achievements.

"It's just business, Mary."

"They're also concerned about Rick."

"Why?" Emma dragged her fingers through her wavy blond hair.

A spark of temper shot into Marilyn's gut at the memory of the partners' accusations. "They said his lifestyle wouldn't reflect well on their practice. They implied Rick was a partier and a womanizer. He's neither."

Emma straightened. A pensive expression settled over her sharp features. "What makes them think he is?"

Marilyn crossed her legs. She tapped her bare right foot to the staccato beat pounding at her temples. "They read about the night he and the other players went looking for Barron Douglas in that Cleveland bar."

Why had the team's captain gone bar hopping the night before a game anyway?

"Rick should have known how it would look for him to be in a bar." Emma's gaze dropped to Marilyn's Monarchs T-shirt before lifting again to her eyes. "He should have thought about how his actions would affect you, personally and professionally."

"He was trying to help a teammate. You'd do the same thing for me, wouldn't you?"

Emma shrugged. "Of course. We're friends."

"The players care about each other."

Emma shook her head. "You're Rick's wife. His first loyalty should be to you."

"I don't blame Rick for looking for Barron."

Emma's gaze bore into Marilyn's. "Then why are you here?"

The question almost stole her breath. "Because the media is all over Rick now that the Monarchs are winning. That kind of constant public scrutiny wasn't part of my life plan."

Emma smiled. "Ah, your famous plan."

Marilyn shrugged. "You laugh, but I put a lot of thought and hard work into that plan. I moved across the country to escape my parents' celebrity and just as I begin to develop my own identity, I get caught up in the media storm of my husband's celebrity."

Emma spread her arms. "I'd be frustrated, too. It

makes it harder that Rick doesn't understand what he's putting you through."

Marilyn wished he did. She uncrossed her arms. "I'm returning home Wednesday."

Emma's green eyes darkened with concern. "Did I say something to upset you?"

"No." Marilyn's knees were unsteady as she stood. Her bare feet sank into the plush pink carpeting. "Rick leaves for Miami in two days for the Monarchs' first game against the Waves. He and I agreed that I'd move back home while he's away."

Emma stood, too. "You don't have to leave. You can stay as long as you'd like."

Marilyn shook her head. "Thank you for the offer, but I don't want to impose on you any longer. Besides, I want my own things around me."

"You're not an imposition. We've been friends since college. Just remember I'm only a phone call away. We can still talk whenever you need to."

"Thanks. I just need to think things through." Marilyn started toward the bedroom, but Emma's voice stopped her.

"Mary, it's fine to be supportive of Rick's career. But don't forget your own."

Marilyn's smile felt stiff. "Good night."

"Good night." Emma's wishes followed Marilyn into the nearby guest bedroom.

Marilyn leaned against the closed door and exhaled.

It's fine to be supportive of Rick's career, but don't forget your own.

She crossed the thick carpet to stand beside the bed. Marilyn pulled Rick's jersey over her head and held the material to her nose. It didn't carry his scent, soap, and sandalwood, anymore.

She and Warrick supported each other's careers to the best of their abilities. She'd missed so many of his games when her patients went into labor. But he attended as many hospital functions as his schedule would allow. And he was a generous donor to their causes. She smiled, recalling the way his wicked banter kept her from being bored out of her mind during those forced-fun events.

But what about now? Could she adjust her life plan to this unexpected development in her marriage? Should she?

3

Warrick's pulse kicked when he heard the key turn in the front door Tuesday evening. He stepped into the hallway as Marilyn entered. "I wasn't expecting to see you tonight." He'd been sure she'd wait until he was out of the state before moving back into their home.

Marilyn hesitated, then pulled her key from the lock and secured the door. "I didn't mean to interrupt you."

"You're not interrupting anything. This is your home, too." How many times would he have to remind her before it sunk in? "How did your meeting with the clinic partners go yesterday?"

She set her suitcase beside her on the hardwood flooring. "It went well. My references and my credit report are good."

Warrick's gaze dropped to Marilyn's mouth. She was biting the corner of her lower lip. What wasn't she telling him?

He closed the distance between them and took her suitcase. "When will they give you their decision?"

"Hopefully, any day now." Marilyn followed him farther into their home.

"I know how important having your own practice is

to you. You'd be an asset to any clinic. They'd be stupid not to accept your offer." *Don't talk too much. Don't let her know that you're nervous.* Warrick mounted the wide polished maple staircase.

"Thank you." Her voice trailed behind him. "I thought I'd sleep in the guest room tonight since you're leaving tomorrow afternoon anyway."

Warrick welcomed her words. "It'll give us a chance to talk."

"What more is there to say?"

"You can start with whatever you're not telling me." At the top of the stairs, Warrick turned right toward the guest bedroom and set her suitcase on the bed.

"Weren't you in the middle of something when I arrived?"

He recognized stalling tactics when he heard them.

Warrick crossed back to the doorway and stared down into his wife's chocolate eyes. Marilyn's soft jasmine scent floated up to him. "I was preparing for the Waves but it can wait. What's wrong?"

Marilyn squeezed past him to wander farther into the room. "I'm concerned about the partnership."

"Why?" He tracked her agitated movements.

She shrugged a slender shoulder beneath her off-white blouse. "Janet and Dionne seem more interested in having a connection to my parents than in what I can bring to the partnership."

"Why do you think that?"

"They recounted my parents' praises as though they were submitting their names for canonization." Marilyn toed off her sensible black flats. "I want this partnership on my own merits, not because of who my parents are."

Warrick watched her finger the dust catchers on the dressing table—votive candles, figurines, and bottles of lotion. "Maybe it's both, honey. They wouldn't check your references and credit if your professional background didn't matter. They'd have just rubber stamped your offer."

"Maybe you're right." Marilyn moved past the table and closed the window blinds against the growing shadows outside. "I've worked hard to build my career as Marilyn Devry-Evans. I thought I'd finally stopped being Terrell and Celeste's daughter."

"You have." Warrick watched her jerky movements, sensed the tension circling her. What else wasn't she telling him? He tried to lighten the mood. "Janet and Dionne will realize you'd be a good fit for their clinic. What's not to love?"

Marilyn stiffened at his question. She faced him from across the room. "They do have one concern about me."

Her expression filled him with dread. "What?"

"You."

Warrick's eyebrows jumped up his forehead. "What about me?"

She twined her fingers together. "They're concerned that the media attention on you could reflect badly on their practice."

His anger melted the ice that had settled in his gut. "What does my press have to do with their practice?"

Marilyn met his gaze. "Negative coverage might make patients wonder why Dionne and Janet allowed me to join their practice."

Warrick crossed his arms. "What did you say?"

"That the media coverage is a misrepresentation of the truth, if not outright lies. They amount to deliberate smear campaigns against you."

Her outrage calmed him. He wasn't alone. She still believed in him. "Were they satisfied?"

"No." Marilyn's eyes scanned the room's warm wood

and green decor. "The press is a large part of the reason you and I have arrived where we are."

The weight returned to Warrick's back. "I know."

She hugged her arms around her torso. "Janet and Dionne's comments are another reason I'm just not certain I can be a celebrity's wife."

He stilled. "What do you mean?"

"The media's personal attacks against us affect me professionally."

"Those aren't even real reporters." Warrick clenched his hands. They were damp with sweat. "They're gossip columnists. You shouldn't pay attention to them."

Marilyn swung her right hand toward the room's two windows. "Even if I don't, they do."

"The public will take their cue from you." Warrick struggled to keep his tone reasonable. "You handled Janet and Dionne well. People will eventually stop asking you about the gossip because they'll know you don't give it any credence."

Marilyn smoothed her hand over her hair. "I spent the first twenty years of my life trying to meet the standards my parents had set with their high profile. Now I have to defend myself from media attacks because of my husband's fame." She pulled the clip from her hair and drew her fingers through her thick tresses. "I had other plans for my life. I hadn't intended to live it with a camera in my face."

Warrick leaned his right shoulder against the doorjamb as the pressure beat against him. "I know this is hard, Mary. The negative attention is new to you. But I've been dealing with it since college. It does get easier."

"I can't wait that long." Marilyn's voice trembled.

Warrick heard his heart beating. "What are you saying?"

"Your celebrity is affecting our marriage. Now, it's

also affecting my career." She paused for forever. "Maybe we should get a divorce."

Marilyn's words echoed in his head. *Maybe we should get a divorce. Maybe we should get a divorce. Maybe we should get a divorce.*

Warrick's body shook. The room spun. If he weren't leaning against the threshold, he would have crumpled to the floor. Marilyn's face, stiff and pale, went in and out of focus.

"You want to divorce me so you can get your partnership?" His lips were numb. If only his heart were, too.

Marilyn raised her hands, palms up. "Our relationship is already under a lot of strain."

"So you're going to throw it away for your career."

"Rick, it's—"

He left the room, closing the door with quiet restraint behind him.

Maybe we should get a divorce. Maybe we should get a divorce. Maybe we should get a divorce.

Warrick's legs carried him down the hall toward the master bedroom. On autopilot, he found a pair of socks and his running shoes. Minutes later, he jogged down the stairs and out of his home. A cool evening breeze softly kissed his heated cheek and wrapped the scent of spring around him. Warrick blinked the sting from his eyes. He had to keep moving. He didn't know what would happen if he stopped. And he was afraid to find out.

"Get your head in the game, Rick." DeMarcus sounded like he was chewing nails. The same nails he'd use to pin Warrick's ass to the wall after this debacle, otherwise known as Thursday's game one of the Monarchs' Eastern Conference Championship series against the

Miami Waves. His coach was using the team's final time-out to make that clear.

Standing on the sidelines surrounded by exhausted teammates and an apoplectic head coach, Warrick wiped the sweat from his brow with his right forearm. He hadn't spoken with Marilyn since Tuesday night. Was she watching the game?

DeMarcus got in his face. "Are you hearing me, Rick?"

Warrick flinched. At DeMarcus's caustic tone or Marilyn's request for a divorce? "I heard you, Coach."

Would Marilyn stay with him if the media gave him positive press? Would that make a difference or was she opposed to any type of coverage?

Warrick glanced at the clock. Twenty-nine seconds remained to the game. The Monarchs were down by 12 points, 98 to 86. No way were they getting back into this contest. All they could hope for was a more respectable final score. A loss was a loss. But no one wanted to be blown out.

DeMarcus continued growling at him. "Burress is getting into your head. You're missing rebounds, breaking plays. Focus."

The buzzer sounded. Warrick followed his teammates onto the court. Vincent Jardine, the Monarchs' center, inbounded the ball to starting forward Anthony Chambers. The shot clock gave the Monarchs a fresh twenty-four seconds. Warrick felt Marlon Burress leaning against him. He pushed back, keeping his arms free.

Burress pitched his voice to be heard above the roar of the Waves' fans. "You never answered me. You and your shortie getting back together?"

"Mind your business." Warrick mentally kicked himself for responding to his opponent. Again. *Block out the noise.*

He watched Anthony dribble to the paint, then pass the ball to Serge at the post. A swarm of green and white Waves jerseys covered him. Warrick drew closer to the paint, ready to grab the ball if Serge couldn't get to the basket. The game clock counted down to seventeen seconds. The shot clock flashed off.

Burress was on his back like white on rice. "Heard your shortie moved out. Been gone long?"

Warrick strained to shut out Burress's words and focus on the game.

Maybe we should get a divorce.

Get your head in the game.

Serge kicked the ball ahead to Warrick. Warrick missed the pass. Walter Millbank, the Waves' near-seven-foot shooting guard, slapped the ball aside right into Burress's hands.

"Are you here to play?" Vincent snapped the question as he raced back up the court.

Warrick gritted his teeth as he also gave chase. How had he missed that grab?

Burress jumped to the basket for an easy layup and another two points for the Waves. Vincent recovered the ball with seven seconds left to the game. He raced back down the court. Warrick hustled to the basket. He could hear Burress's footsteps behind him.

The Monarchs set up in the paint and around the perimeter. The Waves covered them. Three seconds remained to the game. The Monarchs now trailed by 14 points, 100 to 86.

"You know your wife saw that." Burress's taunt was breathless. "Wonder what she thinks about your game now."

Vincent lobbed the ball to Anthony, who passed it on to Warrick. Warrick caught the ball with his right hand and jabbed his left elbow into Burress's gut. An eagle-eyed referee blew his whistle to stop the clock. He called a well-deserved offensive foul on Warrick. It was his fourth foul of the game. Warrick tossed the ball to the referee. His steps dragged as he went up court to the basket.

The Monarchs and Waves lined up in the paint, waiting for Burress to take his free throws.

"Focus on the game, Rick." Serge's French accent sharpened as he hissed the command.

Burress made the first basket, increasing the score to 101 to 86. He missed the second basket.

Jamal jumped for the loose ball, then heaved it across the court. The ball caught air, coming up short. The game clock buzzed at zero seconds. Final score, Waves 101 to Monarchs 86. Blowout.

Warrick turned toward Vom Two, the tunnel that led to the visitors' locker rooms. Guilt dragged on his body. He'd allowed Marlon Burress so deep inside his head that if he sneezed, Burress would be torn apart. Not a completely unpleasant image.

Hours later, Warrick sprawled on top of the covers on the hotel bed. He replayed his game. What could he have done better? He reran the postgame conference. What could he have explained more clearly? He relived his argument with Marilyn. What could he do to save his marriage?

A knock on his hotel room door startled him. He glanced at the radio alarm clock beside his bed. It was after one in the morning. The sound came again. Warrick ignored it.

The knock was louder, firmer, and accompanied by a voice. "It's Marc. Open the door."

Warrick recalled the look on DeMarcus's face as the

team rode back to their Miami hotel. He never wanted to see that look on his coach's face again.

He rolled off the bed and padded barefoot across the room. He opened the door and stepped aside. "What can I do for you, Coach?"

"What the hell's going on with you?" DeMarcus strode into the room, still wearing his black European-style suit. He looked as tired as Warrick felt.

Warrick had discarded his suit coat and tie. The first two buttons of his white shirt were undone. "It's after one in the morning, Coach. Do we have to do this now?"

DeMarcus turned toward him, loosening his silver tie. "Talk fast."

Warrick swallowed a sigh and closed the door. "You were right. I let Burress get into my head. It won't happen again."

DeMarcus studied him for several intent seconds. Finally, he shoved his hands into the front pockets of his pants. "I don't get you, Rick. On the one hand, if it weren't for you, we wouldn't be in the conference championship. Hell, we wouldn't have made it to the play-offs."

"It was a team effort." Warrick shrugged off the accolade and stepped around DeMarcus. He folded his body into one of the room's doll-sized armchairs.

DeMarcus circled to face him. "The team came together under you. You changed the chemistry."

"I can say that about you."

DeMarcus ignored his interruption. "You're hot on offense, strong on defense, and have the mental game. But tonight, you came up with crap. What happened?"

The criticism was as hard to take as the compliments. "I wasn't ready for Burress's trash-talking."

"It's more than that."

"No. It's not." Warrick lied without flinching.

DeMarcus gave him another long, silent stare. "You'll be ready by Saturday?"

"Yes, Coach." He hoped.

"You'd better be. No one steps up when you're off your game."

Warrick shifted restlessly in the stingy chair. "We have eleven other guys who can step up."

DeMarcus arched a cynical brow. "Jamal?"

Warrick sighed, a deep exhale that didn't relieve the knot in his gut. "All right. Ten." He stood, hoping to bring the conversation to an end. "I'm sorry I let you down, Coach. I'll get my mind back in the game by Saturday."

DeMarcus claimed the matching armchair and looked up at Warrick. "I don't blame you for the loss, Rick."

Warrick clenched his teeth and settled back into his seat. Obviously, DeMarcus wasn't done. "I appreciate that, Coach."

DeMarcus shrugged. "I blame myself. I thought the team could lean on you, but I was wrong."

The backhanded criticism was a punch to the solar plexus. How had his career fallen so far? A couple of years ago, he'd been the team's captain and a starting player. Now he was coming off the bench because the current team captain was on the Injured List while he rehabbed at a substance abuse facility.

Warrick forced a smile. "Nice try, Coach. But that mental game works better on a rookie."

DeMarcus's grin turned into rueful chuckles. "I said the same thing when my coach tried that line on me. It was during my final season in the league."

That was the year after DeMarcus's mother had died, Warrick realized. "Real sensitive guy."

DeMarcus smiled at Warrick's sarcasm. "He did what he felt he had to do to win. We should take a page from his book. Do you have what it takes to be a winner, Rick?"

He didn't think about it. He didn't hesitate. He just answered. "Yes."

"That's what matters. It doesn't matter what the media writes, what fans say, or what opponents do on the court. All that matters is what you believe."

"I believe in this team and myself." *And I believe in my marriage.* "We can win the conference, Coach."

DeMarcus nodded. "Then fight for it. Nothing worth having ever comes easily."

Warrick's heart beat faster. "You're right."

He was going to fight for both rings, the championship ring and his wedding band. He knew what he needed to win the conference championship—a strong defense and a relentless offense. What did he need to save his marriage?

"Rick had a tough game last night." Emma shook dressing over her chicken Caesar salad.

The hospital cafeteria was almost empty on this Friday afternoon as Marilyn joined her friend for a late lunch. She popped open the tab on her can of diet soda and took a long drink. "In all of the series, the Monarchs have struggled with the first game."

"They may need to have someone else play against that Miami Waves guy they've matched Rick with." Emma stabbed several lettuce leaves and a chunk of chicken.

Her friend knew less than she did about basketball—which meant Emma was clueless about the sport. But she spoke as though she were on the coaching staff.

Marilyn squelched a smile. "It was one game, Em. I

don't think Marc Guinn should throw out the game plan just yet."

Emma swallowed the forkful of salad. "Well, I hope Rick does better tomorrow night."

"He will." Marilyn warmed with pride each time she thought of her husband's contributions to get his team to the play-offs for the first time in fifteen years. But was the price he was paying worth it?

Emma gathered more salad. "Have you heard from the clinic partners?"

"No, and I don't think I will." Marilyn spooned up her Italian wedding soup.

Emma's eyes narrowed. "Stop being so negative. Of course they're going to call you. They'll probably offer you the partnership."

"But who will they want, me or the Devrys' daughter?"

Emma's tone was exasperated. "Who do you want to be?"

Marilyn sighed, part irritation, part frustration. "Marilyn Devry-Evans. That's who I am. I think we've met."

"Come on, Mary. Everyone is defined by someone, whether it's your kids, career, or spouse. Someone defines you."

Marilyn spoke with measured calm. "I'm aware of that and it makes sense on some level. But these other identities shouldn't overshadow who I am."

Emma snorted. "This is the opportunity you've wanted for years. If they offer it to you, whether they want you to be Marilyn Devry, Marilyn Evans, or Marilyn Monroe, you'd better grab it."

Marilyn spooned more soup. "They don't want Marilyn Evans, remember?"

"Have you heard from Rick?" Emma's question interrupted Marilyn's gloomy thoughts.

"He hasn't returned my calls." Her heart was like a dead thing in her chest.

Emma shrugged one shoulder. "Well, when you first moved out, you didn't return any of his calls, either."

Marilyn lowered her spoon and pushed away her soup. The tiny meatballs and barley weren't as appealing now.

"I asked him for a divorce." She drew her gaze from her lunch to her friend.

Emma dropped her fork. Her green eyes widened and her red lips parted. "Do you *want* a divorce?"

Marilyn crossed her arms and leaned them on the table. She studied the sanitized gray and white room. The blue soda vending machine in the corner gave the space its only splash of color.

Her eyes returned to Emma. "I don't know. When I imagine my life without him . . . I'm still in love with him."

"Then why did you ask for a divorce?"

Marilyn shook her head in a helpless gesture. "I traveled three thousand miles to escape the media scrutiny of being the Devrys' daughter. Then I married an NBA player. Now I'm being scrutinized as Rick Evans's wife."

"I've always admired you for wanting your own identity. But you have to make the decision about a divorce for yourself. Don't let the media make it for you."

Marilyn clenched her fists. "The media is the reason my marriage is falling apart."

Emma gave her a searching look, the remnants of her salad apparently forgotten in front of her. "I agree. I'd never have married someone who lived in front of the camera. It was bound to cause a strain on your personal life. And now it's hampering your career."

Marilyn leaned back in her chair, crossing her arms and legs. "I never wanted to choose between my marriage and my career."

"I know. All I'm saying is that, if you really do love Rick, there's got to be another solution to your problem rather than a divorce."

Marilyn pulled her hand over her hair. "Like what?"

"I don't know. But if your marriage is worth it, you'll figure something out to save it and your career."

Marilyn swallowed the dry lump in her throat. "I'm still in love with Rick. I just don't want to share him with millions of NBA fans. And I don't think being married to a professional athlete should make my private life fair game."

Emma leaned into the table, moving closer to Marilyn. "Well, no matter what happens, I'm here for you."

"I know, Em."

They were as different as oil and water, but somehow they'd maintained a friendship that had spanned sixteen years. Emma's advice against marrying a professional baller had been the only time they'd seriously disagreed. Had she been right?

Emma grinned. "If you do get that divorce, you should go for the house and a big alimony."

Marilyn's brow furrowed. "I don't need alimony. I have a job. And I wouldn't ask for the house. It was his before we got married."

"So what? You both live there now. And, if he paid you alimony, you wouldn't have to work." Emma returned to eating her salad with newfound gusto.

Marilyn glanced at her soup. She still wasn't hungry. "I enjoy working. I love what I do."

"I suppose you love Arthur, too." Emma's voice was dry.

Marilyn's nose wrinkled at the mention of the grouchy hospital administrator. "I could live without his micromanaging everyone."

Emma's green eyes glowed with triumph. "And you would—if you fought for alimony."

"I'm not going to ask for alimony." Marilyn's tone was final. "My parents had wanted me to marry a doctor. I became one instead. I'm not going to give up my career to sit at home, waiting for Rick's check."

"I would." Emma shrugged again. "But it's your choice."

Marilyn shook her head with a mixture of amusement and disbelief. Yes, they were oil and water. Sometimes it surprised her that they were friends.

4

The last time the press had written about the Monarchs, they'd skinned the team alive. Warrick had been sleeping alone for the past month because of the press. So why was he sitting in the Miami Waves Arena's conference room Saturday morning, waiting to start this interview with Kirk West of the *New York Horn* instead of preparing for tonight's game?

Troy Marshall.

Warrick slid a glance at the Monarchs' vice president of media and marketing sitting beside him. Troy had insisted the team needed this interview to help with publicity. Did the marketing executive know what he was asking? Probably not, and Warrick wasn't eager to enlighten him.

With his classic features and close-cropped hair, the media executive looked like a male model. Well over six-feet tall and physically fit, the desk jockey also looked like a professional basketball player. But Troy hadn't played competitively since his college years at Georgetown University in Washington, DC.

Warrick returned his attention to the sports reporter across the table. Kirk held his pen with surgical precision above a blank page in his notepad. The audio device in the center of the circular, blond wood table was recording.

Kirk's sharp blue gaze dissected him. "Rumor has it that you and your wife are separated. How is that affecting your game?"

Warrick shot a look at Troy. This interview was going to help the team with publicity? How?

He gave Kirk a stony stare. "Are you a sports reporter or a gossip columnist? The lines are blurring."

Kirk's cheeks darkened with an angry blush. "Fans are paying a lot of money to watch you play. They have a right to know whether you're going to give them one hundred percent on the court or if you're going to be distracted."

"Is that the fans' question or yours?" Warrick truly wanted to know.

Troy rested a hand on Warrick's shoulder but kept his gaze on Kirk. "Questions about Rick's personal life don't belong in this interview. You know that, Kirk. When the Monarchs are on the court, it's all about the game. That's what you can tell the fans."

Warrick's muscles relaxed. He'd been angrier than he'd realized. Troy's support went a long way toward defusing his temper.

Kirk looked at Troy. "The fans are already asking what happened to Rick's game. He's the one who carried the team to the play-offs."

Irritation surged through Warrick. "There are thirteen Monarchs. It took every one of us to get to the conference championship. Put that in your article."

Kirk pressed the tip of his pen against the blank page. "But if Marc Guinn hadn't benched Barron Douglas in favor of playing *you*, the Monarchs would have lost their final game of the regular season and missed the play-offs."

"You're speculating." Warrick frowned.

Kirk gestured with his pen. "It's not speculation that, when you have a good game, the team wins, and when you don't, they lose."

Warrick shook his head. "You can say that about all of us—Vinny's rebounds, Serge's jumpers, Tony's assists. It's simple mathematics. When we score more points than the other team, we win."

Kirk narrowed his eyes. "Why are you reluctant to admit that, with Barron on the bench, you're the team's de facto leader?"

Warrick swallowed a sigh. *When will this ordeal be over?* "Not having Barron on the court with us is a great loss for the team. No one can fill his role."

Kirk lowered his pen. "Why won't you accept the team's leadership role? Are you afraid of the responsibility?"

The reporter was baiting him. And it was working. "Why are you determined to single out one player? Is it too much work to interview all of us?"

"Rick." Troy's warning tone reminded Warrick not to push the media too far. Fair or not, they always had the final word.

Kirk's thin face flushed to the roots of his blond hair. His blue eyes narrowed. "I've interviewed the key players of all thirty NBA teams. Your chemistry is what makes the difference for the Monarchs."

Warrick leaned back in his seat. "We don't have individual stars. We play as a team. That's what we're going to have to do to earn the title." He couldn't have the media singling him out continually. It was causing dissension in the team.

Kirk arched a brow. "Well, since you aren't interested in individual accolades, I guess it doesn't bother you that you were passed over for Defensive Player of the

Year or that your name hasn't been mentioned for Most Valuable Player. You're probably used to being passed over for recognition in the league."

Warrick kept his features controlled. He pushed back from the table and stood. "I have a game to prepare for."

He didn't look back. He didn't say another word. Warrick crossed to the door and left the room.

He couldn't have cared less for individual accolades. What he was after was his team's support. Twelve years ago, the franchise had drafted him to bring home the NBA Championship trophy. With each passing season, the fans and his teammates had lost faith in him. And he'd failed to impress his head coaches.

Yes, the reporter had struck a nerve. Why would he expect the league to present him with honors and awards when the Monarchs and their fans didn't believe in him?

Marilyn jerked awake at the telephone's sudden shrieks. Who was calling so early on a Sunday morning? Was Warrick all right? Was it one of her patients? What time was it?

She grabbed the receiver for answers. "Hello?"

"Did you see today's paper?" Celeste Devry's tone was disapproving. That wasn't unusual.

Marilyn wilted with relief, then tried to focus on her mother's question. "I haven't seen the day."

"Don't be smart, Marilyn."

The green digits of the radio alarm clock beside the phone read three-twelve. On Sunday morning. Was her mother kidding?

Marilyn closed her eyes. "What are *you* doing up? It's after midnight over there."

She refused to believe her mother was already dressed with her hair perfectly arranged and cosmetics flawlessly applied. At this hour, that was too much to expect, even for Celeste Devry.

"Have you seen the article in the *New York Horn* about Rick?"

Marilyn opened her eyes and frowned toward the ceiling in the dark. "You live in San Francisco. How did you get a copy of the *New York Horn*?" Why *would she get a copy of the* New York Horn?

"We don't get that paper. We read the article online. It was posted at three A.M. That's midnight our time."

"That's three A.M. my time, Mother."

"After the media reported that whole bar-hopping business with Rick last month, your father and I got one of those Google message alert services for Rick's name."

Her mother *had* to be kidding.

Marilyn closed her eyes again. "I'm not interested in what the media have to say about my husband."

The article couldn't be that bad. The Monarchs had won the game in Miami last night. Warrick was coming home this morning. Her heart leapt with anticipation—then stilled. He was returning to Brooklyn, but not to their home. She'd moved back in and he'd offered to make other living arrangements. Where would he stay?

"You should be concerned." Celeste's tone carried a bite. "They're blaming *you* for Rick's poor performance Thursday night."

Marilyn's eyes shot open. She sat up in her king-sized bed. "How am *I* at fault?"

"They're saying your separation is a distraction for him." Celeste made a tutting sound. "This is outrageous, Marilyn. The media are speculating on your marriage. This can't be allowed to continue."

Marilyn pinched the bridge of her nose. "We can't stop them. The press will print whatever they want, whenever they want, regardless of whether it's true."

"These personal attacks aren't hurting only you. They're damaging the Devry name. We can't allow these smears to our reputation to go unchallenged." Celeste spoke with increasing anger.

"They aren't attacking *you*, Mother. They're aiming at *me*."

"You're a Devry. By targeting you, they're attacking the whole family."

Her mother was trying to make her feel guilty. It was working. "I'm sorry you feel that the entire family is under assault. But I'm afraid there isn't anything we can do to prevent the media from writing these stories."

Celeste's sigh was dramatic in its weight. "Your father and I warned you that marrying Rick was a mistake. What *is* a 'professional athlete'? He plays a game for a living, for pity's sake. How can he be expected to take anything seriously?"

Marilyn bristled at the attack against her husband. "This isn't Rick's fault. He didn't ask the press to badger him."

"He should take responsibility for his own shortcomings instead of trying to blame you. He plays basketball. All he has to do is put a ball through a basket. How hard could *that* be?"

Celeste Margot Whittingly Devry had probably never touched a basketball in her entire life. What qualified her to judge Warrick or his career?

Marilyn drew in a deep breath, then exhaled slowly. "Is Rick quoted as blaming me for having a bad game?"

"How am I supposed to know what he said?" Her mother's response was indignant.

Marilyn held on to her patience. "You read the article. I doubt he said anything about me. Rick doesn't want the media discussing his personal life any more than I do."

"Then tell these reporters to stop."

"They won't listen to us." Marilyn enunciated every word in an effort to help her mother understand. "They believe these stories sell papers. They think this is what the public wants to read."

Celeste emitted a short, harsh breath. "Well, if *you* won't stop them, your father and I will."

Marilyn squeezed her eyes shut and did a rapid ten count. "What are you going to do, Mother? You and Father don't subscribe to the *Horn*. You aren't advertisers. Are you going to buy the paper, then shut it down?" She could envision them doing that.

"No. We'll sue them."

Marilyn tightened her grip on the telephone receiver. "Don't do that."

Celeste sniffed. "Why not? You and Rick may be afraid of the media, but I'm not. *They* should fear *me*."

Save me from bossy, arrogant parents who believe the world should live in dread of them.

Marilyn pursed her lips. This wasn't a conversation she needed to have. Not at three o'clock on a Sunday morning. Not before her first cup of coffee. Not. Ever.

"Mother, what do you think would happen if you sued the *Horn*?"

"They would stop printing this nonsense."

"You're wrong—"

"Don't take that tone with me, Marilyn Louise Devry-Evans. I'm *still* your mother."

Marilyn closed her eyes and strained for patience. "I apologize. But I need you to understand that a lawsuit against the newspaper for printing articles about Rick written in good faith will only make the situation worse. It will draw even more unwanted attention to us."

Celeste made another tutting sound. "Am I supposed to just sit here on my hands like you and Rick are doing?"

"I'm certain that, if the article is as bad as you say it is—"

"You don't believe me?"

Marilyn gritted her teeth. "I'm not saying that, Mother. But I'm certain Rick has already discussed it with the Monarchs' media executive."

The silence dragged on longer than Marilyn thought was necessary. She could hear lowered voices in the background. Were her parents conferring over whether to respect her wishes on how to handle the media? That was so unfair. Did she direct her mother's promotional efforts for her philanthropic campaigns? Or tell her father how to brand his investment firm? Why did her parents think they had better insight into her marriage and Warrick's career than she and Warrick did?

Her mother's voice was grudging when she finally responded. "We'll give you one more chance. If these articles continue, we'll handle the matter our way."

Like hell they would. "If it's the damage to the Devry name that's causing you such concern, I'll just stop using it."

Marilyn recradled the receiver with restraint. It was almost half past three in the morning. The room was still dark, but she couldn't go back to sleep—not because of the media but because of her parents. They made her feel as if she were sixteen years old and needed permission to date the neighborhood bad boy.

No, she definitely wouldn't be going back to sleep. Marilyn swung her legs over the side of the bed. She glowered at the phone. Yes, she was sixteen again. Her parents were telling her what to do, and her friends were telling her who to date. Warrick was the only one encouraging her to be herself. But could she be herself if she stayed with him?

* * *

Warrick unlocked the front door of his home late Sunday morning and crossed the polished hardwood entryway. He left his travel bag at the foot of the stairs, then continued down the hall. Marilyn stood in the kitchen, as still as a statue.

His gaze moved from the rolling pin raised in her right hand to the cordless phone gripped in her left. "What are you doing?"

She spoke at the same time. "You scared the *crap* out of me. I thought you were a burglar. I was getting ready to crack open your skull with this." She waved the rolling pin.

He glanced again at the weapon. "That would have hurt."

"That was the point." She set down the rolling pin and leaned heavily against the blond wood and white-tiled kitchen island.

Guilt shivered through him to see her so shaken. "I'm sorry. I told you I'd be back today."

Marilyn looked up, pressing her right hand against her heart. "You said you'd be back in *Brooklyn*. What are you doing *here*?"

Warrick shrugged. Since she was no longer armed, he took the chance of moving closer. "I live here." He almost smiled at the confusion that blinked across her honey features.

Marilyn's brows knitted. "You said I could move back in."

"You can." Warrick stopped less than an arm's length from Marilyn, crowding her. He leaned a hip against the island.

Marilyn stepped back. "But you'll be here, too."

He searched her chocolate eyes. They were wary but warm. "It's a big house, Mary. You'll have as much—or as little—room as you'd like."

Marilyn dragged a hand through her glossy, dark brown hair. "Rick, I need time to think about where we're going—and what we're going to do about us."

He moved closer. Her jasmine scent teased him with memories of happier times. "Why do we have to be apart for you to do that?"

Marilyn walked away from the island in the center of their silver and white kitchen, increasing the distance between them. "Because I can't think when you're around." She stood with her back to him.

Her voice was low and frustrated. But her words were like an aria to his soul.

"Then maybe we're supposed to stay together." Warrick's gaze moved over the green T-shirt hugging her torso and the black biker shorts tracing her curves.

She sighed. "Rick . . ."

"We've been apart for four weeks and you haven't made a decision. You need a new strategy."

She threw him a skeptical look over her right shoulder. "What would you recommend?"

Two long strides carried him to her. "Instead of thinking about the things that are trying to tear us apart— and I'm not minimizing them—remember why we got married in the first place."

Warrick drew his fingers through her loose hair. Marilyn's sharp intake of breath made his knees weak. He wasn't too late. He hadn't already lost his wife.

But did he have what it took to keep her? He didn't even know what that was.

Marilyn turned. Her movement brought her closer to him. Warrick wrapped a loose embrace around her waist. She could pull away from him if she chose to. She didn't move.

"I remember. But I don't know if it's enough."

"It is for me."

Marilyn's gaze shifted from his, then returned. Her eyes were dark with uncertainty. "I need to decide on my own, Rick. I don't want you to influence me."

But it was all right for Emma to influence her?

Warrick crossed to the kitchen doorway. "Like I said, Mary, the house is big enough for both of us. I'll stay in the guest room until you make your decision."

"I need to be alone to think." Marilyn's voice followed him down the hallway.

Warrick strode to the staircase. "Then *you* can leave."

"And go where? I can't stay with Em any longer."

Warrick's shoulders relaxed. A small victory. He mounted the steps. "I don't know what to tell you."

"You're not being fair, Rick." Marilyn climbed the stairs behind him. "You let me think you'd move out so I'd move back into the house."

"I never said I was moving out. You made that assumption on your own. I can't control what you think." If he could, he wouldn't have been sleeping alone for more than a month.

"You lied to me."

Warrick carried his travel bag to the now empty guest room. "What are you afraid of, Mary?" He put down his bag and faced his wife. "That you won't be able to fall out of love with me?"

"It's not a matter of how I feel about you. I didn't sign up to be a celebrity's wife."

He hooked his hands onto his hips and ignored the stir of anger. "No, you signed up to be *my* wife, in good times and in bad. I guess this is the bad part."

Marilyn stepped back as though she were under

attack. "You didn't tell me you were a magnet for the media."

"And you didn't tell me you'd run at the first sign of trouble." Warrick held Marilyn's gaze, forcing her to face the truth about what she was doing.

Marilyn hesitated in the doorway. "I'm not running, but I'm thinking about it."

"I won't give you a divorce, Mary. I don't like living under a microscope. But I won't give up my job because of it. I won't give you up, either.

The silence was long. Marilyn seemed relieved—or was that his imagination?

"Then we'll have to figure out something else, won't we?" She turned away.

Warrick listened to her footfalls taking her back downstairs. Then silence.

He'd expected her to put up more of a fight. Warrick scowled at the room's deep green carpeting. As his first move toward wooing his wife, he probably could have delivered a better homecoming. He scrubbed both hands over his face, then turned to unpack his bag.

No doubt about it, he needed to work on his game—on and off the court.

5

"Dr. Evans?"

"It's Devry-Evans. How can I help you?" Marilyn paused in the Kings County Medical Samaritan Hospital's parking lot Monday morning. She gave the stranger in front of her a visual once-over. Average height, average weight. A drinker with poor eating habits and a vitamin B deficiency. He wasn't one of her patients' husbands and he didn't seem in need of medical attention.

The middle-aged man pulled a business card from the right inside pocket of his brown sports coat. "Kirk West with the *New York Horn*. Can I ask you a couple of questions?"

Marilyn stiffened. She spied the notepad and pen in his hands. "No, you may not." She turned from him and continued across the parking lot toward the hospital. She never wanted to see another reporter—especially one from the *Horn*—ever again.

The reporter kept pace with her. "Dr. Evans—"

"It's Dr. *Devry*-Evans. If you're going to stalk me, at least get my name right." A quick glance at her watch showed it was seven-fifty in the morning. She had more than an hour before her first appointment and she could use every minute of it.

Hospital employees were either walking or running between the hospital's parking lot and its entrance. The high activity was due in part to the shift change. It also was a response to the medical needs of the community.

Marilyn maneuvered around slower-moving pedestrians and yielded to cars and an ambulance as she crossed the parking lot. The click of her low-heeled shoes was barely audible on the asphalt. A warm breeze carried the scent of cut grass and spring blossoms from the nearby landscaping. It also tugged several strands of her hair loose from the clip at the nape of her neck. The tendrils tickled her cheeks before she brushed them back.

"I don't write for the gossip section. I'm a sports reporter."

Like that makes a difference. "I don't care."

"What do you say to people who are blaming you for your husband's bad games?" Kirk's voice was closer to her now.

Marilyn came to a sudden stop. Her blood began a slow boil. "How dare you harass me at my place of work? How long were you waiting in the parking lot?"

The same breeze that ruffled her hair riffled through his shaggy blond locks. A cocky grin brightened his round features. "About thirty minutes. I didn't want to miss you in case you came in early."

Marilyn unclenched her teeth. "You sound so proud of the fact that you were skulking around, waiting to invade someone's privacy. How would you like it if I came to your job and harassed you?"

Kirk turned pages in his notepad. "There's a simple solution. Give me a quote and I'll leave."

His audacity took Marilyn's breath away. "Speak with

my husband. *He's* the basketball player, not me." She started to walk again.

Kirk followed her. "But I want *your* perspective. Do you think it's fair that the Monarchs fans blame you when the team loses?"

Why did the fans blame her? That's what baffled her. She wasn't even on the team. Marilyn stepped onto the curb. The entrance to the hospital was within her sight but still several yards away. "You *cannot* follow me into the hospital. This is where I work."

Kirk dogged her footsteps. Was it arrogance or disrespect? "Then answer me out here and I'll leave you alone."

Marilyn sped up. "I'm a private citizen. I don't have to grant you an interview. You're wasting your time. Leave. Me. Alone."

"The public is interested in you."

"That's too bad."

"Give me one quote and I'll leave you alone." He adopted a wheedling tone. "Just a few words. Do you think you should be blamed when your husband plays poorly?"

She would never give him a quote. He wouldn't be able to print it anyway. "I have nothing to say to you. Go away."

"Is there a problem?" A gravelly male voice interrupted them.

Perfect.

Marilyn briefly closed her eyes, then turned to the hospital's administrator. "Good morning, Arthur. There's no problem. This man was just leaving."

Arthur Posey surveyed Kirk from the top of the reporter's too long, windblown hair to the tips of his battered brown loafers. "It sounded as though you were asking Dr. Devry-Evans for an interview."

Kirk extended his hand. "Kirk West. I'm with the

Horn. I asked Dr. Evans for a quote for a story we're doing on her husband."

Arthur regarded the younger man as though Kirk had introduced himself as a leper. "This is a hospital, not a media center. We deal in life and death here. If you want to speak with Dr. Devry-Evans, make arrangements to meet her elsewhere."

Kirk let his hand drop. "I'm just asking for one quote. It'll take five minutes."

Arthur's stare should have turned Kirk into a pillar of salt. "Leave now or I'll have security remove you."

Why hadn't she thought of that? She watched the men exchange steely stares. Several hospital employees gave them curious looks and wide berths on their way to the hospital's entrance.

Kirk nodded. "All right." He looked to Marilyn. "I'll call you later."

"Please don't." Marilyn was inflexible. She kept her eyes on Kirk as he walked away. "Thank you, Arthur."

"I sent him away for the hospital, not for you."

Marilyn straightened her shoulders and met Arthur's cool silver stare. She ignored the disdain stamped on the older man's bony features. "I know, and I'm glad you did."

He arched a thin, black brow. "Are you? Growing tired of the limelight?"

At this rate, her teeth would be ground to the nub by the end of the week. "I've never sought the limelight."

His smile was stiff. His eyes were cool. "And yet you married a professional athlete. That's like marrying the president, then being surprised that you've become the First Lady."

Marilyn was tempted to shake Arthur's tall, thin body until his teeth rattled. But he was six inches taller and twenty years older than her. Besides, he was her boss. "Believe what you like." She turned to leave.

He fell into step beside her. His brown briefcase ensured she didn't get too close. "Thank you. I think I will. In the interim, please make sure you don't bring any more reporters onto hospital grounds. In case you've forgotten, our patients take priority. We can't have disruptions or distractions to our mission."

Our mission. He made the hospital staff sound like Templar Knights on a holy crusade.

Marilyn's eyes stretched wide with incredulity. "I didn't ask Kirk West to come to the hospital."

"If that's true, how did he know when you would arrive?"

Marilyn swallowed a sigh of frustration. "He waited for me in the parking lot."

She hated Arthur's false smile. "I find that hard to believe."

"It's the truth. He just showed up."

Arthur reached past her to open the door. He was chivalrous, even as he pissed her off. "That's a good story."

"Why won't you believe me?" Marilyn entered the bustling hospital lobby. She took a deep breath, inhaling the satisfying scent of antiseptic as she waited for Arthur.

"Because people like you love living in the spotlight. That's why someone with your options would continue to work outside the home. You feed off being the center of attention." Arthur's black dress shoes echoed against the tiled lobby almost in unison with Marilyn's flats.

Marilyn gaped at him. "What are you talking about?"

Arthur adjusted his grip on his briefcase. "Why are you here?"

Her boss was asking her to defend herself and her work. The question hurt. It was tempting to pretend not to understand it but that was the coward's way out.

She wasn't a coward, despite what Warrick had said yesterday.

Marilyn faced the older man. She adjusted the strap of her mud brown backpack higher on her shoulders. "I'm a doctor, and I'm good at what I do. That's why I'm here and that's why I won't give up my career."

Arthur gestured around the lobby. "The staff is distracted. Patients are complaining and now reporters are gathering in our parking lot. There's only so much I can tolerate and you're coming dangerously close to that line."

Marilyn swallowed resentment and fear. The taste was bitter. "I understand."

Arthur shook his head. He seemed confused. "Your husband is a multimillionaire. You don't need the money."

Cold seeped into her pores. Marilyn arched a brow. It was an attempt at bravado to mask her trepidation. "You're beginning to make me feel like you don't want me here."

Arthur dragged a hand over his thinning gray hair. "Your presence has become disruptive since your husband has started drawing so much media attention."

Marilyn tightened her grip on her backpack. "That wouldn't be a problem if people worried less about my personal life and more about the hospital and our patients."

"But you don't have to be here. You don't have to work."

Marilyn blinked in mock surprise. "I wish you'd told me that eight years ago—before medical school and my residency."

Arthur shrugged. "You know now. So why are you still working?"

"Would you ask the same question of a male doctor?"

"Yes, I would."

She believed him. "I love what I do. I wouldn't give it up even if I hit the lottery."

Marilyn turned toward the obstetrics and gynecology unit. She manufactured a brisk and confident gait as she strode away from Arthur. For years, she'd wanted to be a baby doctor. So her presence was a distraction for the hospital? Too bad. She wasn't giving up her dream for anything. Arthur would just have to deal with her.

Marilyn hesitated. She glanced around the hallway as people maneuvered around her. Was that the way Warrick felt about his career? His passion, commitment, and talent had led him to be one of the few players who succeeded in the NBA. His dream had come true just as hers had. How could she then ask him to give that up? But what would happen to them if he didn't?

"Lena, you're progressing wonderfully." Marilyn spoke with satisfaction after completing her patient's prenatal screening later that afternoon. She removed her gloves and closed the manila folder in which she kept Lena Alvarez's medical files. "You're right where you should be in your third trimester."

"It's not as though this is my first time." The very pregnant mother of three wiggled into a more comfortable reclining position on the examination table.

Marilyn grinned. "Do you have any questions for me?"

"Yes." Lena rested the palms of her small hands on her belly. "When are you and Rick Evans getting back together?"

Marilyn's smile faded. Had she heard the other woman correctly? "Excuse me?"

Lena's Puerto Rican accent was more pronounced

as she spoke louder. "I said when are you and Rick Evans getting back together?"

Marilyn's gaze darted around the tiny yellow and white exam room. "Lena, when I asked if you had any questions for me, I meant questions that pertained to your health—"

"This does concern my health." Lena rubbed her belly through the white paper gown. "The play-offs are causing me stress. Stress isn't good for the baby. Evans needs to keep his mind on the game. He doesn't need the distraction of an unhappy home."

Marilyn's cheeks heated. Had everyone lost their minds? When had her home life become an acceptable topic of public discourse? "Lena, I like you—"

Lena's expression softened into a smile. "I like you, too, Doc."

Marilyn shook her head at the woman's antics. "I'm not going to discuss my personal life with you." It was incredible that she was even having this conversation. Where was the hidden camera?

Lena's big brown eyes widened. "Why not? Every time I come here, your nurse takes my height and weight, and asks me if I'm sexually active." She gestured toward her belly with a comical expression. "All I want to know is if you and Evans are getting back together. You don't have to tell me what he's like in bed— unless you want to."

Marilyn blinked. She must be the last sane person on earth. "I have no intention of discussing my sex life with you. My private life is private. It doesn't have anything to do with the way my husband performs on the court."

Lena stopped rubbing her belly. "Why else did he play like garbage the first game of the Miami Waves series?"

Marilyn stood. "That was Thursday. The Monarchs won game two Saturday. How do you explain that?"

She froze. The team had won Saturday night. But when she'd seen Warrick Sunday, she hadn't even congratulated him. Instead she'd yelled at him for coming home. Marilyn's heart was heavy. When had things between them become so crazy? And why?

Lena smiled. "You must be getting back together."

"That's it, Lena. We're not having this conversation." Marilyn offered Lena her hand to help her sit up. "I'm his wife, not his coach. It's not my responsibility to explain his performance."

Lena held on to Marilyn. "Well, if you're so concerned with my health, you'll straighten up your marriage, Doc. Otherwise, I'll have a heart attack, and that won't be good for the baby."

Marilyn pinched the bridge of her nose. No one listened to her so why did she bother to say anything? The next time someone asked about her marriage, she'd just recite the stages of fetal gestation.

She released Lena's hand. "Take care of yourself, Lena. I'll see you in two weeks."

Marilyn pulled the examination room door closed to give Lena privacy to get dressed. She then strode down the hall, past the nurses' station to the desk she used during her shift. She lifted her backpack onto its surface.

"Where's Rick living these days?" Emma's voice directly behind her startled Marilyn.

She spun around, pressing her hand against her chest. "*Why* are you sneaking up on people?"

Emma wrinkled her nose. "Sorry. So where is he?"

Marilyn dropped her hand and took a calming breath. "He's home." She turned back to her desk.

"With you?" Emma sounded incredulous. She came around to search Marilyn's face. "He said he was moving out."

Marilyn's tense features eased into a wry smile as she relived Warrick's homecoming. "He never actually said that. All he said was that I could move back in."

Emma dropped into the stiff green chair beside the desk. "He lied to you."

"No, he didn't." Why did she feel defensive?

Emma rolled her eyes. "Lying by omission is still lying. But it doesn't matter. You can move back in with me."

Marilyn settled in to the brown desk chair. "No, but thanks. The house is big enough for Rick and me to live together while we figure out what to do." Warrick was right about that.

Emma's eyes widened. "You're going to stay there with him? Suppose he puts the moves on you?"

Marilyn frowned at Emma's question. "He's my husband. Besides, Rick's a gentleman and I'm an adult. He won't do anything that I don't want him to do."

Emma's lips thinned. "And what do you want him to do?"

Marilyn deliberately misunderstood her friend's question. "I want him to help me figure out what *we* should do."

"You know what he's going to say."

Yes, she did. "Would that be so wrong?" Marilyn smoothed both palms over her hair, checking the clip that restrained the mass at her nape. "I didn't even know who he was when we first met."

Emma crossed her legs and adjusted her red skirt over her knee. "That's sad."

Marilyn shrugged. "He wasn't famous at the time. A lot of people didn't know who he was, including you. Then the Monarchs made the play-offs."

Emma pursed her lips. "Now his picture's in all the

papers and his game highlights are on all the television stations."

If Marilyn didn't know better, she'd think her friend was jealous of her husband's success.

"Once the team made the play-offs, we couldn't go anywhere without people recognizing him." She spun her chair toward the desk. Her restless fingers released the fastenings on her backpack. "They stare at us when we go out to eat or pass him their movie tickets to autograph when we're at the theaters. We've stopped going out."

Emma shook her head. "I couldn't live like that. I'd feel like a prisoner in my own home."

So did she. Is that the way Warrick felt? Why hadn't she ever asked him? "He always responds to the fans with good humor. But he can never relax. I can tell it puts a strain on him."

"I meant you." Emma sighed. "If I were you, I'd hate not being able to go out without people harassing me and my husband. You get married so you can share your life with another person. *One* other person. Because of Rick, you have to share your life with an entire city."

Marilyn was proud of Warrick's success. But the constant public attention was the inevitable dark side of celebrity. "It's not his fault that the fans give him so much attention."

"Whose fault is it?"

"The media's." With a finger, Marilyn traced an imaginary pattern on the surface of her backpack. "And they're getting worse. This morning, a reporter tried to follow me into the hospital for an interview."

Emma's green eyes widened. "You're kidding. What did you do?"

She didn't want to relive that event. "Arthur showed up."

"Oh, no." Emma squeezed her eyes shut.

"Oh, yes. The good news is he got rid of the reporter. The bad news is he blamed *me* for causing a disruption in the parking lot."

Emma opened her eyes again. "That's not fair."

"That's what I said. But you can't reason with Arthur—unless you're a member of the hospital's board."

"You're right. So while Rick's becoming famous, his fame is ruining your career."

It sounded worse when Emma said it. "Don't you think that's exaggerating the situation?"

Emma counted her fingers. "Reporters are following you to work. Your boss is blaming you for the media disruption. And Janet and Dionne still haven't accepted your offer to join their clinic." She dropped her hands. "To top it off, patients are complaining about you whenever the team loses."

Marilyn frowned. "How do you know what they're saying about me?"

Emma waved a negligent hand. "I've heard them talking in the waiting rooms."

Marilyn's gaze slid away. "Talk about being unfair."

"Maybe Rick or his coach should tell people to stop blaming you."

Should he? "That would only keep the topic alive. If we ignore it, hopefully, it'll go away."

Emma grunted. "I'm not so sure about that."

Marilyn slid her hand into her backpack, reaching for the treatment notes she'd worked on overnight. Her fingertips brushed the sharp edge of an unfamiliar object. She opened her backpack wider and pulled out a gift-wrapped package.

"What is it?" Emma stood behind her.

"I don't know." Marilyn read the gift label. "To M, From R." She tore at the wrapping, knowing Warrick used too much tape to harbor any hope of preserving the paper.

Marilyn's lips stretched into a broad grin. Sandy and Danny smiled at her from the cover of the *Grease* compact disc.

"I thought Rick didn't like musicals."

Marilyn's smile broadened. "But he knows I do. And *Grease* is my favorite."

"That's such a guy thing to do." Emma straightened away from Marilyn. "A couple of songs won't make everything better."

"Speak for yourself." Marilyn used her scissors to slit open the compact disc wrapper. "You're welcome to stay and enjoy the songs with me, if you'd like."

"No, thanks." Emma turned to leave. "I agree with Rick. People don't just spontaneously break into song."

Marilyn loaded the compact disc into her laptop. She sighed as "Summer Love" played softly on the computer's drive. If only she and Warrick could overcome their relationship obstacles with a few songs and a couple of dance moves the way Sandy and Danny had in *Grease*.

6

Warrick came slowly awake Tuesday from his midday nap to the sound of the ringing telephone. What time was it? Three-thirty in the afternoon. The alarm would have gone off in another thirty minutes, giving him just enough time to get to the arena and warm up before game three of the Eastern Conference Championship.

The phone rang again. Thinking wistfully of another thirty minutes of sleep, Warrick hit the alarm's off button and shed the bedsheets. He strode down the hall-way to use the master bedroom's telephone extension. He should have been napping in that room. The answering machine picked up the call before he could.

He cleared his throat. "Hello."

"Rick?"

"Hi, Dad." Was he wrong to wish he hadn't answered the phone?

"Were you sleeping? You should be getting ready for the game." John Evans's voice was sharp, his tone disciplinary.

After this morning's workout, his body had needed the two-hour rest before tonight's game. But try explaining that to his father. The older man had cheated him of thirty minutes and criticized the other ninety.

Warrick sat on the edge of the king-sized bed. "I am getting ready. What can I do for you, Dad?"

"Napping before the game didn't help you Thursday night. You looked as though you were sleepwalking. Everyone said your head wasn't in the game. Marlon Burress made a fool of you."

After thirty-four years, Warrick had given up hoping for positive feedback from his father. Nothing he did was ever good enough. "Thursday was a tough loss, but we won Saturday."

"Which only goes to show that you're inconsistent." His father pounced on a new line of attack. "Your team needs to be able to depend on you. But from game to game, they don't know which one of you will show up, the sleepwalker or the playmaker."

Warrick's patience was wearing thin. "The series is tied."

"That's why you'll never be a champion." John was accusing. "You're satisfied with the series being tied at one apiece. You had an opportunity to be ahead two to nothing but you blew it."

Warrick stood. He didn't need this. "I have to get ready for tonight's game."

John grunted. "You've always chosen to run from the truth rather than admit when you're wrong."

Warrick gritted his teeth to keep from defending himself. It never did any good. "As much as I enjoy our talks, Dad, I have work to do." He checked the clock on the nightstand. The green liquid crystal display numbers read three thirty-eight. He needed to get to the Empire Arena by five o'clock—three hours prior to the game—for his pregame ritual warm-up and preparation.

"What did Mary say about your game?"

Warrick gripped the receiver. Nothing. She hadn't asked about the loss or the win. What did she think about the first two games? Did she even care anymore? They used to talk about his games and her deliveries. When had that stopped?

He pulled his attention back to the phone conversation and his father. "She wasn't as critical as you."

"Everyone is talking about your separation. Why did I have to read about it in the paper?"

Because failure wasn't a subject one broached with John Evans. Warrick swallowed hard, part regret, all frustration. "I'm sorry."

He'd hoped the response would end the conversation. That strategy had worked in the past.

"You're not going to win Mary back unless you get your act together."

Was his father gloating? He had to end this call. "I appreciate your concern—"

"She's a medical doctor. She saves lives. You play ball and you don't even do it well. How do you expect to hold on to a woman like that?"

The barbs were flying faster now, eliciting both fear and anger, two emotions that were always present during exchanges with his father. John Evans had erred on the side of discipline rather than affection. In fairness, he'd taken his paternal responsibilities seriously. Warrick wouldn't have achieved his dream if it weren't for his father. For that, he'd always be respectful. But now, he needed to get the older man off the phone.

He took a deep breath. The scent of jasmine lingered in the room, filling his head, easing his tension. Marilyn. "Dad, it's getting late. I've got to go. Give Mom my love. I'll talk with you later." He hung up before his father could respond.

Warrick rotated his head, trying to relax the muscles

in his neck. His father's idea of a motivational speech was to identify your most vulnerable area and put a bullet in it.

He wandered toward the room's dressing table. His gaze lingered on their wedding photo before landing on Marilyn's ring box. Holding his breath, Warrick opened the case. He exhaled. It was empty. At least she was still wearing her rings. That was a good sign, wasn't it? He closed the box.

You're not going to win Marilyn back unless you get your act together.

He was beginning to wonder how he'd won her heart in the first place. He studied their wedding photo. She looked so happy with him. They'd held each other so tightly. Now other people were coming between them.

Marilyn hadn't married him for his celebrity. The media attention was tearing them apart. She wasn't with him for his money; she had plenty of her own. Then why had she married him? And why wasn't that reason enough anymore?

Burress shot the basketball over Warrick, raising the Miami Waves to an 81 to 76 lead over the Monarchs during game three at home. Two minutes and seventeen seconds left to the third quarter. Warrick caught the condemnation in DeMarcus's eyes. He'd hear about that play in the locker room. He turned, ignoring the twinge in his back as he jogged up the court.

Barron Douglas stood behind DeMarcus in a bronze three-piece suit. The Monarchs captain wasn't ready to travel with the team, but he'd show his support during every home game—a constant reminder that Warrick wasn't supposed to be here.

"Am I that good or are you that bad?" Burress's laughing taunt came from behind him.

Warrick ignored the words that echoed the question in his mind. Burress shadowed him as Warrick found his position at the post. Monarchs' center Vincent Jardine dribbled the ball past half-court, slowing the tempo of the game and taking control of the shot clock. The Waves' Chad Erving danced in front of him, bending low and waving his arms. Jarrod Cheeks guarded Serge at the left perimeter and Phillip Hawk hampered Anthony at the right.

"You're kind of slow tonight. You feeling all right?" Burress's tone was meant to irritate. And it was working. Why wouldn't the other man stop talking?

Warrick was tangled in Burress's coverage. His opponent's left hand braced his waist. His right hand stretched over Warrick's shoulder. Warrick extended his right leg and turned his torso to claim more room. He clenched his teeth at the shooting pain around his waist.

The shot clock was at nineteen seconds. Warrick gestured Jamal to the left corner with an impatient wave of his hand. When would the rookie read the game plan? Walter Millbank trailed Jamal.

With his teammates in place, Warrick opened his hands for the ball. Vincent kicked it to him. Burress pressed in to intercept the pass. Warrick stepped forward to block Burress's access. He wouldn't let the other man show him up again. Warrick made the catch with his right hand and twisted his body to protect the ball. His back protested.

His opponent pressured him, crowded him, jockeyed for position. He held Burress off with his back and shoulders, skirting the edge of his third foul. Warrick dribbled the ball, dancing forward, trying to find a good look for the basket. He had nothing. The shot clock counted to thirteen seconds. Two minutes and four seconds remained in the third period.

Warrick watched his teammates shift position, crossing in and out of the paint, circling the perimeter. The Waves stuck to them like a bad odor. Burress bedeviled him, waving his arms in Warrick's face and jumping up and down.

Serge shook off Cheeks and worked his way open under the basket. A window of scoring opportunity. Warrick took it. A split-second decision to pass him the ball.

Jamal lost his man as Millbank launched his seven-foot body into the lane. The Waves forward came up with the steal. The Monarchs fans groaned their displeasure. The Miami big man powered past the flat-footed Monarchs. Warrick chased after him. His back muscles tightened with every move. His knees protested at every step. *Play through the pain. Just play through it.*

Burress dashed past him like a locomotive. Warrick dug deeper to pick up his game. A foot from the basket, Millbank launched himself into the air, reaching for the hoop.

No!

Warrick launched himself beside the Miami Wave forward, straining higher, farther, stronger. Wanting it more. He extended his body. Warrick found the ball above the net with the tips of his fingers. One knuckle deep. He smacked it aside.

Rejected!

Monarchs fans went wild. Shouts of approval bounced off the court and echoed around the arena. Relief sapped his adrenaline. Warrick felt himself falling. He slammed to the ground. White-hot pain exploded in his back, blanking his thoughts and taking his vision. He writhed on the court, gritting his teeth against the agony. His body felt like a human torch. Warrick squeezed his eyes shut.

Hands grabbed at him, trying to keep him still. He wanted to shout, "Don't touch me!" Instead, he allowed them to calm him and eventually help him from the court.

Minutes later, Warrick sat in a straight-back chair in the lounge outside the Monarchs' locker room. One of the trainers had taped an ice bag to his waist. His feet were propped on a nearby seat. On the television mounted to the wall, his teammates were giving away game three midway through the fourth quarter.

Barron strode into the lounge in his bronze suit. The diamond studs in his ears winked at Warrick. "You're good?"

"I'm good."

They both ignored his lie and focused on the Monarchs' desperate struggle to prevent a game three slaughter.

Barron broke the awkward silence after a few possessions. "There's a lot of pressure out there."

"It's the play-offs." *Just tell me I played like shit, then leave me alone.*

"I couldn't handle the pressure." Pain and disappointment thickened the other man's voice.

Warrick shifted his gaze from the television to the back of Barron's head. His thick cornrows were shorter now. "You'll be back next season."

Barron turned to him with a chuckle. "You were always my wingman, on and off the court." He sobered. "There's a lot of pressure out there, bro. The other guys, they're icing you out. I can see it. But that shit doesn't matter." He jerked his head toward the televised game. "You're just as good as the rest of those fools and better than most. Take that to the bank."

Warrick watched his captain leave. Barron's words had done more to heal his back than the trainer's ice pack and massage.

Warrick's heart contracted at the familiar scene. Across the room, Marilyn had fallen asleep on the sofa. Her slender body half sat, half lay on the dark brown cushions. Warrick smiled, imaging she hadn't fallen into sleep willingly.

He crept farther into the family room and gazed down on her, careful not to disturb her. The corner lamp cast highlights on her dark brown hair. The thick tresses fanned out behind her shoulders.

Marilyn's cheek rested on her folded hands. She'd changed into her hot pink shorty pajamas after she'd returned from the hospital. The outfit bared her well-toned arms and long, shapely legs. Warrick's smile widened at the sight of toenails painted a glittery purple.

He rescued the universal remote she'd tucked against her stomach and switched off the television and cable box. His brows knitted. Had she caught any of the game after she'd returned from the hospital? She must have. What did she think of how he played tonight? Did his poor numbers and the team's loss make her think less of him? Were his father and Marlon Burress right?

Warrick carefully returned the remote to the center of the table and checked his silver Movado wristwatch. It was after one in the morning. Marilyn looked so relaxed and peaceful. He didn't want to wake her. Maybe he could carry her upstairs. He'd had an ice bag around his back for the better part of the fourth quarter. After the game, the trainer had worked his knotted muscles until he'd felt loose again. Maybe he could risk the movement. He wanted to risk it. He needed to hold her in his arms. Warrick stepped closer to the sofa and leaned toward her.

Marilyn's eyes snapped open. She blinked twice, then stretched, rolling onto her back and raising her arms above her head. "Hi."

Warrick grinned. "Hi, yourself."

She gave him a drowsy smile. Her voice was groggy. "Thank you for the *Grease* CD."

He touched her cheek. Her skin was soft and warm. "You're welcome."

She lowered her arms. "What are you doing?"

Warrick straightened. "I was going to take you upstairs."

Marilyn suddenly seemed wide awake. She struggled into a sitting position. "You can't carry me anywhere. You've hurt your back."

She'd seen the game. Warrick tensed. "I could've carried you. But, since you're awake, we can walk up together."

Marilyn's chocolate eyes darkened with concern. She searched his features as though trying to read his thoughts. "How are you feeling?"

"My pride hurts more than my back." Warrick reached beside her to turn off the lamp. The hallway light strained to illuminate the family room. He offered her his hand. Marilyn's palm felt small and delicate in his hold.

She rose to her feet with his assistance. The care in her dark gaze made his knees shake. "Would you like me to give you a massage?"

Warrick hesitated. After the trainer's ministrations, he didn't actually need Marilyn to massage his back.

"That would be great, if you don't mind?" Warrick loosened his black necktie, pulled it free of his collar, and shoved it into the front right pocket of his gray suit pants.

Marilyn moved past him to lead the way upstairs. "Of course, I don't mind."

The thought of Marilyn's hands on him, her fingers pressing into his muscles, her body close enough to warm his, was almost enough to send his back into spasms. "I'd appreciate it."

She tossed him a cheeky smile over her left shoulder. "We need to get you ready for Thursday night's game."

Warrick mounted the stairs behind her. His gaze settled on her gently swaying hips. The pink pajama shorts cupped her firm bottom.

"I didn't play well tonight." He'd felt compelled to make the admission, but now he wished he hadn't.

"I'm not an NBA expert, but I think you did play well tonight, although you played better Saturday. The team still won."

Surprise eased his frown. Even though she resented his career, she was still watching him play?

Warrick followed Marilyn down the hall to their bedroom, shrugging out of his suit jacket as he walked. "You saw Saturday's game?"

"Of course." She sounded startled by his question. "Even I could see you were brilliant that night."

"Thank you." Her praise warmed him. But then, he'd always felt that she believed in him—until she'd asked for a divorce.

Warrick strode to the closet to hang up his jacket. He pulled his shirt free of his pants to unbutton it. It felt odd dressing and undressing in the master bedroom, but sleeping down the hall. How long would this continue? And how would it end?

"I don't think anyone could play with that level of

intensity every night." Marilyn's voice carried from across the room.

Warrick turned from the closet and wandered to the dressing table to drop off his cuff links. "My game needs to be consistent. My teammates should be able to count on me to come through when they need me."

He sounded like his father, but the old man had been right.

"That's a lot of pressure on you."

He came to a stop at the foot of their bed and unbuttoned his shirt. "A professional should be able to play at a high level every game, especially during the play-offs."

"You know better than I do." There was a shrug in Marilyn's voice. "But I think you're being too hard on yourself."

He removed his white shirt and undershirt. Marilyn's eyes darkened and her throat muscles moved as though she were swallowing. Her reaction to him went a long way toward restoring the confidence battered by tonight's game. It was good to know he could still turn his wife on.

Warrick was tempted to remove his pants, but was afraid his blatant reaction to her would make her turn away. "Are you ready?"

Her eyes were on his torso even as she gestured toward the bed. "Lay down on your stomach."

Warrick stretched out on the mattress. He folded his arms to form a pillow for his head and relaxed his shoulders.

Marilyn straddled him, one smooth thigh on either side of his hips. Warrick closed his eyes and swallowed a groan. Maybe this hadn't been one of his smarter ideas. Having his wife this close to him without being able to love her might damage his back irreparably.

"Where does it hurt?" Her voice was a husky whisper.

He wished he could tell her. "Near my waist."

Her soft, slender fingers tested his taut muscles. "Here?"

He didn't know. He didn't care. *Just touch me.* "Yes."

She pressed into his lower back muscles and a groan slipped through.

Marilyn stilled. "I'm sorry. I didn't mean to hurt you."

"No, that felt good." Warrick's erection flexed in agreement.

A comfortable, intimate silence settled between them for several minutes. Warrick closed his eyes and pretended their marriage had returned to normal.

Marilyn's gentle words interrupted his illusion. "Your career is taking a hard toll on your body, especially your back and knees."

Warrick opened his eyes. He stared across the large room toward the green Venetian blinds masking the windows. Marilyn had called them sage.

"It's not my career. It's the other players." Marlon Burress had been even more zealous in his defense once he realized Warrick's back was flaring up.

"You don't have to do this anymore." Her tone remained soft, her words measured.

Warrick tensed beneath her touch. "What are you saying?"

"Relax." Marilyn rubbed his bunched muscles with her palms.

Warrick's body obeyed her command. "What do you mean?"

Marilyn's massage continued up toward his shoulders. "You have a sizable savings. You've been very prudent with your investments. You could retire."

Warrick frowned. "And do what?"

"Well, other retired athletes have done commercials. Doesn't Michael Jordan do underwear commercials?"

Warrick grunted. "Jordan can get away with doing underwear commercials. He has six championship rings."

"Then you can do something else. You have enough money that you can take your time and figure out what you want to do. And I make good money."

"I'm not living off my wife." His voice was flat.

"It wouldn't be forever." She used extra effort to ease his newly knotted muscles. "Only until you decided what you want to do next."

Warrick struggled to remain relaxed. "I'm not done with basketball."

Marilyn continued her soothing massage and hypnotic tone. "You don't have anything to prove."

Warrick lifted his head to meet her eyes. He felt cold and isolated when her hands fell away from him. "What's on your mind, Mary?"

Marilyn moved to his side before returning his gaze. "I heard your conversation with your father." She jerked her chin toward the phone on her nightstand. "You probably didn't realize you were taping the call."

Warrick rolled over and got to his feet in one motion. "No, I didn't."

Behind him, Marilyn shifted on the bed. "I didn't mean to listen. When I got home, the machine showed it had one saved message. I was just checking it."

"It's all right." Warrick stepped away from the bed.

Could this day get any worse? His father's words had followed him onto the court. Now they were getting between him and his wife.

"He's wrong, you know." Marilyn's tone was tentative.

"What about?" He heard her rise from the bed.

"Your father implied you weren't good enough for me. He's wrong."

Warrick turned toward her. "Then why are we sleeping in separate rooms?"

Marilyn twisted her fingers together. "I don't know whether I can live with everything that comes with your popularity. That's not how I envisioned our life together."

They were right back where they'd started. Their marriage had morphed into a merry-go-round. "Then why haven't you left? What's keeping you here?"

She looked as though he'd slapped her. "It's not as though I can turn off a switch and not be in love with you anymore."

Warrick crossed his arms. "You're standing in front of me, telling me you love me. But you admit you have one foot out the door. Which is it?"

Marilyn crossed her arms as well. "Both. You never warned me you were a star when we were dating."

Warrick's chuckle surprised even him. "How would that have seemed?" He extended his hand. "Hi, I'm Rick Evans and I'm a star."

Marilyn slapped away his hand. "So you admit you misrepresented yourself."

Warrick dropped his arm. "No, I don't. I told you what I did for a living. I play for the Monarchs. I'm not a star."

"The Monarchs changed."

"I won't apologize for that."

Marilyn shook her head. "The quest for the ring. I'll never understand it."

Warrick arched a brow. "I hope that's not true."

Marilyn turned and put more distance between them. "You want to be the best. Your competitive drive is what got you to this point. But it's also the reason the media and all of New York think they're entitled to have an opinion on our private life."

Warrick's shoulders were heavy with regret. "I don't like that part of my career, either. Unfortunately, society takes privacy as payment for success."

Marilyn raised her eyebrows. "You mean *your* success. When I pictured spending the rest of my life with you, I thought it would be you, me, a couple of kids, maybe a cat. I never imagined we'd also be sharing our lives with the greater New York City metropolitan area."

"We're not sharing our lives with them." How could he make her understand?

"There are stories about us in the news every day. They question your abilities. They ask readers whether I'm good enough for you. How do you think that makes me feel?"

He could imagine. It made him feel pretty crappy. "It doesn't matter what they think."

"That's easy to say. It's not as easy to put into practice."

Warrick put his hands on Marilyn's shoulders. "Try, Mary. All that matters is what we think—you and me— and I think you're perfect for me."

Marilyn frowned. "It's not just what they write about me. I don't like what they're saying about you, either."

Thank God she still believed in him. After his father's phone call this afternoon and his teammates' reaction in the locker room tonight, he'd felt as though no one did.

Warrick squeezed her arms. "I can handle the media criticism. I've been dealing with it since college. What they say doesn't matter. Your words carry a lot more weight with me."

She looked sad. "We can't even go out without people mobbing us for your autograph. Doesn't that bother you?"

"Yes, it does."

Marilyn held his gaze. "But you're not willing to do anything about it."

"You mean retire? Would you?"

"My job isn't disrupting our lives."

Warrick felt a stir of irritation. He dropped his hands from her. "How many dinners have been interrupted by your patients going into labor? How many times has your pager gone off while we were making love?"

Marilyn's cheeks darkened with a blush. "I'm a doctor. My patients need me."

"And I'm just a baller." Warrick heard the bitterness in his words.

Marilyn settled her hands on her hips. "That's not what I meant. At. All. Don't put words in my mouth."

He was at the end of his rope. "If you believe in me, why isn't our love enough to save our marriage?"

Marilyn expelled an impatient sigh. "We aren't adolescents anymore, Rick. We need more than love to make our marriage work. We have to be realistic about what it takes to make a lifelong commitment to each other."

"And what does it take?"

"I haven't figured that out yet. But I don't want to raise our children in the media spotlight."

Warrick caught his breath at the image her words painted. He wanted to raise a family with Marilyn so badly he could taste it. But he also wanted to play basketball. "I'm not ready to give up my career, Mary. The Monarchs have a chance to win it all. That doesn't happen every season."

"I'm not asking you to retire this minute. You could retire after the finals."

He was glad she believed the Monarchs would make it to the finals. But he didn't want a combination championship-retirement party. "Michael Jordan has six championship rings, and he and his wife raised a family."

She gave him a flat look. "You're not Michael Jordan and I'm not his wife."

"You're the one who brought up Jordan."

Marilyn threw up her arms. "That's because you want to be just like Mike."

Warrick shook his head in denial and frustration. "Now who's putting words in whose mouth? I've wanted to play pro ball my whole life. Of course I want a championship ring. Who doesn't want to be the best in his field?"

"But you don't need a ring to prove how good you are. There are plenty of athletes in the Hall of Fame who don't have a ring."

Warrick rubbed his forehead. She was guessing, but she was right. "Once a celebrity, always a celebrity."

"What does that mean?"

"Retirement didn't end the media's fascination with Jordan. They still follow him around. And he's not the only celebrity parent on the planet. There are plenty of them."

"I never wanted us to be among them." Marilyn dropped her gaze. "You're not giving me much hope."

"And you aren't giving me any." Warrick turned and marched out of the room.

As irritated as he felt, walking away from her tonight was hard. He'd never be able to walk away from her for forever.

7

Nine o'clock in the morning was late enough for the sun to put pressure on Warrick as he jogged beside the Monarchs' franchise owner, Jaclyn Jones. He was dragging. He hadn't gotten to bed until after two in the morning and even then he'd had a restless night. But he'd been doing this morning jog—usually around the Empire Arena with Jaclyn—every day for the past twelve years. They had an agreement that, if she was at the arena by nine o'clock, they'd run together. If not, it was understood Warrick shouldn't wait for her.

"How's your back?" Jaclyn ran beside him. At six-foot-one, the former Women's National Basketball Association shooting guard was still in game shape although she'd retired from the game years ago.

"Better." Warrick's pace was slightly slower on the mornings he ran with Jaclyn. Speed wasn't the point. He was running for distance and aerobic endurance. He'd work on his time splits later in the afternoon.

"It healed overnight? That's incredible."

Warrick gave her a suspicious look. Her neon yellow T-shirt was almost brown with sweat. "I'll be one hundred percent by Thursday's game."

"Tomorrow night? That's nothing short of a miracle."

Did he detect mockery in her tone? "What's your point, Jackie?"

"Nothing." She gave him an innocent look that wouldn't have fooled anyone. "I'm just surprised that your back took you out of the game last night, but this morning you're doing laps around the marina and vowing to be in playing shape tomorrow."

Warrick controlled the tension in his voice. "We're lucky to have good trainers. Between the ice and massage, my back's a lot looser. Mary gave me a massage last night, too."

Jaclyn's eyes widened. "Is that a good sign?"

Warrick wiped the sweat from his brow. "She doesn't think so."

"I'm sorry." Jaclyn sounded almost as disappointed as Warrick felt.

"So am I."

They continued in silence for several feet. The quiet between them was introspective but comfortable. Warrick breathed easily—a deep breath in, a long breath out. The air was salty from the marina. The cool sea breeze regulated his body temperature. Warrick leaned forward as they came to the first short incline. The strain pulled at his quads and his glutes. He picked up the pace of his breathing.

"Maybe the ice and massages did help." Jaclyn's words broke his pensive silence. "Or maybe the pain was in your head."

Warrick stumbled and caught himself as he crested the incline. "You think I was faking it?"

"Of course not." Her response was fast, firm, and disgusted. "I know you better than that. But I think it's possible that your back pain was more psychosomatic than physical."

Warrick struggled with a sense of betrayal. "Are you questioning my mental toughness?"

Jaclyn blinked as though someone had turned on the light in a very dark room. "Where are you getting these allegations?"

"Your own words."

"You act as though I don't know you." She continued before he could speak. "I know your parents' idea of encouragement is emphasizing whatever shortcomings they think you have."

"They don't—"

"I've seen them do it, Rick." Jaclyn's voice was thin and breathy as though she was running outside her comfort zone.

Warrick slowed his pace. "I can block out their criticism." He could. He'd just have to work harder. "I'm not weak."

"If you were weak, we wouldn't be in the championship game." Jaclyn's voice was stronger now.

"Each win is a team effort." Warrick wasn't buying her denial.

He led Jaclyn around the turn in the asphalt pedestrian path and started back toward the arena. The course beside the water was brutally cold by winter but comfortably cool in the summer. Along most stretches, he enjoyed the smell of the marina. At other points, the stench of dead fish tested his gag reflex. Still, he loved running along the water. Warrick slowed his steps further.

Jaclyn kept pace with him. "The team's contributions are important. But don't undermine your role in the wins, Rick."

He shook his head in exasperation. "If my role is so important, why are you questioning my mental toughness by suggesting my back pain's in my head?"

"For as long as I've known you, you've held back all

of your insecurities." Jaclyn exhaled. "You don't defend yourself when people criticize you, regardless of whether they're justified. Instead, you become quiet and the stress manifests itself as backaches, headaches, and knee problems."

"If you haven't noticed, I'm defending myself right now." His tone was dry. "So maybe your theory is wrong."

"No, it's not." Jaclyn paused. "You're arguing with me now to avoid discussing the cause of your stress."

Warrick snorted. "When did your law degree become a license to practice psychology?"

"When we became friends."

Her soft response took the edge off his temper. "We've already talked about my problems."

"Yes, but not how you feel about them."

Warrick blew out a breath. The arena—and his escape—was still too far away. "Ah, the feelings discussion."

"Are you really going to let machismo stand between you and the championship?"

Warrick's mental brakes came on. The worst part was she knew she'd gotten to him. That's the kind of insight that came with twelve years of friendship. She was the bratty younger sister fate wouldn't let him avoid.

"I'll get us started." Jaclyn's tone held a wealth of concern. "There's tension at home and on the team because of the media. You don't know where to stand to get out of the storm."

How did she know? His gaze shifted away from her sympathetic eyes. "That sums it up."

Their hour-long run was almost at an end. They'd gone just over eight miles. The arena was coming into view. Two more miles—and freedom.

"You're probably thinking that it's time you made a choice."

He gave her a blank look. "What?"

"You're probably wondering which one to give up, marriage or career?"

His irritation stirred. Maybe she didn't understand after all. "Which would you choose?"

"Neither." Jaclyn's laughter was as carefree as a woman in love. Marilyn used to laugh with him like that. "We're competitors, Rick. We don't make choices. We find a way to have it all."

His smile was reluctant. "How?"

She shrugged and sped up. "The team needs you and you need the team. You want Mary and she still loves you. You just have to convince your teammates and your wife they can't live without you."

Warrick wiped the sweat from his brow with the back of his left forearm. "You make it sound easy."

"I know that it's not. But I also know that both the team and Mary are worth fighting for."

She was right about that.

Warrick jogged beside his friend and franchise owner. Jaclyn Jones had played to win in the Women's National Basketball Association. She'd brought that same intensity to the Monarchs' front office. If she were in his position, she'd find a way to save her marriage and career. Warrick didn't doubt that. The question was, could he do the same?

"How's Rick's back?" Emma took her prepackaged meal from the cafeteria's microwave oven and peeled the plastic film from its container. Steam and mouth-watering fragrances floated free.

Marilyn led Emma away from the microwaves and found an empty table for them. She removed the lid from her Tupperware bowl and took a moment to savor the scent of her recently reheated leftover spaghetti with ground turkey. "He seems much better."

At least he'd seemed better last night. He'd been gone before Marilyn had risen that morning.

She stirred her lunch. Her stomach growled, expressing its disapproval of her eating so late. Despite the unconventional lunch hour, the cafeteria was crowded with other hospital staff, medical professionals, and administrators who hadn't been able to break away before two P.M.

Emma swallowed a forkful of her lasagna. "I heard some of the patients talking about his bad game this morning."

Marilyn gave the other woman a sharp look. "Did they say anything about the other twelve players on the team?"

"Don't get defensive."

Marilyn scowled. "He's my husband. Why shouldn't I be defensive?"

Emma pursed her lips. "All they're saying is that he's not playing up to his potential."

"The media wouldn't be stalking us if he wasn't one of the best players in the league." Marilyn twirled her spaghetti around her fork. "That's the problem. If he was the horrible player these so-called fans seem to think he is, we'd have more privacy."

Emma swallowed a sip of her diet soda. "Have you talked about this with Rick?"

Marilyn suppressed a frustrated sigh. "I have and he understands, but there's nothing he can do about it."

Emma sliced into her lasagna. "Maybe he can get another job."

Marilyn spun spaghetti onto her fork. "That's easier said than done, Em."

"All that you're asking is for him to get a job that's not as much in the public eye." Emma ate more lasagna. "Did you tell him what the clinic partners said?"

"I won't ask him to change his career to satisfy people he doesn't even know." She'd been starving a minute ago; now Marilyn's appetite was almost gone.

Emma gestured toward Marilyn with her plastic fork. "How about changing his career to satisfy you?"

"I knew what he did for a living before I married him." Maybe they should change the subject. But she didn't have anyone else to talk with about this and she really needed a sounding board.

Emma sipped her soda, then lowered the can. "Have you heard from the partners yet?"

Marilyn made herself chew, then swallow the spaghetti. "I don't know what to make of their silence." But every time she thought about the partnership, her stomach muscles knotted.

Emma narrowed her eyes. "And if they do call you, who will you be, the Devrys' daughter or Rick Evans's wife?"

"I'm going to be Dr. Marilyn Devry-Evans." Marilyn wasn't reliving this argument. "I've told them I'm not bringing my parents into this partnership. Rick isn't a part of this, either."

"But the partners are concerned about what his image will do to their practice." Emma fed herself another forkful of lasagna.

Marilyn took a long drink from her bottle of water. The ice-cold liquid soothed her. "What would you do if you were me?"

Emma straightened in the bright orange hard-plastic

chair. "I'd realize that I had to make a choice between my job and my husband."

Marilyn's breath lodged in her throat. "Why?"

Emma made a face, part surprise, part impatience. She counted her fingers. "The partners told you they're concerned about Rick's image. Your boss warned you that he doesn't want the media disrupting the hospital. Your patients are turning against you because your husband has lost his basketball magic." Her friend spread her hands. "It's obvious that if you want to get back to a normal life, you're going to have to leave Rick."

There was a buzzing in Marilyn's ears. "You think I should sacrifice my marriage for my career?"

"It's not just your career. He's turned your whole life upside down."

"But what *you're* proposing would turn my life upside down again."

Emma's regard was steady. "It would be different if you were happy in the relationship, but you're not. I warned you not to marry him."

Her friend's condemnation stung. Marilyn took a moment to pull her thoughts together. "Every relationship goes through a difficult period. No marriage is perfect one hundred percent of the time."

"But you said yourself that, even though you may love Rick, you don't think you can live with him."

It hurt to have those words repeated back to her. "I'm hoping that Rick and I can work things out."

"What if you can't?"

She didn't want to think about that. She didn't want to consider that she couldn't have a happily-ever-after with Warrick.

* * *

"Lena, you're appointment isn't until next week. How are you?" Marilyn pulled the door to the examination room closed behind her later that afternoon.

Lena Alvarez, her pregnant patient who was close to her final trimester, sat fully clothed on the examination table. Her café au lait skin glowed in the ruby red, scoop-necked cotton dress. She'd propped her over-burdened silver purse beside her. "Not so good, Doc."

Marilyn's heart thumped once with concern. She crossed to stand in front of her patient. She took Lena's wrist and checked her pulse. "Are you in discomfort?" She counted the seconds on her silver Rolex.

Lena gently slipped her wrist from Marilyn's grasp. "Only my heart."

Marilyn lifted her gaze to Lena's. "What?" She sensed the other woman was nervous but not in distress.

Lena rested her hands on her stomach. "I appreciate everything you've done for me and my baby since my last doctor retired. I do. But I'm going to have to find another doctor. I wanted to tell you in person."

Marilyn glanced at Lena's stomach, rounded in her sixth month of pregnancy. "Why?"

Lena squared her shoulders and raised her chin. "I don't want my baby delivered by a doctor who doesn't support the Monarchs."

Marilyn's lips parted in shock. Her eyes stretched wide. "Excuse me?"

"I don't want—"

"Lena, your reason doesn't make sense. What do the Monarchs have to do with your pregnancy?"

Lena's rounded cheeks flushed. She poked Marilyn in the chest with her right index finger. "You see? You don't care about the Monarchs. If you did, you wouldn't have to ask that question."

Marilyn's eyebrows crinkled with confusion. Were Lena's hormones triggering her irrational behavior? "Of course I care about the Monarchs. My husband works for them."

Lena rubbed her stomach. "Then why are you putting the team—putting your husband—through this?"

"Through what?" This must be some sort of dream, some sort of nightmare. She'd walked into a parallel dimension. Marilyn stepped back and lowered herself into the examination room's chair.

Lena wiggled into a more comfortable position on the table. Her tone was just short of strident. "Can't you see what the tension is doing to him? What it's doing to the team?"

Marilyn studied the petite woman. Lena was passionate in her defense of the Monarchs. She honestly believed Marilyn was hurting the team. Medical schools didn't prepare their students for sports fanatics. At least her medical school hadn't. How should she approach this situation?

Marilyn drew a steadying breath, catching the hint of antiseptic beneath the vanilla-scented room freshener. She crossed her legs and folded her hands. "Lena, what do the Monarchs have to do with my ability to safely deliver your baby?"

"This doesn't have anything to do with *you*." Lena scowled. "It has to do with me and the fact that I don't want the first person who touches my child to be the person responsible for the Monarchs losing the championship. My husband agrees with me."

Oh, my word. If Lena and her husband could, they'd arrange for their baby to enter this world fully dressed in a Monarchs' home uniform, complete with sweatband, mouth guard, and Air Jordans.

Marilyn was the last sane person in this room. She

had to pull herself together. The health of her patient depended on it. "Lena, you're entering your final trimester. This isn't a good time to change obstetricians."

Lena's expression became mulish. "This isn't my first pregnancy. I have three children. I know how it's done. If need be, I'll deliver the baby myself."

The other woman would do just that. And her husband—another Monarchs fanatic—would help her, making his hands the first to touch the next generation of Brooklyn Monarchs lunatics.

Heaven help us all. Marilyn clenched her jaw to keep it from dropping open. She studied the expectant mother's stubborn chin, tight lips, and determined eyes. "I don't like to talk about my personal life with my patients."

"We've had *this* conversation before. You know the date of my last period, but *your* life is this *big secret.*" Lena raised her hands and wiggled her fingers.

Marilyn ignored Lena's interruption. "Rick and I are going through a difficult time right now. But we're trying to work things out."

"No, you're not."

Marilyn's head jerked back at Lena's forceful denial. "Excuse me?"

"Why are you always asking to be excused? It's not me you should be asking. It's poor Rick."

Marilyn's head began to hurt. "What are you talking about?"

"You're getting a divorce."

Shock made Marilyn's facial muscles lax. "No, we're not. Where did you get *that* idea?"

Lena gave her a skeptical look. "The papers say you're getting a divorce." She reached into her crowded purse and pulled out a folded newspaper section.

Marilyn took the gossip section Lena offered and

stared at the item on the top. According to the *Horn*, an anonymous source claimed Mrs. Evans had filed for a divorce from Brooklyn Monarchs shooting guard and twelve-year NBA veteran Warrick Evans. They'd referred to her as *missus* instead of *doctor*. They couldn't even get that right.

"I don't want my baby delivered by someone who would break poor Rick's heart." Lena sounded serious.

The words in the newspaper's announcement wavered in and out of focus. The sheet went black, then white. An anonymous source? Really? From where had the newspaper gotten these lies and why did it print them?

"This. Isn't. True." Her words were thick and rough as she pushed them through her rapidly compressing vocal chords.

"Why would the newspapers lie?"

"To increase sales." Marilyn handed back the paper. Her muscles were stiff. Her temper was straining. "It's my marriage. I would know whether I've filed for divorce—and I haven't."

Lena stared at the folded publication. Her certainty seemed to be wavering. Marilyn no longer cared. Nothing she said would change the other woman's mind.

She stood. "There are several O-B-G-Y-Ns on staff at this hospital. They're all excellent. I can recommend with confidence any one of them."

Lena looked from the gossip section to Marilyn and back. She stuffed the paper back into her purse and struggled to stand. "All right."

Marilyn assisted Lena to her feet. "I'd be happy to meet with your new doctor to ensure your continuity of care."

Lena frowned her confusion. She settled her purse on her left shoulder. "What?"

Marilyn forced her neck and shoulders to relax. "I'll tell your new doctor whatever she or he needs to know to keep you healthy and ensure you deliver another strong baby."

Lena rubbed her hands over her pregnant belly. Her troubled brown eyes met Marilyn's. "Thank you."

Marilyn forced a smile. "You're welcome." She needed to get away. She wanted to be by herself. She reached around Lena to open the door.

Lena caught Marilyn's forearm. "I'm sorry, Doc. I do like you, but . . ."

Marilyn waited a beat after Lena's hesitation. "But you love the Monarchs more." Lena nodded miserably. Marilyn pulled the door open. "I understand." No, she really didn't.

She stood back and watched Lena leave the examination room. The expectant mother of three wasn't her only patient who also was a Brooklyn Monarchs fan. How many more patients would believe she was divorcing a beloved member of their treasured team? What did this mean for her practice at the hospital or potential partnership with the clinic?

8

Arthur Posey looked even more uptight than usual in his smoke gray pinstripe suit. The hospital administrator hovered near the break room table Marilyn usually used as her workstation. Marilyn had watched enough vampire movies to know better than to invite him closer. She wouldn't ask what he wanted, either. She returned his stare in silence. Arthur could say whatever he had to say—or not—without her prompting.

The administrator sighed. "I understand one of your patients has left your care."

"That's right. Lena Alvarez." Every muscle in her body tensed. Why was Arthur here?

He clasped his hands in front of him. It was a pose that wouldn't encourage creases in his perfectly pressed suit. "It took some effort to convince her to stay with the hospital under the care of another physician."

Marilyn's mind raced to stay ahead of him. "It couldn't have taken that much effort, Arthur. She told me she would make an appointment with one of the doctors I recommended before she left today."

Why was he pretending he'd been the one to change Lena's mind?

Arthur's eyes widened, a barely perceptible indication of surprise. "Still, Kings County Medical Samaritan is not in the habit of sending our patients to other hospitals."

"I know." She gave him a patient look, which took all of her amateur acting skills to pull off.

"I told you this would happen." Arthur drew closer without her invitation.

"That what would happen?"

He stood beside her chair, crowding Marilyn. "You're disrupting this hospital."

She frowned, confused. "Lena's devotion to the Monarchs clouded her judgment about her care."

"Your husband's connection with the Monarchs is costing us patients."

Had Arthur lost his mind? "No, it's not."

"You're alienating patients and losing credibility as a physician among your peers."

"And my supervisors?" Marilyn stared him down.

Arthur's lips thinned. "You're trying to live in two worlds."

Marilyn arched a brow. "How did you draw that conclusion?"

Arthur looked down his nose at her. "You're trying to be a celebrity and a doctor. You're either one or the other. You can't be both. Not at this hospital."

Marilyn was losing the battle with her patience. She pushed herself up from her chair, forcing Arthur to take a step back. "Ah, yes. I'm sure lab coats are all the rage among Brooklyn celebrities." She glanced down at her clothing. "And I'm just dripping with pearls, diamonds, and rubies, aren't I? Do you like my tiara?"

Arthur looked as though he'd just sucked a lemon. "It's not the clothes you wear. It's your attitude. You think you're special, that everyone should pay homage to you because you're married to an NBA player and the two of you have almost as much money as God."

This from an administrator who expected hospital staff to kiss his ring. Marilyn's face and neck burned. "Don't pretend to know anything about me or my lifestyle."

"It's more than Lena's leaving. You have reporters congregating in the parking lot. Patients complain about the newspaper stories about you. Other patients are leaving the hospital."

Marilyn had been angry before. She was incensed now. She released a slow breath. "Every statement you've made has been an exaggeration. Tell me, Arthur, what's really bothering you?"

He remained silent.

Marilyn prodded him. "Is it envy? Do you wish the media were harassing *you*? Perhaps you're bitter. Weren't you ever picked for a team at school? Or is it more materialistic? All of the above?"

Arthur sneered. "Rick Evans is a basketball player."

Why did it rile her so when people disrespected her husband's profession?

Marilyn shrugged with forced nonchalance. "You're a paper pusher."

Arthur unfolded his hands and clenched his fists. "I'm a hospital administrator."

"That's what I said."

He glowered at her a moment longer, then smoothed his wine red tie. "I'm giving you one final warning. You've already received one for causing a major disruption at this hospital."

"That reporter's presence wasn't a major disruption." Marilyn felt as though she were speaking through cut glass to a stone wall.

"Are you contradicting me?"

"Yes, I am."

Arthur held his hand up like a traffic cop when Marilyn tried to continue. "I'm not finished." He lowered his hand. "If you bring even one more disruption to this hospital, I will terminate your hospital privileges so fast your head will spin."

Marilyn narrowed her eyes. "Are you threatening me, Arthur?"

"That's not a threat. It's a promise. Our mission is to save lives. Your lifestyle is impeding our mission. I won't allow that to continue."

"My personal life has nothing to do with my work at this hospital." Marilyn enunciated each word. "Judge me on my patient care, not your personal prejudices."

Arthur gave her one last, long glare. "You've been warned. But don't worry. Your husband makes good money. You won't starve."

Marilyn returned his stare. "Am I supposed to sit on my sofa with my eight additional years of education and training?"

"Go to your husband's games. Attend charity balls." He arched a brow. "Isn't that what your crowd is supposed to do? Be seen at fashion shows and theater openings?"

"It sounds as though *you* want to do that."

Arthur turned to walk away. "Pity I'm not a ball-player."

Marilyn watched him leave. She'd suspected jealousy was the motivation behind his behavior. How did she convince him she wasn't playing at being a doctor? She couldn't lose her job, especially if she were about to lose her marriage.

* * *

Marilyn cast her gaze over the other three women sharing the table with her in the quaint Italian restaurant Wednesday night. She had nothing in common with them, except they were all either married or engaged to a Brooklyn Monarchs player.

This status granted them free membership to the Monarchs Wives Club. The club's main purpose seemed to be organizing fund-raisers and other community improvement events. Since her hospital hours didn't often allow Marilyn to attend the Monarchs' games, her involvement with the club seemed the next best way of supporting Warrick's career. But she always felt underdressed and out of place when she was with them. Marilyn swallowed a sigh and stuck her fork into another ravioli square.

The other women wore chunky accessories, expensive clothes, and perfect makeup. Even Peggy Coleman, who looked like she could give birth to Roger Harris's baby at their table, appeared as though she was ready to pose for an *Elle* magazine fashion spread. Marilyn resisted the urge to adjust the collar of her blue Ann Taylor button-down blouse. She smoothed her hair, checking the clip at the nape of her neck. Even if she had the glamorous wardrobe, she wouldn't have had time to go home and change after work before meeting the other club members for dinner.

She studied her plate of vegetable ravioli swimming in marinara sauce. It had been the least expensive entrée on the menu and the portion size closely resembled an appetizer. Still, the cost of her meal alone was more than the total cost of a dinner when she and Warrick used to dine out.

Susan Williams cut into her chicken parmesan. "The casino night theme idea for the homeless shelter fundraiser is the bomb. We should rent a real casino."

From where would they get the money for that?

Marilyn looked at the other two women seated at the elegantly set square table. They looked indecisive, an expression they'd worn to perfection for the past half hour.

She turned to Susan. "There aren't any casinos in Brooklyn. Besides we need to keep our expenses low to raise as much money as we can."

Susan, who'd married Monarchs point guard Darius Williams more than four years earlier, shrugged a bony shoulder. "Then we'll drive to Atlantic City. It's not far." Her mocha brown cheeks flushed and her dark brown eyes glittered with excitement. "A trip to Atlantic City would be the bomb. It would add to the glamour of the event."

Peggy rubbed her belly. "I don't know, Susan. I'm six months pregnant. I can't drive to Atlantic City. I'd have to stop every ten minutes to pee." She patted her left hand over her hair. The twenty-four-carat pink diamond engagement ring sparkled against her baby fine ash blond hair.

Susan kissed her teeth. "There are rest stops all over the interstate. Just pull over and use one."

Marilyn coughed as her bite of ravioli traveled down the wrong pipe. She caught her breath, drawing in the heady scents of rich spices and tangy tomato sauce. Heaven. She swallowed a drink of water from her glass. "Keeping it in Brooklyn would also guarantee that more people attended."

Susan's expression was frustrated. "You just said Brooklyn doesn't have any casinos."

Count to ten. "The church's fund-raiser doesn't have to be in a casino. We could hold it in the Morning Glory Chapel's recreation room."

Susan's lips formed a perfect O. "A rec room? That's so tacky."

Faye Ryland, point guard Jarrett Hickman's longtime girlfriend, nodded. Her orange-tipped dark brown bangs swung across her eyes. "That's a good idea. The fundraiser is for the Morning Glory anyway. Atlantic City is three hours away. Shit. A lot of people aren't going to want to make the trip. Especially at night."

Marilyn sipped her ice water. "And especially with gas prices so high."

Susan gave her a shrewd look. "But that's not a problem for you, right? You can afford it."

Here we go again. "So could most of the people on our guest list. The point is, the less they have to spend to attend the event, the more they'll spend *at* the event."

Susan's constant and transparent attempts to find out how much she and Warrick made was one of the reasons she disliked the Monarchs Wives Club meetings. Surely, the club's president knew Warrick's salary—as well as the salary of every other NBA player—was posted on the Internet, much to Marilyn's dismay. Maybe Susan did and she was only after Marilyn's income figure. Well, that information wasn't for public consumption. Their friends, family, neighbors, and perfect strangers already knew too much about them.

Faye waved a forkful of pasta. "Mary's right. When are we going to have this party anyway? It feels as though we've been talking about this shit for months."

Peggy shifted in her chair. "That's because we *have* been talking about it for months."

Susan traced her glass of wine with the well-manicured tip of a black-polished fingernail. "The first Saturday in August. The players and coaches should be over the championship loss by then."

Marilyn looked at the other women in surprise.

"They could actually win the conference championship. In fact, they may even win the finals."

Susan's laughter was genuine. "Maybe the view from the owner's box is a little rosier, but those guys will have to play a lot better if they're going to win."

Peggy's gray eyes clouded with confusion. "Why were *you* invited to the owner's box? None of us have ever been there."

Faye looked resentful. "Yeah. What makes you the shit? You hardly even come to the home games and you've never been to the away games."

Susan spoke before Marilyn could answer. "You know, you really should travel with Rick to the away games."

"Why?" Marilyn sneaked a peek at her Rolex. How much longer would she have to be here?

"Why?" Faye mimicked Marilyn, then barked a laugh. "To make sure your man isn't creeping around on you with these groupies."

Marilyn ignored a stirring of irritation. "Rick doesn't creep around."

"How do you know?" Susan took the tone of a prosecuting attorney cross-examining a hostile witness.

Peggy rubbed her belly. "Oh, honey, wake up and smell the coffee. All men cheat."

Faye shook her head as though with pity. "Other women are treacherous. They're always trying to get your man. And what man can resist no-strings booty?"

Peggy nodded, her hands still on her belly. "Remember the club in Cleveland? Rick went with them. What do you think they were doing there?"

Marilyn frowned at the knowing looks and the shaking heads. "They were looking for Barron."

The whole team had been concerned over Barron's self-destructive behavior.

Faye gaped at her. "You really believe that shit?"

Marilyn ignored their rolled eyes and snickers. "Yes, I do believe my husband. Don't you believe yours?" She met the other women's eyes with an expression meant to shame them. If it weren't for her love for Warrick, she would have taken her purse and left already.

Susan's cheeks flushed. "I want to."

Peggy's gaze slipped from Marilyn's. "So do I."

Faye snorted. "Shit. I couldn't care less as long as he's coming home to me and paying my bills."

Marilyn ignored the younger woman and focused on Susan and Peggy. "Then why don't you?"

If they didn't trust their men, why did they remain in the relationship?

Susan lifted her chin. "Because only a fool would believe her husband wouldn't be tempted by all those young skanks throwing themselves at him. But until I have proof that he's cheated, why should my kids and I leave? We'll just stay put, thank you very much."

Marilyn cut into one of the remaining two raviolis. They were the size of half dollars. She chewed pensively. "You don't have proof that he's cheating on you. You've been to all of his away games and he's never cheated on you. Still, you don't trust him."

Susan's silent stare didn't intimidate Marilyn. "What about you? It's all over the news that you're getting a divorce."

She really hated these meetings. But Warrick attended her hospital functions and made generous contributions to its fund-raisers. For that, Marilyn would at least assist the Monarchs Wives Club with their fundraisers. The events were for a good cause, after all.

She returned Susan's steady stare. "Rick and I aren't getting a divorce."

Susan cocked her head to the side. "Are you sure?"

Marilyn arched a brow. "Very sure."

"Because I know a great lawyer." Susan leaned closer to her. "I've been doing my research—just in case."

Marilyn blinked. "Why are you still with Darius if you have one foot out the door?"

Susan shrugged, sitting back in her chair. "Isn't that what you're doing?"

The accusation slapped Marilyn across the face. It stung more because she couldn't deny it. Susan was right. She was doing the same thing. And she didn't have the excuse—the reason?—of children to explain her indecision. It was time to choose.

What had awakened her? Marilyn lay on her back in her king-sized bed. Memorial Day was three days away and already the heat index was unusually high. The temperature hadn't wakened her, though. Maybe it was the noise coming from her kitchen or the smell of turkey bacon climbing the stairs.

Marilyn kicked free of the sheet that wrapped around her legs. She climbed from her bed and padded to the head of the staircase. A deep breath drew in the scent of breakfast. Her mouth watered. Hopefully, Warrick was cooking enough for two.

Beneath the sound of her growling stomach, she heard his voice. Her lips eased into a smile. She loved his singing.

She crept down the staircase on her toes, taking careful, quiet steps. If he heard her, he might stop singing. She'd hate for that to happen. Marilyn paused in the hallway. She stood as still as the warm cream walls, listening to his impromptu concert. She sighed as the words to Luther Vandross's "Stop to Love" carried to her in Warrick's strong baritone. His voice was summer warm and silky smooth. It made the muscles in her abdomen dance.

Marilyn closed her eyes and leaned against the wall for support. Warrick sang a little longer about the importance of stopping to appreciate the love you have. She frowned as the sound of pans, plates, cupboards, and drawers competed for attention with his singing.

His footsteps tapped across the kitchen, drawing closer to the hallway. What was he doing? Where was he going? Marilyn grew cold in the bronze silk camisole and matching shorts she'd worn to bed. He couldn't catch her spying on him. How embarrassing! Without stopping to think, she spun into the sitting room behind her.

She listened as Warrick's bare feet carried him down the hall. She held her breath as he drew closer to the staircase just feet from their sitting room. She stiffened as he paused.

There was a hint of laughter in his voice. "I'd intended to serve you this breakfast in bed but it would taste just as good in the sitting room."

Marilyn's face burned. She stepped into view. "How did you know I was here?"

Chuckles rumbled up from his naked chest. "I heard you come downstairs, but I didn't hear you go back up." Warrick walked toward her, wearing gray gym shorts and nothing else.

Her attention dropped to the tray in his hands. It balanced two plates of bacon and scrambled eggs, and two glasses of orange juice. Then his words registered. "Why were you going to bring me breakfast in bed?"

His sexy smile wavered just a bit. He stopped less than an arm's length from her. "I'm courting you."

Marilyn's mind went blank. Her heart melted. "Oh."

Her laughter was nervous. "Does anyone even use that word anymore?"

Warrick's midnight eyes smiled. "All right. I'm trying to get into your pants."

Her gaze caressed his well-muscled chocolate torso, then dropped to his long, powerful legs. "It's working." Her voice was husky.

"It is?" The boyish pleasure in his smile made her laugh.

She tossed him a playful grin. "Scrambled eggs and bacon are very seductive."

Marilyn took the tray from him and carried it to the maple and glass coffee table. She placed each of the plates, silverware sets, and glasses of orange juice onto the table before settling into an armchair.

She saluted him with a forkful of scrambled eggs. "This is great. Thank you."

"My pleasure."

Marilyn noticed the wicked twinkle in his midnight eyes.

They enjoyed the breakfast in comfortable silence until Marilyn's curiosity got the better of her. "How early did you get up this morning?"

Warrick sensed her nerves were as unsettled as his. The feeling reminded him of their first morning-after three years ago. He'd second-guessed every word and gesture, and had known she'd been doing the same. They'd laughed at themselves, then made love again.

He tucked the memory away. Warrick's eyes caressed Marilyn. Her gold camisole highlighted the honeyed tones of her skin. The material flowed from her sculpted shoulders and over her full breasts like a waterfall. It left nothing to his imagination, especially not the reaction she was having to him.

"Early enough to cook your favorite breakfast." Warrick balanced his plate in one hand and held his fork in the other.

She teased him with her tone. "Ah, yes. Your grand seduction. We've never had a problem in the bedroom, Rick. It's all of the interference outside that's putting the strain on our marriage."

His grip tightened around his fork. "Our marriage is between you and me."

"Tell that to the media and your fans." She gathered a bite of egg with her fork. "They seem to think they have a stake in our relationship."

"Only if you let them."

The flash of regret in her eyes scattered the last remnants of humor. "One of my patients left me yesterday."

Warrick's eyes widened. "Why?"

Marilyn hesitated. "She doesn't want her baby delivered by a doctor who would divorce Rick Evans."

"We're not getting divorced." Warrick stood firm, masking his fear.

"That's what I told her."

His thoughts spun with relief. Did she mean it? "And?"

"She didn't believe me. She'd read about our pending divorce in the newspaper and the newspaper wouldn't lie. Her words."

Warrick released a frustrated breath. "I'm sorry, Mary. Sometimes fans get carried away. But that's not a reflection on you."

Marilyn dropped her fork onto her nearly empty plate. "I've cared for her since the start of her pregnancy. She's entering her third trimester. And now I'm not going to be there for the delivery."

Warrick heard raw disappointment in Marilyn's voice.

He wanted to find the reporter who'd falsely written that he and Marilyn were divorcing and make sure he never lied about them—or anyone else—ever again. He wanted to hold his wife and reassure her that her patient would return and no other patients would leave. But he couldn't do any of those things.

He stood and lowered his empty plate to the tray on the coffee table. "The reason your patient left is her issue, not yours. Don't let it get to you."

She lifted wide, troubled eyes to his. "How could I not? Arthur blames me. He's threatening to fire me if I cause any more disruptions in his hospital."

Warrick's spine stiffened. How dare someone threaten his wife. "You aren't causing disruptions. The hospital's patients are."

Marilyn stared at the remains of her food. "I wish things would go back to normal and everyone would just leave us alone."

Warrick rubbed his forehead. "It doesn't matter what people say outside our marriage. I'm the only person who can tell you how to be my wife. And you're the only person who can tell me what you need in a husband."

She stood. Her body seemed tired. "What I need in a husband is not to have to share him with eight million other people. Can you give me that?"

She wasn't the only one who wanted things to return to normal. How many more times would they have this same argument? Warrick implored, "What can I say or do to convince you that you're not?"

Defeat clouded her chocolate eyes. Warrick wanted to demand she not give up on him, on them. Instead, he watched her walk away.

If she couldn't tell him what she wanted to hear, how would he know what he needed to say?

Warrick stacked the tray with their breakfast dishes and carried it into the kitchen. He'd stopped defending himself to others long ago. He'd realized in high school that neither reasons nor excuses would persuade his parents to believe in him. What made him think he could persuade his wife?

9

The Monarchs had split their home games against the Miami Waves in the Eastern Conference Championship series. Warrick had hoped to win both of them. He stood in the locker room of the Empire Arena where he and his teammates had retreated after the slaughter that was game four. He'd showered and was halfway dressed. But their fans' jeers and boos still thundered in his brain. His ears should be bleeding.

It was well after eleven o'clock Thursday night. His body was exhausted from the thrashing Marlon Burress and his Waves had dealt him during this fourth game of the best-of-seven series. But he knew his mind wouldn't let him sleep when he got home. He'd relive this loss in his nightmares.

"What's going on in your head, man?" Jamal's tone punched at Warrick.

Warrick met the rookie's angry eyes over his left shoulder. "Probably the same thing that's going through yours."

Jamal grunted. "You're not living up to your media hype, *superstar*."

Ice settled in Warrick's stomach. He'd never asked for

reporters to focus on him and forget the team. "I know I didn't play my best game tonight. I'm sorry."

"Didn't play your best game?" Jamal snorted. "You played like shit."

"So did you, Jamal." DeMarcus stormed into the locker room like a thundercloud. His presence increased the tension by a factor of ten.

Jamal spun toward the team's first-year head coach. "Rick's buying into his media hype."

"He thinks he's our savior." The disgust in Anthony's olive eyes chilled Warrick. "As if all he has to do is walk onto the court and he'll bring home the trophy."

DeMarcus's anger was unmistakable as he addressed the forward. He lifted his left hand and spread his fingers. "There are five men per team on the court at any one time. Where the hell were the rest of you?"

Jamal jutted his chin. "Rick needs to stop thinking about the hype and get in the game."

Fire burned in DeMarcus's gaze as it took in the players. "The team is more than one man. All of you need to get your heads in the game."

Warrick froze. After benching him at the beginning of the season, DeMarcus was the last person he'd expected to defend him. In fact, he wasn't used to anyone defending him. He forced himself to continue buttoning his shirt. The task was difficult as shock had rendered his fingers numb.

Anthony jerked on his shirt. "We're not the ones the media is treating like the second coming of the Messiah."

Jamal tossed a sneer over his shoulder at Warrick. "You ain't got game."

Every game, he did his best. Sometimes it was enough; sometimes it wasn't. Tonight, it hadn't been and he'd be the first to admit it.

DeMarcus hooked his hands on his hips. "Rick's game wasn't the worst tonight. You have that honor, rookie."

Serge tied his shoelaces, then stood. "Barron was supposed to be starting in this series."

The Frenchman's words blindsided him. Warrick opened his mouth to say something—anything.

But DeMarcus spoke first. "Barron took himself out of the play-offs so he could get well. Was his absence the reason for your poor performance?"

Serge looked away.

Why was DeMarcus continuing to deflect blame from him? He hadn't played as well as he could have, as he *should* have. He was willing and able to accept that responsibility. Why wouldn't DeMarcus let him?

Jamal slammed his locker door shut. "Even with a hangover, Barron's a better leader on the court than Rick."

Warrick stared at the rookie. *Was that true?*

DeMarcus's chuckle was dry and devoid of humor. "How quickly everyone's forgotten. If it weren't for Rick's winning basket during the last game of the season, none of you would be here."

Warrick's shoulders dropped. No one cared about past accomplishments. Professional sports was a what-have-you-done-for-me-lately? culture.

The pressure increased as one by one Warrick's teammates refused to meet his eyes. Jamal, Serge, Anthony, Vincent—all of them turned away from him. It hurt.

Warrick cleared his throat. "I'll play better Sunday."

DeMarcus glared from Warrick to the other players gathered in the locker room and back. "We're two games away from elimination. *Everyone* has to play better Sunday."

Serge adjusted his tie before securing his locker. "What is it they say? Shit rolls downhill."

Warrick frowned at the Frenchman. "What does that mean?"

Serge looked at Warrick. "It means that when you have had a bad game, we all get blamed. When you play well, no one knows who we are. We are just the supporting cast."

Warrick braced his legs and forced himself not to rock back on his heels at the surprise attack. "I've never taken credit for that win. Or any win. I know victory is a team effort."

Jamal sneered. "And that's what you've been telling all the papers. We don't need you to defend us, man. We can defend ourselves."

"No, we cannot." Serge shrugged. "Not unless the media listens to us. But they are too busy listening to Rick."

"I didn't elect you to speak for me." Anthony's tone made him seem like a nine-year-old child in a thirty-year-old's body; a thirty-year-old with a 1970s throwback natural. "I can speak for myself—"

"*Enough.*" DeMarcus's command cut through the resentment in the room like a machete. "The media are not on this team. We win or lose with the people in this room. Making Rick the goat is not going to get us the ring. We all need to raise our game." He expelled a rough breath before checking his wristwatch. "Let's go. They're waiting for us at the press conference. All of us."

Warrick shrugged into his suit jacket and swallowed a sigh. Whatever the media chose to ask him about tonight's game, their questions couldn't be harder than his teammates'.

* * *

Marilyn had fallen asleep curled up on the sofa with the television on again. The tension torturing Warrick's shoulders and the nape of his neck eased. She may resent his career, but she still watched his games. That had to mean something. She'd had a long Thursday of her own at the hospital. She'd have another long day tomorrow. His gaze flickered to his silver Movado wristwatch. Correction. Today. It was after one in the morning.

Warrick loosened his tie further. He crossed the family room with silent steps. Even in sleep, Marilyn wouldn't release the universal remote. She lay with it pressed to her stomach. Warrick eased it from her to switch off the television and cable box. He laid the remote on the coffee table and stared down at Marilyn. When had he last seen her looking so relaxed and content while awake?

He rested his right hand on her shoulder and leaned closer. Her jasmine scent surrounded him. "Mary."

Marilyn blinked several times before focusing on him. "What time is it?" Her voice was low and rusty.

Warrick continued in a whisper. "One. Let's go up to bed."

She sat up, setting her bare feet on the hardwood floor. Her green nightgown exposed her toned arms and long legs. She lifted her gaze to him. Her eyes were dark and sad. "I'm sorry the Monarchs lost."

With those five words, his tension and fatigue returned with a vengeance. He was sorry she'd witnessed the debacle. "Thanks."

"Do you want to talk about it?" She sounded tentative.

"No, thanks." After the confrontation in the Monarchs locker room and the interrogation at the postgame press conference, there was nothing left to say. The Monarchs' losses used to be status quo. Now they led the local nightly news.

Marilyn pushed herself to her feet. "All right."

Had he offended her? "How was your day?"

She started toward the hallway. "Fine."

When had they stopped talking with each other? How had their conversations devolved to *No, thanks; All right;* and *Fine*?

He wouldn't accept that. "Did Arthur give you any more trouble today?"

Marilyn stopped at the foot of the stairs. She wouldn't look at him. "We used to talk about our days. This is another example of how the Monarchs' miracle season has changed us."

Warrick flinched. Marilyn had quoted the nickname the press had given his team's championship run. "I'm sorry. It's one in the morning. The postgame press conference was tense. I'm all talked out."

Tense was an understatement. Reporters had put his every move and emotion under a microscope.

Marilyn faced him with irony in her eyes. "I'm not going to read the newspaper to find out how you're feeling."

He scrubbed his hands over his face. "That's not what I'm saying."

He should have left bad enough alone with *No, thanks; All right;* and *Fine*.

She spread her arms. "Then tell me how you're feeling."

"Are you a psychologist now, too?"

She stepped back. "I'm sorry."

Warrick took a long step forward, catching her arm before she could turn away. "No, I'm the one who's sorry." He released her. "I'm tired and not thinking straight."

Marilyn's voice softened. "I know the fans booed

the team." She raised her hand as though reaching for his jaw, then let it drop to her side without achieving her goal.

Warrick flinched. The echo of the crowd's disgust still reverberated in his head. "It's probably all over ESPN now. They'll replay that from now until the next game Sunday night."

"Tell me how you feel."

He couldn't bring himself to say the words. "How would you feel if someone jeered at you in the delivery room?" He forced a smile.

Marilyn still looked sad. "I'm sure it bothered you. It bothered me." She hesitated. "Are you feeling discouraged?"

"No." He knew she wouldn't stop until he answered her questions. He admired her tenacity—but not tonight. "I'm embarrassed, frustrated, and tired. But I'll be fine after I get some sleep. In the morning, we have to prepare for Sunday's game."

Marilyn's expression eased. "That's all I wanted to know." She turned to mount the steps.

Frowning, Warrick followed her. "We're two games away from elimination, but there are three games left in the series."

"I know."

Did she think he was a loser? Is that the reason she wanted a divorce?

"There's no reason for us to give up." On the championship or their marriage.

Marilyn continued up the stairs, not bothering to look back. "No, there isn't."

At the top of the stairs, he took her arm. "What are *you* thinking?"

She returned his gaze for several silent moments. "I want you to win this championship, Rick."

He blinked. Was he dreaming? Had he fallen asleep standing up without realizing it? He'd go with that. "I'd have thought you'd want the season to end. Why do you want us to win the championship?"

"Because it's what you want."

God, if only she'd give him everything he wanted. The thought gave him a sweet ache in his gut. "You realize that, if the Monarchs win the conference championship—"

She pressed the fingertips of her right hand against his lips. "*When* you win."

His lips itched to kiss her fingers. She lowered her hand before he gave in to temptation. "*When* we win the championship, the media attention will increase. Have you thought of that? It would be the Monarchs' first championship in more than ten years. A win will extend our season for another month, too. Could you handle that?"

Marilyn's gaze was steady on his. "I know how much the championship ring means to you. Whatever we decide about our marriage, I'll never root against you. Ever."

Besides, "Yes, I'll marry you," those words were the sweetest she'd ever spoken to him.

He cleared his throat. "Whatever *you* decide. I know what I want. You."

Her features softened. Her body relaxed. Her eyes darkened with the same need and yearning that twisted inside him. "I want you, too."

She stepped into him, lifted up on her toes, and pressed her lips to his. Lightning flashed inside him. His body tightened with desire. Suddenly, Warrick wasn't sleepy anymore.

He swept Marilyn off her feet without breaking

contact with her pliant lips. Warrick cradled his wife in his arms as he carried her to their bedroom at the end of the hall. The feather-light touch of her fingers left a path of heat from the crown of his head to the nape of his neck. She sighed his name, parting her lips for the sweep of his tongue. Her taste heated him from the inside out.

Warrick crossed into their bedroom, not stopping until he reached the bed. He freed Marilyn's legs, then held her close as he let himself fall backward onto the mattress. She laughed as she landed with a bounce on top of him. The carefree laughter of a woman in love. His muscles tightened at the sound. He held her close and kissed her deep, thirsty for the joy that had all but drained from their marriage.

Marilyn's body softened against him. The scent of jasmine clouded his mind. Her arms and legs moved restlessly over his. Her kisses scorched him. Her caresses burned him. Her desire branded him a champion. She needed him, wanted him, believed in him. In her embrace, there wasn't room for doubts.

She broke their kiss. With fast, efficient movements, Marilyn undressed him. A tug here, a yank there and he found himself wearing nothing but his underpants. Her desire for him was almost painfully exciting.

He tried to smile through his arousal. "I didn't know you were a magician."

Marilyn's grin was mouthwateringly wicked. "It's not magic. It's motivation."

His eyes tracked her tongue around her lips. His body throbbed. "You're still dressed."

She rolled to his left side and lay on her back. "How motivated are you?"

Warrick's laughter eased the tightness in his chest

and beyond. He raised up on his side and played with the top button of her nightgown. "Highly."

Marilyn held her breath as Warrick's long, nimble fingers released the remaining buttons of her gown and peeled apart the edges. The tip of his finger traced the curve of her breast. Marilyn's nipple puckered. Her breath exhaled on a quivering sigh. Her eyelids drifted closed.

Warrick's body was above her. His heat was around her. His mouth was on hers. And when his tongue slipped past her lips, her toes curled. Marilyn kissed him back, hard and deep. She strained into him, rocked under him. His hard, hot palm traveled up her thigh, over her hip and past her waist to cup her bare breast.

When had he removed her clothes?

Marilyn groaned and released his mouth. "Now who has the magic?" Her voice was husky.

Warrick's sexy grin left her breathless. Marilyn sighed as he kissed the spot behind her ear. She moaned as his teeth nipped her neck, shivered as his tongue trailed her collarbone.

His lips and tongue followed a path over her breast. Marilyn held her breath. Her right nipple pinched tighter as he drew closer. She gasped when his mouth closed over her breast, stroking its tip and suckling her nipple. Marilyn's hips undulated beneath him. Blood rushed hot and fast through her veins. Her heart pounded in her ears. She gripped the bedsheets in her fists.

Warrick raised his head. He blew a soft, warm breath over her nipple. Marilyn bit her bottom lip at the intense feeling. Her body wouldn't—couldn't—remain still. She pressed the tips of her fingers into the taut muscles of his back. Her hips strained toward Warrick. His hips pressed into hers. Two strips of clothing—his and hers—separated her from what she wanted most.

"Rick, I need you now." Her words were thin and brittle in her ears.

Warrick released her breast. His left hand followed her curves to her hips. Shifting his body, he slipped his hand inside her lingerie. Marilyn groaned as she felt herself dampen against his fingertips.

"I need you, too, Mary. I'll always need you." His words husked against her ear.

Warrick moved down her body, kissing and licking her exposed skin. He pulled her silk underwear—the last remaining article of clothing—from her pliant body and stood to shed his briefs. Marilyn's thighs went lax at the sight of his full arousal.

He climbed back onto the bed. Marilyn rose to her knees to meet him. As he knelt before her, she skimmed her fingernails over the spare flesh of his torso, marveling again at his strength and power. She lifted her gaze to his midnight eyes and lowered her right palm to cup him. His hips pressed into her hand. Marilyn stroked him until he grew even hotter and harder to her touch. Warrick's body shook and he reached for her. Marilyn pressed him onto the mattress and straddled him.

She swallowed hard as she lowered herself onto his rigid erection. Warrick gripped her hips, helping them settle into a rhythm that was fresh yet familiar. She rocked with him. She worked her hips against him. Her heart pounded in her chest. Her breath caught in her throat. She closed her eyes and arched her back.

Warrick slid his large, hot hands up her torso to palm her breasts. Marilyn moaned as he massaged her sensitized skin. She rode him harder and faster as he rubbed her nipples and pinched their tips.

He drew his hands back down her body, inching closer to her thighs. Marilyn spread her legs wider. Warrick strained upward, lifting her. Her body grew hotter, damper. Her abdomen shivered as his fingers trailed over her. He slipped his hand between them and touched her. Stroked her. Explored her. Marilyn's inner muscles pulled tighter and tighter until her body shattered. She screamed. Her muscles trembled on the waves of release.

Warrick's back arched, filling Marilyn deeper, lifting her higher. His body exploded, shaking Marilyn again. Spent, she collapsed onto him, breathing in his scent, soap and sandalwood; listening to his heart echo the wishes in her own.

Warrick pulled his black BMW into the front row of the Empire Arena's parking lot Friday morning. He collected his sports bottle and unfolded from his car. He inhaled the tangy breeze carried from the marina. A gentle wind swept over him and rustled the trees that lined the sidewalk in front of the arena's rear entrance.

After activating his car alarm, he stepped onto the sidewalk for some easy stretches before his jog. He scanned the lot. Jaclyn's car stood a couple of spaces from his, but she wasn't anywhere in sight. He was doing this morning's run solo. That was a little disappointing.

A movement in Warrick's peripheral vision drew his attention to the building. Troy appeared from the rear entrance and crossed to him. His suit coat was missing. The sleeves of his pale yellow shirt were rolled to his elbows. He'd loosened the brown and yellow tie he wore to coordinate with his shirt and brown pants. But it was the tightness of the media executive's features that set off an alert system in Warrick's mind.

"What's going on?" Warrick drained the water from his

sports bottle as he tried to read the other man's body language.

Troy stopped an arm's length from Warrick. "The *Horn* wrote an article on your possible reconciliation with Mary. It's in today's paper."

Troy's words were wonderful news. But his stance—wary and stiff—warned Warrick that another shoe was ready to drop.

Warrick's attention dipped to the newspaper in Troy's hand before returning to the executive's face. "The morning after game four, they're more interested in my marriage than our loss?"

"This story ran on the front page of the gossip section."

Warrick's neck muscles tightened. "How bad is it?"

Troy sighed and offered him the paper. "The article comes with pictures."

Warrick tucked his water bottle under his arm and accepted the newspaper. His mind was clouded with confusion. What did Troy find so objectionable about the *Horn* running an article about Warrick and Marilyn's reconciliation? Although, he and Marilyn had never actually separated.

He flipped the paper to the page Troy had folded open. Warrick's attention was drawn to the photo that overshadowed the story.

His sports bottle fell to the sidewalk. His eyes stretched wide. "Son of a—"

10

Marilyn's nude back was framed in the color photo dominating the front page of the *New York Horn*'s gossip section. Her arms were raised toward his shoulders, baring the curve of her left breast. His hands were spread on her hips.

Warrick saw red. He was angrier than he'd ever been in his entire life. His fists crushed the page. "How in the *hell* did they get this photo?"

A shadowy memory taunted the edge of his mind. A movement outside his window. Jesus! He'd been right.

"It's obvious they took the photo around venetian blinds." Troy bent to rescue the sports bottle that had fallen from Warrick's numbed grip.

The media executive's words were muffled beneath the blood roaring in Warrick's ears. Warrick spun on his heel and started toward his car.

Troy's hand caught his arm, pulling him to a stop. "Where are you going?"

Warrick turned to glare at the other man. "I'm going to find that photographer and bury his camera so far up his—"

"Jackie's already spoken to the newspaper's publisher." Troy's grip tightened on Warrick's forearm. "She's threatened him with legal action if he doesn't immediately give us all of the camera discs and take down the photos posted to their site—"

"There are photos of us on the Internet?" Warrick's question was just short of a roar.

"She got them to agree not to print or post any of the photos ever again."

Warrick shook off Troy's hold and continued toward his car. "I'm going to sue that rag into bankruptcy." His voice was as rough as tree bark and colder than ice.

"Rick, I know you're angry. I would be, too. But you've got to calm down." Troy's voice came from behind him.

Warrick deactivated his car alarm and opened his trunk. "I have to call Mary."

Troy tossed the water bottle into the car. "Shouldn't you calm down first?"

He pulled his cell phone from his gym bag and pressed the speed dial code for his wife's cellular number. After several rings, a recording came on. "Dammit. I'm being sent to her voice mail. Mary, call me as soon as you get this message, okay? I love you."

He had similar results when he called Marilyn's work phone number. Warrick disconnected the call after leaving a message on that machine as well. He dropped the cell phone in the front pocket of his running shorts, then slammed the trunk closed. The violent act didn't ease his temper.

"I can't reach her." Warrick's muscles vibrated with tension.

Troy laid his hand on Warrick's shoulder. "I understand you're angry. But don't do anything that will keep this story alive."

With his pulse pounding in his ears, Warrick could

barely hear the other man's words. His car alarm beeped as it reset.

He looked at Troy, but he couldn't focus on his friend's face. Warrick's vision was too blurred by anger. "What gives them the right to violate my privacy, my wife's privacy? We were in our home with the blinds closed."

Troy let his hand drop from Warrick's shoulder. "I know this is hard, but think about Mary."

He *was* thinking about Marilyn. Without responding, Warrick spun on his heel and circled his car.

Troy followed him. "Now where are you going?"

Warrick deactivated the alarm a second time. "To get the photos."

"The discs are on their way." Troy's arm stretched from behind Warrick. His hand pressed against the driver's side door to keep it shut. "So what are you really going to do?"

Warrick looked at Troy from over his shoulder. "This doesn't concern you."

Regret flashed in Troy's eyes. "I'm your friend. Yes, it does."

Warrick crumbled the *Horn* in his fist. His car alarm reset again.

He turned to clench the paper in front of Troy's face. His throat worked as he pushed the words past his rage. "Imagine this was Andrea. What would you do?" He had the satisfaction of seeing Troy's face darken and his jaw clench.

"I'd want to make the photographer eat his camera. I'd . . ." Troy stopped himself. "Rick, tearing apart the *Horn*'s offices wouldn't help Andy or Mary. Jackie's taking care of this."

"*I'm* Mary's husband. This situation is *my* responsibility." And his fault. *He* was the reason a photograph of his wife in the nude was plastered to the front page of a newspaper's gossip section.

"Your way isn't constructive." Troy spoke carefully.

The cool breeze coming off the marina didn't ease Warrick's temper or his guilt. He tightened his grip on the paper. "Do you know what this will do to her? To her career?"

"I know what you're saying. But are you going to the *Horn* for Mary or for yourself?"

That pulled him up short. Warrick jabbed a finger toward Troy. "I do the press conferences and one-on-one interviews. I stepped aside as captain when Barron arrived. I sat on the bench when Jamal was drafted. All for the team. But I *will not* sit quietly while my wife is disrespected, not even for the team."

Troy's eyes dimmed with disappointment. "And I wouldn't ask you to. This isn't about the team, brother. This is about Mary. What will you do when you get to the *Horn*?"

"I told you not to worry about it."

"Are you going to give the photographer a beat down? Take a swing at the editor-in-chief?"

Warrick held his silence. He would neither confirm nor deny the other man's suspicions.

Troy didn't wait for a response. "You know the *Horn* would jump at the opportunity to charge you with assault. Think of the number of papers they would sell with that headline and those photos. But what would happen to Mary?" Troy nodded toward the paper crushed in Warrick's fist. "As her husband's reputation was being shredded in the press, that photo would be on rotation on television stations across the country. Networks would show it every time they talked about your assault trial."

"This is bullshit." Warrick stepped around Troy,

needing some space. But he couldn't run away from the truth of the other man's words. He stared across the parking lot, the events Troy described playing out in his mind.

The media executive continued. "I agree. If we didn't have to worry about the repercussions, I'd go with you. But in the long run, we'd only cause our ladies more problems."

Warrick pulled his cell phone from his pocket. "I need to talk with Mary."

He walked away from Troy and toward the marina. Warrick hit the speed dial for her cell phone number and waited. A strong breeze pulled against his jersey. Overhead, trees bent but didn't break in the wind. Sunlight glared at the blue gray water. Marilyn's phone rang several times before tossing Warrick into her voice mail.

Why wasn't she answering?

Marilyn stared at the newspaper spread across the top of the desk. A six-by-nine-inch color photo exposed her during one of the most intimate moments of her life. Her skin burned with outrage and agony. The ringing in her ears was her cell phone, screaming for her attention. The buzzing in her head was her blood, rushing through her veins. Any moment now, her alarm clock would go off and she'd wake from this nightmare. At least, she prayed that's what would happen next.

"I'm waiting for an explanation." Arthur loomed just behind her in the break room.

Her cell phone went silent, but the buzzing in her head grew louder.

"I don't have one." Marilyn couldn't look at him. Her head spun. Her vision went in and out of focus. Was she going to throw up?

Oh, my God. She was on the edge of hysteria. Her muscles shook. She clenched her fists to make them stop.

Arthur's tone hardened. "The board of trustees will want an explanation."

Her desk phone rang.

Warrick! It must be him. Who else would call now and so persistently? She was desperate to talk with him. The team's loss to the Waves last night . . . The photo in the newspaper this morning . . . How much more could he handle? But Arthur was obviously determined to manipulate this incident. Marilyn was fighting for her career. As much as she wanted to speak with her husband, she'd have to call Warrick back after she'd dealt with Arthur.

Marilyn took a deep breath and forced herself to meet Arthur's gaze. "What do you want me to say? I didn't take the photo myself. I didn't ask for it to be taken and I didn't pose for it, either."

Why? When? How . . . ?

Oh, my God. Warrick had been right. Someone must have been hiding outside their kitchen window a few weeks ago, while she and Warrick were . . .

Marilyn squeezed her eyes shut. She was going to be sick. She inhaled long, deep breaths, pulling in the hospital's familiar scents—bleach and iodine.

Arthur folded his hands in front of him. "The hospital cannot condone this behavior."

Marilyn's pulse drummed in her ears. She knew what he meant, but she'd make him say it. "What behavior would that be? The photographer sneaking around my property taking pictures of my husband and me without our knowledge or permission? Rick and I don't condone that, either."

Arthur's thin cheeks pinkened. "You know very well

the behavior to which I'm referring is the photo the newspaper printed of you engaged in that act."

Marilyn arched a brow. "So you blame the *Horn* for printing the photo? So do I."

She was probably grinding centimeters from her teeth. Marilyn knew full well that Arthur wasn't blaming the person who'd taken the photo or the newspaper that had reprinted it large and in color. Dear God, the photo was huge! No, instead Arthur was blaming her and Rick—and they were the victims. She clenched her fists tighter.

Arthur released his hands and sucked in a deep breath. "If you choose to engage in that act, you should do so in the privacy of your bedroom."

Shock and anger fueled Marilyn's burst of laughter. "We were in the privacy of our home."

He jerked a finger toward the newspaper. "With the windows wide open."

"The blinds were closed." She punched her right index finger against the photo. "These shadows are the blinds."

"You should have made certain they were properly closed." Arthur's voice shook with inexplicable outrage.

Marilyn stared at him. "Why? On the off chance that some unknown photographer would sneak onto my private property and press his telephoto lens against my window?"

Arthur stabbed a finger toward the *Horn*. "Look at the paper. It's not an impossibility."

Marilyn was approaching the end of her patience. "What do you want from me, Arthur?"

His expression stiffened more, if that were possible. "I want an explanation, something that I can give to the board."

"Fine. Tell the board a trespasser came onto my property and took an unauthorized photograph of my husband and me doing what married couples do in the privacy of their home."

Arthur's nostrils flared. His lips thinned. "You think this is funny? Is this a joke to you?"

Marilyn's eyes stretched wide. "Do you hear me laughing? A photo of my husband and me is plastered in a newspaper that's circulated to all of our neighbors, friends, and family. To perfect strangers. There's nothing funny about that."

Arthur looked down his long, aquiline nose at her. "If you can't take this incident seriously, perhaps this hospital isn't the right fit for you."

Marilyn narrowed her eyes. "What are you saying, Arthur?"

The administrator gave her a flat stare. "I'm revoking your hospital privileges."

"What?" Marilyn forced the word past her numb lips.

Suddenly, Arthur didn't seem as angry at the world. "Your lifestyle doesn't suit the reputation that this hospital wants to present to the community."

Marilyn blinked. "Are you kidding me? You do realize that Rick and I are married? Married people have sex, Arthur. How do you think *you* got here?" *Much to my regret.*

Arthur looked disgusted. "Do not compare yourself and your lifestyle to my parents."

Perhaps Arthur's parents only had sex the one time. She probably would have sworn off the act as well, if he was the result.

Marilyn spun her chair to face her nemesis. "On what grounds are you claiming to dismiss me?"

"Moral grounds." Arthur's voice was cold enough to give her chills. "The fact that you and Rick are married doesn't make it any more acceptable for you to flaunt your sexuality in such a public forum. Patients expect a higher degree of morality and professionalism from their caregivers."

Marilyn's mind screamed at the injustice of the accusations Arthur threw at her. "Why are you holding me to a higher moral standard than the other doctors in this hospital?"

Arthur had the audacity to look baffled. "What are you talking about?"

"Oh, come on, Arthur." Outrage gave Marilyn the strength to stand. "You know damn well several physicians on staff are having affairs with other doctors—and with their patients. Therefore, how can you claim to dismiss *me* on a morality issue?"

"Several patients have already left because of you." Arthur drew himself up even straighter.

Would someone please remove the stick from the administrator's butt? "One patient, Arthur. And although she left my care, she's still with the hospital."

"Hannah DeSuza cancelled her afternoon appointment with you and informed the nurse she was transferring her care to Downstate." There was satisfaction in Arthur's tone. It contradicted his supposed concern over keeping patients on the hospital's record.

Marilyn frowned. "No one informed me of Ms. DeSuza's cancellation."

"They informed me." His meaning was clear. He was the final authority. "My decision isn't up for debate, Mary. Your access to the hospital has been revoked. If you leave quietly, I'll be more inclined to give you references."

Ice spread across Marilyn's chest, even as her face burned with anger and embarrassment. "I don't think that will be necessary, Arthur." She collected her purse and her backpack. "Something tells me a reference from you wouldn't be the career booster you seem to think."

She circled the hospital administrator and strode to the elevators. Marilyn could feel the stares of patients and former coworkers following her down the hall. She refused to look back.

Warrick went weak with relief when Marilyn's number appeared on his cellular screen. He stepped off the running path outside the arena and answered the call. "I've been trying to reach you for the past hour. Did you get my messages?"

"I know about the article and the picture. How are you feeling?" Marilyn's voice was raised over the background traffic noise playing through the connection from her end.

Warrick's frown was puzzled. Why was she outside? He wiped the sweat from his brow with the palm of his left hand. "I'm fine. It's you I'm worried about."

"Are you sure? I know you were upset about the team's loss last night. Now that photograph turns up in the *Horn*."

Why wasn't she angry with him? Instead she was worried about him.

Warrick turned toward the marina. Watching the water helped to calm him. "I'm all right, Mary. Really. Now tell me how you're doing."

"I've been better." Marilyn's tone was dry. "Arthur revoked my hospital privileges."

"What?" Warrick turned from the water. "Why?"

"He said we were immoral for flaunting the fact that we have sex outside the bedroom."

Warrick saw red. Again. "Son of a—"

"He's never been one of my favorite people, either."

"We didn't pay that photographer to take our picture. The newspaper did."

"I tried explaining that to him. It didn't work." Marilyn's reasonable tone was faked. Warrick heard the underlying anger.

"I'm so sorry, Mary." How could he ever make this up to her? Was this the final straw that ended their marriage? He wished he could see her, study her expression, read her body language.

"So am I."

"Jackie threatened the *Horn* with legal action to get them to turn over the photos and agree never to print them again."

"The damage has been done, Rick. I feel as though I've been victimized repeatedly by the photographer, then the newspaper, now my ex-boss." Her voice wobbled on her last words.

Warrick died a thousand deaths. "Are you on your way home?"

"Yes."

"I'll meet you there." Warrick started jogging back to his car. "I don't want you to be by yourself right now."

Marilyn sniffled. "No, I'll be fine. I need a little time to clear my head. And you and the team need to practice so you can beat the Waves in Miami on Sunday."

Warrick gripped his cell phone. "The team can wait." His tone was hard.

Marilyn expelled a breath. "You say that now, but you'd regret it Sunday."

"No, I wouldn't."

"Yes, you would. Besides, we're a one-income household now. We can't afford the fine you'd have to pay for missing practice." Marilyn's response was a weak attempt at her normal humor. She was hurting and trying not to show it. Warrick had always found her inner strength attractive. But today, it made him feel worse.

"I'd pay it gladly."

Marilyn exhaled a shaky breath. "I know you would. But, please, I just need some time alone right now. And maybe when you win the finals, this will all have been worth it."

His heart was breaking. "I don't think so."

The situation with the newspaper running a photo of their lovemaking illustrated Marilyn's point. *She* wasn't the celebrity. In fact, neither of them had signed up for such a prurient invasion of their privacy. The media had gone way too far. It had lost any sense of decency.

Warrick slowed to a walk. He'd give her the time she'd asked for to process these latest events. "I can't believe Arthur fired you because of the newspaper's lack of morals."

"You know, 'ex-boss' would sound a lot better if I'd gotten to keep my job and he'd lost his."

Warrick forced a brief laugh. "You're right. Are you sure you don't want me to come home?"

"Positive." The word came out on a breath. "I've never been fired before. I want to be alone right now."

Warrick wanted to break something. Rip something apart. Pummel the photographer and the newspaper editor and cause them the kind of pain they were causing Marilyn. Why couldn't he protect his wife?

"Mary, I'm really sorry."

"So am I." Marilyn's voice was choppy with grief.

"I'd tear that newspaper apart, but it would only give the media another excuse to show that damn photograph." Warrick ran his right hand across his forehead.

"Then we'll have to come up with another idea." Her voice was getting stronger as her temper seemed to rise.

"I'll keep working on it."

"When will this nightmare end, Rick?" Marilyn's voice was barely audible.

The sea breeze worked to cool him off as his wife's words tore him in two.

"I don't know." His throat muscles flexed as he made the admission.

Marilyn sighed. "Will it ever?"

He hesitated. "I don't know that, either."

"That's what I was afraid of." She ended the call without waiting for a response. It didn't matter. Warrick didn't have a response to give her.

11

Marilyn was home at half past ten on a weekday morning. How strange. She locked the front door, took off her shoes, and wandered into the family room. The numbness was wearing off. The house was silent as though it, too, were in shock. She'd been fired. And regardless of what Arthur had said, she knew for him this day was the culmination of a two-year dream.

Marilyn put away thoughts of Arthur's vendetta. She had to call Janet Crowley and Dionne Sproles, the clinic partners. As much as she wanted to bury her head in the sand, she had to deal with this—the sooner the better. But what should she say?

Did you see the photo in the Horn *of my husband and me making love? What did you think?* Marilyn shuddered with nausea.

How many people had seen that photo? Coworkers, patients, neighbors, friends?

She wouldn't think about that right now. She couldn't. If she did, she'd never make the phone call.

Marilyn crossed the family room. The polished hardwood floor was cool beneath her stocking feet. Her hand hovered above the black cordless telephone. Hopefully, the clinic partners were more reasonable than Arthur.

What if they weren't?

Arthur had fired her on the spot. Could this photo also cost her the clinic partnership?

What was she going to tell them?

The truth.

She lifted the handset, took a fortifying breath, and entered Janet's direct phone number. The senior partner answered on the third ring. "Good morning, Mary."

Marilyn froze. Caller identification. It eliminated social pleasantries and jump-started conversations. At this moment, she deeply resented the telephone feature. She could have used the icebreaker.

"Hello, Janet." She resisted the urge to clear her throat and adopted a brisk, businesslike tone. "I assume you saw the photo in today's *New York Horn*."

"Indeed I did." Janet sounded smugly amused. "It looks like you and your husband are getting back together."

Marilyn smoothed the hairs on the back of her neck. "We were never apart."

"That's not what the papers reported."

Marilyn heard the thin woman's superior tone and pictured her condescending expression. She gripped the phone to rein in her temper.

Stay focused; don't allow the other woman to distract you. "I wanted you to know that our kitchen blinds were closed."

Janet's hum slid down the phone line. "I'd wondered what caused the shadows on the top and bottom of the photo. Still, your blinds must not have been closed all the way." More smug amusement.

Marilyn turned away from the telephone's base to pace the family room. "They were. The Peeping Tom who took that picture snuck onto our property and pressed his camera lens against our window."

Janet chuckled. "Still, Mary, no one can blame you for wanting to show off your husband. I'm certain all the women in the tristate area are even more jealous of you now. Well, those who aren't married to professional athletes themselves, that is."

Did the clinic's senior partner really think she would have staged that photo? What kind of person would consider going into business with an exhibitionist? And did she want a business partner who believed her capable of such behavior?

"I'm not an exhibitionist." Marilyn was inflexible.

Janet laughed again. "I would be."

The conversation was degenerating. "Listen, Janet. I just wanted you to be aware of how this situation came about. I wanted you to know the truth while you're considering my application."

Janet's pause was unnerving. "Marilyn, you'll recall that when we last discussed the possibility of your joining the partnership, Dionne and I voiced our reservations with your husband's lifestyle."

Marilyn's grip on the cordless phone tightened. "And I assured you that my husband does not have the kind of lifestyle that would negatively impact the clinic."

Janet huffed a breath. "Well, the photograph that appears enlarged on the front page of the *Horn* illustrates otherwise."

Marilyn's temper stirred. She wouldn't allow this attack against her husband. "First of all, that photograph does not appear on the *newspaper's* front page. It appears on the front page of the *gossip* section. And, since I don't engage in gossip, if someone else hadn't brought it to my attention, I never would have seen it."

"Well, I only happened across it myself," Janet stuttered.

Marilyn ignored Janet's interruption. "Second, making love with your spouse is not generally viewed as a high-risk or immoral act."

"Be that as it may, it would be wiser for you and Rick to confine your intimacies to your bedroom." Janet's pompous response grated on Marilyn. "I trust your bedroom is on a higher floor and photographers wouldn't be able to peek into it."

Marilyn told herself to breath. Giving in to her anger against her prospective business partner wasn't wise, especially since she was unemployed. "Yes, Janet, our bedroom is on a higher floor. Thanks for your concern."

Janet must have missed the irony in Marilyn's words. "You're still under consideration but so is everyone else. We hope to make a decision within the next few days."

They'd been saying that for weeks. "Thank you. I hope I'll be hearing from you shortly. This is an opportunity I would dearly love."

"We'll be in touch. Either way." Janet disconnected the call without waiting for Marilyn's response.

Marilyn recradled the cordless phone. Janet's parting comment hadn't been encouraging. "We'll be in touch" was the mother of all noncommittal responses. Still she held on to hope that she'd get the partnership with the women's health clinic. With it, she'd fulfill her goal of being her own boss and—more importantly—having a positive impact on the community. And she could set her own hours. Maybe then she and Warrick could start a family, provided they could ever get out from under the media's spotlight.

Marilyn turned to leave the family room. The phone rang, stopping her in midstride. Could it be Janet again, calling to discuss the partnership further? Hope was almost painful. Marilyn crossed her left fingers and grabbed the receiver with her right hand. "Hello?"

"What in the *hell* were you thinking? Your father almost had a heart attack when he saw those pictures of you on the Internet. What were you thinking?" It was hard to understand her mother's words as she shrieked into the phone, but Marilyn caught the gist of Celeste's hysterical rant.

She closed her eyes. She'd forgotten her parents had established a Google Alert account to receive notices when she and Warrick were mentioned in the media. A headache blossomed from the center of her forehead like a mushroom cloud.

How often would she have to defend herself? "We were in our own home." She opened her eyes, glaring at the shadows across the hardwood floor. "Don't you and Father ever make love outside the bedroom?"

"Watch how you speak to me, young lady." Celeste Devry's voice whipped across the phone line. "Your father and I have never had sex in front of an open window."

"Neither have Rick and I." Marilyn's tone was hard with disappointment. Her own parents were casting her and Warrick as the villains. Why couldn't anyone see they were the victims?

"Come home."

Marilyn frowned. "What?"

"You heard me. Come home. Now." Celeste sounded like a drill sergeant directing new recruits. "This has gone far enough. Your father and I have worked too hard and too long to build this family's reputation as people our community can look up to. Honorable, respectable, philanthropic members of society. In one day, you've destroyed all of that. Now there are naked pictures of our daughter taking booty calls on the Internet."

Marilyn's thoughts were spinning. "What do you mean photos on the Internet? There was one photo and it was in a newspaper."

"On the *New York Horn*'s Web site, there are at least half a dozen pictures of you and Rick in all kinds of poses having sex." Celeste sounded apoplectic.

"Oh. My. God." Blood roared in Marilyn's ears. She couldn't catch her breath. Was she going to faint? "Mom, I have to call you back."

"Do not hang up on me." Celeste chewed the command. "Pack your things and come home. I told you not to marry a basketball player. He's a professional child. He makes his money playing a game."

Marilyn's knees were knocking. She stumbled across the room and tumbled into an armchair. "I did not marry a child." Her words were sharp and angry despite her chattering teeth. "I married a responsible adult. This isn't Rick's fault. It's not my fault, either."

"Then whose fault is it?" Celeste spat the question. "Who told you to open your blinds and have sex on your kitchen table?"

Marilyn bent over in her chair, rocking herself. Why was this happening? And why was her mother blaming her?

She held on to her control with sheer desperation. A respectful daughter would not speak to her parent in anger, no matter how many buttons her mother pushed. "You should be yelling at the photographer who violated our privacy and the publisher who gave his approval to post those photos."

Dear God, were there really photos posted to the Internet of Warrick and her making love? Was Warrick aware of them? Had he seen them? If so, why hadn't he told her? If not, how was she going to break this news to him? He didn't need any more distractions. She needed him to win the conference and the finals so they could move on with their lives.

"We should never have allowed you to move away from home." Some of the steam drained from Celeste's tone. "As a child, you always needed direction and you obviously haven't outgrown that."

Direction? More like commands. She never had the choice or opportunity to think for herself. She'd always planned to go away to college, if only to escape her parents' control.

"Mom, I'm thirty-three years old. I've been making my own decisions for a long time."

"Look at where it's gotten you." Celeste's temper was stirring again. "Naked photos of you posted to the Internet."

"I prefer to concentrate on my medical degree."

"Of course." Celeste snorted. "That reminds me. I tried the hospital before calling you at home. The system said yours was a nonworking number. Why is that?"

This was a never-ending nightmare. Marilyn pinched the bridge of her nose. "I was fired this morning."

"Oh, my God. Was it because of the photos?"

Marilyn swallowed a sigh. "Yes, Mom. It was because of the photos."

Celeste's building anger communicated itself across the phone lines almost three thousand miles away. "Marilyn, this relationship with Rick is ruining your reputation and destroying your career. You don't have to stay with him. Come home."

"Mom, this isn't just a relationship. This is my marriage."

"You made a mistake, but you can do something about it."

Marilyn shook with impatience, outrage, and embarrassment. Was her marriage a mistake? The disloyal whisper snaked across her thoughts. Her mind recoiled from the suggestion. But she'd been successful at the hospital at first. After her marriage, her relationship with Arthur had deteriorated.

You'd still have your job if it weren't for those photos. The traitorous thoughts continued.

If it weren't for Warrick's celebrity, she wouldn't have photographers creeping onto her property and peeking through her windows.

How do you know when love isn't enough?

"My marriage isn't a mistake." Her voice lacked conviction.

"You married a professional athlete. You were obviously acting out against the strict upbringing your father and I gave you."

"I was thirty-one when I married Rick. I wasn't acting out." Acting out hadn't influenced her parents when she'd been sixteen.

"Age has nothing to do with it." Celeste dismissed Marilyn's argument like sand shifting through her fingers. "Your marrying a ballplayer was a clear message to us."

"Then maybe you can explain it to me."

"Don't be fresh, Marilyn." Her mother's disapproval didn't faze her. "Your choice of husband told us you were rejecting the structure we gave you in favor of a more irresponsible lifestyle."

Marilyn rubbed her eyes with her thumb and middle finger. "Mother, you have to separate Rick the man from Rick the ballplayer. Those are two different people."

"We can't." Celeste's tone was firm. "Whatever Rick does ends up in the news and reflects on our entire family. Think about that the next time you want to pretend that your marriage wasn't a mistake." On that note, Celeste disconnected the call.

Marilyn slammed the handset back onto its base. How could her mother blame Warrick? He was as much a victim as she was.

But Celeste was right. Warrick's celebrity had placed her in an untenable position. It had embarrassed her family. It had cost her her job and had hurt her chances of joining the clinic.

The serpent whispered in her ear again, "How do you know when love just isn't enough?"

A reporter stood in Warrick's driveway. For Warrick, it didn't matter whether the other man worked for the *Horn,* some other print rag, a television station, or the devil. Warrick's foot itched to floor the accelerator and drive over the little anchor and his camera crew. Instead, he maintained his speed as he directed his black BMW into his driveway, forcing the television crew to leap from his path. It was small satisfaction.

Warrick stopped his car before continuing past his remote control private gate and into his garage. He unfolded himself from his sedan. "You're on private property. Leave."

As though he hadn't made himself clear, the pudgy reporter ignored Warrick's warning and stuck a microphone in his face. "Rick, what went through your mind when you saw the *Horn*'s photos of you and Mary?"

Warrick glared at the squat broadcaster. He'd never even seen the man before. What gave the stranger the right to invade Warrick's privacy? Why did he think he could refer to Marilyn so casually, as though she were a one-night stand and not his wife?

With Herculean effort, Warrick kept his hands at his sides. "No comment."

The worst thing Warrick could do was get into an

exchange with the vipers circling him. Microphones and video cameras were jabbed toward his head. Flashbulbs scorched his vision. He masked his expression, returned to his driver's seat, and pulled his car into his garage. On how many channels would footage of this media swarm appear?

After parking his car and securing the garage, Warrick let himself in through his back entrance. He controlled his urge to slam the door before setting the main lock, dead bolt, and chain. He crossed his kitchen and walked through his home.

What were his neighbors thinking? They were probably considering buying homes in a quieter area. The media saturation was turning his teammates against him, putting a strain on his marriage, and now possibly alienating his neighbors. The only ones enjoying this circus were the media.

The curtains over the front windows of his brownstone were closed. It was barely two o'clock in the afternoon. Marilyn loved fresh air and natural light. The fact that she'd been forced to change her habit because of the newshounds prowling the sidewalk in front of their home was an additional burden. One more thing to include on his list of transgressions.

"They've been here since noon."

Warrick's gaze followed the sound of his wife's voice. She stood in the threshold between the hallway and the family room. Her face was pale, her features drawn. "Are you all right?"

Her chocolate eyes glittered with anger. "They were aiming their cameras toward the house, taking photos and videos through the windows. Why would they do that?"

Because they lacked a sense of decency. Because the more scandalous the photo, the more money they'd make. Because they'd lost all sense of humanity. All of the above.

Warrick ran his right hand over his forehead. "I don't know."

Marilyn was still wearing the light gray slacks and pale blue blouse she must have worn to work. But she'd pulled the clip from her hair, which now spilled behind her shoulders in soft dark waves.

She hugged her arms around herself. "I don't want to be trapped inside my home behind triple-locked doors and drawn curtains. That's no way to live. How long is this going to last?"

Warrick shook his head. "I don't know that, either."

Marilyn locked gazes with him for several long, silent moments. What was she thinking? What did she want? If it was in his power, he'd get it for her. Anything.

Warrick followed her as she turned back into the family room.

"My mother called." Her voice was brittle. "My parents have seen the *Horn*."

The muscles in Warrick's shoulders bunched. "They live in San Francisco. How did they get a copy of the paper?"

Marilyn's tension communicated itself all the way across the room. "They set up a Google Alert notice on us."

Warrick shut his eyes. "Son of a—"

"I know."

Warrick's eyes opened. His forehead tightened with a scowl. "I'm sure this situation hasn't helped me win them over."

Marilyn's parents had disliked him since *Hello*. Celeste and Terrell Devry were probably at this minute filing divorce papers for their daughter.

"But the article isn't the only thing online." Marilyn's statement dragged Warrick from his unpleasant imaginings to his equally unpleasant reality. "Mother said there are at least half a dozen photos of us on the *Horn*'s Web site."

Warrick's brows shot up his forehead. "That many?"

"Did you know about this?" Marilyn's troubled gaze searched his.

He shifted his stance in the family room's threshold. "Troy mentioned the images to me, but I had no idea there were that many of them."

Marilyn's lips parted. "Why didn't you tell me?"

"Jackie told the *Horn*'s publisher to remove those photos this morning. By the time I went to the site, they were gone."

Marilyn threw her arms up and paced in a small, agitated circle. "You *still* should have told me."

"I didn't want to upset you even more." Warrick spread his arms. "I'm angry and embarrassed enough for both of us."

Marilyn fisted her hands. "That's my decision to make, Rick. Not yours." She spun away from him and paced farther across the room. "I had to find out from my mother. She caught me completely off guard."

"I'm sorry." He'd been saying that a lot. Did the words still mean anything to her?

He wanted to go back to the way things used to be between them. How much longer would they have to weather this storm? And where would the gusts carry them?

"I can't believe this." Marilyn muttered the words under her breath.

She stood frozen in a far corner of the room, almost hidden in shadows. She pressed the heels of her palms against her eyes. Her shoulders slumped.

This was what Warrick had been trying to avoid. Maybe he should have told her. She did have the right to know. But the damage already had been done. Knowing the images had been posted to the Internet could only cause her pain. She'd experienced enough of that because of him. Still, he wasn't ready to let her go. He wasn't strong enough.

"What can I do?" Would she let him hold her?

She stepped from the dark and looked at him in disbelief. "This isn't just about me, Rick. Mother said you were naked in those photos, too. Aren't you horrified? Doesn't that make you furious?"

His temper stirred. "I'm angrier for you. You don't deserve any of this."

"Neither do you. But you're still not angry enough to do anything about it." She swung her arm toward the covered windows. "And now those jackals are swarming our home. When will they have crossed the line? When will you defend yourself?"

Warrick stared at her. "Mary, I'm not going to defend loving you."

Her shoulders slumped again. She buried her face in her hands and started to cry. Hard. "How many people have seen me naked? This is a nightmare. Why won't they leave us alone?"

Warrick rushed across the room and gathered her in his arms. He didn't care whether she wanted him to hold her or not. He needed to touch her, to comfort her.

He gathered her against him, pressing her head against his heart, and murmured into her ear. "We'll get through this together."

She tightened her arms around him, digging her fingers into his back. "How?"

He held her closer and kissed the top of her head. "I don't know. But it will be all right. I promise."

"How can you make a promise like that?" Marilyn's words were muffled against his chest. "These people are crazy. You can't promise that they'll suddenly come to their senses."

"No, but I can promise that the media has a very short attention span." He heard the heavy irony in his own voice. "In a minute, they'll find someone else to vilify, like Tiger Woods or LeBron James."

Marilyn was silent for several moments. She stopped crying and slowly relaxed in his embrace. "I wouldn't wish these constant attacks and public humiliation on my worst enemy."

"I wouldn't mind if Arthur experienced this. Maybe then he'd understand how invasive the media is and how unfair he was to fire you because of them."

Marilyn pulled away to look up at him. Her cheeks were flushed and her lashes were spikey from tears. "You're right. Arthur's the exception."

Warrick lowered his head and kissed her. He couldn't help himself. The temptation was too strong. His mouth moved gently over hers. His touch was meant to soothe and perhaps heal. He tasted her tears, still wet on her lips. He sipped them from her. He nibbled her full, lower lip, then ran his tongue across the seam of her mouth. Marilyn wrapped her arms around him and pulled him closer. He sighed at her acceptance and deepened the kiss. She moaned into his mouth.

Reluctantly, Warrick pulled back. "I have to fly to Miami tonight for Sunday's game."

Leaving her this time would be the hardest it had ever been. It wasn't that the media had prepared to camp outside. They had a security system to prevent break-ins. But Warrick wasn't fooling himself that their marriage wasn't still on shaky ground.

She sighed. Her breath was warm and soft against his neck. "I know."

"Come with me." His tone was urgent.

Marilyn stepped away. "I can't, Rick."

Her response didn't surprise him. But it did disappoint. She'd yet to travel with him on an away game, and he really wanted her there. "Can't or won't?"

12

Marilyn scowled. With her puffy eyes and congested nose, she wasn't certain the expression was effective. "Your career is taking off and you have the media attention to prove it. However, mine is in shambles—also because of your media attention."

"I've apologized for that." Warrick sounded frustrated. Well, so was she.

"This isn't your fault. I don't need an apology." Marilyn led the way out of the family room. "I need a job. Arthur fired me. And Janet is hesitant to offer me the partnership with her clinic." She mounted the stairs.

"A change of scenery will help clear your mind." Warrick's optimistic prediction floated up from behind her.

"There's media in Miami, too, Rick." Marilyn's tone was dry.

"But they won't be camped outside your door or pointing cameras through your hotel window." Warrick was persistent.

Marilyn spoke over her shoulder. "I seem to remember a photo of Jackie and Marc taken outside Marc's Miami hotel room. The picture was plastered all over the New York papers the next morning."

Warrick sighed. "I remember that, too."

At the top of the stairs, Marilyn turned toward the master bedroom—their room, in which they'd made love last night. Now she couldn't get the ugly idea of their photos posted to the *Horn* Web site out of her mind. She rubbed her eyes. The media would *not* ruin the memory of last night for her.

"You don't need me in Miami and I can't leave Brooklyn right now." Marilyn pulled her pink shorts and cropped white T-shirt from the closet. She tossed them onto the bed and unbuttoned her blouse.

Warrick crossed his arms over his chiseled chest. Every muscle—and there were many—in his well-defined arms flexed. "Are you blaming me for the photos?"

Marilyn faced him. "No. I blame the media."

Without another word, Warrick left their bedroom.

Marilyn exhaled on a trembling breath. As cowardly as it might have appeared, she wasn't ready to leave the house. Her technophobic parents had found the photos on the Internet. How many of the other people she knew had seen them? The kid at their grocery store checkout? The old man at the fruit stand? The guys at the fish market? Maybe she should do her food shopping in New Jersey for a while.

She changed her clothes, washed her face, and brushed her hair. It was easy to keep feelings of turmoil at bay if she focused on tedious tasks. Her uncertain career didn't plague her. The disaster of her marriage couldn't worry her. The existence of those photos didn't twist her stomach into knots.

Marilyn turned to leave the bedroom, still preoccupied with the mundane. Dinner. The weather.

A familiar melody rose from downstairs, filling their brownstone's high-ceilinged rooms. Olivia Newton-John's pitch-perfect soprano accompanied the music. From its opening notes, Marilyn recognized "Hopelessly Devoted to You" from the musical *Grease*. It wasn't the song that caused her to pause in uncertainty in the upstairs hallway. It was the person who was playing it.

Marilyn hurried down the stairs, allowing the music to draw her into the family room. Warrick stood in front of the compact disc player. He used the remote control to lower the volume, then tossed it onto the sofa.

Marilyn stared. "You hate this song."

"But you love it. And I love you." He offered her his hand.

Marilyn went to him. She shivered as his strong arms wrapped around her and the day drifted away. Under her hands, his muscles flowed with the music. She drew closer to him, sharing the warmth from his body. Warrick rested his cheek on the top of her head and tightened his hold around her.

He hummed along with Olivia for a few stanzas. The deep, soothing sound was like a magician's spell. More of her tension disappeared. She let his movements and his magic carry her away.

Warrick's lips brushed against her hair as he added his baritone to the song, expressing his hopeless devotion to Marilyn.

Marilyn's heart sighed.

Olivia Newton-John wrapped up the song, promising to hold on to the end. Warrick straightened, drawing her with him so that her feet left the ground, and pressed his lips to hers. Marilyn's eyes drifted close. She wrapped her arms around his shoulders and held on tight.

She was floating. Her head spun from his taste. Her pulse raced from his touch. She shivered as his mouth moved from her lips to her cheek, her chin, then down her neck. Marilyn tipped her head back and held her breath as Warrick licked his way to the pulse at the nape of her neck.

His hands pressed her closer to his strength. They raised her up and held her steady as he loved her. Warrick's mouth returned to hers. He cherished her with his touch. In his kiss, she sensed the same devotion he'd sang of.

Marilyn parted her lips on a sigh. "Rick."

His tongue stole inside. Marilyn drank him in. His feel, his taste, his scent. She stroked the roof of his mouth with the tip of her tongue and her toes curled. She caressed the sides and his teeth and her stomach did flips. She reacted to his scent, his touch, his taste as desperately today as she had their first time.

Marilyn wrapped her legs around Warrick's hips and held him tight. Warrick cupped her hips and pulled her closer to him. Her breath hitched in her throat. Marilyn's hips rolled against his in response to his touch.

This is what she did to him. And his heat turned her bones to jelly. Her body was weightless, warm, and wet.

Had she moaned or had he?

Warrick leaned over. Marilyn's arms and legs slipped from his body, and she landed on the mattress.

Marilyn's eyes flew open. Her gaze circled their bedroom. "How did we get here?"

Warrick grinned. He braced an arm on either side of her head. A low chuckle rumbled in his chest. "Magic." His words whispered against her lips and her thighs went lax.

Marilyn's arms rose of their own accord, twining around his neck. Her fingertips trailed the smooth, hot skin from the base of his head down his long neck. They dug into the deep muscles of his shoulders and back.

Marilyn groaned. "Too many clothes."

"You're right." Warrick's breath tickled her ear. Marilyn's body shivered.

Warrick stood beside the bed, pulling her with him. Their clothes disappeared between licks, kisses, and caresses. Soon, there was nothing between them; nothing that mattered in this moment. There was only the two of them and their passion.

Marilyn reached out. She stroked her fingers over Warrick's well-sculpted torso, his deep pectorals, and six-pack abdominals. Her right hand hovered over his full erection before cupping him. His hips flexed, pushing himself against her palm. Marilyn felt a rush of pleasure and power at his response.

"Tell me what you want." Warrick's words were a husky request. "What would make you happy?"

Marilyn's fingers traced the hard angles of his features. She cupped his face with her palm and looked deep into his midnight eyes. "You. You make me happy."

Warrick bent his head. She rose on her toes to meet him. His mouth covered hers and she parted her lips to accept his tongue. He swept inside her mouth as his hips again pressed into her hand. Marilyn stroked him. She smiled as his body shook against hers. It thrilled her that this big, strong man ached for her as much as she yearned for him.

Warrick pressed her onto the bed behind them. The hunger between her legs made her restless. Warrick soothed her with a touch. His broad palm stroked from her thigh to her waist and higher to her breast. He deepened their kiss as his long, talented fingers drew closer to her breast. Marilyn felt her nipple tighten in anticipation of his touch.

He played her body like a musical virtuoso, plucking and strumming her breasts until her hips swung in rhythm and her arousal pooled in her core.

Marilyn tore her lips free of his spell. "Rick, come inside me."

"Soon."

Warrick moved down her body, stopping at her left breast. He suckled her sensitive flesh. His tongue swirled around her areola and his lips nibbled at her nipple. Her fists pulled at the bedsheet when he lifted his head to treat her right breast to the same intense caresses. Marilyn moaned. Her body tossed and twisted beneath his weight. Muscles deep inside her pulsed with an almost painful pleasure.

"Please, Rick." Marilyn's voice was thin and unrecognizable. "I need you now."

Warrick released her breast. "Soon."

He breathed the word against her damp skin. Every muscle in Marilyn's body strained.

Warrick moved lower. He kissed her hip bones and licked her navel. Marilyn's hips lifted toward his chin, silently begging for this most intimate of kisses. Warrick touched her. She felt her moisture dampen his fingers.

"Are you ready for me?" He whispered the question against her curls.

"Yes." Her response was choked.

Warrick lifted her hips and covered her with his mouth. Marilyn screamed behind clenched teeth. She pressed her head into her pillow. Her body arched, stretching taut. Warrick cupped her hips and worked her against his tongue. Her body responded to his silent commands, rocking, writhing, twisting in his sinful embrace. She commanded him, but she didn't know for what. She pleaded with him, but she didn't know why.

Light exploded behind Marilyn's closed eyes. Her heartbeat thundered in her ears. Her blood heated her veins. Her muscles strained to the breaking point.

Marilyn's release crashed over her. She was drowning under waves of pleasure. She crushed the bedsheet in her fist, trying to hold on. Finally, she flung her arms above her head and allowed herself to be swept away.

Warrick surged up and over her body. He entered her with one smooth, deep stroke, stirring the tidal wave of sensations again. Marilyn gasped. She wrapped her legs around his hips and answered his thrusts as her desire built again. Warrick slipped his hand between them. He gently tapped her spot. Marilyn caught her breath at the almost unbearable ecstasy. Her body soared, then shattered again. Warrick's hips surged into her. He tightened his embrace, then spiraled with her over the edge.

Eons later, Marilyn's breathing returned to normal. She hugged Warrick to her.

He propped himself on his arms above her. "Now I can leave for Miami with the memory of your smile instead of your tears."

Marilyn raised her head and kissed him.

After throwing on some clothes, Warrick packed his travel case for the team's two nights in Miami before helping Marilyn prepare a quick dinner of salad and spaghetti. God, he was going to miss her, even more this time than ever before.

He'd pulled on black slacks and a short-sleeved gray dress shirt for the trip. His black loafers waited near the front door. Marilyn had wrapped her curves in a skimpy bronze robe that made her honey skin glow. Warrick's gaze stroked over her slender back, rounded hips, and well-toned legs. If people knew what the conservative Dr. Devry-Evans wore away from the hospital, they'd probably swallow their tongue depressors.

The phone rang, distracting him from his mental

image of what she looked like beneath the stingy robe. Marilyn caught him staring at her.

Her chocolate eyes laughed at him. "Do you want to answer the phone?"

Warrick shrugged. "Not really. It could be a reporter."

The twinkle left Marilyn's eyes. His joy went with it. Marilyn finished draining the spaghetti. He gave the salad a final toss and set the bowl on the kitchen table. By the fourth ring, the answering machine picked up. Warrick crossed the hallway into the family room. He reached the phone as the caller identified himself with his words.

"Rick!" His father's bellow startled him. The noise bounced off the walls. "Why are you bare-assed in the paper?"

His mother screamed in the background.

Warrick reached for the receiver.

Marilyn's gentle hand restrained him. "You need to prepare for your trip."

Warrick sought her steady gaze. It was as though she hadn't heard—or chose to ignore—the anger in his father's voice.

John Evans continued his tirade. "You always had to be the center of attention."

Warrick knew that wasn't true; still his father's words hurt. He tugged against Marilyn's hold. "He's going to keep yelling until I answer the phone."

Marilyn's gaze compelled him. "He'll eventually run out of tape."

"Then he'll call back."

John's tirade almost drowned Warrick's words. "I know you're there. Pick up the phone."

Warrick pulled his attention from his wife and stared down at the answering machine. Marilyn released Warrick's arm to turn down the volume on the phone until they couldn't hear his father. Warrick stared fixedly at the machine. That plan was bound to backfire.

Marilyn's long, cool fingers turned his face toward hers. "Dinner's almost ready."

"I'm not sure that was a good idea."

Marilyn dropped her hand. "If you'd answered his call, what would you have said?"

Warrick's shoulders tightened. "I don't know." He hadn't wanted to take his father's call, but it would have been better to get it over with.

"You wouldn't have said a word." Marilyn gripped his shoulder. "You would have stood there and let him tear you down without saying anything to defend yourself."

His features tightened. Was it anger, embarrassment, or both? "You don't know that."

"You never defend yourself." Her chin was tilted at an angle from which he knew he couldn't persuade her. "That strategy may make *him* feel better, but how does it help *you*?"

It doesn't. "There's no point in defending yourself to him. Dad doesn't listen. But ignoring him isn't the answer."

"I know." Marilyn waved a negligent hand. "Ignoring your father will only make him angrier. Call him when you get to Miami. Right now, you need to eat. Then you have a plane to catch."

Without waiting for a response, she pivoted on her bare feet and marched back to the kitchen. Warrick's gaze returned to her well-rounded posterior.

He followed her to the kitchen. "What am I supposed to say to him?"

Marilyn shook her head. "I don't know. The truth doesn't seem to matter."

"What do you mean?"

Marilyn faced him, settling her hands on her hips. The robe crept another inch up her thighs. "If you had defended yourself to your father, you'd probably say the same things I tried to say to my mother. We were in the privacy of our own home. The venetian blinds were closed. The photographer pressed his camera lens against our window. None of that mattered to her."

Warrick wasn't surprised. Celeste Devry lived to assign blame. "So how am I supposed to make amends to our parents?"

Marilyn dropped her arms. "We don't have to make amends. We're the victims."

"You're blaming the media?"

"Aren't you?"

"Yes, but they aren't going away."

"I know. I also know the championship is important to you. I want you to win it all this year. Maybe then, you can retire."

Warrick took a moment to form a response. He strode to the table and dished some of the salad into their bowls. "Retire to what? Pull my rocking chair into the sun and watch the day go by?"

She turned on the burner under the pan to reheat the spaghetti sauce. "You majored in accounting and minored in business administration. You can do a lot of things with those degrees."

"I'm a basketball player. That's who I am."

Marilyn shook her head. "Playing basketball is what you do. You're Rick Evans. You have the ability, intelligence, and drive to do whatever you choose."

Her words frustrated him even as they healed the fresh wounds his father's tirade had cut. "Then I choose to be a basketball player."

"Do you intend to keep playing until you're sixty-five?" Marilyn served the now sticky spaghetti onto the dinner plates. "I've done some research. Thirty-seven, thirty-eight is old for a basketball player. You're almost thirty-five."

Warrick stored the leftover salad in the refrigerator. "I love basketball."

"I know." Marilyn's answer came from behind him.

But did she understand? "Growing up, basketball was all I had. When I couldn't earn my mother's attention or my father's approval, I had basketball. It never belittled me. It never made me feel worthless. And, if I failed, tomorrow was another chance."

"Why haven't you ever told me this?" Marilyn's voice was emotional.

Warrick faced her. He hadn't meant to upset Marilyn. "I've never told anyone. Don't feel sorry for me, Mary. A lot of kids have it worse."

"But you've fulfilled your dream, Rick. And you'll be in the Hall of Fame. I'm certain of it."

That was an honor he hadn't dared to consider. But he wasn't ready for his career to end. Searching her eyes, Warrick saw that Marilyn was, and her silent ultimatum was harder to bear than his father's bellowing condemnations.

Warrick considered ignoring the knock on his Miami hotel door Saturday night. After a brutal workout and practice, he was hungry, tired, and sore. Dinner and bed. That's all he wanted. He needed to be well rested for the Monarchs critical game five tomorrow night against the Miami Waves.

He recognized Troy through the peephole. The marketing executive stroked his goatee with a distracted air. Warrick pulled open the door and stepped aside to let the other man in.

Troy wore a tan suit. His pale pink shirt was open at the collar, displaying a short, thin gold chain. He looked like he'd just stepped from the South Beach section of an expensive men's clothing catalog. But the expression on his friend's face didn't bode well for Warrick's evening plans.

He closed the door. "What now?"

He hadn't meant to sound so hard. The Monarchs' executive obviously didn't relish his role as messenger. But how much could a person handle at one time? His marriage was on the rocks, his team's championship was in jeopardy, his starting position was in question, and what little regard his parents and in-laws had for him had been zapped by the prurient paparazzi's photos. Screw happiness. Money couldn't even buy peace.

Troy entered the room and offered Warrick his BlackBerry. "Sit down and press play." The look in his eyes made the muscles in Warrick's gut clench.

Warrick stared at the BlackBerry, his arms at his sides. What was this about? More gossip? Dammit, not more photos. "Just tell me."

"You have to see this." Troy extended the BlackBerry toward him.

Warrick took the device and strode toward the bed. He dropped onto the edge of the mattress. His body felt heavier than it had after the three-hour practice. He stared at the screen. It showed the home page of a New York television station's Web site. The image in the video box was of a woman surrounded by reporters with microphones. Warrick knew what it felt like to be hemmed in by so many overanxious people wielding microphones at your face. He grew tense just watching her.

The woman appeared to be in her mid- to late thirties. The camera framed her to midtorso. Her thick reddish brown curls framed a round brown face painted with dramatic cosmetics.

Warrick glanced at Troy one last time before pressing the play symbol. The male anchor's voice-over introduced the subject of the video clip as Jordan Hyatt. According to the anchor, Jordan's publicist had contacted the local media to schedule a press conference. Her client claimed to have explosive information about Brooklyn Monarchs shooting guard Warrick Evans.

Warrick frowned at Troy. "I don't even know this woman."

Troy returned his stare without responding. Warrick switched his attention to the video clip of the woman holding court to a small nest of reporters outside a large apartment building. Some press conference.

"Thank you all for coming." Jordan Hyatt offered a small, excited smile. "I'm certain you'll realize your time has been well spent once I share my news with you." She paused for effect.

It worked. The reporters shouted questions, clamoring for her information.

She waved her hands to quiet the noise. Her heavily made-up face glowed with pleasure. "As I said earlier, my name's Jordan Hyatt. J-O-R-D-A-N. H-Y-A-T-T. And Warrick Evans is the father of my unborn child."

13

The BlackBerry slid from Warrick's lax hold. He stared dumbly as the device seemed to bounce onto the hotel room's thin dark carpet in slow motion. Troy crouched to retrieve it.

The movement snapped Warrick from his stupor. "Do you believe her?" His voice was cold, controlled, unlike the frenzied fury building inside him.

"Of course not." Troy's surprised response came without hesitation. "Everyone who knows you, knows you have too much integrity to cheat on your wife."

What about the people who *didn't* know him? Did they think he was a lowlife who would get one woman pregnant while married to another? Why did it bother him what strangers thought? He didn't know why, but it did.

Just as it bothered Marilyn.

Warrick stood from the bed. His movements were stiff as he prowled the room. He moved past the cherry-wood combination chest of drawers and television, and circled in front of the matching laminate writing table and cushioned chair. His heart raced in his chest. His breathing came too fast.

He stopped before the wall-length window and glared through the sheer white curtains at downtown Miami at night. "Why did she do this? What does she hope to gain?"

"Fifteen minutes of fame." Disgust deepened Troy's response. "You saw her. She was eating up the attention."

Warrick spun from the window. "At the expense of my marriage? My wife's reputation? My reputation? How selfish could one person be?"

"Pretty damn." Troy crossed his arms over his chest.

Warrick's hands clenched and unclenched with the urge to punch something. He resumed his pacing. "I've got to call Mary."

"You need to calm down first."

"I know." Warrick caught Troy's concerned expression. "How did you find the link? Was it one of those Google Alerts?"

Troy hesitated. "Andy sent it to me."

Warrick froze. Andrea Benson, Troy's girlfriend and the new features writer for *The New York Times*, was in Brooklyn. He squeezed his eyes shut. "So Mary already knows."

"Probably." Troy answered on a sigh of resignation.

Warrick scrubbed his face with his hands. "Son of a—"

"Listen, Rick. I know you need to talk with Mary, but I need a few minutes first."

He faced his friend. "For what?"

"To try to prepare you." Troy dropped his arms. "This has spread all over New York. It's probably followed us to Miami."

Warrick crossed the room again. "Doesn't anyone care about the play-offs? Why is my sex life so much more important?"

"Sometimes the media plays to the lowest common denominator."

Marilyn was right. The media's criticism of his game was one thing. It wasn't as easy to shake off their personal attacks.

Warrick hooked his hands on his hips. "First the photos, now this. What's next?"

"You may not want to ask that." Troy's tone was dry. "The media attention was bad before. It's going to get worse."

A pulse beat viciously in Warrick's temple. "The media printed naked pictures of my wife in a newspaper, posted photos of us making love on a Web site, and gave a crazy woman airtime to accuse me of cheating on my wife. How could it *possibly* get worse?"

"I know you're frustrated."

"That's an understatement." Warrick dropped onto the bed. He propped his elbows on his knees and gripped his head with his hands. "I want them to leave us alone."

"So do I."

He lowered his arms and raised his gaze to Troy's. "What do you suggest I do? Call a press conference?"

Troy smoothed his goatee. "It would be your word against Jordan Hyatt's, which would keep this story alive. We need something more so we can kill it."

"Like what?" Temper propelled Warrick from the bed. He marched back to the window. "Photos of me not having sex with her? How do you prove a negative, Troy?"

"Andy's investigating Jordan Hyatt's background, her personal and professional connections. She's looking for a concrete link we could use to discredit her."

Warrick turned to consider the other man. "What if she doesn't find one?"

A confident smile curved Troy's lips. "She will."

Warrick rubbed the back of his neck. "Why would she help me? Is she doing this for the story?"

"She's doing this for me." Troy's voice cooled.

Warrick was treading sensitive ground because of Troy's romantic relationship with the reporter. "My personal and professional lives are on the line. So are Mary's. I have a right and very good reasons to ask what's motivating the people who offer to help me."

Troy narrowed his gaze. "Andy's proven she's a fair reporter. She cares about the truth."

"You're right. I apologize." Warrick turned back to the window. "I'd almost forgotten decent reporters existed." He heard Troy's approach.

His friend squeezed his shoulder. "They do. Jordan Hyatt has had her fifteen minutes of fame. But we'll discredit her."

Warrick wasn't as confident. There was too much at stake. "What if Andrea doesn't find anything?"

"Andy's persistent. She'll find something. She knows how important this is to the team. And to me."

"Thanks." Warrick took an easier breath.

He remembered well Andrea Benson's persistence. She'd been dogged in convincing Barron "Bling" Douglas, the team's captain and starting point guard, to join a rehabilitation center to help recover from his alcohol abuse. Barron had eventually agreed. And Warrick had replaced him in the starting lineup.

Warrick faced Troy. "I hope it's sooner rather than later."

"So do I." Troy glanced at his thick silver wristwatch. "You need to call Mary and I've got to get Jackie up to speed. You're not alone in this, Rick."

The marketing executive crossed the hotel room and walked out the door. Warrick recalled the scene in the locker room after the previous game, the message his father had left on his answering machine, his wife's request that he retire from the NBA.

He wasn't alone? It sure as hell felt that way.

Janet Crowley's clipped speech came down the telephone line. "Dionne and I have discussed at great length the impact of your joining our Linden Boulevard Women's Health Clinic."

Marilyn was certain they had. In fact, if she was a betting woman, she'd lay odds the partners had discussed her application within the past hour. Right about the time the local television station had aired Jordan Hyatt's press conference. She slid forward on her fat, coffee-colored couch and muted the high-definition television in front of her. She'd heard enough of the broadcaster's analysis of that woman's lies.

What would motivate someone to destroy a good man like Warrick Evans? Jordan Hyatt deserved a special place in hell.

Marilyn's left hand trembled as she held the land line's receiver to her ear. There wasn't any background noise on Janet's end of the call. Did the other woman also have her television on mute? Marilyn didn't doubt it was still on.

She struggled for a confident tone. "Have you made your final decision?"

"Yes." Janet spoke without emotion. "We no longer believe you would be a good fit for the clinic. Your negatives far outweigh the benefits."

She was certain Janet considered her marriage to Warrick a negative. That knowledge burned like acid in her gut. Marilyn closed her eyes. Janet's decision wasn't a surprise. But Marilyn had wanted so badly to be a partner with that clinic. The opportunity to be her own boss and set her own hours was very attractive. Even more enticing had been the clinic's focus on women's health management, which was her passion.

She swallowed to ease the tightness in her throat. "This is because of Jordan Hyatt's press conference, isn't it?"

Janet hesitated. Hadn't the clinic partner anticipated that question? Or had she expected Marilyn to simply thank her and hang up?

Welcome to my world, where nothing is ever as neat and tidy as you think it should be.

"Dionne and I have expressed to you on more than one occasion our concerns regarding your husband's lifestyle." Janet's tone was stiff and defensive.

"Jordan Hyatt is lying." Marilyn bit the words as her anger stirred again.

But why was she lying? What did she want? Money? Fame? Warrick?

"I'm sure every wife wants to believe her husband is a saint and that she's the only woman who could ever hold his interest. But that's not always the case, is it?" Arrogant amusement laced Janet's words.

Marilyn's palm itched to reach into the telephone and slap Janet's face. It was fortunate for the other woman that they weren't having this conversation in person.

She surged from her sofa and strode the length of the room. Marilyn tipped aside the oatmeal-hued venetian blind to peek at the sidewalk. There were even more reporters skulking in front of her home this evening than had been there before Warrick left yesterday. If they were waiting for her to say something to them, they could hold their breath—forever.

Marilyn turned from the window. "How many professional athletes do you know, Janet?"

"I don't mix with that crowd." The other woman sniffed her disdain.

Marilyn tightened her grip on the receiver. "Then on what are you basing your judgment of my husband?"

Janet sighed. "The lifestyle of star athletes is well documented."

"All of them?"

"Enough of them."

Marilyn switched the receiver to her right hand to ease her left fist. The fingers of her left hand tingled as circulation returned. "You and I are very different."

"I suppose we are." Janet sounded bored.

"You're a status conscious, judgmental elitist." She stopped short of adding "bitch." How could she ever have entertained the idea of becoming partners with such a pretentious person?

"Excuse me?" Janet's question was sharp.

"And I'm not." Marilyn ignored her. "Yet we're both O-B-G-Y-Ns."

"I resent that." The clinic partner's tone bristled.

Marilyn narrowed her eyes. "And I pity people who judge all athletes by the negative behaviors of some of the extremely few players the media cover." Marilyn's voice shook as her temper grew. "Until you know even *one* of them personally, don't. Judge. Any."

Janet's intake of breath was long and deep. "I don't see a call for your hostility."

Marilyn's words rolled right over the clinic partner's response. "I didn't meet my husband at a club, Janet. He doesn't frequent casinos or bars or strip joints. Do I seem like the kind of person who would marry someone like that?"

Janet stuttered. "Who knows what a woman would do for a man like that once he got his hands on her?"

Marilyn's words came to a stop. She frowned. "Do you think he's sexually enslaved me?" Intriguing.

"How would I know? However, the photo of the two of you in the paper was fairly provocative." The other woman sounded almost jealous.

Marilyn braced her left fist on her hip, brushing the soft cotton material of her pleated brown shorts. "Rick would rather spend a quiet evening at home with me than a night on the town with the fellas. Do you think you'll ever see that on TV? Neither do I."

She exhaled. Where had this rant come from? It had been building for weeks, possibly months. She felt lighter and freer now that she'd gotten those words off her chest. Her thoughts were clearer. Maybe she should thank Janet.

Maybe not.

Her cell phone rang from across the room. Marilyn hurried to the end table. *Please let it be Warrick.*

Emma's text message read, "I saw the news! Are you all right? Want me to come over?"

Marilyn responded with one word, "Yes!" She dropped her cell phone into the front pocket of her shorts.

Janet cleared her throat. "Be that as it may, Warrick still has an undesirable image. His behavior reflects on you as his wife. Your husband's behavior would also reflect on Dionne and me as your partners. Neither of us believe that image is well suited to the clinic."

Marilyn's attention shifted to the television screen. The station finally had moved on to something other than the Jordan Hyatt fairy tale.

She took the universal remote from the black marble coffee table and turned off the TV. "I know the real man. If you'd rather believe the media than trust my judgment, then you're right to forgo our partnership."

"Or perhaps you're misguided." Janet's tone was cool.

"I'm not." Marilyn's voice was cold. "Besides, this media frenzy will disappear once the season's over."

"I guess we'll see Monday morning." Janet seemed dubious.

Marilyn scowled. The Monarchs' season wouldn't end Monday. The team would win the Eastern Conference title as well as the NBA finals. It was what Warrick wanted, and he wouldn't let anything stand in his way.

She crossed the family room back to the telephone base on the ebony marble corner table. Marilyn squared her shoulders beneath her green T-shirt and the near crushing disappointment of not getting the clinic partnership. "Thank you for calling me with your decision, Janet. I appreciate the courtesy. I hope you and Dionne will be very successful with the clinic."

"Marilyn, when you've had enough of your husband's antics, give us a call." Although Janet's words were calm and confident, they didn't mask her urgency. "Dionne and I are interested in everything else you would bring to the partnership."

Everything else meaning her parents? Marilyn's disgust was self-directed. She'd wanted the clinic partnership. Unfortunately, her desperation had blinded her to how high a price the other women had required. It sickened her how close she'd come to paying it.

"I can't believe I let someone like you try to tell me my husband isn't worth keeping." Could she ever forgive herself? "He's a better person than you could ever dream of being. I wouldn't trade him for your partnership even if your clinic was the only game in town." It took all of her control not to slam the receiver onto the telephone base.

Marilyn left the family room to get a glass of ice water from the kitchen. Her thoughts were scattered. Her muscles were shaking with reaction.

How could she have been so blind—and desperate?—to have ever considered a partnership with Janet Crowley? She may not have been certain where her marriage was heading—the overwhelming media attention was still a concern—but she knew her career path could never lead her into business with the affected parasite.

Her cell phone chimed in her front shorts pocket, startling her from her thoughts. Marilyn retrieved the device. The cellular display identified Warrick as the caller. She selected the answer option with fumbling fingers. "How are you?"

Warrick's mind went blank. He hadn't expected that greeting from Marilyn. But he should have. She'd asked the same question when the *Horn* had published the photo of them in their kitchen. "I've been better."

"So have I." Some of the tension had drained from her voice.

"Mary, I don't know Jordan Hyatt." Warrick enunciated each word. "I've never met her and I'm certainly not having an affair with her. I'd never, ever be unfaithful to you."

"You don't need to convince me of something I already know."

Warrick exhaled the breath he hadn't realized he'd been holding. Thank God she still trusted him. He sank into the cushioned chair beside the writing table. "I wanted you to hear me say the words."

"Why did she call a press conference to tell the greater New York City metropolitan area that she's pregnant with your child?" Marilyn's words tumbled over each other.

"I don't know." He didn't understand why the media was trying so hard to destroy his marriage, either. Were they that desperate for sales? Or had he somehow offended every publisher in the city?

"Are you *sure* that you've never met her?"

"I'm positive." Warrick stared into the middle distance of the view outside his window. Where was Marilyn? The kitchen? The family room? Wherever she was, he wished he could be with her right now.

"Maybe you signed an autograph for her or she attended one of the team's fund-raisers." Her voice was strained and breathless.

Warrick sorted through remembered encounters with Monarchs fans. "Most of the people who approach me are kids. There are a few grown men and women who . . . don't dress like her."

"I can imagine." Marilyn's tone was dry. "What are we going to do?"

Outside his hotel room, Warrick heard other guests walking the halls, talking and laughing. They didn't seem to have a care in the world. He had to believe this media-manufactured drama would end soon.

Warrick rose to pace. "Troy said Andrea Benson is researching Jordan Hyatt's background to find out what or who put her up to this."

"Andrea Benson? Isn't she a reporter?" There was reservation in Marilyn's response.

"We can trust her. She won't write a salacious piece about us."

"The articles she's written about you in the past seemed fair. But I don't want any more stories about us in the newspapers—or on the television or the radio. I've had enough."

So had he. "I can't ignore Jordan Hyatt's lies."

"Then sue her for slander. I'm done with the media. Let's take her to court."

In the background, Warrick identified the sound of ice collecting in a glass. Marilyn was in the kitchen pouring ice water. Not a good sign.

"Think about that, Mary." He dragged a hand over his head. "A lawsuit brought by a married professional athlete against a woman who is not his wife yet claimed to be pregnant with his child would generate a lot of media coverage."

The sound of the faucet running carried to his cell phone. Glass hit the tiled counter with unnecessary roughness.

"You have a point." She didn't seem happy about it. "But if we can't avoid the media, we should at least control the message."

She reminded him of Troy. "What do you mean?"

"If Jordan Hyatt can call a press conference, so can you."

14

Warrick's stomach turned at the thought of discussing his personal life in front of a camera. "A press conference would keep the media coverage focused on her lies. It would be my word against hers. I need to know why she's trying to discredit me."

"And while we're keeping silent, the media and that woman will shred your reputation. Doesn't that bother you?"

"Yes." More than he thought possible. "But there's nothing I can do about that right now. We need to wait until Andrea gets information about Jordan Hyatt's background."

"I wish you'd at least tell the media you're not the father of that woman's baby. Defend yourself."

"It won't do any good." Warrick kneaded the knot at the base of his neck.

"We're not talking about your father, who never listens to anyone but himself. At least try it." Marilyn's frustration was loud and clear.

"The press won't listen. Instead they'll try to goad me into a reaction they can feed to all of their outlets." As frayed as his temper had been lately, it wouldn't take much goading to get him to snap.

"Jordan Hyatt told all of New York that you cheated on me." Marilyn's voice was tight. "Our friends, neighbors, family, your teammates heard her. All that I'm asking is that you set the record straight."

What could he say to convince her that waiting was the more prudent course? "It bothers me that there are people who will believe her lies. But you're the only person I have to defend myself to and you already believe in me."

Marilyn's sigh was soft. "I don't want people to think badly of you. You're a good person, Rick. A great person. You don't deserve this."

Warrick's heart twisted. God, he wished she were near him. Her words weren't enough. He wanted to touch her. Hold her.

He sat on the edge of the bed, propping his elbow on his knee. "What you think is all that matters to me. Our marriage is about you and me. Don't let what other people think about us affect that."

Marilyn hesitated. "What is this really about, Rick?"

"What do you mean?"

"Are you reluctant to talk with the press because of the Monarchs?"

He stiffened. "This has nothing to do with the team."

A beat of silence traveled through the line. "Janet Crowley called."

Warrick dreaded the reason behind Marilyn's abrupt change of topic. "The clinic partner?"

"I'm not getting the partnership." Her disappointment was audible. "Janet and Dionne believe our lifestyle is too disruptive for their practice."

Warrick scrubbed a hand over his face. *Son of a—*

"Mary, I'm so very sorry. I know how much you wanted a partnership with that clinic."

"Your silence may be good for the team, Rick, but it's hurting me. It's hurting us."

Warrick stood, hoping to soothe his agitation. "Mary, our choices are speaking up now and keeping her lies in the news or waiting until we have the proof we need to discredit her."

"But we don't know what we're looking for or how long it will take for us to find this information."

Warrick closed his eyes at the desperation in her voice. "It shouldn't take that long." He hoped.

"And in the meantime, you'll stay quiet to avoid any media coverage that could distract the team and cost you the series."

Guilt pricked him although the charge wasn't completely true. "I have to consider how my actions will affect them."

"What about me, Rick?" Her voice was tired. "I don't want to take a backseat to the Monarchs."

Marilyn ended the call. Warrick held on to his cell phone, prolonging their connection while the silence stretched and bore down around him. He couldn't shake off the weight of her words or quiet the questions chasing each other in his mind.

Should he hold a press conference? Was he asking Marilyn to take a backseat to his team? Who was Jordan Hyatt and why in the hell had she chosen his life to ruin?

"Jordan Hyatt must be mentally unbalanced." Less than half an hour later, Marilyn sat in the kitchen with Emma. She was nursing a second glass of ice water.

"Why do you say that?" Emma had barely touched her first glass.

Marilyn looked up in surprise. "Why else would she claim to be Rick's lover? She must be delusional."

Emma searched Marilyn's eyes. "I know you don't want to hear this, but I'm asking as a friend."

No good ever came from "friendly questions" that began with those words. "What is it?"

Emma took a breath. "Are you sure Rick isn't cheating on you?"

Marilyn squelched the urge to toss Emma out onto the street. Emma was only looking out for her best interests. Wasn't she? "I'm positive. Rick and I spend most of our free time together."

Emma pursed her lips. "I know. Now that you're married, I hardly ever see you."

Marilyn blinked. Was that resentment in her friend's voice? "So when would he have time to have an affair?"

Emma snorted. "Don't be naive, Mary. With the hours you work, Rick's home alone a lot of nights. He also travels a lot during the year and you never go with him."

"I have—had—a job. Besides, I trust him."

"You wouldn't be the first wife of a professional athlete who trusted her husband only to have him make a fool of her." Emma folded her arms on the table and leaned forward. "Would you like me to list the cheaters' names alphabetically or by sport?"

Marilyn didn't recognize the woman seated across the table. "Don't judge my husband by the bad experiences you've had with men."

A spark of anger lit Emma's green eyes. "Sooner or later, they all break your heart."

"Not Rick."

"Yeah, I could tell from that photo in the *Horn*."

Marilyn caught her breath. "That's not funny, Em.

That photograph was mortifying. It also cost me my job and my parents' respect."

Emma cocked her head. "What about the partnership? Have you heard from Janet or Dionne?"

Marilyn eased her throat with a sip of water. "They've declined my application."

Emma sat back in her seat. "Your job, the partnership. This has gone too far. Why are you still with him?"

"If I allow the media to destroy my marriage, I would be letting it go too far." The media, her boss, her mother. Should she now add her friend to the list of outside forces trying to come between her and Warrick?

The disappointment in Emma's eyes reminded Marilyn of her mother. "When we were in college, you said you didn't want to be thought of as the Devrys' daughter."

Marilyn nodded. "That's right. I wanted my own identity."

Emma crossed her arms and legs. "Instead of marrying a doctor as your mother wanted, you moved three thousand miles away and became a doctor."

"That's what I wanted to do." What was Emma's point?

"Then almost as soon as you got your medical license, you married an NBA superstar and became Mrs. Warrick Evans."

"It's Dr. Marilyn Devry-Evans." Marilyn stood and crossed to the sink. She wanted distance between herself and Emma. Was the width of the kitchen enough?

"You gave up your identity."

"No, I didn't."

"He cost you your job."

She spun back to face her friend. "*Arthur* cost me my job."

"Why do you always defend him?"

"Why are you attacking him?" Marilyn planted her hands on her hips. "A true friend would focus instead on helping me prove to the media and the public that Rick is a good man and Jordan Hyatt is a liar."

The telephone rang, shattering the tense silence. Marilyn glanced over her shoulder toward the hallway. "Rick suggested screening the calls to make sure they aren't reporters."

Emma pushed back her chair. "He has you cowering in fear inside your own home? That's ridiculous."

Marilyn's eyes widened as she watched Emma hurry from her kitchen. Her honey blond curls waved behind her.

"Em!" Marilyn arrived in the family room seconds too late.

"The Evans residence." Emma turned away from Marilyn.

Marilyn clamped her hand on Emma's shoulder. "Hang up." She hissed the command.

Emma shrugged out of Marilyn's grip. "Yes, she's right here." She extended the cordless telephone receiver to Marilyn. "It's your mother."

Marilyn snatched the phone from the other woman and covered the mouthpiece. "Are you crazy?"

"He has you afraid to answer your own phone. *That's* crazy." Emma circled Marilyn on her way to the front door. "We'll talk later. I'll let myself out." Emma strutted to the front door.

What had gotten into her?

Marilyn turned her attention to the telephone. She braced herself for the coming storm. "Hello, Mother."

"Your husband's *mistress* held a press conference." Celeste was shouting.

Marilyn may never forgive Emma for answering her

phone. Her friend hadn't done her any favors. "Rick doesn't have a mistress."

"And she's *pregnant*." Celeste spat the words.

Marilyn pinched the bridge of her nose. "Don't believe everything you hear, Mother. Is that the only reason you called?"

"What's happening to you, Marilyn?" Celeste sounded genuinely concerned.

Marilyn's shoulders sagged. She was tired and coming to the end of her patience. "Since Jordan Hyatt called her bogus press conference, my phone's been ringing off the hook, Mother. Everyone's eager to vilify Rick and question my judgment. But instead of tearing us apart, these attacks have made me even more determined to save my marriage."

"What is there to save?" Celeste's voice hardened. "Your marriage is over. You're the only one who doesn't know it."

"Not the only one. Rick doesn't know it, either."

"That man is cheating on you." The words and tone were mean.

She could add her mother to the list of people calling her naive. But none of them knew Warrick, so who were they to judge? "No, he's not."

"Is that what he told you?" Disdain lay like a carpet over Celeste's words.

"He didn't have to tell me. I know my husband."

"The wife is always the last to find out."

"He's not a cheater."

"All men are cheaters." Celeste's words flew like knives from her lips. "Your father's a cheater."

Marilyn's body shivered with shock. She couldn't have heard her mother correctly. "What?"

"Your father's a cheater." Celeste repeated the accusation with a slow and careful delivery.

"You're. Lying."

"Why would I lie?" There was a shrug in the words. "For sympathy? The truth certainly doesn't paint me in a good light. In fact, it adds credence to your father's allegations."

Marilyn's ears were ringing. Her lips were numb. She couldn't understand what her mother was saying. "What are you talking about?"

Celeste's chuckle was bitter. "Your father claims I'm more interested in social status than sex."

Marilyn shook her head, hoping to clear her mind of the image her mother's words painted.

"Is that why he had an affair?" She still didn't believe it. Her father cheated on her mother? Impossible. Her father was a hardworking, devoted family man. He wouldn't cheat. "Why did you stay with him?"

Celeste sniffed. "A divorce would have been too embarrassing. And he promised never to stray again."

Marilyn hesitated. "Why did he stay with you?"

Celeste's laughter was amused this time. "Perhaps he's more interested in social status than sex, too."

"When did this happen?"

"Oh, it's been a couple of years now." Her mother tried to sound indifferent, but there was hurt in Celeste's voice.

Her father had been unfaithful. The affair had happened years ago. She'd had no idea. The information was too difficult to process. It was a side of her parents' relationship she hadn't needed to know.

Marilyn rubbed her eyes. "Why are you telling me this, Mother?"

"Why does a mother confide anything to her daughter?

Because she doesn't want her child to make the same mistakes she's made."

Marilyn hugged herself with her free arm. "So you think I should leave Rick."

Celeste snorted. "I didn't think you should marry him in the first place."

Marilyn remembered well her mother's objection to her marriage. Neither of her parents had given their blessing.

She stared across the room at the framed photograph of herself and Warrick on their Hawaiian honeymoon. He looked happier and much more relaxed than she'd seen him all year. If only they could return to that exact moment in time when they were just Warrick and Marilyn, not the Monarchs' superstar shooting guard and his wife. His celebrity was taking a toll on him—on them. They hadn't signed up for this.

No, you signed up to be my *wife, in good times and in bad. I guess this is the bad part.* Warrick's words were like a talisman for her to hold on to.

"I'm going to save my marriage, Mother."

"Then you're a fool." Celeste's accusation stung.

Marilyn's lips twisted. "Like mother, like daughter."

"How dare you say that to me?" Her mother's reaction lacked heat. Marilyn heard more uncertainty in those seven words than her mother had revealed to her in Marilyn's entire thirty-three years.

"I dare because it's true. You said Father admitted to having an affair, but you remained married. I know Rick hasn't cheated on me. Yet you've demanded that I end my marriage and come home. Before you issue fiats on what everyone else should do, make sure your own decisions are unimpeachable." Marilyn disconnected the call with much more control than she felt.

Warrick was right. Their marriage was about them.

No one else's opinion of their relationship mattered. Still, Marilyn looked forward to proving everyone—Janet, Emma, Arthur, and her mother—wrong.

The Monarchs took possession of the ball during Sunday night's game in Miami. The shot clock started its countdown.

"What are you gonna do about your kid?" Marlon Burress's taunt needled Warrick as he was certain the Waves' shooting guard had intended.

The Monarchs led game five of the Eastern Conference Championship by an amazing—for them—nine points with less than four minutes left. The series was tied at two. Warrick didn't want the Waves to claim a third win. Apparently, neither did his teammates. But the harder the Monarchs fought to maintain their lead, the more incendiary Burress's comments became. The other player was getting to Warrick. He was already in foul trouble.

The shot clock ticked down to twenty seconds. Warrick was out of sync with the rest of his team. He jogged back to the Waves basket. But he was a step behind Serge and the intended play. A step too far to claim the pass the forward sent him. Vincent hustled back to save the play and send the ball back to Serge.

"Stay sharp, man." The center's voice balanced the knife's edge between anger and frustration.

The shot clock read eighteen seconds.

Serge was trapped behind the perimeter. His defender, Jarrod Cheeks, frustrated his efforts to move in to the basket. Serge dribbled twice before passing the ball to Anthony on the line.

Warrick wove his way into the paint, trying to dislodge Burress from his shadow. The shot clock drained to fifteen seconds. He struggled to hold off Burress's blocks almost as hard as he fought not to react to his opponent's words.

Burress continued to dog Warrick's steps. "You gonna keep the baby?"

"It's not mine to keep." Warrick could have kicked himself for responding.

Anthony danced around, taking three more seconds from the clock. But he couldn't shake the Waves' Phillip Hawk. Warrick raised his hand to indicate he was open. Ignoring Warrick in the paint, Anthony pitched the ball to Jamal at the right perimeter.

"That's no way to talk about your child." Burress's smile was amused and a little mean. He'd gotten a rise out of Warrick and wouldn't let up until he got another.

Ten seconds remained on the shot clock. Jamal dribbled once, twice before taking the shot. Warrick followed its trajectory up and over his head. It stopped just shy of the basket's rim before beginning its descent. Eight seconds were on the shot clock.

Warrick stepped forward and leaped to meet the ball. He tipped it into the basket, then dropped back to his feet. The ball went through the net, extending the Monarchs' lead to eleven. Warrick didn't pause to react. He turned and ran back up court. Seamlessly, he shifted from offense to defense. Three minutes and twenty-three seconds remained in the game.

Burress's tireless voice followed him. "I don't know how you could creep out on a woman who looks like your wife. I've seen her picture." The Waves' star smacked his lips.

Warrick saw red. He stopped on a dime at midcourt. He spun and twisted the front of Burress's white jersey in his fist, then shoved the other man backward. Burress's trademark smile of smug superiority barely registered in Warrick's anger-soaked mind. The referee's whistle sounded far away, coming closer as the ringing in Warrick's ears quieted.

Otto Nunez, one of the officiating crew members, pried Warrick's fingers from Burress's white home jersey. "That's your sixth personal foul, Evans. You're out of the game."

Burress smoothed his jersey. He inclined his head before trotting to the foul line. Roger Harris, the Monarchs shooting guard, came off the bench and jogged across Warrick's line of sight.

What had just happened?

He swung his attention to the sideline and was slammed by DeMarcus's disgusted glare. Warrick crossed to the bench. Burress made both of his free throws, dropping the Monarchs' lead back to nine.

Being benched during any game was frustrating. Having to sit out the final minutes of a critical championship game was a special kind of pain. Warrick had never felt so helpless, not even when DeMarcus had benched him at the beginning of the season.

For the next three minutes, Warrick's stomach muscles twisted as the Waves attacked the Monarchs' lead. The Waves fed off his team's growing fatigue and uncoordinated defense. Walter Millbank made Jamal look dazed and confused. Phillip Hawk threw Anthony off his game. Jarrod Cheeks rendered Serge ineffective, and Burress took advantage of Roger coming off the bench cold.

As the Monarchs' lead drained, Warrick's guilt grew. His ineffective play against Burress was doing the team more harm than good. He'd let his team down. He'd let himself down. He'd let Burress get the better of him.

Vincent was left to mop up mistakes and mend broken plays. Through the center's efforts, DeMarcus's play calling, and judicious use of the Monarchs' remaining time-outs, the team came through game five with a battered and stingy two-point lead. And Warrick had come to a hard-earned realization.

Maybe Marilyn was right. If he couldn't be a play-maker for the team, maybe it was time to think about retiring.

15

"That photo of you and Rick together on the kitchen table is *hot*." Susan Williams bit her bottom lip and shook her right hand as though she'd burned her fingertips.

Marilyn blinked at Monarchs' point guard Darius Williams's wife, who sat across from her at the restaurant table. "Susan, I'm not thrilled to have my personal life photographed and blown up all over the gossip pages."

"Don't forget that shit was uploaded to the Internet, too." Faye Ryland, point guard Jarrett Hickman's longtime girlfriend, added helpfully.

Marilyn glared at her chicken parmesan. "No, Faye, I can't forget."

What did those other photographs look like? Did she even want to know? She took a bite of her lunch. It tasted like cardboard.

The Monarchs Wives Club was meeting at its usual Italian restaurant on Memorial Day, the day after the Monarchs' game five nail-biter. Why weren't they talking about the win? Maybe then, she could enjoy her meal.

"Well, at least you looked good." Peggy Coleman, who was pregnant with shooting guard Roger Harris's baby, rubbed her belly. Her peaches and cream complexion glowed as she sent Marilyn a Mona Lisa smile.

"Yeah." Susan waved her fork with gusto. "Who would have thought you had such a great figure under those ugly, androgynous clothes? You need to show off those curves, girl."

Marilyn frowned down at her lavender two-piece pants suit. What was wrong with her outfit? Although she was still underdressed compared to the other women's latest fashions and expensive accessories. Had they ever worn the same outfit twice?

Peggy's smile widened. "Mary's clothes aren't bad. Besides, you've just come from work, haven't you?"

Marilyn took a bracing breath, drawing in the scents of marinara sauce, oregano, and cheese. "I'm not with the hospital anymore."

Her throat almost closed over the admission of failure. Marilyn sipped her ice water with lemon. The glass was cool and wet against her palm.

Faye clutched Marilyn's wrist. "You're not? That's great. Now you have more free time to help with the charity auction. We need to sell a shitload of tickets. We have to impress Jackie Jones."

Marilyn pushed her chicken parmesan around the plate. "Of course, I'm glad to help as much as I can. But I also need to find a new job."

Susan made a comic face. "What? Why?" She cast her gaze around the table. "Your husband is the second highest paid player on the Monarchs' roster. Why do you need a job at all?"

Marilyn winced. Susan must have found the Internet site listing the NBA players' salaries. Wonderful.

"I may not *need* a job, but I enjoy my career." Marilyn sliced her chicken parmesan. Fragrant steam rose from the well-seasoned dish.

Susan chuckled as she twirled her fork around the center of her linguine and clam sauce. "As a doctor, you probably know all kinds of ways to get rid of Rick's mistress without leaving a trace."

Marilyn stilled. She lifted her eyes and pinned Susan with a steady gaze. Her voice was firm and even. "Rick does not have a mistress."

Susan's brown eyes narrowed. "That woman . . ." She looked to the other two women at the table for help. "What's her name again?"

"Jordan Hyatt." Faye was helpful yet again.

Marilyn's lips twisted with wry amusement. Susan was more likely to forget her own name than the identity of key people involved in a social scandal.

Peggy shifted in her seat and shook back her salon-styled blond tresses. "She called a press conference to tell everyone she's carrying Rick's baby. Why would she do that if it isn't true?"

Marilyn's muscles tightened. "I don't know why she lied. But I do know she's not pregnant with my husband's baby."

Peggy's smile spread. "I think it's beautiful that your faith in Rick is so steadfast."

Marilyn regarded the other woman with bafflement. "I don't have any reason not to trust him."

Her mother must have said the same thing about her father once. But then he'd cheated on Celeste. Marilyn still couldn't fathom that. She'd always considered Terrell Devry to be a trustworthy, honorable person.

Susan chewed, then swallowed a forkful of linguine. "Are you going to confront Jordan Hyatt?" Her tone was almost gleeful.

"No." Marilyn tried another bite of her chicken parmesan. It still tasted like expensive cardboard.

Faye's jaw dropped. "Girl, if you think she's punking your man, you *have* to confront her. Shit, you *have* to."

Was she really having this conversation? Marilyn blinked at the other three women at the table. They'd regressed back to elementary school and her classmates were egging her on to fight the new girl.

What little appetite Marilyn had completely disappeared. "I'm not going to speak with her. That would legitimize her claim of being part of my husband's life. She's not."

Beside her, Faye rolled her brown eyes. "This isn't about making her legitimate. It's about representing *your* role in Rick's life."

Marilyn scowled. "My role isn't in question."

A slight smile curved Faye's lips. Her lipstick was a dark plum, which complimented the brighter plum highlights in her hair. Very edgy. "For a doctor, you're not real bright. You're a professional athlete's wife. Groupies are always challenging our role."

Marilyn shook her head. "I don't want my entire identity to be the wife of a basketball player."

Faye turned in her seat to face Marilyn. "That's stupid. You're Rick Evans's wife and he's a ballplayer."

Marilyn spread her hands. "But that's not *who* I am."

Susan waved her fork. "You think you're different from us because your husband used to be the Monarchs' captain and you're a doctor."

Marilyn's temper stirred. "I've never said that."

"You've thought it." Faye shrugged a shoulder.

Marilyn gaped at the other woman. "No, I haven't."

Peggy sent her a confused look. "Do you think the only reason for the Monarchs Wives Club is to organize social events?"

"That's all we talk about." Marilyn searched their

features. She saw patience and curiosity. But she didn't see judgment or disdain. It was refreshing.

"Shit, that's all we talk about with *you*." Faye moved her neck. "We talk about other things when we travel with the team or call each other on the phone."

Marilyn frowned. "Like what?"

Peggy shifted in her seat in the pregnant woman's constant quest for a more comfortable position. "Like what we're going through as the girlfriend or wife of a professional ballplayer."

Faye sighed. "Yeah. It's not all money, fame, and game. There's a lot of shit we have to deal with, too."

Susan gestured with her fork. "Family members telling us how to live our lives or asking for money. Jealous friends. The media. Basketball groupies trying to steal our men."

"Ha! Look at her face." Faye pointed a finger at Marilyn and laughed. "You know the score."

Marilyn was dazed. "Only too well."

Faye snorted. "No one understands like we do 'cause we're going through the same shit."

"That's the real purpose of the Monarchs Wives Club. That's the reason it started." Peggy flashed a grin. "Even though some of us aren't wives *yet,* we're all here to help each other cope with issues that our family and friends can't understand because they've never experienced them."

Susan put down her fork. "People think money can buy happiness. It can't."

"Hell, no, it can't." Faye leaned into the table. "The basketball season is long and there are far too many lonely nights."

Marilyn smiled as her companions burst into laughter. "You ladies really do understand."

Peggy leaned back in her chair. "Yes, we do."

Marilyn sobered, thinking of how embattled she'd felt for so many weeks. Between the media, her boss, her mother, and the woman she'd considered a friend, she could have used the sage advice of these veterans of the celebrity athlete wars.

She looked at the trio through fresh eyes. She'd thought she'd known who her friends were, but it had been these ladies all along. "I wish I'd realized sooner that I could have confided in you."

Susan pushed her plate aside and folded her forearms on the table. "You know now. Tell us what's on your mind."

Marilyn stared at her plate of half-eaten chicken parmesan. "My best friend and I have known each other since college. But lately, I've begun to wonder if she has my interests at heart."

Faye leaned back and crossed her arms. "One of *those*."

Susan shook her head. "We've all been there."

Peggy rubbed her belly. "Yes, we have. We can help you with this."

DeMarcus planted himself in front of the Monarchs locker room door. His arms and legs were akimbo. A familiar scowl twisted his features.

"'Home court advantage' literally means you have the advantage over your opponent because you're playing on your home court." His speech was slow and deliberate as though he was explaining a complex concept to very young children. "Who wants to tell me what happened tonight." He glared around the room. "Anyone?"

"We lost. *Mon Dieu*." Serge's French-accented words were burdened by disgust.

Warrick smiled at Serge's appeal to God. He shrugged

into his cream shirt and hooked the buttons. The Almighty was more inclined to help those who helped themselves. Unfortunately, the Monarchs were hell-bent on hurting themselves.

"Why did we lose?" DeMarcus's voice was insistent.

Warrick sat on the stool in front his locker and put on his shoes. He recognized the coach's tone. No one was getting out of here until they gave DeMarcus the impossible—the reason the Monarchs had lost game six of the Eastern Conference Championship.

"We lost because Rick believes his own hype." Jamal shouted the accusation at Warrick. "They talk about how you're the leader of the team. You're no leader."

"They make Rick out to be a superstar." Anthony cast out blame. "Like he's the second coming on the court."

Warrick's back stiffened as his body absorbed the verbal blows. He breathed in deeply. The smell of sweat had been replaced with soap and cologne. But it would take more than water and cleansers to wash away the stench of defeat.

Jamal snorted. "Yeah. Right. You're a superstar. As soon as you stepped onto the court, I knew we'd lose."

Warrick stood and faced the rookie guard. "Is that why you gave Kirk West of the *Horn* that interview? Because you knew we'd lose if I played tonight?"

Jamal hesitated. "I thought you didn't read about sports during the season."

Warrick had started following the sports coverage in self-defense against the media's attacks. "If you didn't expect me to read the article, why did you give the interview?"

Jamal's chin shot upward. He planted his feet. It was his standard defensive pose when in a confrontation. Too bad he didn't use that stance on the court. "To set the record straight. You ain't no superstar. You're an old, washed-up has-been. We won game five with you on the bench. You started the game tonight, and we lost."

Warrick studied the teammates he no longer knew. Only weeks ago, they'd come together to support Troy when the media executive had temporarily lost his job with the franchise, and again to try to keep Barron Douglas out of trouble as he fought personal demons. Now that team unity had dissipated like smoke, and a wall of jealousy and resentment had built up between him and the other players.

If he were honest with himself, he'd admit this post-season wasn't the joyride he'd fantasized. Winning wasn't even fun anymore and there were too many fingers pointed his way when they lost.

Was it worth it?

"That's not what I saw." DeMarcus turned his dark, displeased stare on Jamal. "We lost because every one of you played like children instead of professionals. I didn't see a team on the court. I saw five individuals."

"That psychology shit is crap." Jamal turned on Warrick. "All you need to do is stop buying into your own media hype. You're not the East Coast Kobe Bryant. You're Rick Evans. And before Barron became a drunk, you were riding the bench with them." He jerked his thumb toward Darius.

Anthony crossed his arms. "You've lost your way, Rick. You've put yourself above the game. Blessed are the meek for they shall inherit the earth."

Warrick considered the other players. Their body language wasn't lost on him. He felt as shut out from the group in the locker room as he'd felt on the court earlier tonight. He'd been on the team before any of them. Now he was on the outside looking in. The Empire Arena used to be his second home. He'd once been surrounded by teammates as close as a second family. Now, he stood alone.

Jamal groaned. "We're tied at three games apiece. Again. Why do we always have to go to seven games? Why can't we win a series in four or even six games, and on our home court?"

Anthony sighed. "We may not even win the conference series."

Jamal threw Warrick a dismissive glance. "He's messing up our chemistry. He should be benched. We proved in game five that we could win without him."

His father's criticisms were coming out of Jamal's mouth.

You don't have what it takes.

You're not good enough.

Marlon Burress is making a fool of you.

But the rookie wasn't his father.

Warrick slammed shut his locker door. The sharp snap of metal striking metal sounded like a bullet firing in the tense room. The abrupt and absolute silence made Warrick more aware of the anger pounding in his chest.

He confronted the brash young player from across the locker room. He didn't trust himself to get too close. "Jamal, if you defend your assignment as well as you blame me for our every loss, Walter Millbanks wouldn't have scored twenty-two points on you tonight, including his personal best four three-pointers."

Jamal's cheeks flushed. His eyes spun around the room. "Hey, man, how was I—"

"Did anyone mail you a copy of the playbook, Jamal?" Warrick spoke over him. "Have you taken it out of the packaging? I bet the binder's still pristine. If the issue is that you don't understand the plays, maybe you should have stayed in school longer instead of coming out of college your freshman year."

"Look, man—"

Warrick maneuvered past him and continued talking. "Speaking of reading comprehension, Saint Anthony reads the Bible. A lot."

Anthony's eyes narrowed at the hated nickname. "I do."

"And he never misses an opportunity to remind us of his knowledge of the Word. I've learned a lot from you, Saint Anthony."

"I'm glad." The tension in his tone belied his statement.

Anthony's attitude disappointed Warrick the most. He could have sworn envy was one of the seven deadly sins. Why was the Bible-quoting starting forward giving him so much grief?

"I've learned a person could quote chapter and verse from the Good Book without having a clue of the meaning behind the words."

"I do know—"

"My favorite quote is from Matthew chapter seven, verse one: 'Judge not that ye be not judged.'"

He turned from the forward to Serge. "Every season, you ask to be traded to a winning team. You're on a winning team now, man. Make the most of it."

Warrick's gaze passed over Vincent, Darius, Roger, Jarrett, and the rest of the Monarchs' players. "I'm not going to defend myself, and I wouldn't ask you to. We're teammates. There's only one question we have to ask and answer. Do we have each other's backs?"

Warrick strode back to his locker, collected his gym bag, then crossed to the door. DeMarcus nodded before holding it open for him.

What did DeMarcus think of the things he'd said to his teammates?

Did it matter?

"See you at practice in the morning, Coach." Warrick left the locker room.

He felt freer, healthier, as though a weight had been lifted from his shoulders. Tonight, he was glad he'd spoken his mind to his teammates. Marilyn would say it was long overdue. And she would be right.

But what would be the fallout of his speech and how would it impact the final game of the Eastern Conference Championship on Saturday?

16

Thankfully, the diner near the Empire Arena was almost empty. Marilyn and her companions had missed the Thursday morning breakfast crowd and beat the lunch rush. Still, she kept her voice low as she questioned the two women on the other side of the table. "Why did the other Monarchs freeze Rick out of the game?"

Jaclyn Jones glanced at Andrea Benson. Before either woman could respond, Marilyn spoke again. "Tell me the truth. I attended the game with the other Monarchs wives. I saw what was happening."

"I know. I saw you." Jaclyn was stunning in a deep orange dress that hugged her perfect figure. Her dark brown curls cascaded wildly past her shoulders.

"So did I." Andrea stirred creamer into her coffee. In brown slacks, matching jacket, and tan shell, she made a much quieter appearance than Jaclyn. Still, she exuded a sexy confidence that commanded as much attention as the Monarchs' owner.

"I'm sure every sports reporter in the arena saw me." Marilyn couldn't mask her contempt for the media. "They seemed almost as interested in me as they were in the game. I felt like a specimen on a Petri dish. That's one of the reasons I'm not reading the paper or listening to the news this morning. I'm tired of their criticisms and innuendos."

Why hadn't she received a Google Alert update from her mother? A voice mail message probably was waiting for her at home.

Marilyn returned to the reason she'd asked the two women to join her that morning. "Why were the other players keeping Rick out of the game?"

Andrea laid her teaspoon beside her mug. "Most of the press is giving Rick all the credit for the team's success. His teammates resent that. They're taking their jealousy out on him."

Jaclyn sipped her mug of coffee. "The media's placing all the blame for the team's failures on Rick's shoulders as well."

Marilyn bristled. "Aren't these grown men? Why are they acting like spoiled children? Rick wouldn't talk about it, but I know his teammates' behavior bothered him."

The cozy diner was fragrant with the scent of freshly baked pastries. Marilyn's gaze settled on the display of cookies, brownies, bagels, and muffins. But in her mind's eye, she saw the expression on Warrick's face during the game and drive home last night. He'd looked cold, distant—and hurt. She'd felt his pain like a knife in her chest. Marilyn had wanted to rush the court and shake his teammates until their eyes rolled back.

Jaclyn's voice pulled Marilyn from her thoughts. "Marc told me Rick finally gave the other players a piece of his mind after the game."

Marilyn blinked. "Rick didn't say anything about that."

Their table grew silent as a server arrived to pour more coffee. The rich hazelnut scent wafted up to

Marilyn as the dark brew spilled into her cup. Finished with their table, the young man moved down the aisle.

Andrea lowered her coffee mug. "Good for Rick. What did they say?"

Jaclyn shook her head. "Nothing, but Marc thinks Rick's words made an impression on them. Today's practice should be interesting."

"I hope so." Marilyn cradled her coffee mug. The ceramic surface was warm against her palms. "They should know Rick and I didn't ask the media to spy on us and gossip about our lives."

"You're right." Jaclyn reached across the table to squeeze Marilyn's forearm. Her smile didn't conceal the concern in her eyes. "How are you holding up?"

Marilyn sat back in the chair and crossed her legs, trying to appear as confident and in control as the women seated in front of her. "I'll be better once Rick and I can respond to Jordan Hyatt's lies. I've done some Internet searches. So far, I haven't learned anything helpful, though. Have you?"

Andrea gave a wry smile. "Our target is on LinkedIn, Twitter, and Facebook. And she's very chatty. I've learned quite a bit about her."

Jaclyn shifted in her seat to face the reporter. "Like what?"

Andrea pulled her notebook from her large, brown bag. She turned several sheets before stopping on a page. "She's thirty-four years old, the youngest of three children, all daughters. Grew up in Rutherford, New Jersey. Graduated with a degree in business from Rutgers University."

Marilyn gasped. "That's Rick's alma mater."

Andrea's sherry gaze found Marilyn over the top of her notebook. "I know." The reporter returned her attention to her notebook. "She lives alone and hasn't had a serious relationship in—and I quote—'more years than I want to count.'"

Jaclyn pounced on the quote. "If she hasn't had a serious relationship in years, is she claiming the father of her unborn child was a one-night stand?"

Marilyn wanted to pace the diner. She settled for uncrossing her legs. "But according to her, she and Rick have been together for months, so which one is it? Has she been in a serious relationship with my husband or has she been alone?"

Andrea raised her mug. "She does seem to be contradicting herself."

"Now even the fans have turned against him." Marilyn hugged her arms around herself. "Why would that woman claim to be pregnant with my husband's baby? What does she want?"

"So you *don't* believe her." Jaclyn sounded relieved.

Marilyn shot her attention to the Monarchs' franchise owner. "Of course not. I know my husband." Even as she said it, traitorous thoughts invaded her mind. *You thought you knew your father, too, but he's cheated. Is there any man you can trust?*

She shook her head to silence the poisonous voice.

Andrea shifted her gaze from Jaclyn to Marilyn. "Has Jordan Hyatt or her lawyer contacted Rick?"

Marilyn frowned. "No. Would that prove she's lying?"

Andrea shook her head. "As you asked earlier, the question isn't whether Jordan Hyatt is lying. The question is what does she want? Money? Notoriety? And how long is she willing to keep up her charade?"

Marilyn worried her lower lip. How much more of this could she and Warrick take? "When Rick and I were first dating there would be occasional interviews at the arena. Now almost every afternoon and some mornings, the cameras gather outside our home. Neither of us had imagined that, barely two years later, we'd experience this level of media pressure."

"I know it's not fair." There was empathy in Jaclyn's cinnamon eyes. "Our players' fame helps with ticket sales. But it's a lot to ask of their families."

Andrea folded her forearms on the table. "The media's in a constant race to break the biggest news story first. A star player's infidelity is a big story. But the press was wrong to run with only Jordan Hyatt's claim. We don't even know who she is."

Jaclyn sat forward. "Rick loves you, Mary. A lot."

"I know. And I love him. It's the situation that's making me unhappy." Marilyn sighed. "This isn't what we envisioned for our marriage. At least it's not what I thought it would be like. Perhaps I was naive."

Andrea spread her arms. "Does anyone know what to expect when they marry a celebrity?"

Marilyn stared blindly at her coffee. "We'd only been dating for three months when he began hinting at marriage. But I wasn't sure. I knew I loved him, but I wanted a little more time. Marriage is a big commitment."

Jaclyn looked at the four-carat monarch cut diamond engagement ring on her finger. "Yes, it is."

Marilyn admired the ring, too. "I'm certain you and Marc will be very happy together. You have a lot in common and you know what to expect from each others' careers."

Jaclyn gave her a wry smile. "It's still a life-changing decision."

Marilyn nodded. "Before we were married, Rick convinced me to move in with him. But it's not that big of a step from living together to getting married."

Andrea glanced at Jaclyn before returning her attention to Marilyn. "Troy's been talking about moving in together."

A smile tugged on Marilyn's lips. "Are you ready to be Mrs. Troy Marshall?"

Andrea's eyes widened with concern. "I'm still trying to rebuild my career."

Marilyn chuckled. "The day we returned from our honeymoon, Rick wanted to talk about starting a family."

Jaclyn frowned at her left hand. "Marc started talking about kids right after I said yes to his proposal."

Marilyn shrugged. "I guess I believed the fairy tales growing up. You fall in love with your Prince Charming, get married, and live happily ever after. The reality is the wedding isn't the end of the story. It's the beginning of another."

Andrea sighed. "No one ever told us how the second story ends."

"No, they didn't." Marilyn had met Andrea during a recent event the Monarchs hosted to celebrate making it to the Eastern Conference Championship. She'd liked the reporter immediately. "Whoever said, 'Love conquers all' wasn't married to a celebrity."

Jaclyn's brow knitted with concern. "You don't think it's true?"

Marilyn's gaze dropped to her engagement and wedding rings. "I don't know if love's enough."

Warrick's teammates were pretending the postgame confrontation in the Monarchs' locker room Wednesday night had never happened. The players were already at the facility where practice would begin in less than an hour. Several of them were stretching with yoga bands on the court. Others were jumping rope, each turn smacking against the high-gloss hardwood floor. The rest were tossing shots at the baskets suspended from the ceiling's perimeter.

Warrick ignored his teammates and focused on the basket in front of him. He bounced the ball three times for luck, sighted the backboard for a clear shot, and bent his knees. Nothing but net.

"You haven't missed a shot yet." Serge's words coming from behind him proved at least one of his teammates couldn't entirely ignore him.

Warrick crossed to retrieve the ball, catching it just as it tried to roll away. When he turned to face the Frenchman, he found all of the Monarchs had gathered around the perimeter.

"We need dependable free throws." Warrick returned to the charity line. His teammates' expressions varied from Jamal's obstinacy to Vincent's customary implacability.

"You play well in practice." Jamal left unspoken his well-known contention that Warrick struggled in game situations.

Warrick tucked the ball on his hip and met each of the other players' eyes. "Is there a point to this?"

The other men hesitated, looking at one another for guidance. Finally, Vincent spoke up. "Yeah. There's a point. You were right to call us out. This series hasn't been easy on you. The media has been invading your privacy—"

"Yeah, they stuck a camera in your window. Damn!" Jamal laughed even as he shook his head. The other players glared at him. "Sorry."

Jamal wouldn't be Jamal if he didn't say something inappropriate and asinine. The question was, were his comments intentionally provoking? Warrick turned away from him as Serge spoke.

"We shouldn't have added to your strain with our childish resentment." Serge hooked his basketball in the crook of his right arm.

Jarrett Hickman shook his head. "Yeah, I wouldn't change places with you on a bet."

Roger Harris grunted. "Neither would I."

Vincent let his jump rope pool onto the court beside him. "We talked after you left the locker room Wednesday night. You were right and we're sorry."

A chorus of mumbled agreements accompanied nodding heads.

Serge's shrug was a gesture only he could make look intelligent. "It is as you said. I've been wasting this opportunity. I finally have my wish of being on a competitive team but I haven't been playing my best. That is going to change."

Incredible. For once, he'd defended himself and it had made a difference. The burden—or at least a large part of it—that Serge had referred to had been lifted from his shoulders.

Anthony cleared his throat. "I haven't been living the Word as I should have. Thank you for helping me to see that."

Vincent grinned. "Well, hell, Saint Anthony. I'd be glad to point out your hypocrisy every time you show it, if that would help you."

Anthony glared at the center. "I'm not a hypocrite."

Vincent frowned in mock confusion. "Then what do you call it?"

Some things would never change.

Warrick jumped in just as Anthony opened his mouth to respond. "This conversation isn't helping." He addressed Anthony. "Tony, we're all human. Let's put the rest behind us. We've got a championship to win."

"Hold on." Jamal looked around. "I've got something to say. Rick called me out, too."

Warrick nodded, bracing himself for the rookie's response. "Go ahead."

Jamal hesitated. His gaze was hurt and uncertain. "You said I couldn't read."

"I never said you couldn't read." Warrick stopped him before Jamal could take a breath. "I asked if you had trouble learning the plays."

Jamal ducked his head. "I do."

Warrick sighed. "You said you couldn't remember them. Why didn't you ask for help?"

Jamal looked up. "Will you help me?"

"Of course." Vincent stepped forward and wrapped his arm around the younger man's shoulders. "We've got your back."

Vincent released Jamal. He turned to Warrick as their teammates returned to their prepractice warm-ups. "Why didn't you call me out the other night?"

Warrick shrugged. "Why haven't you attacked me this postseason?"

Vincent returned his shrug. He scooped up the discarded rope and tossed Warrick a grin before crossing the court.

Warrick shook his head at Vincent's lack of response. His teammates were back and as close as they'd ever been. It was a relief. But was it enough to carry them through the critical game seven of the Eastern Conference Championship?

Almost three hours later, Warrick walked out of the training room. DeMarcus and Troy waited for him near the practice court entrance.

Warrick stopped a pace away from them. "What's up?"

"We need to talk." DeMarcus's voice was somber.

What is it now?

Troy gestured toward the bleachers. "Let's sit for a minute."

The court smelled of wood polish and sweat. The dozen practice nets that circled the court had been lifted and the basketballs piled into the black wire carts near the door.

Warrick changed direction, joining the other two men near the stands. "What's wrong?" His voice was sharp with worry.

Practice had ended almost an hour ago, but he'd stayed to have a trainer work out the tightness in his legs and lower back. Now the tension was returning.

Troy scowled at DeMarcus before meeting Warrick's eyes. "Nothing's wrong. We didn't mean to give you that impression."

"Then why do we need to talk?" He dropped his silver and black Monarchs gym bag to the floor beside his feet, but he didn't sit. He was anxious to get home and spend as much time with Marilyn as possible before leaving for Miami.

With the series tied at three apiece, the Monarchs had one of two choices—win and advance to the NBA finals or lose and spend the rest of the summer wondering what they could have done differently.

Or, in Warrick's case, spend the summer repairing his strained marriage.

Troy smoothed his silver and blue patterned silk tie over his ice blue shirt. "Everything is fine. But Marc and I wanted to talk with you about Andy and Jackie."

He was even more confused. "You want advice on your love life?"

"No." DeMarcus stood beside him with arms akimbo and legs braced on the gleaming hardwood court. He still wore his black Monarchs T-shirt and silver shorts.

"We want you to ask your wife to stop meddling in our relationships."

Warrick gaped at his coach. "What?"

Troy settled onto a bleacher. "Smooth, Guinn. Really smooth."

DeMarcus shrugged. "You're the media guy. Spin it."

Troy frowned at the coach, then looked at Warrick. "Andy and Jackie spoke with Mary this morning."

"Why?" Warrick sat beside Troy. This was going to take a while if he had to pry every word from his friends.

DeMarcus was almost eerily still as he loomed over Warrick. "Jack wanted to check on Mary. She knows the press coverage has been hard on her."

Warrick's brows knitted. He still didn't see a connection. "I appreciate that. But what does it have to do with your relationships?"

Troy smoothed his goatee. "Apparently, Mary said some things that scared our ladies."

The brakes squealed on Warrick's tumbling thoughts. "Like what?"

DeMarcus pushed his hands into the front pockets of his silver shorts. "Jack and I want to start a family. I want to get an earlier start than she does, but I was bringing her around to my way of thinking. One morning with Mary and I'm back to square one with Jack."

Troy added his piece. "I've been trying to get Andy to move in with me. She thinks I'm moving too fast. She said she needs her space." He grunted. "Andy lives in a shoe box apartment with two other women and a little girl. She'd have more space if she lived with me."

Warrick burst out laughing. He couldn't help it. "None of that is Mary's fault. Jackie will make a great mother—when she's ready."

DeMarcus sighed. "Neither of us is getting any younger."

Warrick ignored him. Jaclyn wouldn't appreciate them talking about her age. "And Andrea's address isn't the issue."

Troy spread his arms. "She spends most nights at my place anyway."

Warrick shook his head, tossing his friends a shaming look. "You both need to learn to compromise. That's part of the relationship game. I don't know how you got to this stage of your life without realizing that."

Troy propped his elbows on his thighs, his hands hanging loose between his knees. "So speaks the old married guy."

Warrick sobered. "That's the key. I'm the married one." Though for how much longer was anyone's guess.

DeMarcus rubbed his hand over his close-cropped hair. "All I'm saying is that it would be helpful if Mary could talk about the positives of starting a family. She's an obstetrician. She must have something good to say about having kids."

Warrick pushed himself to his feet. "Sorry, Coach, but I'm not going to ask my wife to lobby for you. You're on your own."

"All right." Troy stood as well. "I understand your reluctance to ask her to speak on our behalf. But maybe you could ask her to ease up on the Independent Ladies platform while we're trying to convince our ladies that they need us."

Warrick couldn't hold back a smile. "If your girlfriends really needed you, it wouldn't matter what my wife said. Now, fellas, I need to get home." He lifted his gym bag onto his shoulder and started to leave, but turned back as an idea came to him. "Coach, wasn't your father a high school teacher?"

DeMarcus nodded. "Both of my parents were. Why?"

Warrick cocked his head. "Do you think he could create a study plan to help Jamal learn the playbook?"

A spark of interest lit DeMarcus's black eyes. "I'll ask him."

Troy smoothed his goatee. "How's Mary holding up?"

"As well as could be expected." Warrick's grip tightened on the gym bag's strap. "Short of a media blackout, I don't know what to do to help her."

Troy offered a smile. "Just continue being the perfect husband you'd have us think you are."

Warrick appreciated his friend's attempt at levity. "I wish I was the perfect husband. Then I'd be able to shield her from the media."

DeMarcus held his gaze. "There's nothing you can do. The media will play itself out. Once the finals are over in June, baseball season starts. The reporters will be Jeter's problem."

Warrick gave a mock wince at DeMarcus's reference to the New York Yankees' shortstop. "What do you have against the guy?"

"Nothing, but he's not one of my players." DeMarcus grew serious again. "Don't let the media distract you from your game. You've got to find a way to quiet the noise."

Warrick saw the look in DeMarcus's eyes. His coach knew what he was talking about. DeMarcus's mother had died the summer before his last season as a player in the NBA. He'd still managed to quiet the noise and lead his team to a third title.

"You're right." But Warrick had more than the title on his mind.

* * *

Warrick caressed Marilyn's back, from her shoulder to her waist. Her body was warm and soft as she lay on top of him. Tonight's lovemaking was the memory he'd hold on to as he traveled to Miami tomorrow afternoon, not the image of her brittle with tension, locked inside a darkened house, hiding from reporters.

Every kink and ache, every knotted muscle of his body was relaxed. He stroked his hand back up to her shoulder. He turned his head into the curve of her neck and inhaled her scent, jasmine and sex.

Marilyn shifted above him. She pressed her mouth against his and coaxed his lips apart. Warrick didn't need persuading. He stroked his tongue over hers.

Marilyn broke the kiss. She raised her head and met his gaze. "I still can't believe you rented *Grease.*"

He brushed her hair back from her face. "Neither can I."

Marilyn laughed and smacked his bare shoulder. She tucked her face into his neck. "Thank you, Rick. I wish we could stay in bed and watch movies forever."

"Not always *Grease,* though." Warrick felt her smile against his skin.

"Fair enough." Marilyn rose to look at him. Her expression sobered. "I also wish movie nights were enough to save our marriage."

17

Warrick froze. "What do you mean?"

Marilyn rolled off him to lie on her back to his right. "I know what you're doing, Rick. The *Grease* sound-track, the dancing, breakfast in bed, movie night."

"I'm wooing my wife. I told you from the beginning that's what I was doing." It had seemed like a good idea. Was she telling him it wasn't working? What should he do now?

"But we danced in the house because your fame would get us trampled at the club. You made me break-fast in bed—"

"It wasn't breakfast in bed." Warrick rolled his head on his pillow to look at her. "You'd sneaked downstairs before I could bring it up to you."

"It was still incredibly sweet. But it was a reminder that, whenever we go out, people continually interrupt us to talk about the team or the game."

Warrick frowned. "It wasn't supposed to be a re-minder. It was supposed to be romantic."

"It was." Marilyn gestured toward the television. "And we had movie night in bed because at the theater, people ask for your autograph."

"What are you saying, Mary?" Warrick wasn't sure he wanted to know.

"You don't have to win me over. I'm in love with you. It's our lifestyle that I'm uncomfortable with."

"I can't change that."

She hesitated. "Is this what you want? Don't you feel like a prisoner in your own home unable to go out because of fans and the media?"

He'd dreamed of playing in the NBA for as long as he could remember. But in his fantasies, he hadn't imagined what that achievement would do to his private life. "It's not an ideal situation. But if it weren't for the fans, the franchise wouldn't exist."

"You're right." Marilyn heaved a sigh. "I've never experienced so much exposure, though, not even growing up as the daughter of Terrell and Celeste Devry."

Warrick studied her profile. He could barely make out her features in the gathering dusk. "The media isn't parked outside our house anymore."

"No, but we still can't go out." She turned to him. "I wish we could go back to the way it used to be when it was just the two of us."

"So do I."

"Those days are long gone, though. Aren't they?" Her voice was soft, wistful.

"They'll come back. It'll just take a while."

Marilyn waited a beat. "Why didn't you tell me you confronted your teammates in the locker room after the game Wednesday?"

The question blindsided him. Warrick searched his memory. Jaclyn must have told her when they met this morning, which meant DeMarcus had told his fiancée last night. He should have anticipated that. "I didn't want to talk about the loss."

"I could tell." Marilyn prompted him when he remained silent. "Is everything okay with your team-mates?"

Warrick gave a ghost of a smile. "Yes. I think we'll be fine."

"I'm glad." She shifted in the bed. "I'm proud of you, you know."

Warrick stared at the ceiling. "Oh, yeah?"

"Not many people make it to the NBA and not many NBA players get to their conference championship. You've accomplished both. I just wish it hadn't come at such a high price for us."

Warrick watched Marilyn adjust the sheet more closely around her. It was like she was putting up a protective shield between them. So much for warm, soft memories as he traveled to Miami. "What can I do to make the situation better, Mary?"

She rubbed a hand over her face. "I don't know. I just know I want my privacy back, and my career."

Warrick felt her frustration coming between them. He reached out and, with his index finger under her chin, turned her face back to his. "Just give me until the end of the postseason. Then baseball will start and the cameras will turn to Mariano Rivera and ARod."

His lips curved as he sensed her confusion. She probably didn't recognize the names of two of the New York Yankees' biggest stars. But that wasn't important now. Her response to his request was. He held his breath and waited for her answer.

"What about next year?" Her voice was a whisper.

Warrick dropped his hand. "I can't predict what will happen next season."

"Will the media harass us again? Will all of this start over?"

He went back to staring at the ceiling. "God, I hope

not." Warrick took a risk and reached for her hand. He relaxed when her fingers entwined with his.

Marilyn reached behind her head and pressed the switch on top of the headboard. The light above the bed jumped on. The shadows slid back. "Why haven't we heard anything else from Jordan Hyatt? What is she waiting for?"

Warrick rose up on his right elbow and studied Marilyn's illuminated features. "I don't care about Jordan Hyatt. I care about us."

Marilyn turned onto her side to face him. "You said that we can't ignore her and I agree with you. But Andrea and I haven't found any useful information."

"That makes three of us." He lay back down.

Marilyn tensed. "How much longer are we going to wait? She's granting interviews but we're not even releasing comments."

"Something will turn up, Mary. Give us time."

Marilyn squeezed his hand. "I feel as though we're running out of time. Game seven is Saturday. Are we going to have to deal with Jordan Hyatt during the finals?"

"I hope not." The idea made his blood boil.

Marilyn tossed in the bed. "The media is putting enough pressure on us without the Jordan Hyatt story."

"Don't let them." Warrick reached behind his head and pressed the lamp switch. The light winked out and the shadows rolled back deeper than before.

"How do you do that? How are you able to block out the press?"

Warrick rolled his head on the pillow to face her silhouette in the dark. "When you want something badly enough, you make it work. That's why love is enough for me, Mary. Why isn't it enough for you?"

He turned onto his side, not waiting for her answer.

In the growing silence, he didn't know what scared him more, that she'd have an answer he didn't like or that she wouldn't have an answer at all.

"I'm surprised you went to see Mary yesterday." Warrick squinted toward the sun as he jogged beside Jaclyn on their regular route along the marina Friday morning. They were nearing the halfway point of their eight-mile jog.

"Why?" Jaclyn sounded a little out of breath, but not enough to prompt Warrick to slow down.

"She doesn't like you." He automatically leaned forward and shortened his stride as they climbed the hill.

"She's not jealous of our friendship anymore." Jaclyn sounded matter-of-fact. "Besides, she's a part of the Monarchs family. I should have gone to see her sooner."

Jaclyn was serious about treating the Monarchs players, executives, staff, and their relatives as one extended family. It was the culture her grandfather and his three franchise partners fostered when they established the franchise almost six decades earlier. Jaclyn worked very hard to continue the tradition.

Sweat rolled down Warrick's bald pate. He wiped it from his brow without adjusting his pace. "I appreciate your concern, but Mary and I are coping with the situation."

"Are you sure?"

Warrick felt Jaclyn's eyes on him, staring as though she hoped to read his mind. He turned toward her and captured her gaze. "Why?"

Marilyn wiped the sweat from her eyes. "Because Mary is depressed. She's struggling under the strain."

"And you're concerned, just like everyone else, that

trouble in my marriage is distracting me on the court."
Warrick's chest compressed with disappointment.

"No." Jaclyn exhaled as she kept pace with him. "I'm
concerned that there's trouble in your marriage. What
can I do to help?"

"Could you get the media to stop stalking me and my
wife?" Warrick kept jogging. He led Jaclyn around the
loop at the five-mile point of their run.

Jaclyn's expression was apologetic. "I'm afraid not.
I'm sorry, Rick. I know the press is a pain."

"That's an understatement." The marina waters were
a brilliant blue this morning. Sunlight danced on their
gentle waves. The peaceful scene did nothing to soothe
Warrick's troubled thoughts.

Jaclyn was silent for several strides. "Maybe Mary
should stay with your parents while you're in Miami."

He gave her a wry look. "If you were me, would you
want your spouse to stay with my parents?"

She gave him a sympathetic look. "Point taken. Does
she have friends she could stay with?"

Warrick banished Emma's image from his mind.
"We'll figure something out. And hopefully our marriage won't fall apart in the meantime."

"What about after the finals?"

Warrick allowed himself a smile. Jaclyn already had
them winning the Eastern Conference Championship
Saturday and moving on to the finals. "If we win the
title this season, great. If not—I don't know. But I won't
make a championship title a bigger priority than my
marriage. I won't put one ring above the other."

"I wouldn't ask you to, Rick. But I think you should
consider your decision about next season carefully."
Jaclyn kept pace with him. She caught her breath
before speaking again. "You know as well as I do that

most athletes don't get even one shot at a championship ring. Don't take this opportunity lightly."

"I'm not." Warrick matched his strides to Jaclyn's, trying to slow his pace. "But this is my marriage. I love Mary. I don't want to lose her."

"You'd sacrifice your dream of a championship title for your marriage?"

Warrick flicked his friend a look. "I want to be a good husband to Mary first. I can't be that when I'm the source of the strain on our marriage."

"But *you're* not causing the strain. The *media* is. Mary knows that." Jaclyn's reasonable tone reminded Warrick of his efforts to explain the media madness to his wife.

"And they'll continue to be a problem as long as I'm an active player."

"You mean as long as you're a public figure, which is what they'll consider you for the rest of your life."

"You won't change my mind, Jackie."

Jaclyn wiped her upper lip with her right wrist. "Will Mary be all right with you giving up your lifelong dream?"

Warrick recalled an image of Marilyn standing at the top of their staircase the night she'd told him she hoped he got the ring this season so he could retire.

Warrick looked at Jaclyn. "It wouldn't be her first choice. But I don't think a divorce would be, either."

Jaclyn shook her head. "I can't imagine the Monarchs without you. And I can't imagine you retiring without at least one ring. I really want that title for you. I'm certain Mary wants that as well. She believes in you, Rick. And she loves you. She wouldn't want you to retire with regrets."

The Empire Arena came back into view. Warrick

checked his watch. They were going to complete their run in less than fifty minutes.

Warrick wiped the sweat from his brow. "Then I've got one of two choices. I can either retire after this season without a ring, if it comes to that. Or I could continue my career until I earn a ring and retire without a wife." He caught Jaclyn's eyes. "Which would you choose?"

Jaclyn returned Warrick's steady stare with one of her own. "The Rick Evans I know would find a way to retire with both." She shook her head and rubbed her eyes. Was it frustration, perspiration, or both? "When did you become such a defeatist?"

Warrick's eyes widened. "I—"

"You told me yourself your father didn't believe you'd make it to the NBA. Well, you did. And several All-Star selections."

Warrick's stomach muscles clenched. Mercifully, they were closing in on the arena's rear parking lot. "What's your point?"

"You'll find a way to get the championship ring and keep your wedding ring. I have confidence in you. You need to have confidence in yourself."

Warrick broke eye contact with his friend and franchise owner. He stared at the arena looming larger as they jogged closer. She made it sound so easy. But it wasn't just up to him. Other teams would have a say in who won the championship. And Marilyn would have input into whether their marriage was worth saving. Right now, he wasn't confident in either outcome.

"It's been a week since Arthur fired me. It feels more like a month." Marilyn jogged to the end of her first lap of Prospect Park. She veered to the left of a slow-moving older couple just as Emma passed the pair on the right.

"It's the stress of the unknown. It always makes time seem longer." Emma's voice was thin and breathy. But to her credit, she didn't ask Marilyn to stop before beginning their second lap.

It was still early enough to be cool on this first Saturday in June. Marilyn's gaze swept over the area. To the right, Prospect Park's Eastern Parkway entrance was teeming with shoppers from the farmers' market stands assembled just outside the park.

Marilyn glanced at her watch. It was almost eight-thirty in the morning. In just over eleven hours, the Monarchs would play the seventh and final game of the Eastern Conference Championship. Would they return home winners and prepare for the long-anticipated finals? Or would they lose and begin their off-season? She wanted Warrick to get his championship ring, but what would that mean for them?

She looked toward the Eastern Parkway entrance again. Almost four years ago this month, she'd met Warrick for the first time at the farmers market. They'd both completed their separate runs and were waiting to buy produce from one of the vendors. She hadn't known who he was. He'd seemed amused—and pleased—by that fact.

Marilyn called herself back to the present and her problems. "I haven't even received one return phone call or e-mail in response to my job applications."

Emma panted. "You probably won't, either."

Marilyn glanced at her friend. "Why not?"

"Because no one wants to hire someone who's tainted by scandal." Emma sounded almost smug. "As long as you and Rick are together, you've got two choices."

"Which are?" Marilyn controlled her increasing agitation with an effort.

"You can either end your career or start your own practice."

Cyclists flew past them on the trail. More serious runners sped by them. Marilyn veered to the left of two parents with their toddler triplets. Triplets. God bless them.

"I'm not prepared to start a practice on my own right now." Marilyn looked over her shoulder at the three small children moving forward on unsteady, chubby little legs. So cute.

"Then you're going to end your career?"

Marilyn inhaled a deep breath in an effort to figure out what to say next. She and the other Monarchs Wives Club members had discussed this. "You sound happy about that, Em. Almost satisfied."

Emma shrugged her shoulders. "I've warned you since you and Rick started getting serious that his career would destroy yours. You wouldn't listen to me."

Marilyn reined in her temper. "I'm trying to save my marriage and my career. I'd appreciate a little support from my best friend."

Emma looked at her in concern. "Are you sure you have a marriage to save?"

The other Monarchs wives had told her she'd have to confront Emma. Marilyn had dreaded this moment. She feared the outcome. She stepped off the pedestrian path and turned to face the woman she'd called "friend" for fifteen years—through college, medical school, and residencies; boyfriends, breakups, makeups, and marriage. "Em, are you jealous of my marriage to Rick?"

Emma's cheeks flushed scarlet. "Jealous? Why would I be jealous of you and Rick?" But her friend wouldn't meet her gaze.

"There's no reason for you to be." Marilyn led Emma farther across the park's lawn. "But you've been criticizing our relationship since the day I told you he'd proposed. Why is that?"

"He's cheated on you." Emma almost spat the words.

Anger clouded Marilyn's vision. "For the hundredth time, no, he hasn't."

"You're beautiful, intelligent, and successful. But that doesn't inoculate you from lying, cheating men."

Marilyn searched the bitter glow in Emma's green eyes. She swallowed, but the lump in her throat was stuck. "All of these years, Em, and I never realized how much you hated me."

"You never appreciated what you had." Emma shoved her hands onto her hips. "You wanted to get away from your parents. You had wealth and prestige and you wanted to throw it away. I would have loved to have grown up in your family. I never would have left."

Talking with this Emma was like meeting a stranger. "You encouraged my applying to medical schools on the East Coast. You said you admired my independence."

"But marriage changed you." Emma's tone was a sneer. "You weren't independent anymore. And you weren't going to return to California."

"I made it clear before I left for medical school that I wasn't returning to San Francisco."

Emma shrugged. "You could have changed your mind."

"But I didn't." Marilyn stared at Emma's defiant expression. "Were we ever friends or did you just want to get in good with the Devrys' daughter?"

Emma nodded once. "We were friends before you became Rick's wife and didn't have time for me anymore. Didn't I warn you he was going to break your heart?"

"You're the one who broke my heart, Em. You'd have done better to warn me about that."

A flicker of uncertainty moved across Emma's round face. She shrugged her shoulders and checked her watch. "I guess this jog is over. I'm going home."

"Good-bye." Marilyn inclined her head, too numb to think of anything else to say.

She watched her former best friend forever turn and walk back toward Eastern Parkway.

Emma merged with the crowd at the park's entrance. With a heavy heart, Marilyn struggled to continue her second lap. This was the hardest summer of her personal life yet. But it wasn't due to the heat. She was hanging on to her marriage by a thread. Her husband's integrity was being publicly debated. She'd learned that her father had cheated on her mother, and the woman she'd considered her best friend since college had been pretending for all of these years.

It was telling that, through it all, the one person who'd remained true to her was Warrick.

18

The Waves had figured out their offense. Warrick stood on the sidelines with his team. DeMarcus had called a time-out. The Monarchs had gone into the half-time with a thirteen-point lead and a silenced Marlon Burress. At that point, Warrick had hoped they'd win and return home Sunday as conference champions.

Warrick lifted his gaze to the scoreboard, 108 to 105, Monarchs. One minute and eight seconds remained to the game. Too much time. At least he wasn't in foul trouble.

DeMarcus shouted to be heard above Lady Gaga's "Edge of Glory" as it competed with the cheers of the Waves fans. "We can't make any mistakes. You can't give them the win."

"It's as though they are reading our minds." Serge smoothed back his dark blond hair, which hung in a damp ponytail behind his head. "They know what we're going to do before we do it."

"We need to open the playbook." Anthony tossed aside his towel.

"We can't." Warrick shut down that option before it gained traction.

He avoided looking at Jamal. The rookie's tension spiked each time he was reminded the shortened playbook was for his benefit. Warrick didn't want the young player's confidence shaken on the court.

DeMarcus pinned him with his coal black gaze. "Rick, you need to get into Burress's head."

Warrick's brows knitted. "How, Coach?"

"You know Burress's game better than anyone else." DeMarcus was impatient. "You know *him* better than his mother."

Vincent clamped a hand around Warrick's right arm. He gestured across the Waves' arena, drawing Warrick's attention to Burress. The Waves player stood with his team on the other side of the court. "Be Burress."

Warrick stilled. He understood what he needed to do. He'd always depended on physical ability and mental strategy to earn victories. Now he had to take his game to another dimension. He had to tap into a skill he'd never exploited before. His teammates needed it. His coach demanded it. But could he do it?

The buzzer sounded.

He was about to find out.

Vincent inbounded the ball over the Waves' Chad Erving. The game clock restarted. The shot clock counted down from twenty-four. Serge worked his way to the post. The Waves' Jarrod Cheeks defended him. Jamal took the left perimeter as Walter Millbank followed him. Warrick made his way to the right perimeter. Burress covered him like body odor.

Anthony couldn't break free of the Waves' Phillip Hawk. He tossed the ball to Warrick. Warrick used his back to block Burress. He stepped into the open lane and claimed the pass. Gripping the ball with his fingertips, he spun to face Burress. He stared into the other man's fevered eyes. He gave the Waves' point guard a small smile. It was a little amused and a bit mean. Burress's eyes widened, then narrowed.

That got your attention.

Warrick would have powered through his defender on the inside for a run at the basket. Burress knew that. His body signaled he anticipated the move. But Warrick had gotten into Burress's head. He'd read his thoughts and knew his intentions. Warrick dribbled once, feinted right, then danced a tightrope around Burress's weak side. He sprang from the court. His jump shot rippled the net. Monarchs 110, Waves 105. Fifty-nine seconds left to the game.

The Waves' Erving claimed the ball. He advanced it up court at lightning pace. The Waves needed time to close the score.

The Monarchs couldn't allow that.

Staying in character, Warrick channeled Burress's trash-talking. "Everybody's going to know my name tonight."

Burress cut Warrick a look, part surprise, part anger. "I doubt it. No one remembers second best."

Warrick laughed. He fed off the power of getting under the other man's skin.

From the sidelines, DeMarcus urged the Monarchs to a faster pace. Warrick played through the fire in his knees and the knots in his back. The Waves center pitched the ball to Walter Millbank. Jamal missed the block but pressured his man in the paint. Unable to take the shot, Millbank bounced it to Burress. Eighteen seconds remained on the shot clock, fifty-six seconds on the game clock.

Warrick moved in hard on Burress, careful not to draw a foul. Funny how silent the Waves' point guard became when he played offense. Burress feinted inside. Warrick anticipated the trickery. Quick as a thought, he blocked Burress on the outside. Burress stumbled but protected the possession. Fifteen seconds on the shot clock.

Burress moved up to draw a charge. Warrick inched back to avoid the foul. He saw the exact instant when Burress realized he was mirroring him. Awareness dropped into his eyes, followed by anger. Warrick gave him the smile, part humor, part meanness. Burress came at him. Warrick planted his feet. Burress's shoulder drove into his chest. Warrick allowed himself to fall to the court.

The referee blew his whistle. "Offensive foul. Number thirty-two." That was Burress's third foul. Three more and the point guard would find himself on the bench. The tables were turning.

The shot clock reset. The game clock drained to forty-seven seconds.

Vincent extended a hand to help Warrick to his feet. The center didn't say a word, but his brown eyes gleamed with laughter. Warrick inclined his head. He arched a brow at the now furious Burress, one more dig before ambling to the free throw line. Warrick bounced the ball three times for luck. The first shot dove through the net, accompanied by boos and catcalls from the Waves' fanatics. The second shot wheeled around the rim before dropping into the basket.

The Waves' Erving grabbed the ball. Vincent guarded him, trying to slow the pace.

And so the dance continued as the game clock wound down. Each time the Miami Waves scored, the Monarchs responded. Burress grew increasingly agitated by the mental game, sending Warrick to the free throw line twice more. He had one foul to give before he was benched.

Warrick came off the charity line. Monarchs 116,

Waves 110. The shot clock turned off. The game clock restarted with eight seconds left. The Waves' Millbank advanced the ball to Erving. The center took off up the court. The Monarchs couldn't take the pressure off the other team. They had to play hard to the buzzer.

In his peripheral vision, Warrick monitored Vincent and Serge as they blocked their assignments from the basket. He guarded Burress in the paint, keeping his eyes on the ball. Five seconds on the game clock.

Warrick spread his arms wide. "Watch and learn."

A muscle jumped in Burress's jaw but he remained silent. He stepped back, preparing for a three-point shot. Warrick gave him just enough room—but not too much. Burress went high. Warrick jumped higher. He slapped the ball away. Anthony caught the rebound and flung it to Vincent. Two seconds on the game clock.

The Waves chased the Monarchs center to midcourt. One second.

The buzzer sounded. The series was over. The Monarchs had won.

Warrick raised both fists into the air, threw his head back, and roared his joy. Jamal leaped onto him and they crashed to the ground, laughing and shouting. The Monarchs bench cleared and charged onto the court.

They'd won the series. They were the Eastern Conference Champions. They were going to the NBA finals. The quest for the ring continued.

Marilyn had screamed herself almost raw watching Warrick and the Monarchs win the Eastern Conference Championship. The title was the culmination of his dream. It also brought him that much closer to the NBA Championship ring and—hopefully—retirement.

She was dizzy with excitement. She should have

watched the game with at least one other member of the Monarchs Wives Club so she could share these feelings with someone else. What were they doing now?

Marilyn reached for her cellular phone to call Peggy Coleman, but the local sportscaster's words stayed her hand.

"We have in the studio with us tonight Jordan Hyatt, the alleged pregnant mistress of Monarchs' forward Warrick Evans."

Marilyn's eyes shot back to the television to see the tall, thin anchor sitting beside the short, plump imposter. "Oh, my God. Are you kidding me?"

Jordan Hyatt's round face was heavily made up, even for the television appearance. And sometime between her first press conference and tonight's interview, she'd had wavy extensions added to her reddish brown hair. She looked like a different person. Who was she trying to be?

Marilyn fisted both hands in her lap and forced herself to watch the program. What did this fraud have to say?

The young man turned to his guest. "Jordan, what's your reaction to the Monarchs winning the Eastern Conference Championship tonight?"

Marilyn's jaw dropped. The media had sunk to a new low. It was obscene that the anchor should ask a woman pretending to be her husband's mistress for her reaction to Warrick's conference title. Never mind that Marilyn would never have agreed to the interview. Jordan Hyatt's appearance on the local news program was highly inappropriate.

Jordan cocked her head flirtatiously and granted the former frat boy a shy smile. "I'm very happy for Ricky. I know this championship has been his dream for a very long time." She touched her stomach and giggled. "And

I'm happy for me and our baby as well. Our son—or daughter—will be very proud of his father."

Marilyn blinked, then blinked again. "This *can't* be happening. Am I actually seeing this?"

The sportscaster's eyes dropped to Jordan's stomach. "An NBA champion for a father. Who wouldn't want that, right?"

Another giggle. Jordan petted her stomach. "Right."

The anchor continued. "Jordan, there are people who think you're not telling the truth about being Rick Evans's mistress. What do you say to those people?"

Marilyn shouted toward the television. "She's lying!" But, of course, the sportscaster didn't hear her.

Jordan lowered her eyes, still stroking her stomach as though it were a poodle. "I'd say those people were very jealous people who envied my happiness with Ricky. Some people are so mean and unhappy themselves that they don't want to see other people happy."

Marilyn's eyes stretched wide. "Is she unstable?"

The program's host frowned. "But Rick Evans hasn't acknowledged your relationship."

Jordan giggled. Was that noise a nervous tick? "What do you expect Ricky to say, silly? He's married. Of course he's not going to admit to being in love with me when he's still married."

Marilyn blinked. "She's unstable."

The anchor looked nonplussed. "Well, if you knew he didn't want his wife to know, why did you call a press conference to announce not only your relationship but your pregnancy?"

Jordan lifted her chin defiantly. "I'm not ashamed of our love."

A wave of nausea washed over Marilyn. She swallowed back the bile.

The anchor waited but Jordan didn't add anything.

"Did you tell him you were going to call a press conference?"

Jordan shook her head. "No."

"Have you spoken with him since the press conference?"

Again her fake curls bounced around her head and shoulders. "He's been busy."

The anchor looked nervous. Perhaps he'd finally realized the mistake he'd made in inviting this poser onto his program. Marilyn leaned forward, anxious to see the make-believe mistress and the so-called sportscaster fall flat on their faces.

The young man looked off camera before turning back to his guest. "What proof can you offer that you're Rick Evans's mistress much less that you're carrying his child?"

A sly smile stretched across Jordan's bright red lips. She looked at her host from under her false eyelashes. "Do you want to hear about his tattoo?"

Marilyn stiffened. *What* did she say?

"Rick Evans doesn't have any tattoos." The anchor tossed another desperate glance off camera.

Jordan straightened in her seat. "Yes, he does. It's on his right hip."

Blood drained from Marilyn's head. How had she known that?

The anchor frowned. "Really?"

Jordan's voice sounded so far away. "Yes. Really."

The host leaned closer. "Are you sure?" His voice was a mixture of shock and sensationalism.

Jordan nodded. "I've seen it myself."

The sportscaster looked uncertain for several seconds more. Jordan's confident expression never wavered.

Finally, the young man grinned into the camera. "Well, ladies and gentlemen, you heard it here first.

And, of course, we'll be watching the situation closely to keep you up to date on the developments." He turned to Jordan. "We'd like to thank Jordan for coming into the studio tonight and graciously giving us some of her time."

Marilyn's muscles were heavy as she reached for the universal remote control. She turned off the television and the cable box, then slumped back into her sofa.

Jordan Hyatt knew about her husband's tattoo. The one on his hip. The only one he had. Only Warrick, his doctor, and she knew of the tattoo.

How was it possible that Jordan Hyatt had seen it? Since Marilyn would never believe Warrick had shown it to her, someone else had to be involved. But who?

"Are you lost?" Warrick paused in front of Marlon Burress.

The Miami Waves star player was propped against the wall near the entrance to the visitors' locker room. Marlon had lost the Eastern Conference Championship. But he still looked like a winner with his air of confidence and his double-breasted navy pinstriped suit.

Marlon gave Warrick a half smile. "I deserved that."

Warrick wasn't amused. "What do you want?"

Marlon straightened from the wall. "To congratulate you. You played me hard. It was a good series."

"Thanks." Warrick didn't want to like this guy.

Behind him, his teammates, coaches, and trainers filed out of the visitors' locker room. He sensed their curiosity. In his peripheral vision, he noticed them lingering in the hallway behind him. A hand clamped onto his shoulder. Warrick looked around and met DeMarcus's gaze.

His coach's dark eyes pinned him. "All good?"

Warrick nodded. "Yes."

DeMarcus extended his hand to his former teammate and longtime friend. "Good series, Marl."

Marlon clasped DeMarcus's hand. "Don't embarrass me with the Nuggets."

"Bus's leaving soon." DeMarcus gripped Warrick's shoulder again before turning to leave. He nodded toward the other Monarchs. "Let's go."

Warrick started to follow them, but Marlon caught his arm. "I'm sorry about the trash-talking, man. Just trying to win by any means necessary." Marlon offered his right hand. "But I crossed the line a couple of times. For that, I'm sorry."

Warrick hesitated. It was the sincerity in Marlon's dark eyes that made the difference. Warrick clasped his opponent's right hand. "Don't do it again."

Marlon nodded as he released Warrick's hand. "I think I learned my lesson."

Warrick hoped so. He enjoyed the Monarchs divisional rivalry with the Miami Waves. But he could live without Marlon's mind games. He stepped around Marlon on his way to the parking lot.

Marlon walked with him. "Listen, good luck against the Nuggets. You're representing the Eastern Conference. Bring back the win."

Warrick met his gaze. "We'll do our best."

They continued to the parking lot in a surprisingly comfortable silence. Security lights kept the night shadows at bay. The smell of the nearby Atlantic Ocean reminded him of the marina.

As they neared the bus, Marlon slapped his back. "I hear your wife's a doctor."

Warrick regarded his opponent with suspicion. He

may have forgiven Marlon but that didn't make them friends.

Marlon was oblivious to Warrick's silence. "You're lucky. She'll be able to take care of all of your aches and pains when you retire." Marlon laughed at his own joke, then turned with a wave. "Good luck. Go get your ring."

Warrick watched Marlon walk to his car.

Retire.

Even when the Monarchs were at the bottom of the league, Warrick had never considered asking to be traded or retiring from the game. Now with his team battling to the top, the word *retirement* appeared with increasing frequency.

Sunday morning, Warrick let himself in through his back door. He was still groggy from the flight. "Mary?"

Warrick turned to secure the lock before crossing the kitchen in search of his wife. Was she waiting for him in the bedroom? Heat filled his body at the image.

He started down the hallway toward the staircase, carrying his travel bag with him. "Mary?"

"I'm in the family room." Marilyn sounded strained.

Warrick found her sitting on the sofa staring at a darkened television screen. He settled his bag beside his feet. "What's wrong?"

Marilyn stood, turning to face him. Her hair was tousled. Her silver Monarchs T-shirt and navy shorts looked slept in. "How does Jordan Hyatt know you have a tattoo on your right hip?"

Warrick's muscles went lax. His right hand touched his hip. He'd gotten the tattoo shortly after he'd met Marilyn. It was a private matter. It wasn't body paint. It wasn't a fashion statement. It was a personal message, one he'd only confided to Marilyn. No one else. And only a select few had ever seen it.

"What makes you think she knows about it?" He struggled with a sense of betrayal. Who could have told this lying stranger about his tattoo?

"Last night, she appeared on a local news show that aired right after the game. She told the interviewer she'd seen it." Marilyn gestured toward his hip.

Warrick winced. How many millions of people watched that show and now knew about his tattoo? "Did she describe it?"

Marilyn wrapped her arms around her waist. "No, but she knew where it was. How is that possible?"

"I have no idea." His eyes narrowed. "Don't you believe me?"

"Before last night, I thought the only people who knew you had a tattoo were me, your doctor, and the team trainers." Her voice sounded brittle enough to break. "Then, Jordan Hyatt popped up on the news telling everyone not only does she know you have a tattoo, but she's seen it."

Warrick paced the gleaming hardwood floor on the edge of the family room. "I've never taken my clothes off for that woman. Before her press conference, I'd never even seen her."

"Then how does she know about your tattoo?"

Warrick stopped midstride. "I can't explain something I don't understand myself."

"She couldn't have just guessed you had a tattoo on your hip." Marilyn bit her bottom lip.

Warrick gave his wife a considering look. "Have you told anyone about it?"

Marilyn gaped at him. "Of course not. I respect your privacy too much to tell anyone your secrets."

"Not even Emma?" He wouldn't put it past Marilyn's so-called friend to gossip about them.

"No one. I wouldn't tell anyone." She frowned. "Have you?"

"No."

"Maybe one of the team trainers or your doctor."

"They've all signed confidentiality agreements for the franchise." Warrick's tone was definite.

"Then how could Jordan Hyatt find out about it?"

Warrick faced his wife, knowing more than a room separated them. That knowledge was heartbreaking. "What are you accusing me of, Mary?"

Marilyn gaped at him. "I'm not accusing you of anything."

Warrick resumed his pacing. "Yes, you are. Some delusional fan—or more likely a pathological liar—has made a false accusation about me and you've chosen to believe her."

Four years ago, he thought he'd found someone who would always believe in him, unlike his parents, whom he could never seem to please. Today, that had changed because of a stranger's words.

Marilyn dropped her arms. "Someone is trying to come between us."

"Who?" He rubbed the small of his back through his dark gray polo shirt. The muscles there were tightening on him.

"That's what we have to figure out." Marilyn pulled her fingers through her hair. Her voice was packed with frustration.

Warrick gathered his courage to ask the question they'd both been dancing around. "Do you think I've cheated on you?"

Marilyn's gaze wavered. "I don't want to believe that."

A large fist slowly crushed his heart. "There's nothing more to say, then."

Warrick reached for his bag. The twinge in his back was nothing compared to the pain in his chest. He left the family room and walked past the stairs back to the kitchen.

Marilyn's voice came from behind him. "Where are you going?"

"I'm leaving. There's nothing keeping me here anymore."

Bare feet rushed across the hardwood floor. A hand tugged on his arm. Warrick turned to look down at his wife. He was looking at a stranger.

Marilyn's eyes were panicked. "You can't leave. We have to figure this out."

"I can't stay here, Mary. Not when you don't trust me." The pain in his chest throbbed like a burn. He couldn't stand here, talking with her much longer.

"I do trust you."

"Those are just words. Your eyes and your voice say something else." Warrick tugged against her hold. "Just because I can't answer your question doesn't mean that I'm lying."

"Rick, wait."

He didn't. He unlocked the kitchen door, then closed it gently behind him. He'd believed in them and their marriage, and tuned out everyone else. But Marilyn had let other people's accusations poison their relationship. She'd listened to the fans who'd thought she wasn't pretty enough to be a baller's wife, the media who accused him and his teammates of a night of debauchery in Cleveland, and now a stranger who'd claimed to be his lover.

Warrick's grip tightened on his steering wheel as he

drove his BMW as far away from their Prospect Heights home as possible.

Marilyn had been right. She wasn't suited to a marriage in the media spotlight. He'd been wrong to expect her to change.

19

If Marilyn had listened to one of the messages Andrea had left Monday morning, perhaps the reporter wouldn't have shown up on her doorstep that afternoon. Marilyn dried her nose with the ragged facial tissue in her fist. She'd wanted to be left alone with her heartache, but obviously the reporter couldn't be ignored. She opened the door and stepped back to let in her guest.

Andrea began speaking the moment she crossed the threshold. "I'm sorry to just show up on your doorstep, but you weren't answering your phone." She turned to face Marilyn. "I know . . . What's happened?"

Marilyn shook her head. Her face crumbled and she began to cry. Again. "Rick left me." The words burned her throat.

"Oh, no."

Maybe it was Andrea's caring embrace. Or maybe it was her soothing voice. Whatever the trigger, Marilyn found herself crying even harder than she had last night. They were deep sobs that wracked every muscle in her body as they were torn from her soul. Her eyes were too swollen to see. She couldn't think. She couldn't speak. She could barely move.

Some minutes later, Marilyn found herself sitting beside Andrea on her thick coffee-colored sofa. "I'm sorry. I've been crying all morning."

"There's no need to apologize. That explains why you weren't answering your phone." Andrea dug into her large brown purse and produced a travel packet of facial tissues. "You can have those."

Marilyn accepted the gift with unsteady hands. "Thank you."

"When did Rick leave?"

Marilyn's head felt as though it was filled to bursting with foam. "Yesterday." She took several quavering breaths. "He didn't even unpack. He came home Sunday morning. We had an argument. He picked up his bag and left."

Andrea was silent for several moments. "Did you argue about Jordan Hyatt?"

Marilyn wiped her nose, then pulled another tissue from the small, soft packet. When would her crying end? "How did you know?"

"I saw her interview on the local sports show Saturday night as well. I was shocked."

"*You* were shocked? I'm his wife." Righteous indignation stemmed her tears. Marilyn surged from the sofa to wander the family room.

"You don't believe Rick slept with her, do you?" Andrea's question carried from behind Marilyn.

"No, but I haven't told anyone about Rick's tattoo. Neither has he. So how would Jordan Hyatt know about it? Who could have told her? Whoever it is, that person is deliberately trying to destroy our marriage."

Marilyn strode from the room.

Andrea's footsteps hurried after her. "Where are you going?"

Marilyn crossed into the kitchen and marched to

the refrigerator. "I need a glass of water. Would you like some?"

"Sure." Andrea sounded preoccupied.

Marilyn opened a cupboard for two large glasses and filled them with ice and water. "I'm sorry. I'm very poor company right now."

Andrea took one of the glasses from Marilyn with a hasty thanks. "Mary, I know how Jordan Hyatt learned about Rick's tattoo. Or at least I have a theory."

Marilyn turned from the refrigerator to face the reporter. Hope eased the tightness in her chest. "What is it?"

"Sit down." Andrea sat beside Marilyn at the table. "As I said, I saw the interview Saturday night, too. And I was stunned. Rick would never cheat on you."

Marilyn fisted her hands in her lap. "I want to believe that. But how could another woman know about his tattoo?"

Andrea reached into her shoulder bag and pulled out several sheets of folded paper. "Because she saw it—but Rick didn't show it to her."

Marilyn frowned. "You're not making sense."

The reporter smoothed the papers on the kitchen table between them. Marilyn glanced at the printouts. Her eyes widened as she realized what the color images represented.

Her hand flew to her mouth, smothering a gasp. "Oh, my word! Where did you get these?" Marilyn didn't recognize her own voice.

There were six sheets, four full-color images on each, of her and Warrick making love in their kitchen. Marilyn was shocked. She was angry. She was embarrassed and ashamed.

"I asked Troy to get them from Jackie for me." Andrea's voice was hesitant. "She'd demanded the photographer and the *Horn* turn over all of the original images they'd taken through your kitchen window. Troy offered the disc to Rick. But he was too angry to take them, so Jackie secured them."

"She should have destroyed them." Marilyn could barely hear herself over the buzzing in her ears.

The contact sheets showed Marilyn and Warrick in some of the most intimate poses. They were kissing, caressing, and undressing each other. Thank the Lord they'd disappeared onto the floor behind the table before they'd progressed any farther.

Andrea reached into her bag of tricks again. "Be glad she didn't." She extended the camera disc to Marilyn. "Now you can."

Marilyn stared at the object. How could something so innocuous have caused so much trouble? No wonder Warrick didn't want to touch it.

She took it from Andrea's hand. "Thank you." Marilyn turned back to the printouts, stealing herself against the embarrassment of seeing herself and her husband together while a complete stranger looked on. "Have you . . . looked at these?"

"Yes." Andrea's voice was without discernible inflection. "That's how I knew Jordan Hyatt had seen them also. In some of these, you can tell that Rick has a tattoo." She tapped a couple of the images.

Marilyn winced. "You're right." She let the sheets drop from her hands. "Now I know how that woman found out what my husband looks like naked."

"She can thank the paparazzi."

Marilyn fisted her hands. "That wretched photographer. What made him think he could invade our privacy? Did he have any idea of the trouble he'd cause? Did he care?"

Andrea squeezed Marilyn's shoulder. "If this had

happened to me, that photographer would have had to take out a restraining order for his own protection."

"I should have thought of that." Marilyn's eyes widened with worry. "You're not going to do a story on these photos, are you?"

"There isn't a story here." She tapped the images of Warrick's tattoos again. "But at least now the mystery is solved."

Marilyn's head felt clearer and her eyes were finally dry. But a burden still weighed on her shoulders. "This is only part of the mystery. I still don't know why Jordan Hyatt is lying about having any kind of relationship with my husband. What does she want?"

Andrea stood with Marilyn, taking her oversized purse with her. "One step at a time."

Marilyn escorted the other woman to the front door. She gave her a hard hug. "I'm very grateful for your help."

"It was my pleasure." Andrea hugged her back before stepping away. "Now go save your marriage."

Marilyn locked the door behind her guest, then ran upstairs to get dressed. She was anxious to bring her husband home.

Warrick's sneakers squeaked against the hardwood Monday afternoon. DeMarcus and Oscar sat on the bleachers deep in conversation on the other side of the practice court. Warrick's gaze dropped to the scouting reports and game plans for the Monarchs' first game against the Denver Nuggets Wednesday night. The papers lay forgotten on the bleachers beside the coaches.

So what were they talking about so intently?

Warrick adjusted his gym bag on his shoulder as he drew closer to the other men.

"All this traveling is beginning to piss me off." Oscar's tone was grouchier than usual.

DeMarcus emitted a surprised laugh. "The play-offs are pissing you off?"

Oscar's features compressed into his default expression of irritation. "Did I say play-offs? I said the *traveling* is pissing me off. You should listen to someone other than yourself once in a while."

Warrick wasn't in a rush to return to the hotel. He stopped in front of the bleachers to listen to the coaches' exchange.

DeMarcus's smile widened. "Unfortunately, we can't play all of our games at home."

Oscar continued to scowl. "If you'd taken us to a better record, we'd have had home court advantage."

"Ease up on Coach, O." Warrick lowered his gym bag to the court beside his feet. "No one thought we'd make it to the play-offs. Now, we're the Eastern Conference Champions. Not bad."

DeMarcus chuckled. "You sound as though we've made it. We're not done."

Oscar grunted. "Maybe *you're* not. But *I* am. We've traveled all over the country. Twice. Now, we're going to fly back and forth to Denver. If the time change doesn't kill you, the damned altitude will."

DeMarcus slapped the older man's shoulder. "But it's the play-offs, Oscar. It's worth it."

Oscar shot DeMarcus a look of mingled aggravation and affection. "Keep telling yourself that."

Warrick laughed. "You sound as though winning a championship is something you do every season."

Oscar snorted. "This may be your first run at the championship with the Monarchs, but I've been here before. I've got my ring. Now I'm old and tired. I'm not looking forward to four-hour flights on airborne sardine cans."

"What are you saying, Oscar?" There was a trace of concern in DeMarcus's tone.

The assistant coach gave the younger man a patient look. "You need to listen harder. I'm saying this will be my last season."

Warrick drew a sharp breath, catching the scent of sweat and floor wax. Oscar Clemente had been the Monarchs' assistant coach before Warrick had been drafted to the team. He'd been the organization's dependable constant through all of its coaching carousels. Oscar Clemente and Franklin Jones—Jaclyn Jones's grandfather and one of the franchise's founding members—had been father figures to Warrick. Franklin had passed away recently and now Oscar was talking about retiring.

Warrick's mind went blank as he tried to process the information. "I can't imagine the team without you, O."

Oscar grunted again. "I can."

"You sell yourself short, old man." DeMarcus's voice was strained. "You're a great coach and a valuable member of the franchise."

Oscar's cheeks turned pink. His gaze flicked to Warrick before returning to DeMarcus. "There are plenty of assistant coaches out there, younger men who enjoy having their circulation cut off in those flying matchsticks."

DeMarcus shifted on the bleacher. "None of them are as good as you. Are you sure you won't reconsider?"

Oscar pinned Warrick with his brown gaze. "Rick would make a good assistant coach."

Shock rattled Warrick's system again. "Me? What makes you say that?"

Oscar waved his hands. "You're doing it already.

You're always talking and teaching, on the court and on the sidelines."

DeMarcus's lips tipped up. He gave Warrick a curious stare. "I hadn't realized constant talking was a sign of a future coach."

Oscar angled his chin toward DeMarcus. "Watch your game film. You never shut up."

DeMarcus arched an eyebrow. "I never noticed that."

"Neither have I." Warrick's thoughts were spinning. Could he go into coaching after he retired? It was a possibility he'd never considered. The job would keep him in basketball. But he'd miss the court.

"And selflessness. A lot of players don't put the team first." Oscar waved a hand from DeMarcus to Warrick. "You two do. And Jardine. The others don't."

Warrick pictured the Monarchs' center. He'd often admired Vincent's game. If he had the look, he'd take the shot. Otherwise, he'd pass the ball. He'd never force it.

Vincent also stayed out of locker room drama. He was the only teammate who hadn't said anything—for or against him—regarding all the media attention on Warrick.

Oscar crossed his arms. "Yeah. You'd make a good coach. Maybe better than Marc."

Warrick laughed. "That's raising the bar pretty high." There was a strange expression in DeMarcus's eyes. "What's wrong, Coach?"

DeMarcus shook his head. "I think I may have just solved a puzzle."

Oscar snorted. "'Bout damn time."

Warrick frowned, but neither man enlightened him.

DeMarcus addressed his assistant coach. "Does Jack know about your retirement plans?"

Oscar sighed. "No."

DeMarcus smoothed a hand over his hair. "She'll probably try to talk you out of it."

Oscar looked away. "Probably."

Warrick considered the assistant coach. Oscar's words were confident but his body language told a different story. His fingers were knotted together. His shoulders were rounded. Warrick didn't care what the older man said. His decision wasn't set in stone.

Still, he'd given Warrick a lot to think about. Coaching. Could it be in his future?

His gaze roamed the practice facility, bringing to mind images of the practice that had ended almost two hours ago. The Monarchs were on their way to the finals. The NBA Championship ring was so close his hand itched.

He turned back to Oscar. "It's your decision when you retire. I just hope you'll continue to help us through the play-offs."

Oscar scowled. "Season's not over yet."

In Oscar-speak, he'd just given his word that he wouldn't leave before the finals were over. Satisfied, Warrick shrugged his gym bag back onto his shoulder. "I'll see you tomorrow morning, then."

Warrick made his way to the parking lot. He slipped on his sunglasses as protection against the 3:00 P.M. sun. Summer was only weeks away.

"Rick."

The sound of Marilyn's voice surprised him. It was unusual that she'd come to the practice facility. But then, she wasn't working right now.

His pulse beat faster at the sight of her hurrying toward him. Her dark brown hair—free of that clip thing—swung frantically behind her shoulders. A brisk marina breeze molded her thin tan T-shirt to her firm curves. Dark brown shorts bared her endless legs from midthigh. She stopped in front of him. He could reach out and touch her.

Warrick fisted one hand in the front right pocket of his gray khaki shorts. His other hand held the strap of his gym bag in a death grip. "What's wrong?"

Marilyn's gaze scanned his features. "Andrea stopped by this morning. She has a theory about how Jordan Hyatt learned about your tattoo."

Warrick shifted his gaze from her lips. "How?"

Her expression was strained. "It appears in some of the pictures that Peeping-Tom photographer took of us in our kitchen."

Warrick gripped his gym bag even harder. "It's on my hip. Did the guy use a telephoto lens?"

"It's true. I saw the photos."

"You're kidding." Warrick felt sick.

Marilyn's scowl cleared. "We can use this information to discredit her."

"How?"

Marilyn's eyes reflected her confusion. "By telling the media that Jordan Hyatt isn't having an affair with you. She only knows about your tattoo because of those pictures."

"And when the reporters demand to know which photo, what am I supposed to do? Show them the pictures of you and I making love?"

The faint dusting of color on Marilyn's cheekbones was answer enough. "Of course not."

Warrick sidestepped her. "That's not my first choice, either."

Marilyn kept pace with him. "We'll figure out something."

We. That word, when applied to them, had been the culmination of a dream.

Warrick paced to his black BMW in silence. He

deactivated the car's alarm and tossed his bag onto the passenger seat.

Marilyn fished her car keys from her purse. "I'll follow you home."

Warrick pushed the door shut. "No, you won't."

Marilyn froze. "Why not?"

He turned his back to her and circled the hood of his car. "I'm not going home, Mary."

"Why not?"

Warrick faced his wife. She was so close he could smell her jasmine scent carried on the cool breeze. "I was never worried about proving myself to the media. They could think whatever they'd like. But I never thought I'd have to prove myself to my wife."

Marilyn's gaze wavered but didn't fall. "It's not that I didn't believe you. I didn't know how she could have known about your tattoo."

Warrick grunted. "It sounded as though you didn't believe me. Have I ever given you a reason to distrust me?"

"Of course not." Marilyn's words came with satisfying speed. But were they only words?

"Then why didn't you trust me this time?" Warrick genuinely wanted to know. Had Marilyn felt confused and uncertain because of the media pressure? Or were they growing apart?

Marilyn's gaze swept the parking lot. Warrick's regard remained squarely on her. His car alarm reset with a chirp.

She returned her attention to him. "Maybe I did have a little bit of doubt because I learned a few days ago that my father recently cheated on my mother."

Warrick didn't hesitate. "I'm not your father."

Marilyn's brown eyes darkened. "I know and I'm sorry, Rick."

"So am I." He turned toward his car and deactivated the alarm.

Marilyn took his arm. "I was wrong to have ever doubted you, even for a second. How can I make it up to you?"

Warrick stared into her eyes for seconds that felt like an eternity. Hurting her was killing him. "I don't know if you can. I needed for you to believe in me. I thought you did. But when I asked you to take a leap of faith in me, you wouldn't."

Marilyn's hand fell away from him. "None of this would have happened if it weren't for that damned photographer."

"Maybe he did us a favor."

She looked stricken. "How could you say that?"

"He's helped us to realize that we don't trust each other as much as we thought we did."

Marilyn didn't recognize the bitter man standing before her. "I think most spouses would have had some doubt in our situation."

"But you aren't most spouses. You're my wife." He cocked his head to the side. "When did you stop trusting me, Mary?"

"The media have caused a lot of upheaval in our lives."

Warrick crossed his arms. "You're hinting at my retirement again, aren't you? I've never even considered asking you to give up your career when the late-night deliveries pulled you out of our bed or when evening labors interrupted our dinner."

"That's different."

"Why? Because it's *your* career?"

Frustration tore through her. "My job doesn't inspire photographers to take pictures of us having sex."

"You have a vision of a perfect life for yourself.

Everything and everyone in its place." He straightened away from his car. "Well, my life isn't perfect. Does it still have a place in yours?"

Marilyn stepped back. "You expected me to take a leap of faith in you, but you're the one who walked away. You're still walking away."

"What am I supposed to do?"

"Fight." She fisted her hands. "If our marriage means anything to you, fight for it."

Pain and anger darkened his features. "I have been fighting to save our marriage ever since you asked for a divorce three weeks ago. I'd have saved myself a lot of trouble if I'd given it to you." Warrick climbed into his BMW and drove away.

Frozen, Marilyn could only watch him. She'd come to bring her husband home. Instead he'd driven farther away.

20

"After a surprising game-one win Wednesday, the Monarchs took a loss tonight." Kirk West of the *New York Horn* was barely visible in the throng of national and international reporters in the Denver Nuggets media room. "Did the Jordan Hyatt interview discussing your tattoo have anything to do with your poor performance?"

"No." Warrick stared down at the sports reporter from the podium in front of the stuffy, overcrowded room Friday.

He'd known one of the reporters would ask that question during this postgame conference in Denver's arena. The Monarchs had stunned the Nuggets on their home court during the first game of the NBA finals best-of-seven series Wednesday night. However, they'd failed to capitalize on that win tonight. Still the media spotlight remained on his bedroom.

Troy Marshall stepped to the front of the room and waved an arm to claim the reporters' attention. "Let's limit the questions to what happened on the court tonight."

Kirk looked smug. "But last Saturday's interview

with Ms. Hyatt may have had something to do with what happened on the court."

"It didn't." Troy's tone was clipped.

A young female reporter toward the back of the room popped up from her chair. "Rick, how's your marriage?"

With an effort, Warrick held on to his patience. "I'm here to talk about basketball, tonight's game in particular. Does anyone have any questions about that?"

A graying gentleman with dark circles under his eyes pushed himself from his seat in one of the middle rows. "You seemed distracted tonight. What was on your mind?"

All variations of the theme. "The game." Warrick stepped away from the podium. Troy joined him as he left the room. "I'm not doing any more of those."

Troy tossed him a sympathetic look. "I'm sorry, Rick. But you have to do them. League rules."

Warrick's muscles tensed as he strode with Troy down the hall toward the arena's parking lot. "The rules don't specify that I'm the one who has to talk with them."

"All right. We'll let Marc handle them from now on." Troy braced a hand on Warrick's shoulder.

The memory of his head coach during past postgame interviews tugged a smile from Warrick's lips. "I don't know who to feel sorry for, Coach or the media."

Troy's tone was dry. "Pity the media. But they brought it on themselves."

Warrick chuckled. "Payback's sweet."

The next morning, after the long, uncomfortable flight from Denver, Warrick made his way to the New York airport's parking garage. Still groggy from the nonstop commercial flight, he searched for his car keys. Since he'd checked in to a hotel near the airport, at least he wouldn't have far to drive.

DeMarcus caught Warrick's shoulder. "Could you give me a ride home?"

Warrick stopped. A survey of the baggage area located Jaclyn exiting the terminal alone. "You usually ride with Jackie."

"I need to check on my father."

That still didn't explain why he wasn't riding with Jaclyn. DeMarcus's body language was relaxed. His eye contact was direct. It didn't seem as though the couple had argued. So why weren't they driving home together? It wasn't his business.

"Sure, I'll take you home."

DeMarcus fell into step beside him. "Thanks."

"No problem." He wouldn't think about the journey ahead, thirty minutes to DeMarcus's house, then thirty minutes back to his hotel. So much for the convenient commute.

In silence, he walked with DeMarcus to his black BMW. He deactivated the alarm and they tossed their suitcases into his trunk. "Which way?"

DeMarcus circled the car to the passenger side. "Take the Jackie Robinson to Eastern Parkway."

Warrick made certain his coach was buckled in to his seat before exiting the garage and pointing his car toward the parkway. The four-door sedan felt a little smaller with the larger-than-life presence of the Mighty Guinn.

A tense silence lasted the first few miles as Warrick drove out of Queens toward DeMarcus's Park Slope, Brooklyn, neighborhood.

Finally, DeMarcus spoke. "You were pretty quiet after the game last night."

Warrick kept his eyes on the road. Freeway traffic was heavy at nine o'clock on a Saturday morning. "Not much to say."

"Not much to say or no one to say it to?"

Warrick didn't answer that.

DeMarcus continued. "You fought two teams to get to the finals—the Waves and your own."

Warrick couldn't ignore that. "We're playing like a team again. We lost last night, but the series is tied. Everything's going to be fine."

"That's because you wouldn't let the other guys continue to shut you out of the team. You have a lot of heart."

Warrick felt DeMarcus's eyes boring in to the side of his head. What did his coach expect him to say? "I don't know about that."

"I do." DeMarcus shifted in his seat. "When I played for the Waves and we were making our first championship run, the media turned their spotlight on me, just like they're focusing on you now."

"I remember that." Warrick shifted in his seat to ease the tightness in his back.

DeMarcus looked away from Warrick. "My teammates tried to shut me out as well."

Surprise loosened the muscles in his upper body. "Even Marlon Burress?"

DeMarcus chuckled. "No, not Marl. He was the only one who didn't shun me."

"Why?" Warrick saw the grin that spread across DeMarcus's face.

"In his mind, Marl is always the center of attention." There was affection in DeMarcus's voice for his long-time friend and former teammate.

Warrick smiled. "I can believe that."

DeMarcus sobered. "Like you, I wanted the title too much to let my teammates' jealousy get in my way.

Warrick checked his car's mirrors and his blind spot

before switching lanes. They were getting closer to the Eastern Parkway exit. "Why are you telling me this?"

"I know what you're going through."

Warrick caught the exit, then maneuvered the weekend traffic as he mulled over DeMarcus's statement. Silence again settled in the car for several miles.

"Turn right at the next light." DeMarcus moved in his seat. "You don't believe me, do you?"

Warrick checked traffic before switching lanes. "That the Mighty Guinn—three-time MVP, two-time NBA champion, and Olympic gold medalist—can understand what a mere mortal is going through?"

"Sarcasm. That's good."

"Sorry." Warrick tossed out the word without conviction.

"Sometimes I forget that you even have any emotions. You should show them more often."

Warrick glanced at his coach and found the other man watching him intently. "Seriously?"

"Yes. You're the leader of this team. If you play tight, the team will play tight."

Warrick's grip tightened around the steering wheel. "You're wrong. I'm not a leader."

"I didn't think so at first, either. But I was wrong. You're doing more harm than good by not accepting your role."

"It's not my role to accept." Warrick sat up to take some pressure off his back.

"You're in the role whether you've accepted it or not." Several silent minutes later, DeMarcus waved a hand at the windshield. "Turn left at the next corner. It's the house toward the middle of the block on the right. You and I are alike."

DeMarcus's words dazed him.

"How?" Warrick activated his left turn signal and

waited for traffic to clear before easing onto DeMarcus's street.

"Neither of us was looking to be a leader. But we'll do whatever it takes to get the W. That makes us leaders by default." DeMarcus pointed toward his passenger window at a narrow brick house. "This is it."

Warrick found a parking spot two doors down from DeMarcus's house. He turned off the engine and popped the trunk open. He climbed out of the driver's seat and met DeMarcus at the back of the car.

DeMarcus adjusted his travel bag's strap onto his shoulder, then inclined his head toward Warrick's trunk. "Grab your bag."

Warrick's brow knitted with confusion. "Why?"

DeMarcus gave him a direct stare. "You're going to stay here until you patch things up with Mary."

Warrick hooked his hands on his hips. "Is that why you had me drive you home?"

"Yes."

"Why the pretense?"

DeMarcus met his stare. "Would you have come if I'd told you the truth?"

Warrick didn't have to consider his answer. "No."

"Jack didn't think so." He started toward his house, calling over his shoulder. "Get your bag and come on."

Warrick glared at his coach's back, half tempted to lock his trunk and return to his airport hotel room. But it had been a long trip. He was tired and he didn't like hotels. He grabbed his bag, shut his trunk, and activated his car alarm.

Warrick followed DeMarcus up the staircase to the front door. "You talk about my wife interfering. That's nothing compared to what you let Jackie talk you into."

DeMarcus's response was a noncommittal grunt.

Julian Guinn, DeMarcus's father, must have been watching for them. He opened the door before DeMarcus even reached it.

"Eastern Conference Champions." Julian pronounced the title with relish. His voice was thick with pride and pleasure.

Julian stepped aside, allowing both men to enter the house before pulling his son into a bear hug. "Good start to the finals, son."

DeMarcus returned his father's grin. "Thanks, Pop."

Julian released DeMarcus. He slapped Warrick on the back, still beaming with a fan's joy and pride. "Good game, son."

Warrick looked at the older man in surprise. A glow of pride warmed his skin and relaxed his tension. "Thank you, Mr. Guinn."

Julian chuckled. "I thought we'd agreed on Julian, Rick."

Warrick smiled. "Yes, sir."

"I knew the Monarchs had it in them." Julian stepped back, apparently not interested in moving the NBA finals discussion from the front entrance of his turn-of-the-century home. "You know, I've watched you play since you were with the Rutgers Scarlet Knights."

DeMarcus set his travel bag on the gleaming hardwood floor. "Pop, Rick already heard this story during our play-off party."

Julian's dark eyes, so like his son's, still danced with excitement. "It's my favorite story." He turned to Warrick. "Never mind. We'll have plenty of time to talk when Marc leaves."

"You're leaving?" Warrick looked at DeMarcus. "How are you getting home?"

"I'm driving him." Jaclyn's voice joined the conversation.

Warrick looked up as the franchise owner crossed into the entranceway.

Jaclyn stopped beside DeMarcus, taking her fiancé's hand. "Don't look at me that way. You think you have to do everything yourself. I knew you wouldn't have accepted a more conventional invitation."

Warrick lowered his bag to the floor. "I appreciate your concern, but I'd already checked into a hotel."

"Isn't this better?" Her voice was soft persuasion.

Warrick looked from the concern in her bright eyes to Julian's welcoming smile and DeMarcus's watchful expression. They'd arranged to have him come here not because he needed a place to stay but because he needed a place to heal. They'd tricked him because they cared. "You're right."

Jaclyn looked relieved. Her chin lifted to its normal cocky angle. "Aren't I always?"

"Oh, brother." DeMarcus lifted Warrick's bag to his shoulder. "Let me show you to the guest room before I throw up the handful of peanuts they served on the plane."

"Very funny." Jaclyn's sarcasm followed them upstairs.

DeMarcus took him to the guest room. He deposited Warrick's suitcase at the foot of the bed. "I've never slept in here, but I'm sure you'll be comfortable."

Warrick stood awkwardly with his arms at his sides. "Thanks, man." The words didn't seem expressive enough. "I mean it."

DeMarcus slapped his arm. "You're more than a valued member of the Monarchs. You're a friend."

He gave Warrick a quick tour of the top floor before

leading him back downstairs. Jaclyn and Julian stood as he and DeMarcus entered the study.

Jaclyn went to DeMarcus. "Are you ready?"

"Yes." DeMarcus hugged his father. "See you later, Pop."

"Drive carefully and congratulations again." Julian released his son to give Jaclyn a hug and a kiss. "Take care of my boy."

Jaclyn smiled. "Always." She turned to kiss Warrick's cheek. "We'll see you tomorrow."

"Bright and early." Warrick hugged her tight. "Thanks."

Jaclyn returned his embrace. "What are friends for?"

Warrick's tension was easing. It was as though a pressure had been lifted from his chest and shoulders. He'd felt on the outside for so long—outside his marriage, outside his team. He hadn't realized the toll that was taking on him, heart and soul.

Julian returned from escorting DeMarcus and Jaclyn to the front door.

Warrick faced him. "Mr. Guinn—Julian—thank you for letting me stay in your home." For how long was anyone's guess.

Julian waved a hand. "You're welcome, Rick. There's more than enough room for the two of us. Stay as long as you'd like."

Warrick crossed to the study's bay window. "I don't know how long it will take for Mary and me to work things out." *Or even if we can.*

"Marriages go through periods of adjustment." Julian's voice carried from across the room. "Being a celebrity, you have a marriage with more to adjust to than most."

Warrick crossed his arms as he contemplated the quiet Park Slope neighborhood outside. "It shouldn't matter what other people say or write about us. It's our marriage—Mary's and mine. We're the only people who should matter."

"That's true, in a typical marriage. But your marriage isn't typical, is it?"

Warrick considered the other man's question. Behind him, he heard Julian moving around.

"Can you cook?"

Warrick wandered away from the view. "A little."

"How about bake?"

Warrick shook his head. "Sorry."

Julian's disappointed expression quickly brightened. "I still have some of Althea's cookies left. Come on."

Warrick followed Julian down the hallway toward his kitchen. He'd known DeMarcus's father was dating Althea Gentry, Jaclyn's administrative assistant. But he hadn't realized the older woman could bake.

Julian fished the plastic bowl of homemade cookies from a kitchen cupboard and put it in the center of the table. "Marriage is a union that involves two individuals who are growing and changing. Sometimes, you grow together. But sometimes you grow apart."

Was that what was happening to him and Marilyn? Were they growing apart?

Warrick chose a cookie from the container. "How do you know which one it is?"

"You don't, at least not right away. It may feel as though you and Mary are growing apart, but be patient." Julian paused as he filled two glasses with milk and carried them to the table. "Between the NBA finals, Mary losing her job, and the two of you living in a media storm, emotions are running high."

Warrick caught and held the older man's gaze. "I want you to know that I have never and would never cheat on my wife."

Julian sat across the table from Warrick and offered

him one of the glasses. "You don't need to explain anything to me."

Warrick took a sip from his glass of milk. The cool drink eased his dry throat. "It's important to me that you don't think I'm a womanizer."

"I don't." Julian sipped his milk. "For the most part, the press left Marc alone when he played for the Miami Waves. He was single, but his social life wasn't interesting enough for them. Still, I know the media can distort a person's image so much that even their families don't recognize them."

Warrick stared into his glass. "I wish my family had realized that."

"Go easy on them, Rick. This situation is hard on everyone." Julian washed down a bite of cookie with a swig of milk. "I'll say this for your Mary, though. There are a lot of women who would have left the minute Jordan Hyatt stepped onto the scene. But your Mary stood beside you. She really does believe in you, Rick."

Warrick considered Julian's words. Marilyn had stood by him. She'd even tried to help him discredit the other woman. She'd never doubted him, never questioned him—until Jordan Hyatt told New York about his tattoo. Was he being unfair just because she was asking questions now?

21

Faye Ryland walked into Marilyn's home and rested her hand on her shoulder. "Girl, you look like shit."

Peggy and Susan joined the other woman in the entryway. They didn't echo Faye's sentiment, but their expressions told Marilyn they agreed. She turned to close her front door, ignoring the lone photographer who slouched against the tree in front of her home, taking pictures. She secured the lock, then led her unexpected guests into her family room.

Peggy lowered herself into one of the two overstuffed coffee-colored armchairs. She smoothed her turquoise and silver maternity dress around her. "Susan told us you'd called to say you couldn't make today's meeting, so we brought the meeting to you."

Marilyn wrapped her arms around her waist. Warrick's worn black Monarchs T-shirt was soft in her fists. "I appreciate your concern, but I'm not really up to company."

Susan wandered the room. Her four-inch red stiletto heels tapped the polished maple flooring. In her flowing crimson top and black yoga pants, she was a dramatic figure in front of the white stone fireplace. She paused to study the framed photos arranged on the blond wood mantel.

"You were a pretty bride." The compliment seemed almost grudging. Susan met Marilyn's eyes over her shoulder. "How many guests did you have?"

"I don't remember. A hundred?" What did it matter? Marilyn glanced at the pearl clock mounted above the mantel. Almost six o'clock.

"What's this? You like *Grease*?" Susan frowned at the compact disc soundtrack that Warrick must have left on top of the CD player.

"Hey, that's good shit." Faye sprang from the sofa. She snatched the case from Susan and sang a couple of lines of the movie's soundtrack.

Marilyn blinked. "You know the words?"

Faye set the case back on the CD player and crossed the room in strappy wedge-heeled sandals. She was wrapped in a figure-hugging minidress. Its jeweled magenta and black patterned cloth matched the highlights in her hair. "Of course. The young John Travolta." She waggled her eyebrows. "Pretty hot."

Peggy shifted in her chair. "The old John Travolta's not too bad, either."

"Shit, I'm hungry." Faye rested her hip against the fluffy sofa and rubbed her flat stomach. "You got anything to eat?"

The sudden shift in topic challenged Marilyn's sluggish mind. She started toward the kitchen. "I'll check."

Susan's stilettos echoed behind her. The sound stopped at the doorway. "This is nice. Do you do a lot of cooking?"

Marilyn faced Susan. The other woman was casting her gaze around the kitchen as though estimating the cost of the state-of-the-art appliances, green and white marble counter, white tiled floors, and blond wood cabinetry.

"Some." Marilyn pulled two packets of tilapia from the freezer and set them in the microwave to defrost.

"What are you making?" Faye nudged Susan from the doorway, then stepped aside so Peggy could enter the kitchen first.

"Tilapia and salad."

Marilyn wasn't hungry, but her guests probably were. The meal wouldn't come close to the culinary brilliance of the Italian restaurant they frequented, but they wouldn't starve. She turned on the oven, then pulled vegetables from the fridge and a salad bowl from the cupboard.

Susan traced her fingers across the stainless steel stove top. "Everything's so clean. Do you have a maid?"

Marilyn nudged the refrigerator closed with her foot and placed the vegetables on the table. "Yes. She comes in twice a week."

"Tilapia?" Faye wrinkled her nose. "I could order us a pizza." She settled her hips against the counter and looked at Marilyn with hope in her toffee brown eyes.

Peggy lowered herself into a kitchen chair at the table. "Tilapia sounds great to me."

The microwave buzzed. Marilyn avoided the other women's gazes as she made quick work of seasoning the four slices of fish. "I don't think you're here for a meal. If that's what you really wanted, you'd have gone to the restaurant."

Peggy rubbed her pregnant belly. "We saw the interview with Jordan Hyatt." There was empathy in the other woman's words.

"I thought so." Marilyn put the fish in a pan and set the pan in the oven. She closed the oven door as she straightened, then faced the other women. Her voice was firm. "Rick has never had an affair with Jordan Hyatt or any other woman."

Peggy, Susan, and Faye exchanged concerned looks. Peggy frowned. "Okay. If you're sure, then we believe you."

"But how did she know about his tattoo?" Susan pulled a knife from the butcher's block. She washed the tomato at the sink before slicing it for the salad.

Marilyn grabbed another knife from the block to chop the lettuce. "She must have seen the pictures that deviant photographer took through our kitchen window."

Susan nodded toward the window on the far right wall. "That one?"

"Yes." Marilyn bit the word through her clenched teeth. If she could get her hands on that photographer, she'd break his fingers.

Peggy peeled the cucumbers. "What did Rick say?"

Marilyn avoided Peggy's eyes. The other woman's gaze seemed to reach into her mind. "He's as upset as I am."

Faye joined the group at the table to cut the carrots. "I didn't see a tattoo." She shrugged. "But then I wasn't looking all that closely. I've got a man."

Susan rolled her eyes. "We all do and they're all fine."

The conversation turned to the NBA play-offs, the physical results of a professional athlete's workout regimen, the sexual benefits, and the restrictions of their healthy diets. Faye's biggest and most frequently voiced complaint was the moratorium on pizza. Marilyn lost herself in the other women's energy, their laughter and their irreverent conversation. By the time they'd finished cooking and consuming the meal, Marilyn was more relaxed than she'd felt since Warrick had driven away from her in the Monarchs' parking lot three days earlier.

Marilyn escorted the other women back to the family room after they'd cleaned the kitchen. "I'm glad you came. I feel much better."

The admission surprised her. She'd never expected to find genuine friendship with these women. She'd at first believed she had nothing in common with them. Meanwhile the woman she'd known more than a decade longer had become worse than a stranger. Marilyn shook off the sadness before it took hold.

Peggy returned to the armchair. "You look better, too."

Susan crossed the hardwood flooring to examine the caramel-colored drapes. "Almost back to your old self."

Faye helped their pregnant friend get comfortable before sprawling onto Marilyn's sofa. "The tilapia was good. But next time we get pizza. I get enough of that healthy shit with Jarrett."

"So what are you going to do about Jordan Hyatt?" Susan wandered the room, touching the framed artwork mounted to the walls and fingering the sculptures placed around the room.

"I don't know yet." Marilyn settled into the other armchair. "I've got to find a way to let people know she's a liar."

Faye sat straighter in the sofa. "Why don't you call your own press conference?"

"That's one idea." Susan circled back to the black lacquered entertainment system in the room's corner. "But it would be even better if you could get her to admit—publicly—that she doesn't know what she's talking about."

Peggy combed her fingers through her ash blond hair. "How is she going to do that?"

Faye scowled. "I mean, the pictures were so small, how could she tell what the tattoo was?"

Marilyn had a mental picture of a light coming on. She blinked in its brightness. "She couldn't."

Peggy's grin spread slowly. "That's right. Now we've just got to get her to admit it in public."

Susan flipped her light brown hair behind her shoulder to get a closer look at the sound system. "I've got that covered. A friend of mine has a popular radio talk show. He's always asking me to convince Darius to go on his show." She looked at the other women from over her shoulder. "Either he's lost his mind or he thinks I've lost mine. I don't give up my man like that."

Faye inclined her head. "I know that's right."

"But he'd lose his mind over the opportunity to have Jordan Hyatt as a guest on his show and Mary as a caller." Susan took another look at the *Grease* CD.

Marilyn gaped. Ice cubes danced in her stomach. "Me? I've never called in to a talk show before."

"Don't worry, Sandra Dee." Susan faced Marilyn, waving the CD case. "Once we're done with you, Barbara Walters will be calling for tips."

Pandemonium greeted Warrick when he arrived home Sunday afternoon. After his four hours of working out and practicing with the team, he'd showered and changed before coming home.

Warrick locked the back door and followed the raised voices to his family room. His entrance brought an abrupt end to the shouting, allowing him to identify the participants if not the reason for the argument.

"Mom. Dad. I would have come home sooner if I'd known you were visiting." His sneakers were silent as he walked farther into the room, taking in the sparks shooting from Kerri Evans's eyes and the tight line of John Evans's lips.

"Are you sure?"

He ignored his father's question and offered his in-laws a socially acceptable lie. "Hello, Terrell, Celeste. It's nice to see you. I didn't realize you were coming, either."

Celeste gave him a dispassionate once-over, taking in his tan khakis and black jersey. "Were you at work?"

He ignored Celeste's biting sarcasm. Warrick knew she didn't consider his profession legitimate work. Hours of training, film and playbook study, and team meetings all amounted to a hobby as far as Terrell and Celeste Devry were concerned. But for him, they'd all added up to an Eastern Conference Championship and a one-and-one game record against the Denver Nuggets in the NBA finals.

Warrick drew closer to Marilyn. He resisted the allure of her jasmine scent. "Why were you arguing?"

She gestured to both sets of parents. "My parents are paying us a surprise visit."

Warrick's brows jumped up his forehead. "All the way from San Francisco? That's quite a surprise." He glanced at Terrell and Celeste. In their formal clothes, they looked ready for a board of trustees' meeting for one of the organizations that benefited from their support. What was behind this impulse trip?

"That's right." Marilyn's smile was tight around the edges. "And, by happy coincidence, your parents came by to see you."

With an effort, Warrick kept an even tone. "Yes, that's great." How many socially acceptable lies was a person allowed in one day?

Celeste managed a delicate snort of disbelief. "Don't

worry. Terrell and I aren't staying long. We're just here to bring our daughter home."

Shock cut through him. "My wife *is* home."

Warrick's words were the reflexive response of a man determined to hold on to the one he loved. But were they true? Where were he and Marilyn going? He might not have known, but he wouldn't allow anyone else to answer that question.

Marilyn searched his eyes, a question and a wish in hers. But he no longer knew without a doubt that their wishes were the same.

Celeste gave him a cool look. "Marilyn has the opportunity of a prestigious position with a well-respected hospital in San Francisco."

"What does she have here?" Terrell looked around the family room as though searching for an answer. "She lost her job because of you. Is she supposed to sit at home while you father children with other women?"

"That's a little bit of the pot calling out the kettle, isn't it, Terrell?" Celeste's laughter was light and brief but with a noticeable edge. "Charming."

Terrell chose silence in response to his wife's mockery. His cheeks bloomed bright red under his dark brown skin. A look of pain crossed Marilyn's delicate features. Warrick wrapped an arm around her shoulders and pulled her close.

"How dare you speak to my son that way."

Warrick was distracted by his mother's angry words. Kerri's knuckles were white from the tight-fisted grip on her navy purse strap. He released Marilyn and crossed to his mother. Cupping her elbow, Warrick tugged her toward the sofa. "Mom, why don't you sit down?"

John Evans's raised voice almost overpowered Warrick's request. "Don't blame my son for that hospital firing your daughter. Rick had nothing to do with that."

"He had everything to do with it." Celeste's neck strained forward from the high collar of her dark blue jacket. "His irresponsible behavior reflected poorly on Marilyn's judgment to marry him. It cost her the job with the hospital and the partnership with the clinic owners."

Kerri strained against Warrick's hold on her arm and jabbed her index finger toward Celeste. "Small-minded people like you cost Mary those opportunities, not my son. Get it right."

"Do you think an irresponsible man would be able to afford a house like this?" John spread his arms to encompass their surroundings. "Would an irresponsible man become a success in the NBA, leading his team to the finals?"

Warrick stared in disbelief at the older couple flanking him. Who were these people? They looked like his parents. They sounded like his parents. But he never would have believed their words had come from his parents.

Celeste scoffed. "Behind every great man is a woman. Your son was lucky to find a woman as accomplished and intelligent as my daughter to help him."

His mother tugged against his hold again. Warrick held on for dear life. He was careful not to hurt Kerri, but he envisioned terrible things happening if he let her go.

Kerri jerked a thumb over her shoulder at him. "My son graduated magna cum laude."

Terrell grunted. "From Rutgers. Marilyn graduated from Stanford. It's a top five school. I think *he* got the better deal."

"Undoubtedly." Celeste adjusted the navy strap of her Coach purse more securely on her shoulder. "Marilyn, are you coming with us or not?"

"I'm not, Mother. I've told you before. This is my home and I'm staying here with my husband." Marilyn's response was quiet, her tone inflexible.

"What are you saying?" Celeste hissed the question. "He's ruined your career. He's ruining your life. You need to get away from him and get your life in order."

"My life is in order." Marilyn arched a brow. "Can you say the same about yours?"

Celeste gasped. "How dare you?"

Marilyn's gaze shifted from her mother to her father and back. "I'll make a deal with you, Mother. I won't pass judgment on your marriage if you'll stop judging mine."

Terrell's eyes widened. "You told her?"

Celeste grabbed her husband's upper arm. "We're leaving."

With her head held high, Celeste dragged Terrell from the family room. Within moments, Warrick heard the front door open, then slam shut.

Warrick was still staring at his parents, who now seemed like strangers to him. He glanced at Marilyn. Her eyes were clouded by sadness. But she gave him an encouraging smile as though prompting him to prolong this rare positive experience with his parents.

He cleared his throat. "Mom? Dad?"

"What?" John's response was characteristically brusque. He stared into the hallway as though expecting Celeste and Terrell to reappear.

Kerri tugged against his hold. "Let me go. I'm not some feeble old woman."

That quickly, everything returned to normal. Warrick released his mother's elbow. "I had no idea you were proud of me."

"Of course we are." John gave up his vigilant watch over the hallway.

In his peripheral vision, Warrick saw Marilyn shake her head.

"I guess I should have read that in between your telling me Marlon Burress was making a fool of me and I was failing the team." Warrick couldn't keep the sarcasm from his tone.

John shrugged. "I'm hard on you because I don't want you to become complacent. You're in the NBA. Great. But that shouldn't be the end of it."

Kerri finally sat in the nearby armchair. She cradled her purse in her lap. "Other people can feed your ego—your fans, the media, Mary." His mother sent a smile in his wife's direction before returning her attention to him.

Warrick dragged a hand across his forehead. "You may not have noticed, Mom, but the fans and the media haven't exactly been kind lately."

Kerri's brows knitted. "That's true. Still, as your parents, it's our job to keep you grounded and remind you that you're not perfect."

"I never thought I was. I'm thirty-four years old. I probably never will be."

His mother rose from the chair and crossed to him. She cupped his cheek with her hand. "But you're pretty darn close."

Warrick gave her a wry smile. "Any chance you and Dad could ease up on me?"

Kerri dropped her hand and turned to her husband. "John?"

His father gave him a curt nod. "But don't let the championship ring go to your head. Come on, Kerri. Let's go home."

Warrick walked with his parents to the front door. He sensed Marilyn following behind him. "We've only played two games against the Nuggets and we split those wins."

"Work harder." John tossed the command over his shoulder.

Warrick smiled at his parent's standard response. "Thanks, Dad."

The encounter was surreal. All of his life, his parents had made him feel as though he wasn't good enough. Today, he learned they were trying to keep him from getting an ego. They'd done their job almost too well.

Once he and Marilyn had bid his parents farewell, Warrick locked the front door and turned to her. "What are the odds of our parents coming to our house at the same time?"

"Your mother said she hadn't heard from you in a week. You weren't returning her calls."

He evaded the question in her eyes. "And your parents?"

She shrugged. "My mother probably thought she'd have more influence over me if she made a personal appearance."

"She underestimated you."

"It wouldn't be the first time."

"That's true."

Her parents had underestimated Marilyn when they thought they could forbid her from marrying him. Almost three years later, they were still miscalculating the strength of her will. Her parents, her best friend, even the hospital and the clinic partners had tried to come between them. But Marilyn had stood by him despite all of that pressure.

Wasn't that evidence that their love was enough? How much more proof did she need?

Marilyn tilted her head and offered him a smile. "Congratulations."

Warrick straightened from the door. "We lost Friday."

"You won Wednesday. Game one on Denver's home court. You looked unstoppable."

He offered her a smile. "Denver underestimated us."

Marilyn gestured to his empty hands. "You're not carrying a bag."

"I've come to get some more of my things." He steeled himself against the surprise in her chocolate eyes.

"I'd hoped you were moving back in."

"I don't think either of us is ready for that."

He'd check out of the hotel yesterday. Julian Guinn's home was the perfect place for him to clear his mind. It was free of distractions, especially since the elder Guinn spent a lot of time with his girlfriend, Althea Gentry.

Warrick felt her eyes on him as he mounted the stairs. He knew he was taking a risk. Marilyn had a point that the media invasion and the fans' intrusions put a lot of pressure on their relationship. Maybe he should retire, but he didn't want to make that decision under pressure.

Reaching the top of the stairs, Warrick pulled a suitcase from the guest room closet. He brought it down the hallway to the master bedroom and filled it with clothes and personal items. He packed quickly, then returned downstairs.

Marilyn met him at the foot of the staircase. She laid her hand on his arm. "Rick, I've never stopped believing in you, no matter what you think. What can I do to convince you to give me another chance?"

Warrick looked down into her eyes. "That's up to you, Mary. Can you handle being a celebrity's wife?"

Marilyn removed her hand. "Let's get through this season."

Warrick stepped back. "That's not enough for me. I

need to know I can have forever with you. All or nothing, Mary."

He turned to leave before the look in her eyes, the touch of her hand, the scent of her skin made him change his mind.

22

Marilyn listened to every word of the radio talk show host's interview with Jordan Hyatt on Monday afternoon. She'd had enough of the chitchat. *Get to the meat of the program.*

She wiped her palms on her denim shorts. Restless steps carried her around her family room. The maple flooring was warm under her bare feet. Her heart reverberated in her chest. Was it nerves or anger? Both?

"When and where did you meet Rick Evans?" LaMarr Green asked with easy camaraderie.

Finally!

Marilyn started another loop of the room. How had Susan persuaded her high school friend to arrange this interview so quickly? In less than a week, she and the other members of the Monarchs Wives Club had devised this plan and were ready to execute it. Now she had to remember all the tips her friends had given her— speak confidently, stick to the script, don't lose control.

"Ricky and I met at a gas station eight months ago. It was after the Monarchs' first regular season home game." Jordan Hyatt's voice was as breathless as an adolescent with her first real crush. "I helped him figure out how to open his gas tank."

What? Marilyn jerked to a stop. She stared at the black stereo system perched on the silver and glass entertainment center. Warrick had bought his BMW sedan more than five years ago. She'd seen him fill his gas tank hundreds of times—without help.

"Really?" LaMarr seemed skeptical. "That sounds like a scene from *Just Wright,* that basketball romance movie starring Queen Latifah and Common."

Jordan giggled. "It does, doesn't it?"

Yes, it does. Marilyn wasn't amused. She hugged her arms around herself. "Ask her how many times she's seen that film."

Unable to hear Marilyn, LaMarr continued. "You don't look pregnant."

"It's still a bit early in my pregnancy." Jordan's response was demur.

"How far along are you?"

"Just three months."

"And how are you feeling? Any morning sickness?" LaMarr sounded like a concerned friend. If Marilyn didn't know better, she'd think the two of them were lifelong pals. Any minute now, LaMarr would offer her milk and cookies.

"No, none." Jordan giggled again.

The sound set Marilyn's teeth on edge. She grabbed the cordless telephone receiver from the end table and punched in the radio show's telephone number. She turned off her stereo and waited for the call to connect.

Was Warrick listening to the program? God, she hoped not. He didn't pay attention to sports writers or broadcasters during the season. He considered them too much of a distraction. She hoped he hadn't changed his mind about that now. The possibility of his hearing what she was about to do made her even more nervous.

Marilyn jumped as the program host answered the phone.

"Good Monday afternoon. You're on the air with the *LaMarr Green Show*. Who's on the line?"

Marilyn swallowed the lump in her throat. *Speak confidently.* "Hello, LaMarr. This is Mary from Brooklyn."

"Hi, Mary from Brooklyn." LaMarr's voice radiated goodwill down the phone line. Nothing in his tone gave away that this call-in had been planned. "What's your question for our guest?"

LaMarr's enthusiasm gave her confidence. Marilyn wiggled her bare toes against the floor and took a long, deep breath. "Ms. Hyatt, you've said you've seen Rick Evans's tattoo. It's on his hip. Is that right?"

"Yes, that's right. And, please, call me Jordan, Mary." Jordan sounded as self-assured as Marilyn was straining to be.

Marilyn shivered in revulsion. She stared blindly across the family room toward the hallway. "Which hip?"

"His right one, next to his hip bone." Jordan's voice grew husky.

Marilyn wanted to reach into the phone and slap Jordan Hyatt's face. Instead, she fisted her hand, forcing herself to lull her prey into a false sense of security. "Is that the only tattoo he has?"

A suggestive laugh. "It's the only one he needs."

"What does it look like?" The silence was sudden but not unexpected.

"It's hard to describe." Jordan seemed flustered.

"Give it a try." LaMarr cajoled.

"I can't." An edge of desperation entered her speech. The Wives had anticipated this reaction. Marilyn pressed the other woman. "Don't you know what it looks like?"

"Of course I know what it looks like," Jordan snapped.

"Then go ahead and tell us." There was a smile in LaMarr's voice. Always the genial host.

"How many questions does she get to ask?" Jordan's voice was sulky. "I don't want to give away *all* of Ricky's secrets."

LaMarr chuckled. "You already told us that he has a tattoo. You might as well tell us what it looks like."

The silence lasted a little longer this time. Marilyn wished she could see the other woman. She closed her eyes and waited for the answer.

"It's a bird."

Marilyn blinked her eyes open. She walked across the room and dropped onto the sofa. Jordan was right. But the tattoo had appeared small and shadowed in the picture. How had she known it was a bird? If she couldn't force the other woman to admit publicly that she didn't have specifics about Warrick's tattoo, how could she convince the public that Jordan Hyatt was a liar?

"What type?" Her voice was tight.

"What type what?" Jordan's confusion seemed feigned.

Marilyn held on to her patience. "What type of bird does he have as his tattoo?"

"A peacock." Jordan's confidence was returning. But this time she'd guessed wrong.

Marilyn exhaled. Only someone who'd never seen the tattoo up close and personal would mistake a phoenix for a peacock.

"Why did he get that particular image?" She rose from the sofa and wandered back to the armchair and end table beside it.

"Because he's a basketball player." LaMarr's laughing

response startled Marilyn. "All NBA players are peacocks."

She wasn't amused. "Why did he get it, Jordan?"

"How many questions are you going to ask me?" Jordan's reply verged on a shriek. "She can't ask that many questions."

There was a shrug in LaMarr's voice. "This is a call-in radio program."

Jordan's sigh was angry. "I don't know why he has a peacock tattooed on his hip. He never told me."

Satisfaction washed over Marilyn. It took away the tension tightening her forehead and eased the weight bearing down on her shoulders. "He wouldn't have to tell you. The reason for the tattoo he chose is written into its design. You would know that if he'd actually shown you his tattoo. You'd also know that it isn't a peacock. But you've never even met him, have you? The truth is you only know about his tattoo from a photo posted to the Internet."

LaMarr's voice bounced with laughter. "Mary from Brooklyn." He spoke her identity pensively. "Would you be Mary Devry-Evans, Rick Evans's wife?"

Pride lent strength to Marilyn's response. "Yes, I am."

Jordan's gasp of surprise cut across the phone line. "You're Rick's wife? Are you going to sue me?"

Marilyn ignored her. For now. "Thank you for your show, LaMarr. I hope you'll be able to attend my press conference Friday."

"Are you going to sue me?"

Marilyn didn't respond to Jordan's question. She recradled the receiver and sank onto the armchair. She remembered the first time she'd seen Warrick's tattoo. He'd told her he'd gotten it shortly after they'd met. She'd stroked her fingers over the words, "Strength from adversity."

Marilyn stared at her wedding photos on the fireplace mantel. She would get back to those happier times. She wanted forever with Warrick even more today than on her wedding day. *Please don't let it be too late.*

She lifted the receiver again and dialed Jaclyn Jones's direct business number. "Hi, Jackie. It's Mary Devry-Evans. Is everything ready for Friday?"

Warrick drained his sports drink, hoping to cool his body and his temper. What good were these practices if Jamal couldn't remember the plays?

"Jamal." Oscar Clemente's voice was a low growl behind Warrick. The assistant coach stood before the bleachers and singled out the young shooting guard. "Are you playing Denver tomorrow?"

"Course, O. Are you?" Jamal laughed at his own joke. He lowered himself to the bottom bleacher away from his teammates.

Oscar grunted. "I'd do better than you."

Warrick set down his empty sports bottle and turned to face the action.

Jamal's laughter stopped. His brows met at the bridge of his nose. "What do you mean?"

"Are you learning the playbook?"

The rookie paled under the older man's glare. "I'm trying really hard, O."

"Try harder."

As though seeking help Jamal's eyes darted to his teammates sprawled on the bleachers. Warrick swiped the sweat from his brow and remained silent. So did the other Monarchs seated around him. DeMarcus stood with Oscar. His expression was implacable. Jamal would have to get out of this one on his own.

"We're up two to one, aren't we?" The rookie's swagger was slipping.

"No thanks to you." Anthony's Christian charity continued to fray as the postseason worn on.

Warrick's patience was unraveling as well. He drew in air heavy with sweat and wood polish.

"Nice one, Saint Anthony." Vincent turned to Jamal. "Shape up, rookie. We need you to remember at least the shortened playbook. If you don't, the rest of us have to pick up your slack to get those wins."

Jamal popped up from his seat. "I'm not asking you to."

Warrick rubbed his hand over his damp head. Jamal could hear them, but he wasn't listening. They needed more drastic measures if they were ever going to get through to him.

"That's true, Jamal." Serge inclined his head. "You haven't asked. Instead you're leaving us without a choice."

"Jamal." DeMarcus's tone demanded attention. "Carry your weight or I'm benching you."

The threat caught Warrick's attention. That was drastic.

It caught the rookie's attention as well. Jamal's jaw dropped. "You'd take away my spot?"

DeMarcus nodded. "You leave me without a choice."

Warrick heard Serge's words in DeMarcus's message. But he also recognized Jamal as the team's best hope of winning the series and the NBA Championship title. The bench players might know the playbook better. But even they'd agree they didn't have Jamal's speed, footwork, or shooting skills.

Jamal stabbed a finger toward DeMarcus. "I helped you get here. I helped you all get here. And now you're going to bench me three games into the finals? That's bullshit. You promised to help me."

Warrick raised his head. "We've worked with you after practice. We've gone through the playbook with you. What more can we do?"

Jamal turned to DeMarcus. "Come on, Coach. This is the finals. You can't bench me."

DeMarcus narrowed his gaze. "What are you willing to do to keep your spot?"

"Anything. I want the ring." The rookie responded without hesitation.

In his answer, Warrick heard himself ten years ago. He'd been willing to do anything for the title and the ring. Now that he was older, he'd tempered his answer. He was willing to do *almost* anything. He wasn't willing to lose Marilyn. But was he willing to risk the title for his marriage?

DeMarcus arched a brow. "Anything?"

"Yes." Desperation tightened Jamal's voice.

"Be at my house by five o'clock tonight." DeMarcus's gaze swept the bleachers. "That goes for all of the starters. My house at five."

"What for?" Anthony asked the question.

"You'll see when you get there." DeMarcus returned his attention to Jamal. "Rick may have saved your ass. Again." The coach blew his whistle. "Practice's over."

Less than an hour later, after soaking in an ice tub to ease the pain in his back and legs, Warrick had showered and dressed in black Dockers and a white short-sleeved shirt.

He crossed the practice court to speak with De-Marcus and Oscar at the bleachers. "Don't you guys have offices?"

Oscar grunted. "Don't want him there. He never leaves."

"That's because you're so warm and welcoming." De-Marcus's rebuttal was dry.

Warrick grinned with relief. The two coaches were getting along well. At the beginning of the season, they'd been so embattled Warrick had thought one of them would leave. But working together, the duo had engineered a Cinderella run that had raised the worst-placed Monarchs to the top of the Eastern Conference and into the finals. He hated the thought of Oscar leaving after this miracle season.

He let his gym bag drop to the court. "What did you mean when you told Jamal I'd saved his ass again?"

DeMarcus lowered the stack of papers in his hands. "You'd suggested I ask my father for ideas to help Jamal better understand the playbook. I think he's come up with a plan."

Warrick's brows jumped. "What is it?"

"You'll see." DeMarcus grinned. His pride in his parent was visible.

Oscar frowned at DeMarcus. "Why didn't you think of that?"

Warrick answered for his coach. "Sometimes we're too close to a situation. It takes someone on the outside to see it more clearly."

"Maybe." Oscar gave in but only grudgingly. The older man's intense gray gaze studied Warrick's as though reading his mind. "You still quieting the noise?"

Warrick shrugged, uncomfortable with the question. The truth was that every day the noise seemed to grow louder. "I'm doing my best. There's a lot at stake."

Oscar grunted again, shifting on the bleacher toward him. "It's the finals, not surgery."

Warrick's gaze swept the nets circling the ceiling, the black wire carts of supplies—basketballs, yoga bands, and jump ropes. Of course, Oscar was right. There was no comparison. Basketball wasn't life and death. But every time Warrick stopped to think about how close he was to the NBA finals title, he was transported back to the twelve-year-old boy who'd been unable to live up to his father's expectations and unworthy of his mother's attention. Warrick had something to prove, at least to himself.

He shook off the past. "I may not have another shot at the title."

Oscar looked from Warrick to DeMarcus and back. "You tanking the finals?"

"No, but I may retire after this season."

DeMarcus rose from his seat on the bleacher. His movements were slow and stiff. "You, too?"

Warrick shrugged. "I've been thinking about it."

"Don't." Oscar's advice was much like the man, brusque and to the point.

"Wait until the finals are over to decide." DeMarcus sat again.

Warrick jerked his chin toward his coach. "You left the game when you were a couple of years older than I am now. You were on top. How did you know it was time to retire?"

DeMarcus drew a hand over his hair. "I had a great career. No regrets. But after my mother died, my priorities changed. The game wasn't fun anymore."

Warrick lifted his gym bag and settled the strap onto his shoulder. "The game isn't fun for me anymore, either." Coaching was looking better and better.

"What was it you just said?" Oscar's frown cleared. "Sometimes you're too close to the situation. It takes someone on the outside to see it clearly."

"There's a lot at stake." Warrick turned to leave. It wasn't only that the game wasn't fun anymore. Like De-Marcus, his priorities had changed.

* * *

The reporters were no longer camped on the sidewalk in front of her house. Marilyn celebrated by entering her home through the front door. It was a beautiful June day, despite the personal clouds following her. She'd had a hard run through Prospect Park and was dripping with sweat. As she crossed the entranceway and mounted the stairs, the sudden ringing of the telephone brought her to a stop. She changed directions.

Marilyn answered the phone in the family room, careful not to drip sweat on the armchair. "Hello?"

"Marilyn. It's Arthur Posey."

Her mind went through twists and leaps trying to determine why she was hearing the hospital administrator's voice again. She glanced at the clock above the sandstone fireplace. It was almost noon on Tuesday.

"What can I do for you, Arthur?" The conversation had barely begun and already she was anxious to end it.

"Actually, Marilyn, the question isn't what you can do for *me*. It's what *I* can do for *you*."

The hospital administrator's voice still made her gums itch. "What would that be?"

"Reinstate you at Kings County Medical Samaritan Hospital."

Marilyn froze at Arthur's words. He was calling to give her her job back? "Why?"

"The board met and reconsidered the decision to revoke your hospital privileges."

Marilyn pictured Arthur in his office, seated in his maroon leather executive chair behind his oversized mahogany desk. Was he alone or was a member of the hospital's board in his office holding a gun to his head? Marilyn couldn't believe he was making this call willingly.

"You mean the board disagreed with your decision? They didn't fire me, Arthur. You did." The word *fired* still stung. It would for a very long time. The unjust reason behind the dismissal made it worse.

"The board and I have decided to give you another chance."

Marilyn gritted her teeth at the pompous statement. "Why?"

"What does the reason behind our decision matter?"

Marilyn paced to the windows in front of her family room. She tipped the curtains to peek outside. Still no reporters. She drew the curtains wide open and let the early afternoon sunlight sweep the shadows from her home.

"*If* I accept your offer—and for the record, Arthur, that's a pretty big *if*—I want to know why you want me back."

Arthur was silent for so long. Was he going to ignore her question?

"We recognize the value you bring to the hospital." He sounded as though he was forcing the words through a restriction in his throat.

"My value?" Marilyn's laughter was disbelieving. "You didn't recognize it before you fired me?"

"We recognize it now."

Same old Arthur. Smug, arrogant, and facetious. His tone matched the man to perfection.

"You fired me less than three weeks ago. Now you're asking me to come back." Marilyn turned away from the window and wiped the sweat trailing from her forehead into her eyes. "I want to know why, Arthur. The truth. I'm not rushing back to the hospital unless I understand what's going on. And I can wait you out."

Though not for long. Her body was cooling in her dampened clothes. She was getting chilled. And she desperately wanted a shower. But Arthur didn't know any of that.

Marilyn heard tapping in the background, like a pen hitting a desktop. Arthur was agitated.

More silence, then a heavy sigh. "Your patients are asking for you."

Marilyn stilled. A thrill raced through her system. "Really?"

She'd been thinking about her patients as well. How were their pregnancies progressing? Were they on schedule? Were there any complications?

"Really." Arthur didn't sound as pleased. "They've been asking for you since the Monarchs won the Eastern Conference series."

Some of Marilyn's pleasure dimmed. In asking for her to return, were her patients expressing their preference for her medical care or were they acting on their Monarchs fanaticism?

Marilyn pushed the question to the back of her mind. "So you're inviting me back because my former patients are asking for me?"

"That's right."

"Is that the only reason?" Although she had a large number of patients, she doubted the hospital considered their preference for her enough of a concern to bring her back.

"The board wants you back. Are you going to accept their invitation or not?"

"The board, huh?" Marilyn smiled with bitter satisfaction. "I take it they didn't support your decision to dismiss me?"

"Not exactly."

"I suppose that answers the question of whether you'll fire me again if the media becomes an issue."

"What's your answer, Marilyn?" Arthur bit the question.

It was Marilyn's turn to be silent. She wanted to return

to practicing obstetrics and gynecology. She wanted to care for her patients again. But did she want to work under Arthur?

Marilyn pulled the clip from her hair and dragged her cold fingers through the damp mass. "I don't have one for you."

"What?" Arthur's response rang with disbelief. "The board is offering you your hospital privileges back."

Marilyn settled her hands on her hips. "You and I didn't get along well the first time. Why are you pressuring me to return?"

Arthur's tone stiffened. "I would think you'd be more appreciative of the board's interest."

Her confusion cleared as disappointment settled in. "The board members aren't happy with you, are they, Arthur? How many of them are Monarchs' season ticket holders?"

"I hate to disappoint you, Marilyn, but none of them have Monarchs tickets."

Marilyn blinked. "Then why are they pressuring you to convince me to return?"

"Any number of reasons." Arthur responded impatiently. "Your patients want you to return. Several of them have been quite vocal." He hesitated. "One of them is the neighbor of one of the board members. And several doctors, led by Dr. Mane, presented the board with their support for your reinstatement."

"Em?" Marilyn's eyebrows shot toward her hairline. *Why would Emma champion her?*

Marilyn paced back to the corner table. "This is a big decision, Arthur. I'm not going to rush into it."

"Then what am I supposed to tell the board?"

"Tell them the truth. I'm considering their offer. I'll call you once I've made my decision." Marilyn recradled the receiver.

The board wanted her back. They valued her for what she brought to the hospital. To them, she wasn't the Devrys' daughter or Mrs. Warrick Evans. She was Dr. Marilyn Devry-Evans. There was a rush of relief, but it was subdued by other concerns. What about Arthur's resentment toward her? And what was behind Emma's support?

The phone rang again as she turned away from the table. Was Arthur calling her back so quickly? She wouldn't allow him to harass her into an answer just so he could look good to the board.

Marilyn smothered an impatient sigh. "Hello."

A hesitant voice responded. "Is this Doctor Marilyn Devry-Evans?"

Marilyn didn't recognize the voice. "Who is this?"

"My name is Betty Waller. Faye Ryland gave me your phone number."

Really? "Why would she do that?"

"Because I explained to her that I had information that would help you with your problem."

Marilyn stiffened. She didn't even know this woman. How could they have anything in common? "What are you talking about? What problem?"

"My daughter, Jordan Hyatt. She's willing to admit she's been lying."

23

Warrick joined his teammates in Julian Guinn's living room. The curtains were open. Corner lamps boosted the waning light from the early evening sun. Through the window, Warrick glimpsed the other turn of the century brownstones in his coach's neighborhood.

The men stood around the room exchanging curious looks. Julian stepped forward to stand with DeMarcus on his left, and Jaclyn and Althea to his right.

"All right." Julian rubbed his hands together. "Marc asked me to devise a teaching lesson that would help Jamal with the Monarchs' playbook."

"That doesn't mean I'm a dummy." Jamal's eyes were defensive as he looked at his teammates.

Julian raised his hands. "No one said you were. People learn differently." He lowered his arms. "One person can remember all the plays after reading them once. Someone else might need to read the playbook a couple of times. Jamal, I think you're a visual learner."

Jamal frowned. "What's that mean?"

Julian clasped his hands behind his back. "You need something to visually associate with a play to help you remember it."

Anthony crossed his arms over his chest. "Isn't that what practice is for? So that he could see what the plays look like?"

Julian shook his head. "Think of practice as a midterm you take in school to see how well you've studied. The games are your final exams. Jamal needs to study in a different way to prepare for those tests."

"But that doesn't mean that I'm stupid." Jamal's expression was aggressive.

"Exactly." Julian gave him a firm nod.

"Then why do I have to do all this?" Jamal raised his chin to a stubborn angle. Still Warrick heard the insecurity in his voice. "We're up two games to one over the Nuggets and tomorrow night we play our second game at home. Why do I have to do this if we're winning?"

Warrick pictured winning game four Wednesday night in the Empire Arena. That would bring them within one game of ending the series and capturing the championship title. Game five was Saturday night in Denver. It would be great for the team and the fans to earn the title at home. But it didn't really matter where they lifted the trophy.

DeMarcus dragged his hand over his close-cropped hair. "You need to learn the plays, Jamal."

"Yeah, man." Anthony shifted to face the younger player. "We can't keep covering for you. If you give a man a fish, he eats for a day. If you teach a man to fish, he eats for a lifetime."

"Thanks, Saint Anthony. Now I know what Jesus would do." Vincent's words were dust dry.

Anthony's olive green eyes glared at the Monarchs' center. "Jesus didn't say that."

Serge rubbed his forehead. "Could we get through one practice without the two of you sniping at each other? I know a three-year-old girl who is better behaved than the two of you."

"Sorry, Serge." Vincent's words didn't hold much sincerity. "Look, Jamal. You're always complaining that we have to take the series to seven games. We wouldn't have to do that if you'd learn the playbook."

Jamal turned his mulish expression on Vincent. "Everything I've got, I leave on the court. It's been good enough to get us this far."

"The finals aren't about being good enough, Jamal." Warrick slipped his hands into the front pockets of his black Dockers. "The finals are about being the best. What are you prepared to do for it? How far are you willing to lift your game?"

The room grew still as Warrick waited for the rookie's response. This answer would determine the rest of their season. They'd need the support of all thirteen players to take home the championship. Without that, the Monarchs would end their season as the also-ran. No one remembered second place.

Slowly, Jamal's muscles relaxed. His stubborn expression eased. "I'm willing to try this—if it will lift my game." He gave Warrick a sharp look. "But my game's already really high."

Warrick recognized the younger man's cockiness as cover for the insecurity underneath. "I know."

"Good." Julian spoke on a relieved sigh. "Let's get started."

Warrick looked to Julian. "What do you need us to do?"

Julian switched his attention to individual players during his explanation. "When you boil them down, each play is tailored to a specific player and designed to maximize his skill at his position. For example, there's a plan designed to get Serge open in the post. Another to get Warrick open in the paint."

Watching Julian, Warrick imagined the high school teacher he must have been. A great one.

"So, how does this work? Am I supposed to stare at Serge and keep repeating his play number like a parrot?" Jamal sounded dubious.

"No, we need a visual representation of the play associated with that player." Julian gestured toward the other side of the room. "Serge, take a seat on the sofa. Tony, go ahead and sit on the coffee table. It's sturdier than it looks. Rick, take the recliner, and Vinny, stand beside the television."

Jamal's expression remained doubtful as the other players took their positions. "What's this supposed to do?"

Julian gestured toward Warrick. "Instead of thinking of Rick's play as Backdoor, remember it as the Recliner Play." He turned to Serge. "Serge is no longer the Post Screen play. He's the Sofa Play."

Jamal hooked his hands onto his hips. "And what's Tony? The Table Play?"

Julian nodded. "And Vinny is the TV Play."

Jamal's brows knitted as he stared across the room at Warrick, seated in the armchair. "Rick. Recliner." He stressed the R sound in both words. A grin spread across his warm brown features. "This is dumb, but it might work."

DeMarcus patted his father's left shoulder. "I don't care how dumb it seems as long as it works."

"Let's run through a couple of plays." Julian displayed a green and blue stress ball. "You guys stay where you are. Jamal's going to walk to his position as it relates to where you're seated."

"Wait a minute." Jaclyn gestured toward Julian's right hand. "Is that a Miami Waves stress ball?"

Julian's cheeks darkened. "Come on, Jackie. I can't just toss it out. Marc played for the Waves for fourteen years."

"He's the Brooklyn Monarchs' head coach now." Jaclyn looked to her assistant. "Althea, please arrange to have some Monarchs stress balls ordered. Julian needs a new toy."

"You know how Jackie feels about the Waves, Julian." Althea shook her head with a grin. "I'll take care of it first thing in the morning, Jackie."

Serge shifted on the sofa. "Julian, how much longer will this take? Whatever is cooking in the kitchen is making me hungry."

Warrick silently agreed with the Monarchs' forward. He drew in another deep breath. His mouth almost watered from the scents of curry, chicken, and vegetables sneaking into the living room.

What was Marilyn having for dinner? Was she eating alone? Warrick shook off the questions and refocused his attention on Julian's lesson.

DeMarcus inclined his head toward Jamal. "The sooner we get started, the sooner we can eat."

Vincent called across the room. "Hey, Coach, did you cook?"

"Yes, I did."

Anthony smiled. "Oh, this should be good. I can't wait."

Althea chuckled. "Jackie, you're a lucky woman."

Jaclyn glowed. "I know."

Julian gave Althea a mock scowl. "And what am I? A consolation prize?"

Althea sent him a suggestive smile. "No, Julian. You are definitely not."

The other players laughed as they teased the couples. Warrick looked away. Jaclyn and DeMarcus were good together. Anyone could see that. And so were Althea and Julian. He was happy for both couples. But looking at them reminded him of all he could lose.

"All right. All right. Let's settle down." Julian sounded like the high school teacher he used to be. Once the room quieted, he tossed the stress ball to Jamal. "Walk us through the Recliner Play."

"Why didn't you tell me you'd spoken to the board about Arthur firing me?" Marilyn found Emma in the hospital's break room cradling a mug of coffee.

Emma looked up at the sound of her voice. "I wasn't the only one who spoke with the board."

Marilyn gazed around the room. At six o'clock Tuesday evening, the overbright gray and orange room was fairly crowded with hospital staff either eating dinner, filling up with caffeine, or both. After almost a month without the bitter brew, Marilyn wasn't keen on the hospital's coffee.

"I know." Marilyn settled into the hard plastic orange chair opposite the other woman. She breathed in the scent of antiseptic, burnt coffee, and someone's fried fish dinner. "But Arthur said you organized the other doctors to speak on my behalf. Thank you."

Emma swallowed more coffee. "Mary, I didn't speak with the board for your thanks."

"That's obvious." Marilyn crossed her legs, then settled her black leather handbag on her lap. "If you'd wanted my gratitude, you'd have told me yourself. Since you didn't tell me, I have to wonder about your motivation."

Emma stared into her coffee mug as though searching

for an answer. "Jealousy is an ugly thing." She lifted her green eyes to Marilyn. "I hadn't even realized just how jealous I'd been of you. You're smart, beautiful, and from a wealthy family. Everywhere you go, people like you. I hadn't even realized that I'd grown to resent being in your shadow."

"My shadow?" Marilyn's voice was thin with shock. "That's ridiculous. You were never in anyone's shadow."

"I was only popular because I know you. And you weren't popular because of your name. People like and admire you because of *who* you are, not *what* you are."

Could that be true? "Maybe after they get to know me. But I see the recognition in their eyes when they hear my name. I know my parents are the reason they want to get to know me in the first place."

Emma shook her head. Her honey blond curls bounced around her shoulders. "The only people who are in awe of the Devry name are your parents. Real people don't hold your name up as a trophy." Her smile was fleeting. "They don't hold it against you, either."

Marilyn arched an eyebrow. "What about Janet and Dionne? Because of my parents, they gave my partnership application special consideration."

"I said *real* people. Janet and Dionne are fake." Emma sipped more coffee. The strong scent and bitter taste didn't seem to affect her. "Actually, you should have pulled your application long before they had the opportunity to turn it down."

Marilyn dropped her gaze to the gray Formica table. "I should have walked away as soon as they suggested I leave Rick."

"Rick's one of the real people." Emma set down her empty mug. "Your family's name never impressed him. That's probably because he'd made his own."

Marilyn sighed. "Rick doesn't see himself as famous. But you never understood that."

Emma sat back in her chair, the match to Marilyn's. "I bought into the professional athlete stereotype of cocky men with too much testosterone. And I was hurt that you had someone more important than me in your life. I had less of your shadow than I'd had before."

"We were still friends, Em." Why couldn't the other woman have seen that?

"I know. I was childish." Emma shrugged. "And I didn't want to share you. I also was jealous of the fact that you'd won again."

Marilyn frowned. "Won what?"

"The happily-ever-after before I did."

"I hadn't realized that we were in competition."

"I know. But in my mind, we were."

"Since when?"

"Since college."

How was it possible that she hadn't noticed Emma's competitiveness before? Maybe she hadn't wanted to see it.

"That's ridiculous." Marilyn crossed her arms.

"I know." Her friend hesitated. "If it's any consolation, I don't think of us as being in competition anymore. I need to compete based on my own talents and stop comparing myself to you."

Relief eased the tension in Marilyn's neck and shoulders. "I'm glad you finally realized that. I'm not interested in being anyone's role model, Em. We each have to develop our own strengths and not compare ourselves to other people."

Emma gave her a steady stare. "You were comparing yourself to someone who didn't even exist."

Marilyn frowned her confusion. "What are you talking about?"

"You were trying to be the perfect Devry offspring by becoming a partner in a high-profile clinic."

Marilyn shrugged off her disappointment. "Yes, well, that didn't work."

"And the perfect Mrs. Warrick Evans to silence the gossip columnists."

She wrinkled her nose in disgust. "No matter what Rick or I do, the gossips won't be silenced."

Emma shook her head. "No one's perfect, Mary. The point is your patients and colleagues admire you. And as far as Rick's concerned, you're perfect just the way you are. I'm going to stop competing against you. But you should stop competing against nonexistent standards of perfection."

Was that what she'd been doing? Unconsciously setting herself to fail by establishing unattainable standards? Why had she done that? "Thanks for the advice."

"I'd better get back to work." Emma stood. "I know it will take a while for me to earn back your trust. But I will. Maybe in time, we could think about opening a practice together. You could take care of expectant mothers and I could care for their kids."

"Maybe." Marilyn watched Emma return to her rounds. The idea of opening a practice together held appeal. A month ago, she would have rushed into the partnership with Emma. But now, their friendship needed time to heal—if it ever could.

"Are you sure you're comfortable taking questions?" There was concern in Troy Marshall's voice as well as in his ebony eyes.

From the back of the room, Marilyn scanned the crowd of broadcast and print media representatives gathered in the Empire Arena's conference room Friday morning. The younger reporters seemed eager. The veterans tracked her movements as though she was chum in the water and they were planning their attack.

She pulled her attention back to the anxious expressions of the trio surrounding her, Troy, Jaclyn Jones, and Andrea Benson. She'd resented these three people at the start of the Monarchs' postseason run. Now as she stood in the rear of the conference room with them, she was grateful beyond words to count them among her strongest supporters.

She glanced at the single sheet of talking points gripped in her right hand before offering Troy a weak smile. "I don't *want* to, but I think taking questions would make the press conference a stronger presentation. What do you think?"

Troy looked grim. "If you're nervous, they'll tear you apart."

She hadn't expected such candor.

Andrea gasped. "Troy."

Jaclyn shook her head at her media executive, then administered a bolstering pat to Marilyn's shoulder. "Think positive. The Monarchs had a convincing win over the Nuggets during their second home game of the series Wednesday night. They're on a roll. That means these vultures can't pick at you for any recent losses."

"And Troy and Jackie will be right behind you at the podium." Andrea offered a bright smile. "If you get a question you can't answer, one of them will bail you out."

"That's right." Troy searched her features. He probably expected to have to bail her out fairly quickly.

"Thank you again for arranging this press conference." Marilyn smoothed the jacket of her caramel suit. She glanced at her talking points again.

Jaclyn nodded. "The media have been hard on you

and Rick. The message you're going to deliver won't stop them, but it will put them on notice. And you're the best person to deliver it."

Troy glanced at his watch. "Are you ready?"

Marilyn raised her gaze toward the podium. It seemed a great distance away. First the radio call-in program and now the media conference. She locked her knees as they began to shake. "Yes, I'm ready."

Troy stepped to the side, putting himself between her and the restless press corps. His broad shoulders blocked most of the camera flashes that tried to blind her even before the conference began.

Andrea stayed behind as Jaclyn and Troy escorted Marilyn to the front of the room. The trip seemed to take forever. Marilyn and Jaclyn stepped back as Troy took the microphone first.

"Ladies and gentlemen, thank you for joining us today. As we mentioned in the announcement, Dr. Marilyn Devry-Evans, wife of Monarchs' shooting guard Warrick Evans, will address the media stories about her and her husband. Dr. Devry-Evans." Troy stepped aside and gestured Marilyn toward the podium.

Marilyn squared her shoulders and strode forward. She scanned the room while Troy adjusted the microphone for her shorter stature. The Monarchs Wives Club was seated toward the back of the crowd. Peggy gave her a Mona Lisa smile. Susan waved with enthusiasm and Faye gave her two thumbs up. Their encouragement helped Marilyn breathe more easily.

She laid her talking points beside the mic and gripped the sides of the podium until her knuckles showed white. "Good morning and thank you for coming." Her voice shook. She cleared her throat as though that would help. It didn't. "This morning, you received a statement from Jordan Hyatt recanting her claim that she's had an affair with my husband and that she's pregnant with his child. She's finally admitted what people who actually know my husband already realized." Marilyn lifted her gaze and stared at the crowd and their cameras. "My husband is a man of great integrity."

She returned her attention to her notes. "Much has been written—and photographed—about my marriage this postseason."

Inappropriate giggles from the crowd pricked her temper. Marilyn let her anger strengthen her voice. "I hadn't realized that by virtue of his profession, every aspect of Rick's personal life was considered fair game to be exposed, dissected, and criticized by the public. However, no matter how you attacked him, he rose above your words and actions, and kept on winning. You claimed he didn't have a champion's mental strength. Yet he kept winning. You chased the lies of a stranger, allowing her to brand him an adulterer. He kept on winning. You turned his teammates against him. And he just kept on winning."

Marilyn blinked back her tears and set aside her notes. "I never realized the value of what I had until I almost lost it. Rick wouldn't allow the media to come between us. But I did. Because of the negative publicity and public criticism, I almost gave up on my marriage. But I've decided not to allow the worst thing in my life, the media attention, to cost me the best thing that could ever happen to me, my marriage. I admire Rick Evans. I'm proud of him. And those are just two of the reasons I love him."

She took a breath and looked out over the crowd. "Are there any questions?"

A tall, heavyset man with short graying hair rose from his seat in the middle of the room. "You're blaming the media, but isn't your failed marriage your fault?

Rumor has it you threw Rick Evans out after Jordan Hyatt revealed he has a tattoo."

Marilyn tightened her grip on the podium. "First, my marriage hasn't failed. And second, I'm taking responsibility for the problems in my marriage. What I'm saying is that I won't allow the media spotlight to cause a strain between Rick and me ever again. In fact, next season, when my husband helps lead the Monarchs to another NBA Championship title, you can turn your spotlight on us again. Just keep your cameras away from our windows."

Applause from Jaclyn and Troy behind her joined with cheers from the Monarchs Wives Club in front of her. Marilyn almost shouted herself.

"Are there any other questions?" She extended the invitation against her better judgment.

Toward the front of the room, a small woman in a gray pantsuit accepted her offer. "During the *LaMarr Green Show,* you indicated there was a specific reason Rick Evans chose to get a tattoo. What is that reason?"

Marilyn smiled. "I'm not going to discuss my husband's tattoo. Ever."

She glanced over her shoulder toward Troy. Marilyn smothered a sigh of relief when he came forward to rescue her.

He must have sensed she wouldn't be able to release her grip on the podium. Instead, he raised the microphone toward his mouth.

"That's it, ladies and gentlemen. Thank you again for your time." Troy turned off the microphone. With a gentle tug on her right elbow, he drew her from the podium.

"I'm shaking." Marilyn's voice trembled.

Jaclyn gave her a hug. "Nervous reaction. You were

great." She stepped back as Andrea, Peggy, Faye, and Susan joined them.

"Girl, you were wonderful." Susan gave her a hard squeeze before releasing her.

Andrea nodded. "I was impressed. I'm sure the other reporters were, too."

Faye grinned. "Way to go, predicting back-to-back championships."

Peggy rubbed Marilyn's arm. "You made us proud."

"Shit, you represented." Faye turned wide horrified eyes toward Jaclyn. "Excuse my mouth."

Jaclyn laughed. "We're in the NBA. I've heard worse." She turned to Marilyn. "Congratulations again. I have some things to wrap up before tonight's flight out. I'll see you all in Denver Saturday?"

A chorus of agreements followed Jaclyn from the room.

Marilyn turned to the other women. "What's next?"

Peggy took Marilyn's arm as Troy escorted them through the conference room's rear exit. "Now, we're going shopping."

24

Julian chuckled. "I hope you can make good on the back-to-back championships Mary just promised."

Warrick stared blankly at the large, high-definition television in Julian's living room. The local channel had just aired Marilyn's press conference in its entirety. His thoughts were jumbled, spinning like a top across his mind. His media-averse wife had called a press conference to tell the country she loved him.

He asked the first coherent question he could pull together. "Did you know she was going to do that?"

Julian aimed the remote control at the TV to turn it off. "Jackie called earlier. But I don't think Mary knew we were watching."

Warrick freed his attention from the now dark television and turned to his host. "Why not?"

"It's obvious. If she'd known you were watching, she would have said 'I love you, Rick.' Instead of 'I love him.'" Julian set the remote on the white-veined ebony corner table. "Besides, Jackie asked me to try to get you to watch the press conference. She didn't say anything about Mary."

Warrick was still dazed. Marilyn had gone on television to defend him to the media and the public.

Julian continued. "Jordan Hyatt's statement came out right before the press conference. For Mary to include it in her notes means she knew about it in advance."

"How could she?" *And why hadn't she called me to talk about it?*

Warrick rose and crossed the room, trying to wrap his mind around what had just happened.

"Maybe she's the one who convinced Jordan Hyatt to tell the truth." Julian's words followed him.

If that were true, Marilyn had gone to a lot of effort to restore his reputation.

Warrick stared out the window at the late afternoon. The trees in front of Julian's home and across his street cast shadows on the sidewalks. "She challenged the press to keep their spotlight on us." Did that mean she was ready for forever with him?

Behind him, Julian shifted on the sofa. "Yes, well, that might not have been a good idea."

Warrick drew a hand over his scalp. "When the media first started invading our privacy, Mary wanted me to retire. She thought if I didn't play basketball anymore, the press would leave us alone."

"It doesn't sound as though she wants you to retire now. It seems like she wants you to win the title next season as well."

"Why?"

"Because she loves you and she knows it's what you want."

"What if I don't win? What if I disappoint her?"

"You heard her press conference, Rick. You can't disappoint her. The only person you could disappoint is you."

"Maybe." Warrick returned to the armchair. "I feel as

though everyone expects me to fail—the press . . . the public . . . my parents."

"You've already won, son." Julian's words were earnest. "You've been through the fire, but you didn't let it consume you. Instead it made you stronger. There are a lot of people who admire you for that, including me."

Warrick pressed back into the chair. "But what would this season—my career—mean without a ring? Nothing."

Julian shifted on the sofa to face him. "Rick, with or without a ring, you're going down in history as one of the greatest Monarchs ever. And ring or no ring, Mary will always love you."

Warrick saw the conviction of those words in the other man's eyes. He hoped Julian was right.

Marilyn entered her home, then locked her front door Friday evening. She was completely worn out from four hours of shopping with the other Monarchs wives. She hadn't even been able to keep up with the very pregnant Peggy. Beneath her Mona Lisa smile, that woman was a live wire.

As she crossed the entryway, Marilyn frowned at the large shoe box balanced in her arms. She still wasn't certain about that purchase. Regardless of what Peggy, Faye, and Susan said, nothing good could come of it.

The phone rang. Marilyn detoured into the family room. She dropped her bags and the shoe box beside the sofa before answering the call. "Hello?"

"Good evening, Marilyn. It's Arthur Posey. You've had three days to consider the board's offer. Have you made a decision?"

Marilyn sank into the nearby armchair. This conversation would undoubtedly take a while. "This is a life-altering decision, Arthur. Do you really think three days is enough time to consider it?"

"Either you want to return to the hospital or you don't. Those are your choices." He sounded at the end of his rope.

"The board must have you under a great deal of pressure." The mental image was deeply satisfying.

"May I have your answer?"

Luckily, Marilyn and the other Monarchs Wives Club members had discussed the board's offer and arrived at a proposal that would benefit the Monarchs and make the idea of working with Arthur again much more palatable.

Marilyn settled back in the armchair and crossed her legs. "Would the terms of my hospital privileges remain the same?"

"Yes, we would reinstate your original contract. Is that acceptable to you?" Arthur continued trying to push her into a quick decision.

Marilyn wouldn't allow it. "I want to add another term to the contract."

"You didn't have any objections to the contract when you originally signed it." It sounded as though Arthur was speaking through gritted teeth.

Marilyn grinned. "Times have changed, Arthur. You dismissed me. Now you want to reinstate me. The original contract is no longer acceptable."

"If you choose to make changes to your contract, I'll have to consult with the board."

Did he think that would dissuade her? "That's reasonable."

Arthur expelled an impatient breath. "What is this term you want us to consider?"

"I want you to do more than consider it. I want the hospital to agree to sponsor a table every year at the Monarchs' annual charity fund-raiser."

"You want us to do what?" Arthur's incredulity sounded a bit exaggerated.

"You heard me." Marilyn was firm.

"How much is the table?" After Marilyn named the sum, he continued. "That's exorbitant. I'll have to get the board's approval."

Marilyn chuckled. "I happen to know that amount is within your budgetary approval. Those are my terms. Take it or leave it, Arthur." It really made no difference to her one way or another.

His pause was a little lengthier this time. "Fine. I'll send the new contract to you tomorrow morning."

Marilyn stood. "And I'll review it when I return from Denver."

"You're going out of town?" Arthur infused his words with as much drama as possible. "I need you to return your signed contract to me A-S-A-P."

"And A-S-A-P is once I return from Denver. Don't worry, Arthur, I won't keep it any longer than necessary." Marilyn returned the telephone receiver to its mount before Arthur could frame a rebuttal.

She swept up her packages, then climbed the stairs to her room. She felt happier and more confident than she'd felt in weeks—despite the dubious purchase in the large shoe box. No good could come from it.

"Hey, stud." Marilyn had to repeat herself before she caught Warrick's attention Saturday evening as he walked into Vom Two, the tunnel to the visiting team's locker room.

Warrick did a double take when he saw her posed on the top of the nearby staircase. *"Mary?"*

The heat in his eyes as they traveled from her thigh-high black boots, over her figure-hugging black minidress to her curled, teased, and sprayed-to-death hair almost made her forget her name. As it was, she struggled to remember the words to Olivia Newton-John and John Travolta's *Grease* duet, "You're the One That I Want." It was a song she'd been singing since her teens.

Finally, the words returned to her and she began her amateur performance. Marilyn gripped the handrail for balance as she descended the steps in the four-inch heels of her boots. With each unsure step, her voice shook, carrying her farther off key. She'd been right. No good could come from the purchase of these outrageous boots. But Warrick's reaction made it worthwhile. His expression eased from stunned to confused to amused.

Marilyn ignored the flashing lights and buzzing cameras she'd known would follow Warrick from the parking lot. Instead, she focused on her husband as she wobbled her way to him—physically and vocally.

She'd reached the chorus where she insisted he was the one she wanted. Barely an arm's length from him, Marilyn stumbled in the high, thin heels and fell against his chest. Warrick caught her to him before he threw back his head and roared with laughter.

It took him a while to catch his breath. Warrick rested his forehead against hers and whispered her name. "Mary?"

"Yes, Rick?" Beneath her fingertips, his muscles still shook with laughter; muscles she looked forward to exploring later.

"That was the worst Olivia Newton-John imperson-ation I've ever heard."

Marilyn grinned. "I suppose it was."

Warrick lifted his head. "What are you doing here? You've never traveled to an away game before."

"I came to wish you luck."

Warrick smiled. "Why would I need luck? You already guaranteed Monarchs fans the championship title during your press conference Friday."

Marilyn's cheeks warmed. "You saw that?"

He pulled her even closer and pressed a quick kiss to her lips. "You were great."

Marilyn cupped his cheek with her hand. "I know how important this title is for you. I want you to get it this season. But if you don't, there's always next season or the season after that."

He grinned. "Let's take it one season at a time."

His midnight eyes darkened as he lowered his head to cover her mouth with his. Marilyn forgot the cameras. Apparently, so did Warrick. As his lips pressed against hers, Marilyn's blood rushed through her veins. Her toes curled in her thigh-high boots. She'd been too long without his kisses. His taste, his touch, his scent transported her to their own private island. Marilyn pressed her fingertips into his muscled shoulders and tried to move closer to him.

"Get a room!"

She blinked as Warrick lifted his head. Marilyn looked around in time to see Jamal Ward toss back his head and laugh as he walked past them and the busy cameras. She stepped back—and lost her balance in her heels.

Warrick's arms shot out. He caught her around her waist and held her tightly. "Are you all right?"

"I think so." She grinned up at him. "Another benefit of being married to a professional athlete. His cat-like reflexes."

His smile chased away his frown. "May I kiss you again?" His voice was low and smooth, seeping into her skin.

She raised her head. "As long as we keep our clothes on."

He drew her closer. This kiss was soft and warm. The buzzing went crazy as the cameras caught their embrace. Too soon, they drew apart, slowly, reluctantly.

Warrick cleared his throat. "I'll see you after the game."

"You'll see me before that if you look into the visiting owner's suite. Jackie invited the Monarchs Wives Club to watch the game with her."

He nodded toward her boots. "Are you sure you can walk in those things?"

"Of course." She turned to leave. After three steps, she wobbled again. "I'm all right." She waved over her shoulder, then continued more slowly.

Marilyn glanced at her watch. The game would start in four hours. She should be able to get to the booth by then.

The Monarchs hadn't come to play. They'd come to win. The Denver Nuggets weren't making it easy for them, though. But then neither had the Cleveland Cavaliers, the New York Knicks, or the Miami Waves.

By halftime of game five, the Monarchs had scraped and battled to an 8-point lead, 87 to 79. As they'd returned to Vom Two, the tunnel to the visiting team's locker room, the Nuggets' arena had rocked with approval from the Monarchs' fans who'd come to the Pepsi Center. It had sounded like a Monarchs' home game.

But the Nuggets had made strategic adjustments during the half, including a decision to be more aggressive than they'd been all series. Now, three minutes into the third quarter, the Nuggets were assaulting the Monarchs' 8-point spread. Warrick and his teammates were left with a tenuous 3-point lead, 91 to 88. And Jamal picked up his third foul.

Warrick jogged back up court with the hotheaded rookie. "No more fouls."

Jamal seemed ready to argue, but must have noticed Warrick's no-nonsense glare. "All right. Sofa play?"

Warrick nodded. "Go."

Jamal found his position at the left perimeter. The Nuggets' Jordan Hamilton joined him. Warrick moved into the paint with Denver's Kenyon Martin. The Nuggets' Danilo Gallinari followed Serge to the post. Gary Forbes dogged Anthony's steps to the right perimeter. Melvin Ely guarded Vincent as he advanced the ball up court. Vincent crossed over, passing the ball to Anthony. Forbes moved in. Anthony shook free, pitching the ball to Jamal.

Jamal reached for the ball, keeping Denver's Hamilton at arm's length. Hamilton flung forward, chopping Jamal's forearm and making him drop the ball. The referee whistled the foul.

Jamal straightened, vibrating with fury. He stepped to his defender.

Warrick moved between them. He settled a firm hand on the rookie's shoulder. "No fouls. Take the shots."

Jamal's dark eyes glowed with anger. Still, he nodded his understanding. Three more penalties and the hot-headed rookie would be supporting his teammates from the sidelines with Barron Douglas, their team captain who'd come to Denver despite being on the Injured List.

Jamal missed both free throws. Undoubtedly, that was the reason Denver wasn't afraid to foul him. They knew his free-throw shooting percentage was pitiful.

The Monarchs battled back and forth with the Nuggets for the rest of the third quarter and into the fourth. With less than two minutes to the game, Denver stole the lead with a series of lucky three-point shots by Forbes. Panic was settling in. Warrick saw it in his teammates. He sensed it in himself. They had to regain control of the game. But Denver wouldn't fade into the night. The Monarchs were going for the win and the championship title. Denver was fighting for survival in the form of a sixth game.

Denver's Gallinari shot a 2-point basket. Nuggets 103, Monarchs 99. One minute and seventeen seconds left to the game. Anthony recovered the ball. The shot clock counted down from twenty-four seconds. Anthony flung the ball to Vincent, who advanced it past midcourt. Twenty-two seconds on the shot clock.

Warrick clapped his hands. "Slow it down. Slow it down." They needed to play their game, not get swept up in the Nuggets' speed.

The Monarchs set up the Table Play, clearing Anthony to take the shot. Anthony dribbled twice, spinning around Gallinari. Eighteen seconds on the shot clock. Gallinari leaped with Anthony, colliding with the Monarchs' forward. Anthony came down awkwardly, landing on his knee.

Warrick stiffened. His teammates froze. He sensed their collective horror as Anthony writhed in agony on the hardwood court. From a distance, the referee's whistle sounded. The noise freed Warrick from his spell.

He jogged forward, reaching Anthony's side as the trainers did. "Hold still, Tony. Hold still."

"My knee, Rick. Oh, my God, my knee."

"They'll take care of you, Tony. Hold still." Warrick rose to his feet.

He watched the trainers help Anthony from the court. Warrick felt his teammate's pain as though it were his own. Pain, frustration, disappointment.

And rage.

Warrick turned toward Gallinari. The other man was jogging toward the Nuggets' sideline.

"Let it go." Vincent grabbed his arm. "It was an accident."

He glanced at Vincent, then looked around for the visiting owner's suite. Warrick could barely make out

Marilyn as she stood with the other Monarchs Wives Club members and Jaclyn. She raised her hand and his tension eased. Warrick followed Vincent to their sideline.

"What are we going to do now? They took out Tony. What are we going to do?" Jamal's voice was shrill with panic.

"Calm down." DeMarcus shot the order like a bullet. "Roger."

Roger Harris, whose pregnant girlfriend was in the visiting owner's suite with Warrick's wife, shrugged off his jacket before coming forward.

Jamal gaped. "Roger hasn't played since the first half, Coach. It's going to take him a minute to warm up."

"He has thirty seconds." DeMarcus was grim. "Rick, take Tony's free throws. Make them. We're down by four. There's seventy-one seconds on the clock. Manage the game."

Warrick hooked his hands on his hips. "We're playing tight."

DeMarcus frowned. "What do you suggest?"

Warrick looked across the court at the Nuggets. They were a younger team. But where Denver had speed and endurance, Brooklyn had heart.

He challenged his teammates with a grin. "Let's have some fun."

Vincent nodded. "We've got your back, Rick."

Jamal's eyes lit up. "Take us home, Superstar."

The referee whistled the game back in. Warrick took to the free throw line and made both baskets. Nuggets 103, Monarchs 101. One minute and eleven seconds.

The Nuggets' Ely took possession of the ball. The shot clock reset. Ely jogged down court. Vincent guarded him close. He bent his knees and spread his arms wide. Ely advanced midcourt. He kicked the ball to Martin. Warrick stepped into the open lane and plucked the ball midair. He blew by Martin and Ely. In his peripheral vision, he tagged Jamal on his right and sent the rookie a no-look pass. Jamal stuffed the basket to tie the game at 103 with one minute on the game clock.

The Monarchs never looked back.

They kept just ahead of the Nuggets, 111 to 109. The game clock drew down to twelve seconds and the final possession of the game. The Nuggets' Ely sprinted up court. The shot clock turned off. The Monarchs set up the triangle defense, luring him deeper into the paint—keeping the Nuggets away from the perimeter and a three-point shot that would win them the game.

Ely pitched the ball to Gallinari, who spun toward the net for the fade away. Serge sprang into the air and rejected the shot. Nuggets fans wailed their dismay.

Jamal picked up possession.

Nine seconds.

"Table!" Warrick shouted.

Jamal hesitated before heaving the ball to a wide-open Roger, who'd replaced Anthony. Roger flew down court. The Nuggets' Forbes closed in from behind.

Seven seconds on the clock.

The Monarchs hustled across the hardwood. Forbes stretched forward and slapped the ball from Roger. Monarchs fans screamed.

Denver's Gallinari claimed the ball on a bounce. He pivoted on one leg and sent it back to Martin. Warrick ignored his swelling knees. He slid into the lane. His right arm shot out, stealing the ball inches from the Nuggets' Martin.

Four seconds on the clock.

Warrick steadied himself. He dribbled once and stepped up to the perimeter line.

Two seconds on the clock. The arena silenced. The air stilled. His vision narrowed to the net.

Warrick held his breath, leaped into the air, and sent a rainbow to the basket. The buzzer sounded as the ball reached its highest arc. Its echo held on as the ball descended and slipped inside the rim. Three points. Nothing but net.

Monarchs 114, Nuggets 109.

Warrick released his breath and sank to his knees.

The Monarchs' bench cleared, sweeping DeMarcus along and raising him to their shoulders. Serge and Jamal raised Warrick from the court and settled him onto their shoulders. Warrick threw back his head and laughed. Confetti fell from the rafters. Balloons lifted to the ceiling. The sound system blared Lady Gaga's "Glory."

Warrick raised his gaze to the visiting owner's suite. Inside, Jaclyn, Julian, Althea, and the Monarchs Wives Club were dancing and jumping around. Marilyn blew kisses through the glass.

The Monarchs were National Basketball Association Champions. Warrick raised his fists and roared in victory.

"Why do they keep playing that video?" Marilyn wiggled closer to Warrick as they lay together in the hotel bed. She buried her face in his bare chest to avoid watching the third replay of her Olivia Newton-John impersonation on the news. Her body warmed again as she inhaled his scent, sex and sandalwood.

Warrick's chest shook with laughter. The hair on his skin tickled her nose. "Are you kidding me? I want a copy of this tape. It's great!"

"I sound horrible!"

"I know!"

"Thanks a lot." Marilyn swatted him. Her hand probably stung more than his shoulder.

Still chuckling, Warrick tucked her closer to him. "Seriously, what possessed you to do that? You must have known the cameras would eat it up."

Marilyn drew back to meet his gaze. "I didn't care that the media was watching or that I can't carry a tune to save my life. I had a point to make."

His smile faded. With a gentle touch he brushed her curls away from her face. "What was your point?"

Marilyn swallowed to ease the dryness in her throat. This was so important. "You're the one I've been waiting for all of my life. If being with you—being Dr. Marilyn Devry-*Evans*—means living in the media's spotlight, then so be it." She would never again be foolish enough to let him go.

Warrick wrapped her in his arms, burying his face in the curve of her neck. "I think I can learn to love *Grease*."

Marilyn laughed in his embrace. "No, you can't. Be real."

Warrick pulled away. "I love you, Mary."

Marilyn closed her eyes briefly to count her blessings, then met his gaze. "I love you, too. You were right when you said our marriage is between us. I never should have listened to my parents, Em, or anyone else."

Warrick stroked a hand across her left arm. "But you didn't. You believed in me despite all the media scandals, even though I'm sure they were telling you to leave."

Marilyn shook her head. "It was the tattoo that almost did us in. I still can't believe the trouble those photos caused."

Warrick broke the brief silence. "Jordan Hyatt's statement didn't explain why she made up that story about an affair between us."

"Her mother told me."

"What?" Warrick pulled back again.

"We met for drinks." Marilyn nodded, studying Warrick's stunned expression. "Apparently, Jordan has had a crush on you since you played at Rutgers. She had a couple of classes with you. Those photos of you on the Internet must have sent her over the edge."

Warrick frowned. "That's disturbing."

Marilyn gave him a quick kiss. "I'll protect you."

"Is that why you did the press conference? To protect me?"

Marilyn was shaking her head before his last question. "I did the press conference to put the media on notice that they weren't going to break us apart, and also to prove that I can handle them. . . . I can handle anything as long as we're together."

Warrick traced a finger across her cheek. "I'm glad, because I can't imagine my life without you."

Marilyn cupped the side of his face and loved him with her eyes. "You never needed the NBA Championship ring. From the day we first met, you've always been my champion."

Warrick closed what little distance separated them. He lowered his mouth to hers and Marilyn tasted victory.

If you enjoyed *Keeping Score,*
don't miss Regina Hart's

Smooth Play

Available wherever books are sold

1

Troy Marshall needed a plan. But when the Brooklyn Monarchs' vice president of media and marketing had read the Twitter message that the professional basketball team's captain was drinking heavily at this trendy Brooklyn nightclub, he hadn't stopped to think. He'd simply reacted.

He navigated the hot, smoky space past the sweaty, gyrating bodies in the darkened downtown club. The bass of a popular urban song pounded in his chest, echoing his heartbeat.

Memories of his own club-hopping years came back to him. Another lifetime, another world. Who had he been and what had he been hoping to prove? Trying to hold on to an image and a lifestyle he'd lost.

Troy mounted the stairs to the club's VIP floor. Two mountains masquerading as men secured the perimeter of the team captain's private section. Their stony stares dared him to approach them. Before Troy could introduce himself, Barron Douglas's voice defused the standoff.

"He's OK." The Monarchs' captain shouted his grudging approval above the driving beat of the club music. His voice was slurred.

Troy's irritation rose. Shit. There were a lot of places he'd rather be at two o'clock on a weekday morning. Like home. In bed. Preferably with a warm and willing female. He'd leave that thought alone for now. He watched impatiently as Kilimanjaro on his left unhooked the purple velvet rope barrier to allow him into Barron's inner circle. He nodded to the large security guard as he walked through.

One of the women stood, separating herself from the pack. She moved toward him with practiced sensuality. Her stilettos' thin heels spotted her an extra five inches. The silver satin of her stingy dress wrapped her generous curves and shimmered against her brown skin. Even in the club's dim lights, Troy could see the avarice in her dark eyes.

"Who are you?" The groupie stood too close. She raised her voice above the club's entertainment.

"A friend of Bling's." Troy looked toward the NBA player. Hopefully using Barron's nickname would reassure him that Troy was there as a friend, not a representative of the franchise's front office.

"Are you a basketball player?"

The woman looked him over. Troy could hear the cash register in her head tallying the cost of his cream silk jersey, black pants, and Italian loafers. Did she think every tall, physically fit, and financially comfortable African American male played basketball?

"No." Troy started to move around her.

She shifted to block him, taking hold of his arm. "What do you do?"

Troy glanced from her to Barron and back. "I look after the players." As an NBA media and marketing executive, that wasn't part of his job. Then why was he here?

Her brown brow creased in confusion. "Like a babysitter or something?"

"Or something."

The groupie's greedy gaze considered him again. "You get paid a lot to do that?"

"Not enough."

"Do you want to babysit me?" She licked her lips as though her offer needed clarification.

In the past, it hadn't mattered whether a woman was interested in him or his wallet. But it mattered now. Troy removed her small hand from his arm. "No. Thank you."

Ignoring the groupie's disappointed pout, he continued toward Barron. He stopped beside the table. Barron scratched his scalp, bared between his thick cornrows. From the sheen in Barron's dark brown eyes, Troy feared alcohol wasn't the only contributor to the player's unnatural high. "Bling, let's talk."

Barron stared through Troy. His gaze wasn't quite focused. His movements were deliberate as he lifted a heavy crystal glass and took a healthy swallow of its brown contents. He put the drink down with a thud. "Talk."

Was the Monarchs' captain deliberately trying to antagonize him? It didn't matter. It had been a long day and Troy was short on patience. But he wasn't going away. "In private."

Barron's sigh was more tired than annoyed. He placed his hand on the shoulder of the big man beside him. "Move."

Barron stood with slow, unsteady movements. Troy tensed with worry. Getting drunk was bad enough, considering Barron was a professional athlete whose season hadn't ended. If drugs were involved, he wouldn't cover for the team captain any longer.

He followed the six-foot-five player past the velvet rope barrier and the human mountains guarding it. They came to the railed landing overlooking the dance floor. Shifting lights irritated him. What effect were they having on Barron in his intoxicated state?

Troy pitched his voice above the dance music. It seemed even louder up here. "What are you doing, Bling?"

The point guard's smile was too bright. "Partying!"

Troy wanted to shake him. "It's after two in the morning. Practice starts in nine hours. You need to bring your A game to the play-offs."

Barron's smile vanished. His glazed gaze hardened. "What do *I* have to do with whether the team does well in the play-offs?" Frustration tightened the other man's stance and strained his voice.

How could Troy reach the basketball player? "You're the team's captain. You represent the Monarchs to the public on and off the court."

Barron curled his lip. "That didn't stop the Mighty Guinn from benching me last night."

Troy should have expected that response. DeMarcus Guinn was the Monarchs' rookie head coach. The media had been stunned when DeMarcus led the perennially losing team to a postseason berth. But DeMarcus had done it with Barron riding the bench at the end of the last regular season game, the game that determined whether the team got into the play-offs.

Was there anything he could say to ease the other man's anger? His temper was probably worse because of his pride. Troy drew from his experience playing for a successful college basketball team. "This is the first time in four seasons the team's gotten to the play-offs. And it's the first time in your career you've made it to the postseason. Isn't that incentive enough for you to give one hundred and ten percent?"

Troy stepped back as Barron swept his arms in an emotional gesture.

"I gave one hundred and ten percent all season." Barron's expression twisted with pain and disappointment. "The Mighty Guinn still benched me in the final sixteen minutes of the game."

DeMarcus had been right to bench Barron. If he hadn't, the players would be preparing to watch the postseason games from their sofas. But Troy kept those thoughts to himself. He'd read somewhere you're supposed to humor drunks. "That's between you and Marc. My concern is that it's two in the morning. The team doesn't need headlines about your early-morning clubbing when the first play-off game is Saturday."

Barron swayed on his feet again. "It's only Wednesday. Well, Thursday. And what do I care about headlines?"

At least the point guard wasn't so drunk he'd forgotten what day it was. "Believe me, you'll care when your name is smeared in the press. So humor me. Let me take you home."

Barron jerked a thumb over his shoulder. "I came with Ten-speed."

Was he referring to the heavyset guy who'd sat beside him in the VIP lounge? "Ten-speed can find his own way home. You're coming with me. Now."

Barron frowned. Would the point guard continue to argue? Troy didn't have time for this.

Barron rested a heavy hand on Troy's shoulder. "Yeah. I guess I'm ready to leave. Thanks, man. How'd you know where I was?"

Troy stared at Barron. "You sent a Twitter message about where you were and what you were doing. Don't you keep track of who's following you?"

Barron shrugged. "I have thousands of followers, man. How am I supposed to keep track of all of them?"

"Try. Andy Benson is following you."

Barron gave him a sloppy grin. "Oh, yeah? That *Sports* reporter? She's hot."

Why did the other man's observation rankle him? "She's a reporter. You need to know who's reading your messages. Do you want the press to report that you're getting plastered at a nightclub during the play-offs?"

Barron scowled. "They've turned against me, too."

"Stop giving them reasons to criticize you." He gestured toward the player. "Do you have everything you need?"

Barron slapped both pants pockets. "Yeah, I've got my wallet."

Troy followed Barron to the steps as a young male server approached. The large, circular tray the young man balanced was burdened with alcohol.

Barron stopped. "Yo, my man. If that tray is for Barron Douglas's private group, take it back. I'm leaving and taking my credit cards with me."

The server switched directions to carry the tray back downstairs.

Barron looked at Troy over his shoulder. "I don't mind their company, but their freeloading gets on my nerves."

Troy frowned. "Then why do you hang out with them?"

Barron started down the stairs. "They want a good time. I want a good time. And they don't hassle me about basketball."

Troy caught the verbal jab. It didn't matter if Barron was annoyed with him. It mattered how he performed during the games. That's why he was pulling the team captain out of the club.

He followed the athlete across the club to the exit. Barron lost his balance several times, stumbling into the club's other patrons. Interesting that he subjected only women to his clumsiness. Troy braced himself, unhappy at the prospect of being dragged into a fight because of Barron's childish antics. He saw a headline in his mind: MONARCHS' CAPTAIN, MEDIA EXEC IN DRUNKEN BRAWL. Luckily, once the men recognized the klutz tripping into their dates was Barron "Bling" Douglas, they were more understanding.

Despite Barron's attempts to antagonize the club-goers, his celebrity got them out of the establishment unscathed. Outside, the cool mid-April breeze seemed even colder after the heat generated by the crush of sweaty bodies in the club. Troy handed the valet the ticket to retrieve his Lexus.

He watched Barron take deep breaths of the early-morning air. "Your friends in the club don't have your back."

"And who does? My *teammates*?" Barron sneered the word.

Troy didn't react. "Yes."

"Those punks don't have my back. They let Coach bench me in the last sixteen minutes of the game." Barron didn't sound as drunk now. Was it the fresh air or his anger?

"You're stuck on those sixteen minutes. Where were you the other thirty-two?"

Barron's face twisted with temper. "I was leaving everything I had on the court. I was busting my ass to make the plays no one else would."

"They couldn't. You wouldn't give up the ball." Troy held up his palm. "What happens on the court is between you and Marc. My concern is the media coverage. The team can't afford negative publicity, not when we're trying to rebuild our fan base and increase revenue."

Anger still sparked in Barron's eyes. "What do I care about that?"

Troy gave the belligerent baller a hard stare. "The negative coverage affects your money, too. Do you want an advertising contract? What company wants to have their product pushed by a drunk?"

The silence between them was tense. It continued when the valet pulled up to the curb with Troy's silver Lexus. He gave the young man a generous tip before getting behind the wheel. His irritation spiked when Barron sprawled unmoving in the passenger seat. "Buckle your seat belt."

The point guard complied, his movement jerky. "Why'd you come for me tonight, man?"

"You mean this morning?" Troy checked his rearview and side mirrors before merging into traffic. "It's my job to make sure the team gets only positive media. It would really help me out if you'd stop screwing around." He let Barron hear his frustration and disappointment.

"So you left your bed—and probably a honey—at two in the morning to make sure the team gets positive press?"

"I wasn't with a woman."

Barron chuckled. "Guys like you are *always* with a honey."

Troy ignored him. "I was working late at home."

Barron's voice was distant. "You think you're going to get some kind of recognition for your hard work? I'll give you some advice, man. Wake up. You think the front office cares that you care?"

Troy pulled up to a red light. He turned to Barron. "*I'm* in the front office."

"At the end of the day, your desk won't protect you. The front office isn't loyal."

"If I weren't loyal, I wouldn't be here."

Barron grunted. "You aren't here for me. You said yourself this is about the franchise."

"And you're part of the franchise."

"Am I?"

Of course he was. He was the Monarchs' starting point guard, their captain. He and the team were inseparable. To protect one, you had to protect the other. And that's exactly what Troy was going to do.

Troy strode into the *New York Sports* newspaper's weathered and worn reception area. The middle-aged woman behind the desk was simultaneously transferring phone calls, typing at a computer, and signing for packages. She stopped typing, transferred the call, and thanked the delivery woman before turning to Troy.

"May I help you?" The question was brisk and delivered with a hint of an Asian accent.

"Troy Marshall to see Andrea Benson."

Her dark eyes studied him as though trying to decide if he was trouble. "Do you have an appointment?"

Maybe he should have called before driving to the newspaper's office. But after reading Andrea's article in that Thursday morning's edition of the *Sports,* he hadn't stopped to think about it.

He tried to win the receptionist over with a smile. "No."

Her cheeks flushed. She lowered her eyelashes and picked up the phone. "I'll see if Andrea's available." She pressed a few buttons. "Andrea, Troy Marshall is here to see you." After a moment's silence, she slid her eyes back to him. "I'll let him know." She replaced the receiver and nodded toward a row of chairs. "She's on her way. Please have a seat."

Troy stepped toward the cracked and battered vinyl chairs. He chose one in direct line of sight of the newsroom. Before long, Andrea Benson walked through the doorway. Troy stood as she came closer. Her long, lithe body moved with a sexy confidence that defied her conservative black slacks, white blouse, and gray blazer. Her honey brown skin glowed. Her straight dark hair swung hypnotically behind her narrow shoulders as she advanced on him across the aging linoleum.

She stopped and offered her hand. The expression in her wide sherry eyes was more curious than welcoming.

"This is a surprise." Her melodic voice reminded him of satin sheets and summer nights. But with her distant manner, he'd never confuse fantasy with reality.

At five-foot-nine, she was almost a foot shorter than his six-foot-four inches. But her energy and assertiveness made her seem even taller.

Her hand was warm and delicate in his. Troy gave her the smile that had won over her receptionist. "Do you like surprises?"

Andrea ignored his question and drew her hand from his. "What can I do for you?"

He glanced behind her at the newsroom before meeting her gaze again. "Could we talk privately?"

She arched a winged brow. "A private conversation? What was wrong with the phone?"

Andrea was his challenge. He needed something more than a smile to charm her, but he still hadn't figured out what that was. "I wanted to talk with you in person."

Her perceptive eyes searched his. "All right." She led him to the newsroom.

Troy had never been to the *New York Sports* offices.

He'd suspected the organization struggled financially. The worn gray carpeting, peeling paint, and battered furnishings confirmed his suspicions.

He was struck by the stench of newsprint and burned coffee, battered by the cacophony of ringing telephones and shouted conversations. The scene brought back memories of his days as a sports reporter. Part of him missed the adrenaline rush of chasing a story. But, on the whole, he'd rather be back on the court.

Andrea turned a corner, leading him around the newsroom's perimeter and into what appeared to be a combination conference and storage room. She turned on the light.

Troy looked around at the room's stained walls and scarred furniture. "Maybe you should turn the lights back off."

Her eyes sparkled with humor, but her manner remained cool. "What's on your mind, Troy?"

She shut the door, closing them into the musty space. Troy quashed the urge to step closer and inhale her soft scent instead. He'd better get this over with before he became even more distracted.

He rested a hip against the conference table and slipped his hands into the pockets of his suit pants. "Let's talk about the article you wrote on Barron."

She remained near the door. "What about it?"

"You weren't fair to him, were you?" Troy tossed the words as a friendly question. But he was here to demand a retraction.

Andrea's eyes widened. "What makes you say that?"

"You accused him of being on drugs without giving him a chance to respond."

Andrea's smooth brow wrinkled. "I never mentioned drugs."

Troy shrugged. He hoped his smile would mask

the frustration roiling in his gut. "The accusation was implied."

"Only if the idea of Barron using drugs is already on your mind." She tilted her head, causing her thick brown hair to sway behind her. "Is it?"

The muscles in Troy's shoulders bunched even as he strained to keep his tone light. "Come on, Andy. You know as well as I do that your article put that idea in readers' minds."

"I quoted people who know Barron. They're concerned about his increasingly irresponsible behavior. And don't call me Andy, Slick. You know I don't like it."

"Why didn't you interview Barron?"

She shrugged. "He refused to speak with me."

"Can you blame him? He knew your article could ruin his reputation. What gives you the right to do that?" He hadn't meant to ask that question.

Color dusted Andrea's high cheekbones. "I speak for the sports fans who want to see a competitive play-off series. I represent the ticket holders who want their money's worth. That gives me the right."

Troy met the challenge in her electric eyes. "Your media credentials allow you into the press section with the other reporters for free. We all know reporters will write any sensational piece—fact or fiction—to get a headline."

Andrea's full red lips tightened. "You know the truth matters to me. That's why I came to you first when Gerry was planting lies about Marc's supposed drug addiction."

Her hard gaze forced Troy to face the facts. He remembered when Jaclyn Jones's franchise partner, Gerald Bimm, had tried to smear DeMarcus Guinn in the media. Gerald would have succeeded if Andrea hadn't warned him and Jaclyn of Gerald's plan. By her actions, Andrea had proven the truth did matter to her. Then what was behind her damaging story about Barron?

Troy leaned more heavily on the conference table and crossed his ankles. "We can't have negative stories about the team, Andy. They're a distraction. Instead of focusing on beating the Cleveland Cavaliers when the series starts Saturday, the players are wondering whether their captain has a drug problem. How does that help anyone?"

"If Barron's on drugs, you can't sweep that under the rug." Her voice was urgent.

"He's passed his drug tests. He's clean."

"Then what's causing his destructive behavior?"

He wished he knew. "That's Barron. That's just the way he is."

"But why?"

Troy dropped his arms to his sides and tried another persuasive smile. "Frankly, Andy, I'm not here to be interviewed. I want you to stop writing negative stories about the Monarchs."